Mr. Cannyharme

Michael Shea

Mr. Cannyharme

A NOVEL OF LOVECRAFTIAN TERROR

Michael Shea

Foreword by Linda Shea

Edited by S. T. Joshi

Hippocampus Press

New York

Published by Hippocampus Press
P.O. Box 641, New York, NY 10156.
www.hippocampuspress.com

Cover art © 2021 by Tom Brown.
Cover design by Daniel V. Sauer, dansauerdesign.com
Hippocampus Press logo designed by Anastasia Damianakos.

First Edition
1 3 5 7 9 8 6 4 2

ISBN 978-1-61498-325-5   limited cloth
ISBN 978-1-61498-324-8   trade paper
ISBN 978-1-61498-326-2   ebook

For Sweet Linda,
a hellish book, for a heavenly babe.

Contents

Foreword

Michael wrote *Mr. Cannyharme* in 1981. He had recently left his native Los Angeles and come back to the Bay Area, a place he knew well from his undergraduate studies at UC Berkeley in the mid-1960s. During that time he would take construction and painting gigs in the day time, and several nights a week—in exchange for rent—man the desk at a men's residence hotel in San Francisco's Mission District.

In the oddly permeable work space of the hotel's "cage" Michael would write—the striking of the keys on his Olivetti typewriter sounding to me much like rain. Foot traffic was light after the neighborhood bars had closed, and only an occasional resident rang the street level bell. He would buzz them in, and check their reflections in the concave mirror at the stair's turning, as they came up the stairs. Often as they'd pass the cage, Michael would exchange in a bit of friendly banter and laughter. He did not seem to mind the interruptions. In hindsight, I think that these little social moments might have provided some inspiration for the novel at hand.

When the editors at Hippocampus Press requested something from me for this first publication of Mr. Cannyharme, I decided to do a bit of research on the history of the neighborhood. Located on Valencia Street, the hotel is just two blocks south from Dolores Park. The Mission San Francisco de Asis adobe church, California's oldest standing building, adjoins the park. Both the Mission District and the city of San Francisco take their names from it.

Spanish Franciscan priests arrived in the area during the late eighteenth century. Father Francisco Palou, a student of the explorer, priest, and inquisitor Father Junipero Serra, is credited with the dedication of the Adobe

9

Mission Church in 1776. At the time, there was a nearby creek which the Spanish called "Arroyo de Nuestra de los Dolores," or Our Lady of Sorrows. For the native people it did prove to be a place of many sorrows.

The native Ohlone had inhabited the coastal region extending from what is now San Francisco to Monterey for 10,000 years. The arrival of Spain was disastrous for them: Spain claimed native lands and the church demanded native souls. They were "converted," enslaved, and then punished harshly for the "heretical" act of attempting to escape and return to their homes. Forced to build the Mission and develop the surrounding farmlands, they had no immunity to the diseases the Europeans brought and succumbed. It is thought that more than 5,000 native people were buried in the grounds surrounding the Mission, and by the 1850s there were only fifty Ohlone living in California.

Tensions leading up to the Mexican-American War (1848) created a mandate in 1834 that forced church properties to be sold or granted to private owners. The missions could only keep title to the church edifices themselves, with small surrounding gardens. The Gold Rush brought an influx of miners and settlers. Plank roads were constructed from the Bay and downtown, to the neighborhood, one forming what is now Mission Street.

The area became a focus for amusements: bull and bear fighting, horse racing, and dueling—the carnival on full display. From 1865 to 1891 Woodward's Garden Conservatory and Zoo covered two full city blocks just west of the future site of the hotel. Much of the Mission SF de Asis' land was developed into housing units for working class families. The Mission grounds also contained the original first colonial graveyard and San Francisco's first Jewish cemetery, and by the end of the nineteenth century there were seven functioning mortuaries on Valencia Street. Black carriages pulled by black plumed horses were a common sight. But in 1900 the city curtailed burials within its borders, the presence of the dead deemed incompatible with progress, new construction, and the health of the living. Between 1900 and 1940 some 50,000 of the city's deceased were exhumed and reinterred in Colma, just south of the city. The colonial and Jewish cemeteries became what is now Dolores Park.

When the Ohlone had inhabited the area of the Mission, it had been filled with creeks and streams. In order to create buildable land, developers created landfill in place of the waterways. During the great earthquake of 1906, the fill was unstable and many buildings fell. Fires started.

In the early 1980s, when Michael and I lived there, the Mission—the sunniest part of the city—was a richly creative place. Not too expensive, it was a good place for artists. It teemed with many languages. Michael loved its idioms and loved being there. Blue-collar working families, many of them descendants of the waves of Irish and Italian and Mexican immigrants, made up its core.

The streets were even more interesting and diverse than they are now: the Hibernia Bank, McCarthy's Bar, Lucca's Deli, La Raza Cultural Center, the Women's Building with its huge murals, the Chinese bookstore, and all sorts of eateries and establishments. Close to the Castro District, there were plenty of gay night spots. It was just barely the beginning of the AIDS epidemic. The Vietnam War and the Summer-of-Love had left their mark and things were changing. Yet there were still a great many traditional working families—and around them the "fringe" was large and held the poor, disheveled, and homeless.

Just one block from the hotel, at the BART Station Plaza, and in front of its surrounding bars, there was a thriving twenty-four-hour hub of drug dealing and prostitutes with their pimps. Descending into the subway or walking to the bank on the corner, one had to catch their eyes. Because of this, many of the "Grand-Dame" residence hotels only rented to men in an attempt to discourage prostitution on their premises. Michael kept a Smith & Wesson in the desk of the cage because who knew who might come through that door at three in the morning. But, as far as I know, he never had to take it out of hiding.

Somehow, all these groups and many more basked in the Mission sun and were functionally tolerant of one another. I remember telling Michael, after we had left the Mission, how much I remembered and liked the novel. I wondered if it would ever be published. His interest was piqued and he gave it a read for the first time in decades after finishing it . . . but then asked me if I thought it to be too harsh. Always contemptuous of those who wielded power over the weak, he wondered if the book was too brutal. I replied that the villains were truly terrible and mythic, but that most of the heroes were women, and that was a good thing. His answer: "Yes. But Jack is such an asshole."

A few years after Michael's passing in 2014, as chance and nostalgia would have it, I was on Valencia Street directly in front of the hotel. The faded paint job and the neon sign were exactly as I remembered. Pressing the streel-level bell, I heard the answering buzz—both unchanged by the years, and after pushing open the heavy metal door and stepping in I found the old chain and padlock to the basement door still on guard. The carpet runner creaked as I went up the stairs, and touched the hammered tin wainscoting. The little concave mirror saw me before I made the turn, and a well-spoken desk clerk from India greeted me from the cage. How is it possible that, with so much recent dot-com gentrification in the neighborhood, particularly on Valencia Street, this funky, low-rent hotel could remain frozen in time?

Michael's amazing imagination bounced off and reinvented the people he met. He would not usually discuss a piece in progress until it was finished and often not for a good while after that. But I very clearly remember the ancient Gentleman who would painstakingly cane his way down the stairs of the hotel in the mornings, wearing a worn peacoat and watch cap, so bent over that when he turned to nod to Michael his one searingly blue eye was level with the desk of the cage.

Many thanks to S. T. Joshi and Derrick Hussey of Hippocampus Press for bringing *Mr. Cannyharme* into the light of day in this wonderful edition—and for seeing the novel as the beautiful, dark, and hopeful masterpiece that I think that it is. Michael would only wish that it has proved to be, for his readers, "a good read."

—LINDA SHEA

A Note on This Edition

Michael Shea's *Mr. Cannyharme* exists in two versions, one considerably longer than the other. After careful examination of both versions and consultation with Linda Shea, I agreed with her that the longer version is to be preferred, as its more detailed characterization and more richly textured prose make it a far more satisfying read, even at the risk of a certain initial slowness in the pace of the narrative. I have made no alterations in the text aside from minor revisions in punctuation in the interests of internal consistency.

Many readers will become aware that the novel is an elaboration of the plot of H. P. Lovecraft's story "The Hound" (1922), a flamboyant narrative of an ageless vampire in Holland. The extent to which Michael Shea has expanded on this core idea, setting it in the gritty San Francisco milieu he knew so well, will make it evident that the novel is far more than a literary pastiche, but instead is the expression of many of Shea's deepest beliefs in the lingering effects of horror and in the power of the human spirit to overcome adversity both natural and supernatural. *Mr. Cannyharme* has waited far too long to achieve publication, but the editor and publisher hope that its emergence will only enhance the high reputation that Michael Shea enjoys as a pioneering author of weird fiction.

—S. T. JOSHI

For crouched within that centuried coffin, embraced by a close-packed nightmare retinue of huge, sinewy, sleeping bats, was the bony thing my friend and I had robbed; not clean and placid as we had seen it then, but covered with caked blood and shreds of alien flesh and hair, and leering sentiently at me with phosphorescent sockets . . .

—H. P. LOVECRAFT, "The Hound"

In Netherlands did old Van Haarme
A vasty boneyard till and farm,
Did plough and plant a funeral field
Where gnarled lich was all his yield,
And parched cadaver all the crop
That e'er the ghoul did sow or reap.

But Carnival Town in latter years
Is where Van Haarme now scythes and shears.
The boggy graves of his natal fief
He's quit for the Carnival's shadow-strife.
It's Poortown's earth he seeds now, and tills,
Where the shambling shadow-folk drift without wills.

I

At Home with the Homeless

Late in the day old Chester Chase walks down the hall from his room, headed for the stairs. His legs have seventy-seven years on them, but usually he's not as tottery as this. Today he walks wide-legged, as if the danger of falling has suddenly increased.

He advances to the barred window of the cage. Elmer, the day clerk, is in there, lying on the couch and watching TV.

"'Lo, Chester." Elmer's a scrawny old rooster in an undershirt. He has thick goggle-glasses and a phlegmy voice, but he's not old the way Chester is old, not near-the-end-of-it old.

"Hi, Elmer." Chester's own voice sounds far and faint to him, like dead leaves blown down an empty sidewalk.

As he creaks down the two flights of stairs to the street, he is seized by sorrow. All the funky details—these walls, these banisters—seem to glow, perilous and precious. In the bubble mirror at the stairs' turning, he sees himself, huge-headed, spindle-shanked, a tottery freak on his way out. Coming to the steel-framed street door—battered and shabby, but implacable and absolute when you're shut outside of it—he hauls it open and steps out. Stands outside of the Hyperion Hotel, his home for the last twelve years.

Chester Chase has just learned that his elder sister Edith, whose slender checks have sustained him these last ten years, has died. She lived in a subsidized apartment. The last installment of her pension bought the coffin she was buried in. In a week, he'll join the homeless. Broke already, he hasn't eaten a bite in the last twenty-four hours. He contemplates the streets he will soon call home.

The sun has just set. San Francisco's Mission District is all rosy and golden. The people, even the raggedest lowlifes, are lit like angels. But Chester knows how it will look in the deep of night—how it will look to the houseless denizen of these streets: all brick and concrete and asphalt, wet with fog. All rock-hard emptiness, and not a door in it that will open for him.

It's been years since Chester has looked at the homeless as normal people do, people with money and time in their pockets. Such people, when they drive through the Mission, or down Market, or through the 'Loin, may know all the social explanations for these roofless souls, but as they look from their SUVs and minivans, you see in their eyes a more primitive response, as if the homeless were a kind of spontaneous alien growth. Normal folk see them as medieval folk saw maggots, which they thought to be conjured from nothing, by sunlight falling on carrion.

Maybe this is because those multi-sweatered shapes, with their glazed eyes and their smudged and sunburnt cheeks, bloom so infallibly in all the expected niches. The bus stops, the doorways, the parks . . . They sprout amid the sparsest plantings that flank the freeways and form clusters on the dirt slopes up under the overpasses.

But Chester Chase has long known that their origins are far more prosaic than spontaneous generation. A great many of the homeless enter the streets from the doors of hotels just like his own, the Hyperion. There's a whole sisterhood of these old residence hotels throughout the city, eighty- and a hundred-roomers still wearing, like faded dowagers, the grand names of their youth: the Continental, the Crown, the Mayfair. . . . The soon-to-be homeless are stepping out their doors all the time. In fact—

"Hey, Chester."

"Hey, Ron."

—here's Ron Ratchett. He used to live here, but mostly is on the streets now. He comes in to sell his food stamps at fifty percent face value to his former fellow tenants, will soon be heading back out to buy some bourbon. A lean guy, going bald in front from a nervous habit of incessantly combing his hair back while he's sweating out jail time for drunk-and-disorderlies. Ron's mellowing, growing more drunk and less disorderly, closing in on his long-term goal: mental erasure. You're rarely arrested any more when you reach that state. They let you stand there, swaying, by your trashcan pulpit, and mutter your slurred sermon. . . .

Chester starts walking. Even Ron's not as bad off as he is—not nearly. He has a quarter of a century in his pocket, like a fortune in the bank, if he just decided to use it. . . .

He walks and walks. Everywhere he notes the homeless, his new countrymen, and searches their eyes. Many are burnouts, their eyes mere emptiness. Many are smug, have beaten the game because they're warmed for the moment by Night Train or pills. But more are mad-eyed, and glare like fanatics when you 'front them. Not insanity, no. It's a fierce, futile insistence they exist, that they are *here* in spite of owning not one square foot of concrete, one square foot of floor, or wall, or roof. . . .

It's after midnight, his terror dulled by exhaustion, when Chester presses the Hyperion's bell and is buzzed back in. Jack Hale is on his graveyard shift in the cage, typing. A big, bearded man, his eyes seem to eat up the typewriter as his fingers poke its keys. A man with a task, and some time left. A man still in the world.

"Hey, Chester! Out on the town?"

"Hi, Jack." Chester finds he has paused. Jack here is the gatekeeper, the Hyperion's rent-collector. Chester's mouth wants to frame some words. An explanation? A plea for some special exemption?

"So you're writing, eh, Jack?" How frail his voice sounds in his own ears!

"Ah, it's nothing serious. A steamy romance. A chimp could write this stuff."

Chester sees a short glass of whiskey by the typewriter, remembers when *he* was a hard-shouldered man who could relish a beer and a bump after work in the shipyards. If he took a shot now, it would knock him on his ass.

He heads down the hall toward his room, feeling more and more ghostlike with each step, passing the doors of long-term neighbors who will still live here next week, when Chester will have ceased to exist for them, will be someone who is gone. Here comes wiry little Rich Rasp, a hot-mop roofer.

"Hey, Chester." And Rich gives him a pat on the shoulder as he passes. The touch stuns him. It seems years since he's had one. His whole body, propped on its pithless legs, becomes painfully distinct to him. This brittle stick is who he is, is all that's left of him. Dazed, he passes Karl Cabron, next door to him. The shy old Hispanic just smiles at him. Is that compassion, a kind of farewell, in Karl's eyes?

He lets himself into his room and locks the door. Sanctuary! He curls on his side on his bed.

Here is harborage. Here is rest. He must cling to it as long as he can. He lies there, straying down paths of memory, dreaming his way back into the earlier parts of a life that is nearing its end.

II
The Night Clerk

One A.M. Jack Hale looks a bit more somber than Chester found him, because what he's typing now is a letter to his ex-wife Erika, the "ex" her doing, a year and a half ago. He never calls her, because he fears that in conversation she will impulsively say too much, blurt out a final refusal, blurt out . . . a new lover? In her infrequent letters she is vaguely warm, indefinite about her doings. She always was in awe of the written word—was that why she stayed on so long, married to a poet?

This letter to her is very definite, full of dates and figures. Eleven thousand saved now, seven thousand of it the advance on his *first publication*. Yes! *The Gamekeeper's Daughter.* (He's less definite about the other four thousand—"savings" he calls it.) He writes. . . . *Why didn't I see this sooner? Commercial fiction! Why did everything have to be poetry, be* literature? *The advance on this one*—Master of the Hounds—*plus savings will put me past 25K by the end of the year. A down payment, Erika! A down payment on* something. *Don't answer me yet. Just say you'll stay open. just say you'll still* think *about it. Losing you—I can see it now— was what it took to blast me out of my old habits. Why didn't I realize how easy this would be? And really, you can't say I didn't try, sweetheart. You know I did! I just didn't see the way!*

He had indeed tried, after twelve years of cheap rentals, of scraping by on his house painting and construction jobs, and her clerical work, had finally gotten unbearable to her. He'd dusted off his B.A. in English, gotten a sport coat with leather elbow patches, and taught at adult schools all over the great L.A. area. But of course he'd started drinking too. Had never touched Erika in anger, but how much better was sullenness, and brooding, and endless, shouted tirades about his Art?

As he is typing *Jack, the one who really loves you!,* a creak of floorboards heralds the reappearance of Rich Rasp in the now deserted hallway. "Hey, Jack," he smiles. Slides a hundred in twenties across the little counter under the bars.

"You be careful up on those roofs now," Jack says, pulls a neatly folded little bindle from his pocket, and slides it across. They part—Jack with a friendly upraised admonitory finger, Rich with a smiling salute.

This, of course, is the part of Jack's new prosperity he's not too happy with. Friends, and friends of friends, are his small-scale customers, maintenance users, many, like Rich, in manual labor, who take the crank for energy. Jack sells only to veterans of the substance he knows fairly well, has used it himself just a few times at parties.

And look how quiet and well-run the Hyperion is. He's not creating any problem here. Indeed, dangerous outsiders would otherwise be coming in to serve his regulars among the residents. It's a sleazy thing to do, OK, though it's still better than what he *was* doing through most of his first year up here: drinking and fighting, hammering himself to pieces.

He opens his notes for *Master of the Hounds.* Bodice rippers are very simple in their form, but since his first slapdash success he's become aware of their potential, the libidinal energy they can hum with if you sculpt them, use their clichés creatively.

His buxom bodice this time is Lupinnia, poor relation of Lord Darcy, who's been given work in the kitchen of Darcy's manse. Here she's under the thumb of the housekeeper, the lofty, disapproving Miss Mandley. Now Miss Mandley is about to send Lupinnia, with a pail of meat scraps, down to the kennels. There, dark, brooding Rackham, Master of the Hounds, holds sway. Lupinnia has already caught the eye of the still, icy blond Lord Darcy—Hunk A. Rackham—Hunk B—she's only glimpsed from afar, but in that glance has seen something mysteriously compelling to his smoldering eyes—

From the manager's suite across the hall at the end of the stairs, a muffled snarl erupts, a shrill answering wail replies—and they're at it again! What is *with* them lately? Bill and Phaasri Patel, the manager and his wife, have started growling and hissing and snarling their way through yet another dead-of-night fight.

The couple could almost be siblings, both mahogany-complected, long-limbed and graceful, with handsome Aryan features. Jack's heard them fighting before, some shouting there from Bill, some fierce wifely haranguing from Phaasri. They work for loftier Patels who own the Hyperion and some other hotels. Though their English is limited, Jack gathers that Phaasri feels that her husband is undervalued and underpaid by these richer relatives.

But these recent struggles . . . Always deep in the night. It's not their volume—they're probably inaudible a few doors down the hall. It's their eerie ferocity, his voice relentless, hers veering toward hysteria. Bill seems to be chanting a guttural litany, while she quavers protest, denial. . . . What are they *thinking* of? They've got Aarti, their twelve-year-old daughter, in there! The kid *can't* be sleeping through this.

They've really settled into it. On and on they go. Jack screws his foam earplugs in deep. He pours another inch of Ancient Age—old AA he calls it—and knocks it back, violating his own strict discipline of two drinks per night of writing.

He can usually get past this and push his work ahead. When he rereads it next day he finds his writing grows sparser, less inspired, once the fighting starts, but at least he can advance it.

Not this time. Tonight there seems to be something about that closeted turmoil that is aimed at him personally, that there's a message in it that he's meant to read. It simply will not drop into the background, however he stares at his half-typed page. As if in some proto-human tongue of snarls and groans the pair of them are calling him, warning him.

This is absurd. He has to stay on schedule. His editor has promised the advance on "ten good chapters and the outline." He can send that in a couple weeks if he can just shut those two out and concentrate!

A delicate sensation of something small and slender in his pocket offers him an inspiration. It's the bindle he has prepared for Bender up in 43. He extracts the little envelope, untucks its flap . . . takes out his knife and nicks out on its point a tiny dune of powder.

We're not talking his Art here. We're talking the manufacture of pulp. Shallow fun by formula.

He snorts it.

Within five minutes he's typing again, drowning them out, all the way back into the tale. At the kennels' open doors, whence breathes out the scent of beasts, timorous Lupinnia, afraid to enter unbidden, calls out quaveringly, "Master Rackham, sir?" Long silence follows, a vague stir of caged bodies her only answer. At length she enters, her wooden clogs knocking on the echoey floorboards. . . .

Near four A.M., Jack straightens and stretches. Utter silence fills the Hyperion. When did they stop fighting? Who cares?

Damn, that went well! At this rate—

He hears a whisper. It has the oddest quality of coming from a considerable distance. He harkens. Only silence now.

He stands up and stretches more completely—feels, in the motion, an effervescence in his blood, a faint seethe of added color in his vision. It's the speed, of course. He's reminded it's a creepy, cobwebby drug, especially late at night when you're alone and hear things.

He steps out into the little staff compound—a short hallway, his door there, Elmer's next to it, the staff bathroom . . . and again, he hears a whisper.

There are syllables in it, almost distinct, and it's still . . . far away. Not directionally marked, but from somewhere else within the building. From the cavernous street-level storage floor beneath his feet? From the fourth floor, two floors above his head? It's in the hotel, is *of* it—that's the sensation.

Well, he should clear his brain anyway. Go on one of his little night patrols. He opens the compound's steel door and steps into the hall. The parched rubber runner of the hall crackles faintly as he treads it: *eekie, eekie, eekie . . .*

The bulbs are sparse and dim, and in their gloom the dark-varnished doors of the rooms seem, ever so slightly, to bulge and contract, as if with the breathing of the sleepers inside. Eerie, and surely the effect of the unaccustomed drug.

Eekie, eekie, eekie . . .

Those first months after losing Erika, he lived in other hotels like this one. He knows that places like the Hyperion are dangerous. Not crudely dangerous like the real flops, like the pusher-and-pimp-infested Mayfair down on Mission, its hallways bellowing with boomboxes, its wastebaskets wicked with dirty needles. The danger of quieter places was more insidious. It was a danger to people who didn't have somewhere else they were headed, and a way to get there, as Jack did.

Because places like this slip your time out from under you. The longer you stay in them, the lonelier and smaller you grow, till you dwindle too small to dare leaving.

Eekie, eekie, eekie . . .

And they all have this same complex smell to them. Somehow it's more distinct in the deep night's silence, as if the odor were like a faint noise drowned out by the day's bustle. A layered aroma: the ghosts of food furtively cooked on generations of hotplates; the stale echo of a million cigarettes; the millennial sad scent of booze, with a *soupçon* of the puke it prompted; and, hovering over all, an exhausted whiff of boxed air rebreathed by a thousand dreaming failures gone before.

. . . eekie, eekie up the stairs . . . Thank God that *he* isn't destined here. Free rent and two hundred a month for the niftiest little writing niche a man could want, a stable clientele of honest working joes he can sell clean, cheap product to, guys who would otherwise have to risk—

What's that he hears? Around the next turning. The soft closing of a door. Steps in the hall.

It's DeeAnn, heading for her own room, obviously just come from someone else's. Her little butt-hugging black micro blends with the gloom, but the bleached quills of her short 'do shine. She's walking quietly for her, meaning her heeled sandals aren't quite knocking the floor as she sashays along. A cheerful, amped-up little woman with more than a few nosefuls in her by this time of night. She turns at her door, smiles, and says—almost at street volume—"Hey, Jack!"

"Shhh!" When he's close he murmurs ironically, "Hi, DeeAnn. Working?"

She stage-whispers, "Can't sleep, Jack?"

"Just stretching my legs." Jack likes DeeAnn. Her heavily made-up eyes make her look like a merry little raccoon. He more or less trusts her, or she wouldn't be the Hyperion's one and only resident hooker. "You *working?*" he repeats.

Her answer is a half-beat slow. "I will be. I'm heading back out to meet Razz." Razz, the hotel's one and only resident pimp, who serves the neighborhood from his rolling trick wagon, a white Caddy convertible. Jack's question was, was she working *here,* just now, in one of the rooms on this hall. She's allowed to trick only three of the tenants of the hotel, older long-term tenants, reliable and discreet. And none of those men room on this floor.

He can't keep his eyes from scoping her tight little rump. He clears his throat. "Well, I know you're respecting our ground rules here. You guys have it nice here, right?"

"Oh, Jack, it's great for *all* of us." Her merry eyes have caught his glance, never missing a trick, though Jack's been careful never to *be* one of her tricks.

She's right about "all" of us. Jack rakes a triple rent off her and Razz, and Bill pockets the extra without "knowing" of the deal. Bill Patel seems to like Jack, but the added sweetener does Jack's job security no harm.

"See yuh, Ja-a-ack." Her friendly taunt follows him to the back staircase. He creaks on up to the top floor.

This floor's no different from the lower two, except that somehow

Jack feels he's entered a stratum of deeper desolation, as if, up here, the hotel's whole sad aura were more concentrated. He treads slowly, a sense of utter loneliness enveloping him. All these boxed sleepers, each lying in his little electrochemical turbulence of dreams. Together they seem to form a great dynamo of solitude, all of them radiating their aloneness up into the night sky. Jack suddenly feels like the night watchman in some forgotten cryogenic warehouse. All these flash-frozen souls have waited for the Thaw a thousand years. They've paid for it in a currency long out of circulation, out of memory. CryoCorp folded centuries ago, its schedule lost, its techs all dust. . . .

Eekie eekie eekie . . . He stops at the rearmost corner of the building. Number 96, in a little cul-de-sac opposite an airshaft. Whose room is this? Jack knows all the tenants, should be able to call up instantly the face that goes with this room number, but for some reason he draws a complete blank. He stares, hypnotized, at the open airshaft window. Under the lifted sash, the darkness of the shaft is a perfect black. It's that blackness that is so mesmerizing. It's impossibly dense. It seems to be the blackest black Jack's ever seen.

The street door sounds its electric death-rattle two floors below. Jack plunges down the nearest stairwell three steps at a time, thudding softly on the balls of his feet, gripping the banisters to swing through the turns. Released from his trance, he enjoys a little game he's played before: reach the cage with minimal noise and buzz the guy in before his second ring. Now he's sprinting tiptoe down the hall. . . .

Makes the bars of the cage, thrusts an arm through, down under the counter, and buzzes the street-door release. Damn, he's good!

The miniaturized man in the bubble mirror, plumpish and severely barbered, is Bender. Even the pens in his pocket-protector are distinct in the micro-image as he climbs with measured steps.

"Hey, Bender."

"Jack." A contained and private guy who does something in computers, his skeptical gaze lingers on Jack's face, a moment of uncharacteristic directness. "I've got something I want to show you. Can you come up when you get off shift?"

"It'll have to be when I'm back from work."

"Fine."

At seven A.M. sharp, Bill Patel steps out of the manager's suite. His handsome, dusky face looks exhausted; the smudges of darker pigment under his eyes look as purple as bruises. He already has one of his wand-like Marlboro 100s going, waves it languidly at Jack with a tired smile. He unlocks the steel door, comes into the cage, and drops exhaustedly onto the couch.

"Ah, Jack," he says, "never marry weeth a wooman!" Above his smile, his eyes look out from somewhere far removed from mirth. Jack makes his standard answer.

"I don't know, Bill. I want *my* woman back." He collects his things, slips his little .38, his midnight protection, into his pocket. The Patels' deep-night battle, which Bill has to know he's overheard, hangs in the air between them. Jack gathers his papers and his typewriter.

"You get something for me, Jack?"

The question completely surprises him. "You mean the rents?" They won't all be in till the end of the week.

Bill looks at him a moment longer, something strange there, ironic maybe. Then he shrugs and waves his Marlboro wand dismissively.

Jack decides on a shower before turning in. As he's standing under the hot water, he recalls his friendly little run-in with DeeAnn . . . her merry eyes . . . her little bubble-butt. His thoughts begin to take a carnal turn.

He thinks of Brittany. Would it be all right to visit her? It's been a week, hasn't it?

It was Brittany's pill connection Squash—massive, imperturbable— who brought her to the Hyperion. Jack ran into Squash in Dolores Park, where the man sometimes did business. "This little fren' of ours streets it round here? She been zonin out way too far. *Way* lettin go of herself."

"She's a sweet little girl," rasped Fat Sal, a rail-thin, caramel-colored woman always after Squash to quit his trade. "She need to be inside a while, fed an' looked after. What about your big hotel down there? Mature man like you would know not to mistreat her."

They brought her by the same day, with a month's rent from their own pockets.

Ill and exhausted, the girl seemed scarcely awake enough to stand upright. Having the room seemed good for the girl. He saw her going out occasionally, more often ran into her headed to or from the shower. For a street person, she seemed inordinately fond of being clean.

He put off asking her for her rent when her advance ran out, but Bill started asking, and he had to knock at her door. She smiled a little loopily—always had a buzz on—and said, "My mom hasn't sent me anything lately, don't have more food stamps to sell for a while. I could get it on with you for the rent. I don't mind at all if that works for you."

Astonished, all Jack could think of to say was, "How old are you?"

"Twenty."

Talk about guilt! Selling crank has nothing on this! Even though he has found Britt to be cheerfully indifferent about sex. Even though he visits her no more than a few times a month. Even though he's always gentle and considerate. Even though he's struggled to get her to stop taking pills, though she absolutely refuses to do this. Even though . . .

He knocks. "Britt? It's Jack. Is this an OK time?" A vague mumble, or just the TV? He ought to peep in, just to make sure she hasn't overdone her pills. He uses his master key.

She's sprawled on the bed watching the tube, head propped by pillows, eyes at half-mast. The hem of her T-shirt discloses, not far recessed within, a triangle of panty crotch.

"Britt? You OK?"

"Huh? . . . oh shrr . . . shrr." Vaguely, she begins struggling to sit up. "Fine . . ."

"You want to shower first?" Guiltily, he knows he's skipped a step, is taking her saying *she's* fine to mean that *it's* fine. She doesn't seem to notice.

"Oh yeah . . ." she says, "wake up . . ." Britt loves bathing. Jack's come to believe the hotel's bathrooms were her main inducement to move in here. She gives him a vague smile. She has pretty features, but her face strikes you as undersized. It's clenched. There's a wariness about it even in her pillhead somnolence.

He helps her into her terrycloth robe and walks her to the nearest shower. Wakened by the water, she'll find her own way back. He returns to her room. Checks the nightstand for her pill stash and finds both Nembutals and valiums, genuine pharmaceuticals, so she's still copping from Squash. Checks the mini-fridge he installed for her: one unpeeled banana, spotty but still viable; a quart of milk, half drunk and still smelling OK; a small box of Grape-Nuts, a third eaten. It's three days since he got her this stuff, so at least she's doing some eating. He closes the fridge.

For some reason, her field jacket—a sturdy khaki garment with many big, buttoning pockets—is hanging off the back of the chair. Is she thinking of taking off? But he checks the pockets and finds them empty.

For a while after Britt moved in here, all her meager belongings remained neatly stored in this jacket's pockets: clean underwear, clean T-shirts, toothbrush, candy bars, food stamps . . . Weeks passed before she transferred her stuff to the little chest of drawers by the bed. Where, yes, it's all still nested, along with a few of the paperbacks she's recently gone through.

She's the readingest young druggie he's ever met. Britt's unlike any pillhead he's ever known. Determined. She didn't just drift from being a druggie to being homeless. She *chose*. She was pursuing a career of being both. It eases his guilt a little, knowing that as soon as she wants to be gone, she will be.

She comes back, hair in wet quills, face a bit more focused. She gives him her little clenched smile. "Hi, Jack!" She falls back down on the bed and, supine, shows her tranked state more plainly, her eyes sliding off fo-

cus, skittish like the bubbles in a level. She spreads her legs companionably, her labia moistly pink in their fleecy ruff.

"You're so lovely!" croaks Jack, dropping his clothes off. He touches
her breasts, her thighs, scrolls the condom on, and gently mounts her. She
eases him into herself.

Gently, tenderly, he couples with her. He understands that for her this
is mere gymnastics, a friendly feat of limberness and rhythm. He accepts
his solitude and seeks a release as unintrusive as he can make it . . . and, as
he nears his crisis, allows himself his shameful fantasy, invariable for him
at this juncture—that her breasts are Erika's more jutting cones, the nip-
ples brown as nuts, her cheekbones Erika's wide, tilted planes, her eyes the
limpid, arctic grey of Erika's . . .

As he begins to come, she startles him. She convulses, and then goes
tense and trembly. Can *she* be coming? He's sure, in the instant of wondering it, that she isn't . . . and then his seed is springing, springing . . .

Afterward she lies so tense, so still beneath him. "Britt? Are you OK?"
She gives him—scarcely moving—a quick little quieting touch. He gathers that she wants him silent, or better yet, gone. Awkwardly he disentan-
gles, rises, and pulls his clothes back on. She isn't trembling now, but
lying absolutely still. She's closed her eyes but he feels her there, wide
awake behind them. In sympathy with her inward withdrawal, he whispers, "You sure you're OK?" She gives him the faintest nod and sketches,
still not opening her eyes, a smile—urgent, it seems, to make him leave.

So he does, and heads for his room, and his own bed.

III
The Trouble with Walls,
and with Windows

As the first gray light is sifting through her airshaft window, Brittany comes stark awake. The tube's still on from last night, some morning talk show. She turns it up and gobbles some nummies and vals—lies waiting for the warm chemical blankie to enfold her, glancing for reassurance now and then at her field jacket, which she's hung on the chair in case she has to pack it and hit the streets fast, blow out of here like a bubble at the first sign of danger. Because fear has been nagging her these last few days.

Here comes her blankie's thick warmth. The very air around her grows radiant, fluffy. On the tube, the painted faces grow more vivid, flex and grimace with earnestness, coin smiles of compassion, concern. So cozy, all this friendly energy these pretty TV people lavish on her! This was what Mom was enjoying all those years, all those nights, propped in her La-Z-Boy. On pills and tubing out, while young Brittany lay in her room alone . . . and later, not alone.

Then a knock. And there's Jack looming above her. Britt's not delighted. She likes Jack. He's a sweet old guy. But so much work it seems, the whole physical transaction. It's as if Jack's come asking for her help unloading a furniture van or a truck full of bricks.

But that's not fair. He's a nice man, really doesn't bother her very often. The work will probably do her some good, help someone else out, and get her out of herself for a change.

Once she's in the shower, lathering the soap into her skin, the chore ahead seems light enough. She rinses and soaps again—loves scrubbing off the fine patina of the day's dirt. Unfortunately, the shower also wakens her, thins her blankie and brings back her larger dilemma. This unlimited hot water, these clean towels, shampoo . . . are all so wonderful, but the price of them is living indoors, inside the same walls, day after day, night after night . . . and that's *not* wonderful. Living boxed in like this is just not *safe*. It's always far safer being homeless, because any home can be broken into—just as it's safer to vacate your body with pills, because any inhabited body can also be broken into.

She belts on her terrycloth robe and heads back down the hall. Take care of Jack. Stop brooding.

Back in her room, she tries to be graceful, inviting, though she's pretty dizzy, hitting the horizontal again. But she strokes his back as he climbs aboard, smiles encouragingly. He's avid, but always considerate. She opens to him and eases, eases him in. The pills enable her to achieve that Zen of inner absenting, inner loosening. Carefully, companionably, she supplies him with the helpful apparatus of her body.

He moves gingerly, cautious, long past the point she needs him to be. Though he's shaking with desire, he squeezes her breasts as if they're fragile as kittens. She's impressed anew by how heavily his need burdens him—a cruel burden, it seems to her. Like her own fear, so relentless, that she's lived with so long. At least Jack's burden can be—

What is happening to the lights? The ceiling bulb still blazes, and the TV tube—but their glare has shrunk down close to the glass. They emit only two little yellowish spheres of light, like dying suns, while a grainy, seething darkness swells around them, a darkness like a boiling of black ants that billows from the walls and floor and ceiling and fills the air.

And as this darkness envelops them, Jack's laboring breath gusts down searingly cold on her face, its frosty volume astonishing, a cold smoke roiling from his mouth, filling the darkness like an arctic blast that wraps her nakedness in icy tendrils. . . .

And as he rears his head back, climaxing, the monstrous thing occurs that Britt already knows is coming, knows is coming precisely because of the dark and the cold, and because Jack's breathing now makes an un-earthly hiss like the breath of the interstellar abyss, a ghostly crackle of ra-dio energy sweeping through infinite void—and because, too, of a stench beginning to tendril around them, the icy charnel stench of some mass grave in a polar wasteland . . .

Jack's shadow-head rears back in the dark. She steels herself. The wall behind Jack crumbles away, and a star-filled darkness silhouettes him, and out of that galactic aperture something reaches and slides itself around his corded throat—

(*lie absolutely still, Britt, absolutely still*)

—a thick and glittery whiteness, a wet, muscled tentacle, fish-belly pale, that swells as it tightens, tightens . . . till Jack's neck crumples with a crushing sound, and the hiss of the void, and the stench of the void, pour in an icy geyser from his gaping mouth.

absolutely still absolutely still absolutely still . . .

The light is back. The air is clear. Jack's himself, is bowed over her solicitously. She reassures him as much as she can without stirring. She makes only tiny, cautious movements of her hand.

She is alone. The light-bulb shines, the tube murmurs, but she does not yet dare to trust their returned reality. Every time a Window opens, it is a test of nerve. Whatever comes through hovers waiting for her terror, waiting for Britt to break and bolt. She will not break cover. She will close her eyes, will lie absolutely *still*.

The endless minutes unfold, the light through her window grows stronger. Thank God for the heavy blankie she has already wrapped her-self in. Thank God for that chemical gravity already ballasting her before the Window's opening. Her blankie, which never fails her. Dear life-saving, soul-saving blankie, which even the things from the Window can-not penetrate, once she is snugged deep inside it.

Britt's outside, crossing the wide lawn of Dolores Park. The sun beams down on her shoulders, a breeze ripples the trees, and she's put the hotel behind her. She's outdoors, she's safe!

But what's this chill she feels? She touches her chest and feels bare skin. Tries to turn around, and finds herself flat on her back.

And comes full awake. She's still lying nude on her bed, and it's full night outside her airshaft window.

Fool! Passing out like that. She carefully rises, sits listening—*feeling*, more precisely, for that faint exhalation of fear from the walls. Plenty of fear in her own heart, but the dread that reaches out for her, that faint, in-human *teasing*, is gone. The Window has closed.

She assembles herself methodically for departure, starting with a fresh throatful of pills. It will be good to be gone from here, good to be outside again, though *no place* is really safe, is it? The last Window, far worse than this one, opened outside. As she packs her coat, she lets it come back—because, till the downers come on, she can't help it.

It happened last year. Fat Sal was with her, on one of her rampages against Squash's lazy, pill-dealing ways, and streeting it with Brittany to spite him. (Though lean and testy as a snake, Sal's a good friend of Britt's.) The hour was long past midnight, find-a-hidey-hole time. Some-where along their westward ramble they had picked up Demetrius, an old wino they knew, and now the three of them were out in the blocks between Haight and the Panhandle, cruising for someplace to sleep.

It was that most unfettered hour of the homeless, when the neighbor-hoods are dead as tombs. All those daytime possessors of the streets have left town for the Land of Nod, and the fog-chilled vagabonds enjoy an empty interval of city ownership. Any nook they can worm into is theirs by right.

They had let Demetrius—a shrunken little man-monkey, half-erased by booze—join them as a kindness. They would see he bedded warm and had the solace of some company, because they had sensed that tonight for some reason he feared his solitude. Demetrius had only rudimentary social gestures left, fractional riffs of camaraderie from the years before his self-lobotomy. He wore a cheap plastic cameo ring, some guy in a wreath, and periodically showed it to you, saying, "Demetrius, see? That's me. Demetrius, see?" Then his smile would stretch his collapsed face, briefly displaying a whole web of wrinkles cleaner than the rest of his skin. In daylight it had a sunburst effect.

They walked past tall Victorians whose gardens smelled powerfully fresh in the citywide silence. At length they chose a house that stood in dimness, equidistant between two streetlights, and threaded their way back between it and its neighbor. Under its back stairs they found a clean little pad of concrete. They could snug up against the house's back wall, with the first flight of stairs like a slanting, ribbed roof above their slumbers.

Britt and Sal had collected newspapers earlier on their cruise, and Britt had scouted more for Demetrius when he joined them. They laid pads of these on the concrete against the wall. Sal curled up on her side, and in moments was snoring softly.

But Demetrius was uneasy and wouldn't lie down. He sat with his back to the wall, seeming more anxious, if anything, now that they had a refuge. Britt sat up with him. He kept breaking into his little riffs, and she kept shushing him, soothing him down with nods and whispers.

". . . when I get that *check* they still owe me, watch out. Get me some teeth and somethin to chomp with 'em, get us some Night Train and piss up a storm. Demetrius, see? That's me." His sunburst grin was just a dim smudge in the stair-shadows, with only starlight sifting down through the gaps in the risers. Britt soothed and shushed him, patting his arm, knowing the contact helped, although her touches must feel a thousand miles away to the old man, sunk as he was in his mental wasteland.

But at last Britt had to sleep. Her body sank down on its paper bed. She curled on her side and was gone.

Soon she was coiling through a meandering dream, which presently became a dream of a rat with a huge tail that was rubbing against her body, rasping and rasping against a part of her body she couldn't quite identify, couldn't quite feel, but knew was hers. Rasping and rasping her, the rat grinned, yellow-eyed.

She awoke behind still-shut eyes and discovered that the rasping was an actual sound, was a rhythmic scraping on the concrete near her head. She opened her eyes.

A fragmentary moon had migrated up over the gap between the houses, and their understairs nook was zebraed with light and shadow. Cautiously turning her head, Britt confronted Demetrius's moon-striped legs. They were working, pistoning uselessly on the concrete. It was his heels that were scraping, trying to gain purchase, kick free of something.

Britt's nerves already knew that a Window had opened. She cringed from the arctic cold and the carrion stench that tendrilled out with it. But her survival instincts failed her. In a reflex of terror, she lifted her head and looked straight at it.

And she was lucky, so lucky. The thing from the Window returned her no notice, was wholly engaged with poor Demetrius.

It had thrust itself from the wood of the wall just above the old man. Its plated midsection was as flexibly girt by the wood as a wader's waist is by the water. Its bug's head was hugely jawed with the thorny mandibles of some colossal stag beetle, and these jaws jailed the wino's arms and his frail chest, their barbs biting through his stiff dirty jacket and into the flesh beneath.

A stripe of moonlight caught Demetrius's upturned face, twisting and working with his agony. He was raving in whispers, pleading with a desperate sanity she'd never heard in him. And then Britt thought she heard his raving answered. She wasn't quite sure, maybe what she heard was just the cold hiss of Outside, the staticky breath of its vastness leaking through the Window's aperture. Yet it seemed the thing did whisper an answer to its prey, "*I know . . . I know . . .*"

What she heard next wasn't in doubt: the rush of the wino's bladder emptying, drenching his pants, as the thing, with a powerful pull, hauled him into the wall. The wall was blank wood again. Of Demetrius, all that was left was a piss-stain on the moon-latticed concrete.

Britt would have bolted, but for leaving Sal there, and she was too frightened to make the stir of rousing her, persuading her away. She huddled on her side, shivering, till the dawn and Sal's waking, telling herself it was his Window, the wino's, not hers. Just as this morning it was Jack's. Jack's, not hers.

Britt's dressed now, and all the pockets of her jacket packed. She slips it on. Tears are streaking down her face. All her grown life her enemy has hounded her, driven her into the streets, made her hunker down and dirty, lurking and looking out, and darting from cover to cover. All her grown life he has made her crouch and cower.

All this a game for her enemy. Because with all her terror she's always escaped, just as the mouse is meant to escape from the cat, again and again and again. Until the final capture.

And this latest kind of teasing—what is she to make of it? This mock murder of Jack, which goes all unsuspected by the victim himself? She fears for him, but just how is she supposed to warn him? Get him to believe? And if he believed, what could she tell him to do? She fears for Jack, but fears much more for herself. It's time to go.

She pulls her Buck knife from her back pocket, opens it one-handed by pinching the blade out with thumb and forefinger, snagging its point on the leg-seam of her jeans, and flicking her wrist. Sometimes, when she's hanging out, if someone unwelcome joins her and her friends, she will practice this little one-handed draw repeatedly, as if absentmindedly. As often as not, the routine will discourage the interloper after a while. Sal loves it and has nicknamed her Blade.

She's never had to use the knife though. Has no idea what she'll do if she ever has to.

She steps out into the hall. As she walks, Bettina Butch, her inevitable pack of Marlboros tucked in her T-shirt's folded sleeve, falls in step with her. "Traveling, Brittany?"

"I guess so."

Bettina's faint smile and nod seem to confirm some thought of her own. "Take care of yourself." She heads down to the street.

Britt pauses by the cage. "Hi, Elmer."

"'Lo, Brittany."

"Is Jack in?"

"Naw, he took off an hour ago, went to get somethin to eat."

"Well . . . would you tell him I took off? I moved out? Tell him I said thanks?"

"OK."

Her escape is as good as made. She can take a last look from that street window at the hall's end. That's one window she's always liked.

She leans out into the cool evening air, framed by the fire escape, looks down on the bustle of the street below, breathes in the smell of the night. A fugitive from the suburbs, Britt has always liked these big, high city windows. Windows you can look out of, discover things from. In her suburban childhood, windows were dangerous leak, where prowlers could get in, and you kept them locked. But this kind of window you could even *escape* from—out onto that wrought iron ladder, and then one quick swing down to the street . . .

Voices behind her. Britt turns.

It's the Indian manager with his wife and daughter, just stepping out of their apartment. They all seem somber, and both of the adults look exhausted as well. When Britt smiles at them, Bill nods, remote. The two females give Britt exactly opposite looks: from the girl, shy admiration; and from the mother, a stony stare. Britt understands. For the child, a coltish twelve or thirteen, she must be adventure incarnate, a young American woman on her own in the world. For the mother, Britt's more what she really is—an addict, diseased with weakness and failure, a threat to the daughter. The woman's beauty somehow makes this speechless accusation crueler.

The pay phone beside Britt rings, a hoarse, old-fashioned caw that startles her. For some reason, with these three beautiful Aryans staring at her, it seems her obligation to answer it.

"Yes?"

In the receiver she hears only live air, the faint hiss of somewhere else, and someone else breathing there.

But that particular breathing . . . it touches her spine with a long-known touch.

And then comes that long-known voice, gritty and sly. "*Have a hunka unka, hunka unka, hunka unka . . .*"

Like a nursery rhyme. Like a lollypop lullaby, in a mocking croon. She stands staring at the Patel family, those beautiful, uncomprehending people, while her terror is sweeping her away inside. She feels like someone a sleeper wave has just snaked offshore for drowning, a person dragged out to die who looks back and catches the eye of someone safe on shore, the soon-to-be-drowned one's eyes saying to the stranger, "*Do you see what is happening to me? Do you see?*"

This isn't like this morning. This voice, Unka Doug's voice, is for Britt herself, for her and her alone.

She hangs up the phone with a bang, plunges past the startled little family, and down the stairs to the street.

IV
Into the Carnival

Jack wakes to the rising roar of traffic and the blaze of sunset out his window. Christ! What kind of sleep was that? He must have awakened a dozen times, but you couldn't call it shallow sleep, because every time he went back under it seemed deep as a well, and it seemed he had every kind of nightmare known to man, but he can't recall a single one of them.

The crank, that's what it was. Stupid! It's enough he's still *drinking*, really. A glass or two of Old AA, in the controlled way he's been doing it, well, so be it. But absolutely no more speed. It's a road he doesn't need to go down.

It's bad enough to be selling it, he reminds himself as he climbs the stairs to Bender's floor. At least Bender's as stable a customer as you could ask for. Just look—

"Hi, Jack. Come on in."

—at his room here. All his computer equipment, arranged on tidy worktables of his own construction. And along the other wall, the man's other avocation: chests and footlockers of collectors' firearms and neatly shelved archives of gun-lore magazines. The guns themselves have never worried Jack. Bender is such a perfect specimen of the obsessive-retentive type that his particular obsession seems secondary. If anything, the revered guns underscore the man's harmlessness. Plump, severely barbered, his clothing crisply ironed, his utterances brief and formal. Jack imagines his bullied childhood, and rather likes him.

"Here you go."

". . . sixty . . . eighty . . . two hundred. Thank you. Jack, I asked you up to show you something."

For the first time in their acquaintance, Bender is opening one of his footlockers. "Look at this, Jack." A hint of fervor, now, in his careful face. "It's a Glock 17, nine millimeter. With this Eclipse suppressor, it's a little over twelve inches long, but this shoulder-rig is a Velcro breakaway. You can carry it silenced and still pull it fast. Here, take it. It's a well-balanced weapon to start with, and see how I've augmented the frontstrap and backstrap? Put more heft in the hand? Swivel it. That's it. Aim here and there. See? Even with the suppressor on, it's got great pointability. Dry fire it, go on. Feel good? Forty decibels net sound reduction in that Eclipse. From a few yards away, a round fired sounds like someone pulling the tab on a beer can."

Jack has never before heard so much speech issue from Bender's mouth. He has a comic sense of being the rube at a big-city car lot. The weapon does feel wonderful, a weighty little scepter of power, but it's completely irrelevant to his concerns. "It's beautiful, Bender, but hey, my little .38 is all I need. It's not like I really have to shoot anyone."

"Of course. That's a perfectly adequate little Smith, no question. What I'm thinking of is mutual profit. This was a windfall to me. I'll trade it to you for half an ounce. With the rig and suppressor, you could get two thousand dollars for this."

That *would* be an unusual profit, especially at Cozzens's low prices. But then, Jack would have to sell an unlicensed firearm, something more dangerous than selling modest doses of speed. Bender is proposing a double risk to him for a sweetener that costs the man himself nothing.

"I don't think so, man. It just doesn't seem worth the trouble."

"I understand completely. Just remember it's not going anywhere. If a taker for the piece should happen to present himself, I'll still be open to the trade."

Jack heads back downstairs. The salesmanship, the articulateness, he hasn't seen these sides of Bender before. It makes him seem less pathetic, more purposive.

"Jack?" There's Elmer in the cage, holding up the office phone. "Call for you!" He hands Jack the receiver below the bars.

"Hello?"

"Hey, Slick." The voice surprises Jack: it's the gravelly baritone of Cozzens. The huge biker deals only face to face, and has never given him a phone number. Jack's always had to drop by his place and hope that he's in.

"I'm home," says Cozzens. "Why don't you drop by?"

"Sure. Sounds good. Couple hours maybe?"

"Tonight. Whenever." Cozzens's great size can be heard in the burr of his voice, but there is an odd delicacy in his hanging up.

Jack's got only Rich's and Bender's cash on hand, but he doesn't like to rebuff this advance from a very profitable connection. He met the man through Willy and Marnie. They are more party pals than friends of Jack's, and he knows even less about Cozzens. The guy makes him nervous. He has startling tawny eyes, feral but waxy—the eyes of an unwell beast. And as he sits weighing, and packaging, and taping, saying little, Jack always feels that the whole transaction is uninteresting to him. That something as yet unspoken is on Cozzens's mind. Well, Jack will have some dinner and go see the man.

Down on the street outside the Hyperion, Jack just stands there a moment, taking in the early evening. The candy-colored neons are coming on, the signals blaze, all the tail-lights and headlights river and roar, and above it all a first shy star or two gleams in the purple sky. The sidewalks throng, the working stiffs—many Latins and Easterners—threading through the lowlifes. And even these drinkers and druggers, these hookers and hardcores, move briskly with a Happy Hour air, as the Mission turns to jewels all around them.

He's right where he should be, Jack thinks. The . . . *romance* of being here strikes him anew. Look at who he's just been talking to: a well-groomed, secretive, low-key kind of madman, followed by a full-blown, outright outlaw. What a world away he is from flat smoggy L.A. A city with history, a city with an underground, a city with color! Here is where magic is to be found. Here is where his first *real* book will be born!

When he has Erika back, they'll move north, live at least within range of the City. How could he have expected to write poetry in L.A.'s wasteland? Here in the Mission is where the real human mysteries live, the grotesques, the misfits, the monsters and archetypes. Here is myth! Here is vision!

A good, sharp appetite is in him now. He strides to the corner and turns down Sixteenth. Halfway down the block is the Silver Dragon. Through the big street window you can see half the neighborhood is in there, and a good fraction of the Hyperion, inching their trays past the steam-table, chowing down at the tables. He goes into the warm food-fog and the music of silverware.

Asians run the Dragon, as they do most of the good greasy spoons around here. These look like Koreans, perhaps a family, the gray-haired matriarch at the register, a man (her son, or younger husband?) and a teenage boy and girl. They're nearly speechless, and their black eyes convey nothing, except perhaps how alien they find this American underclass that they serve. With their veiled faces and avoiding eyes, they might be feeding ghosts. It always makes Jack think of Odysseus in the Underworld, and the ghosts flocking to his trench of blood to drink, and testify.

Take DeeAnn there, setting a speed freak's supper on her tray—two donuts and a cup of coffee. Sometime today she's changed her black micro for a red one, and her lipstick from red to purple. Smiling Jack imagines her testimony.

Know, O studmuffin Odysseus, that I am DeeAnn, daughter of SueAnn, granddaughter of LooAnn exsettera, and that I have spent my years on this glorious green globe whipping head, hand, or ass on anything that breathes and has a hundred bucks, and I have generally had a high old time feeding a righteous, double-barreled crank-hole that I keep locked and loaded in the middle of my face here.

Or what about Razz there next to her—small, slight, black, wearing a leather gunfighter's hat with a band of coins around the crown. A fairly cool, smart pimp who has so far been a trouble-free source of pocket money for Bill Patel, and added job security for Jack.

Yo, Odie-daddy! Know that I am Razz, son of Ma-tazz, and that I pass my time on this swingin sphere pimpin the ears off this skinny white ho, buyin myself slick threads, an' chinawhite skag to mellow my 'tude, an' supreme gas for my rollin Caddy whorehouse, an' that I be known for blocks around as one chill, no-fool motherfucker.

Jack tucks into eggs, sausages, potatoes—dense luscious food—and watches Sixteenth from the window. Some nocturnal renovation going on across the street and down a few doors. What looks like another Asian family painting the interior of a new 'spoon just getting ready to open. The sign's already up: *The Harvest Moon.* Two young people in overalls are rolling yellow paint on the walls. A woman, bulky and frizzy-haired, is directing them. On the night street, the distant group shows as clear as a TV image.

A severely bent figure totters toward the Silver Dragon's door, slowly, slowly caning his way along. This is old Mr. Cunningham. *He's* the one in 96. Why couldn't Jack remember that this morning? The guy's lived there forever and is not easily forgettable.

He's bent almost in half by some senile spinal deformity. His speech is a barely intelligible grunting, yet he apparently preaches the Word— some word, anyway, because crudely printed tracts can often be seen peeping from side pockets of his shabby coat. He has white stubble on his jaw, a vague half-smile, and pale blue eyes. Jack can never quite decide if his expression is pleasant or imbecile. He must be in his nineties at the very least. He inches down to the Dragon once or even twice a day, and the trips take him forever. Jack must have passed him on the way down. Can the man's frailty even manage that heavy glass door?

Well, look at this. The Korean lady has left her post at the register, left Rich Rasp there holding out his money, and is scurrying to the door, opening it for the old man. She ushers him to a table, while her son or husband has promptly taken over at the register.

Are the Koreans converts of Cunningham's? All these customers who stream past them they view like specters, and look who they single out to honor! The woman's bringing him some tea. She carries the saucer in both hands, placing it gently, even *reverently* before him. Why hasn't Jack noticed this devotion before? She stands there talking softly with downcast eyes. The old man is more perched than seated on his chair, has hooked one elbow on the tabletop and can barely lever his head above its level, his face aimed more floorward than forward. Does he give a slight nod of acknowledgment, or is it just a tremor at the strain of his posture? You can't tell from his face if he's even registering her words . . .

"You hear what I axe you? Whoring don't cause deafness, far as I know. I axed you how much money."

Razz is ragging DeeAnn at the table behind Jack. They get like this when they've been out working their traplines three or four days running. Though it's DeeAnn who's been wired and working, it's Razz who tends to get cranky, while she sits there tuning him out, indifferently dunking donuts in coffee, and eating a bite now and then. It's a riff to publicly abuse your 'ho now and then, Jack supposes, but Razz is supposed to keep a low profile near the Hyperion, and the Silver Dragon is practically the Hyperion's dining room.

"Maybe you better listen witchoo twat," Razz is saying, "'cause widdat you be hearin a pin drop across town."

Jack turns his chair to face their table and resumes forking food in his mouth while gazing at them, like a guy having dinner at home as he watches TV. He's much too close to be ignored. Razz has to notice him, "'S happenin, Jack?"

"Hey, Razz, Dee. Am I intruding?"

For a couple seconds Razz's sparky little pupils seem to be shorting out, anger cutting across the wiring in the man's eyes. The pimp is small but cold as a snake, might be dangerous, Jack realizes.

But prudence tells, and Razz smiles at last. "Oh hey, was we too loud? We still like newlyweds, I swear, Jack, we still get so carried away."

"Join us, Jack," says DeeAnn brightly. Though she's an infallibly sociable young woman, there's the glint of another motive in her speed-bright eyes.

"Thanks, guys." He scoots up to their table. It's occurred to him she might have some cash to put into his visit to Cozzens. He uses a low voice he hopes the vivacious DeeAnn will take as an example. "You know, if you can do it like, discreetly, you might want to give me some cash. I'm paying a visit tonight."

"Great idea." DeeAnn instantly opens her little postage stamp–sized purse on her lap. Razz smoothly starts generating some cover talk. "Have a Kool, Jack."

"Thanks."

"I see you eyein that new 'spoon, that Moon place."

"Yeah, I'm gonna try it out."

"That new place sure chap our momma's ass, though, don't it?"

And now Jack sees that the Korean matriarch is still murmuring to Mr. Cunningham, and that her eyes do indeed seem to be fixed on those bright-lit young painters across the street.

"You think she's pissed?"

"Cantchoo tell? Guess she don't like no competition."

"If you need some smokes," says DeeAnn, "take some Marlboros." She's nudging him a pack. He pockets it. "Thanks. I'll drop by your room before I come on shift."

As he rises, he sees that old Cunningham's hand is trembling with some kind of effort. He's pulling something up from the side pocket of his coat. The crooked paw struggles up into view, a little tract pinched between the knuckles. He drops it on the tabletop as Jack passes, and Jack tries to glimpse the text, but the woman scoops it up greedily. Does the old man's pale eye slant Jack a look as Jack passes him?

Walking along the street, he pulls out the pack. Three hundreds. Hell, he can take a cab to see Cozzens. He heads for the Skyscraper Bar for a beer and the use of their phone.

V
A Friend in Need

Brittany has walked for blocks and somehow cycled back to Sixteenth and Valencia. Her blankie now swaddles her, plenty of nummies and vals, but still her terror twists within its envelopment. Never has she been struck like this, twice in one day. The real horror of hearing Unka Doug's voice was that she knew it wasn't the man himself—knew it was the voice of the enemy the man had brought into her life.

Her enemy can tear through anywhere. It's a flimsy world, she knows, for all its concrete and steel and lumber and stone. All its tar-black pavements, its bolted doors, its raftered roofs are paper-thin. She's known this since she was thirteen, but now she *feels* the wormholes on every side and is in a flinching panic. She must take hold of herself. Must.

Little by little, she unclenches. She's outside, can dodge in any direction. It's a big, big city, and if you look long enough you can always, almost always, find a safe spot, a spot to curl up in and sleep. And now she's feeling the good of her blankie, is growing calm at the core. At last! She spit-swallows another nummie, just to be sure. She can ride this out, she's just got to be calm. Don't let them drag you through the wall. *Fuck* them! Stay real. Stay in *this* world. Food. She'll get some food.

But, looking through the Silver Dragon's window, she can't go in. Everyone so at ease in there together, she sees herself as they must see her, a bulky-coated nomad, an alley-spook in a permanent pill trance. From here, in the darkness of her lurking life, the light in there seems too alien to enter.

Then a shock. Someone in there is waving to her. She looks behind her . . . yes, waving to *her*. It's that DeeAnn, gesturing her in to a seat at the table she's sharing with that man of hers, Jazz or something. The gaudy little woman, so much realler than Britt feels, draws her as if by gravity. Britt goes inside. Her gait feels jerky, as if she's a marionette worked by DeeAnn's beckonings.

"Siddown, Brandy! Siddown! You look starving, sweetie. Wanna donut?"

Her pimp, leaning intently toward DeeAnn, doesn't look pleased by Britt's intrusion, while DeeAnn is delighted with this distraction from him. "You looked like an orphan out there, Brandy. For Chrissake, if you're ever hungry you should just tell me, I'll buya something. Sit—I'll get you some coffee too. You want something, Razz?"

The man doesn't answer, and DeeAnn bustles to the counter, her little red microskirt switching, switching like a bright bird's tail. Razz sits looking at Britt—meditating, she's sure, on something mean to say. He's not much bigger than she, but taut with energy and malice. Has a very still, dark face, eyes large and intent, their whites tarnished like old ivory. His lids get lazy.

"You fuckin Jack jus' for the rent?" he asks in a pleasant tone. She just stares at him, a caught-in-the-headlights stare.

"Cos if you are, you fuckin way too cheap. You got a trim little rack on you there. You yo-o-u-ng. Thing is, an amateur just don't understand the market *values*. Jus' for instance, whatchoo charge for a blowjob?"

Britt's hand is moving to her back pocket. It seems she has no control of what she's doing. Her body is doing it, her body still far more electrified by terror than she realized. Draws her knife and snaps it open on her leg-seam, brings it right up into Razz's face. He flinches back and she holds it vertically there, her hand shaking uncontrollably, but her outthrust arm locked.

"How 'bout this?" she shrills, voice quavering uncontrollably. "You let me cut your fucking *throat*, and *then* I'll give you a blowjob!" She sees how wild she looks in his startlement. He makes an uncertain grab for the weapon and she slashes the air side to side, surging to her feet at the same time and toppling her chair with a *whack* behind her, standing there, knife outthrust. Razz seems paralyzed less by this than by the room's sudden silence, the stare of every eye.

"Hey! It's OK, Brandy!" And DeeAnn is putting donuts and coffee between them, righting the chair and sitting Britt down. "Razz honey, I found those bills I thought I'd lost. Thank God, eh? Here they are, sweetie."

Razz regains poise by skeptically counting the little stack of twenties and fifties she has handed him. Britt sits trembling, knife still clenched. Here and there people have gone back to eating, and the matriarch replaces on its cradle the phone she's picked up.

Razz pockets the bills with a flourish, glad to be seen doing it, receiving the little green banners of his power. It is enough. He may exit with dignity. He stands. With his gunfighter hat and black leather sport coat he should look ridiculous, but he doesn't. He looks like one dangerous little motherfucker. "I'll see you at the ride," he tells DeeAnn. For Britt he has only a supercilious look, but it leaves the menace of him with her as he saunters to the door.

She looks around, sees amusement, sees curiosity, and even gets a nod from one or two she knows. That bent old man from the hotel, Mr. Cunningham, can barely lift his head above the table top, but his pale eyes hold hers a moment and seem to laugh at her.

DeeAnn is saying something, touching her hand. "You OK, Brandy? Just relax! Have a donut. Take this coffee."

The coffee is amazing. It seems to warm her right to the heart. The whole room's eating and talking again, their privacy restored. She draws a shuddery breath.

"I'm so sorry, DeeAnn . . ."

"Why? A little cash and sweet-talk. Men are easy. A piece of cake."

"I've never freaked like that before."

"Don't *worry*. They don't call men tricks for nothing. Eat!"

The donut is another revelation. Sweet food! She's hungry! DeeAnn looks on, beaming. What's she doing now, rummaging in her little long-strap hooker purse?

"You should never let yourself get so hungry, Brandy. You're hitting the streets again? You got your bandana on." Britt nods, startled that she's been noticed, *considered* by this bold little woman. "Well, I want you to take this. You've gotta stay nourished. You can't go letting yourself get so wasted you start pulling knives on people—they'll put you in the slammer."

It's a little fold of twenty-dollar bills DeeAnn's giving her now.

She looks at the money thrust from DeeAnn's scarlet nails like pretty little claws, and for some reason realizes that DeeAnn must be just about her own age. . . . Tears fill Britt's eyes again, then scald her face. She can't believe herself. She grips the table, not to start bawling.

"Oh hey now, hey, Brandy! Stop that, sweetie-pie, I'm just givin you a few bucks and a few donuts. Us girls gotta stick together, am I right? Come on, just *take* it and button it up safe, the hell with that. I think you need some *protein* too, you know? I'm gonna get you a hamburger an' some *milk.* I don't know what I was thinking about just getting—"

She's rising, flustered, when Britt reaches out and grips her arm, holding her in her seat, suppressing the tears. Britt never cries! Nor reaches out and grabs people to keep them from leaving her either. She drags her sleeve across her eyes. Why don't her nummies and vals kick in?

"DeeAnn, it's just . . . it's just you're so nice to me. And actually . . ." she smiles, wiping her nose on the other sleeve, "my name's Brittany."

"Oh hey, I'm sorry!"

"No! *I'm* sorry. That thing with the knife—I've never done anything like that. It's just he was talking—"

But the hooker too is indignant. "You did the right thing. He was *try-ing* to scare you. Little guys always have to be extra macho, right? He's no idiot, he knows you're not cut out for the life. Anybody could see that! Your thing with Jack is just right for you. A nice friendly guy, a little convenience fucking, am I right?"

"Right. I just don't really—"

"Hey, anyone can see that, Brandy! It's an attitude thing. It's a lot of work if you don't take an interest in it. If you do, it's like *acting*. I love getting all costumed up, like on stage every night. Of course a counselor I had in County said it was a power trip, right? Just the kind of bitchy shit you expect from a counselor, but maybe it's a little bit true too. I mean, money for nothing! They do the wanking, and I do the banking!"

This surprises a giggle from Britt. DeeAnn grins, pleased to see this guarded, inward girl laughing. DeeAnn has more. "I whale on their woodies and walk with the goodies."

Britt giggles. Offers, "You pound on their groins and pile up the coins."

"Coins? No way!" More giggles. "I strangle their stiffies for twenties and fifties. I socket their rockets and fill up my pockets."

Britt scarcely knows herself. Laughing now, pouring out tears a moment ago . . . Is she going crazy? And laughs some more.

DeeAnn regales her with tales from the street. Warmth, laughter, sweet tastes and smells—Brittany sinks into the haven of these moments.

A thread of anxiety *does* run through it, because she wants to warn DeeAnn. It has dawned on her that the hotel is dangerous *in itself,* apart from Britt's personal nemesis. But if she tries to warn her, DeeAnn will recoil, will still be nice and all, but will shrink back inside from good old Brandy the whack case, a lot farther gone than anyone guessed. . . .

Britt lifts the last donut for another bite, but it smells a little odd. She sets it down again. DeeAnn's saying, of Razz, "He's actually a big help with some things. He's real ingenious about arranging trick spots, I mean besides the Caddy. You know WhizBurger on Eighteenth? They've got . . ."

But what is this smell? Really insistent now. And there's something wrong with the space in this diner. The street windows' half-transparent reflection of the interior has grown much more vivid and seems to reflect far more people than are actually here. . . .

Where are she and DeeAnn? There. There they are. How gaunt and hollow-eyed her own face looks! DeeAnn's faced away, her reflection is of her back side, but there's something not right about it, there's something dark and sticky in her hair, and this smell, this rotten stench, that's where it's *coming* from! That's why it seems so nearby!

But no, that's not something smeared in DeeAnn's hair, that's a big, ragged hole in the back of her skull, that's her brains and clotted gore all black and sticky within the fouled nest of her spiky bright hair!

Britt's on her feet, DeeAnn looking concerned, saying something to her, but whatever she's saying is far and faint. Already Britt is halfway to the door.

Just as she reaches it and thrusts it open, she catches old Mr. Cunningham's pale, pale eye once more. Such a glee in it! *What,* it seems to ask her, *are you going to do about* that?

VI
Monsters in the Earth

Jack tells the cabby his destination and says that he wants her to take Twenty-fourth across the Mission.

"Your dime," she says.

A slower route, but down here the Carnival really swarms, and he likes the show. Here's where the underclass boogies, blind dumb Mortality, playing the Fool at the Fair. His voyeur's face changes color with the passing neons, as he watches the bundle-hugging immigrants hastening past the Nike-d gangsters, watches all the vagrant loners, the bent, the baffled, the burnouts vaguely tottering. All the transactions going on! With a little X-ray vision you could see them, detailed as Dante—in the parking lot back of that liquor store, or the blind alley beyond those dumpsters, behind those dim flophouse windows—all that urgent, secret trade of passions and powders, of vows, violations, viruses. . . .

But now they're past Potrero, the Mission lights are dropping behind, and Jack's drawing near to his own little transaction. It nags him, that air Cozzens has of an unspoken agenda. His cheap rates too, especially for such minor quantities as Jack buys. Jack's a friend of Willy's . . . but there's nothing chummy about the giant biker.

He's arrived. The house is on a small rise, a little cluster of old houses isolated by evolution. Below one side of the knoll, a ghetto playground, dark and empty; below the other, blocks of brick warehouses, their streets equally empty. These few battered Victorians, with their two dim streetlights and weedy yards, form an elevated island of silence, the city's traffic a vast rumor all around.

The windows of Cozzens's house are dark, and its porch is jammed with decayed furniture and boxes of rubbish. Jack has never entered its front door. He follows his customary route down along one side of the house, to the back yard.

This lies below the level of the street. Descending in steep darkness, he enters a spill of light. The yard is an automotive boneyard, filled by the hulks of variously dismembered cars, vans, trucks, and motorcycles. They are all rooted in a net of shadows, half-lit like lunar terrain by wattage flooding from the gaping doors of Cozzens's basement garage.

In this basement bare hundred-watt bulbs blaze everywhere from fixtures, clamp-lamps, and trouble-lights dangling from hooks. All-out war is being waged on shadow. Back in one corner is a flatbed truck with its hood up. Its maw has swallowed the upper half of a man, all except for two big dirty-denimed legs. These stir with the man's toilings deep in the engine-well.

"Cozzens?"

"Half a sec, Chief," his voice booms from beneath the hood. Then the man rises, big as a cave bear, six-six, two-sixty, his thick hair and beard all streaked and tendrilled with stark white. Within this black/white thicket his stark cheekbones and mad tawny eyes beam welcome from their lair. His whiskers are here and there daubed with grease as with some hasty, secret meal.

Jack's never quite easy confronting the man, but there's something dangerously different about his face tonight. What is it? The biker's skin seems to bake in the merciless light. His pupils are black gulfs of . . . rage? Jack stares in Cozzens's face a beat too long without finding his tongue.

"Whatcha starin at, Slick?" The big voice is stony, ominous. The silence they stand in is suddenly loud.

Jack's startled into giving a straight answer. "I can't put my finger on it. You look different."

"You can't put your finger on it. Can you put your dick in it?"

"Hey, I didn't mean to offend you. I'll leave. No problem."

"You'll leave? Don't leave, Ace. I'm cool."

"Is something wrong, man?"

"Wrong? Oh, nothin major, Homes! Hey, you never scoped my cockpit, did you? Let's go back to the vault for our biz, and I'll show you."

In the opposite corner is a heavy door. There's a little table to one side of it where Cozzens usually weighs out his product with a pocket-scale, but now the goon is leading him to the door itself. At no point does Jack, beginning to feel somewhat alarmed, think that he should step through that door with the giant, yet he follows like an obedient guest on the tour. Scared, but curious too.

The door's opening pulls out a waft of odors, a complex gust of leather and batch and hard liquor. Following Cozzens, Jack takes exactly one step inside, just enough to meet the challenge.

Ranged around this smallish room are mattresses, benches, and other less interpretable furniture with shackles and leather straps dangling from it, all upholstered in black leather and chrome studs. There is a lot of other paraphernalia that Jack's eyes flinch away from, but the big posters that cover the walls, these his cringing gaze cannot avoid. The pictures are a carnival of victims bound with chains or handcuffs.

The only thing that Jack can look at to spare his eyes is Cozzens himself, now seated at the corner workbench, where a triple-beam balance stands amid drug miscellanea. Cozzens strikes a pose, grinning like a suburban hubby mugging in his hobby shop for a family album photo.

"Whaddya think, Ace? Is it me?"

Jack realizes what it is he has seen in the biker's face tonight. It's as if the glossy posters have shed a diseased light on that terrible face that reveals its secret: two . . . three . . . four . . . Jack counts five faint, bruise-colored spots on Cozzens's brow and cheeks. Kaposi's lesions. The giant has the Death in his blood.

Monsters in the earth. Cozzens is one of them, the real thing, is old Prokrustes down in his Last Rites Love Nest amid his torture benches, his grinning teeth stained with ancient residues of human flesh.

The biker replies to the look in Jack's eyes. "Yeah. I got the AIDS,

Chief." The big voice has quieted. "Had it a year or two now, but it's comin on fast these last couple months. All those bitches I gave what they asked for are trying to kill me now, a day at a time, from the inside out. And I'm here to tell you: *No fucking way.* I'm gonna kill this fucking death they put in me. I'm gonna kill it dead as shit. All I'm askin *you,* if you get any *word* . . . just pass it on to me."

Jack is meeting those eyes as steadily as he can—delirious yellow eyes!—while he wonders what the fuck Cozzens is talking about. The ogre has risen and stepped over, stands right up close to him, where Jack can smell that his breath carries a light scent of carrion. As he towers so close, he could seize Jack and sink his teeth into him in less than a second. *Here, Ace. Have some of my death.*

"Cozzens," Jack says carefully, "I really don't think I know what you're talking about. Word from *who?*"

"Hey, absolutely!" A palms-out gesture of his blackened hands surrenders the point completely, no hard feelings. "Of course you don't! But look here, Homes."

Out comes Cozzens's huge hand from his vest pocket. It opens to reveal a bright object, a plastic packet, snugly taped, full of whiteness. "I'm *givin* you these five OZs, Ace, and I don't want a dime for 'em. All I want from you is to taste it." He points to where a glass phial stands. "I know you hardly use, I respect that, but I want you to *know* what I'm givin you. This is special even for *me.* Cut it in *half* an' they'll still howl for more."

Jack stares, his mind split into two amazements. On the one hand: five OZs sold in quarters, twenty transactions—fifteen K. Or *double* that figure!

On the other hand: these sums as a gift, a gift from an ogre, for a "word" from an unknown someone that will save the ogre's life.

Jack should run from this. Just bolt.

But consider it a minute. With some help to turn it, maybe through Willy . . . with Willy to find buyers for larger quantities, taking the sales end and ten K for the risk . . . Jack could call Erika and tell her he has thirty-two K in *hand,* soon to be forty with his second advance.

"Cozzens, I've gotta make this clear." A third amazement is tingling up his spine. He's thinking of *doing* this! "I've got *no* idea *who* you're—"

"Ace!" The palms-out gesture. "My man! If you never meet him, if you never hear a word, we're A-OK, you're free and clear. This is a *gift*, Slick! Just take the taste so you'll know what I'm givin. Then it's yours free an' clear! If you hear what I want, you'll know it. Just pass it on to me. 'Nuff said."

Jack finds it strange that he is pocketing the ounces—he hasn't yet decided to. Twenty K, he discovers, has a way of putting *itself* in your hand. He taps a little fraction of a capful from the phial. He doesn't dare hesitate in snorting it—the twenty K commands him to close the deal—but he fleetingly feels something momentous in the little gesture. Fire blooms through his sinuses. He stands there humming like a dynamo.

VII
A Little Bit of the Power

Another cab. Passing that school playground, Jack sees that even at night it's not deserted. Teenage shapes sit in the swings, perch on the monkey bars. Little gangsters, nostalgically haunting the place where they first learned to play, to form packs and to torment the unprotected. The social machine will soon crank them upward and onward, into prison yards, then back to the Carnival streets, and back to the prisons. They are caught in machinery as fixed as the wheeling stars.

The cosmic view—that's meth's allure. Jack's glad he snuffed so little, this stuff is so powerful. It could be cut by *two-thirds* . . . Christ, in grams that could net— No. Leave it strong as an inducement to Willy to take it off your hands. Settle for twenty and dust your hands of it as soon as you can.

He has the cab stop at a Mom 'n' Pop's on the way. Ten minutes later, with a bag of beer and chips, he is climbing Willy and Marni's porch. They have a corner house with a front garden in the quieter streets between Guerrero and Dolores. The living-room windows are lit and the front door, as always, stands a couple inches ajar, laying a yellow slice of light across Jack's shoes.

Just before he knocks, he hears Marni's voice inside. Doesn't quite catch the words, but gathers that an intense conversation is in progress and, on impulse, stands eavesdropping a moment. Hears Willy quite clearly:

"It's not *about* you, babe! You'd just be peripheral. I just need someone I can bring if—"

Marni, cutting in, surprises Jack. Not her words, whose meaning is dark to him, but her fierceness. Marni rarely says two words at a time when they're all together. "You invite him in here, and he is sure as *shit* gonna be dealin with both of us, treatin with both of us."

The sack Jack is holding gives a crackle, and the quality of silence inside tells him his friends have caught it. He knocks instantly, calls out, "Hello in there! Special Corona delivery!"—but feels sure his silent spying's been registered.

Willy pulls open the door. He's a skinny little guy, bare-chested in a leather vest, his hair like a gray storm cloud, his eyes almost black, with a perfect little Chaos spinning in each huge pupil.

"Brewskis and powder. Thought I'd drop by and share."

"OK, big guy . . . Come in." Willy's eyes, for just a moment, show surprise and speculation, as if they have just been discussing Jack.

Most of the living room's furniture and floor are draped and heaped with clothes, newspapers, dishes, every flat surface crowded with glasses, bottles, cans, ashtrays—except the center of the glass-topped coffee table: a dusty-looking square foot of glass. On it, Jack showers a little dune of Cozzens's crank. Willy chops it in rails, his gaze still strange, as if there's something both he and Jack know but won't say. Marni stays cross-legged on the rug—it's her habit with company, like an exotic creature lying low in the underbrush. A beautiful woman—she's some kind of Native American, has huge breasts that not even her roomy sweatshirt can hide, and an animal magnetism in her ripply caramel hair, in the lovely oval of her saffron face. Beneath her usual silence, Jack feels something tensely crouched tonight. He's heard that Willy takes her uptown now and then and pimps her to make the rent on this nice little house.

"Now this is some prime shit," gasps Willy, two lines uploaded. He offers Jack the straw. Jack waves it away. "Naw, I had some." *Had all I'll ever have again*, he mutely vows. Finds himself wondering about Willy.

The man has a decade or so on Jack, is a veteran jailbird, cranker, and boozer. He's sometimes to be seen, when out and about, in a Stetson and calf-high boots, with a hunting knife in a sheath on his belt. A Poet of the

Streets, he calls himself, and on a table in the windowed corner of the room a big old Underwood manual typewriter towers above the clutter.

While Willy may have dashed off some free verse back in the hippie days, Jack's always thought that now he just does drugs and booze and wears the poet sobriquet for style, like his boots and hat. Funny, though. A few minutes ago, when he thought himself in privacy, Willy told Marni she would be "peripheral." In company, his vocabulary's always pure street.

Marni rises and takes the straw. As she bends to the table, Jack can see old razor scars on the part of her forearm that peeps from her sleeve. He's heard that these scars are her own work long ago. Clearly, she's suffered some intimate damage growing up, but having overheard her anger, Jack sees new meaning in the scars: that this woman knows how to cut and slash. She snorts, and hunkers back down into her watching silence. Jack's never seen anyone honk so much, and stay so mute, as Marni can.

"Yeah," muses Willy. "Some *serious* shit." His eyes hold Jack's as they both take swallows of beer. Marni cracks a can of her own and glowers at them both. What's going on here?

"I'm glad you like it Willy, because—"

But before he can go on, the Poet of the Streets says, "Will you answer me a question, Jack?"

"Sure."

"You've been invited to the party, haven't you?"

"What party?"

"*The* party."

Jack blinks. He looks at Marni for help, and is further surprised to see in her eyes how much she dislikes him: she's actually trembling with anger.

"'Invited to the party.' *What* party?"

Willy lets a beat go by. "*What* party? OK, Jack. OK, whatever. Just lemme ask you— What was your prayer? Tell me how you prayed, so that he invited you. Just give me some of the words, man, just some of the fucking *words*."

There is a crash. Marni has sprung up and toppled the big armchair at her side. She turns and storms out of the room.

Jack struggles for a grip. "Willy, you want to know . . . what prayer I prayed, to get invited to *what* party? Willy, man, you wanna hear stuff, but you've gotta *explain* stuff. You gotta give me something here. What party?"

Willy is looking at Jack as if he is an alien being, someone impossibly remote from human experience. It's a look Jack recalls from another talk he and Willy had, a late-night, half-drunk talk over this same coffee table. That night, Jack was into one of his pet raptures about what joy and solace were to be found in writing. Willy, Poet of the Streets, was officially in the guild, and Jack kept goading him to agree that art—that getting something down just right on the page—was a compensation for everything, was full and sufficient payoff for all you'd suffered, all the shit life gave you.

Willy had heard all this before, but this time it seemed to wear his patience out. He looked at Jack in much the same way he's looking at him now. Looked at him and said, "Pays you off for everything, huh? Say Jack, have you ever sucked a cock?"

"Well, no."

"Well, I have. A lot more than once. And I didn't have any choice about it, either."

It had sobered Jack right up and taught him shame for his pompous moralizing. He really saw the man before him for the first time, down there in the lower circle of the inferno it had been given him to tread: a smart, undersized trailer-trash kid sent to prison for a drunken B & E, getting whatever he had in the way of pride and potential beat out of him PDQ, and leaving him his present hollowness that must be poured full of something to get through each day, every day, till his last day.

And now Willy says, with the same bitter, world-away eyes, "Why do I wanna be *invited*? Hey, man, I'm human here too, right? After all the shit and the pain, to have a little fuckin bit of the Power? A little fuckin' bit of the Glory? What, you think you gotta go to college to have a soul? I got one here, big guy. Tell me your fuckin prayer. What'll it cost you to tell me?"

"You pathetic idiot!" This is Marni, stepping back into the living room. She has something massive and silver jutting from her right fist. She holds it up beside her head, aiming obliquely at the ceiling, its stubby barrel with a *big* muzzle, a big, dark nostril for snorting fire. "Don't you *know* there's no fucking magic prayer? Your stupid *words* have nothing to do with it. All you gotta do is grovel at his feet! All you gotta *do* is be willing to betray someone to him, betray them all the way."

"No! I keep *telling* you that's not what he—"

"Shut the fuck up! Just shut *up!*" Now she brings the pistol down, and levels it—at Jack!

He's on his feet instantly, placating palms thrust out. "Whoa! Marni, what're you—"

"Just shut up and listen, Jack Hale. I want you to leave my house right now. I don't care how much you know or don't know, but you're *in* this shit, and I want you right out of here."

"Sure! Sure! But can't you tell me—"

Without glancing down, she fires a round into the floor, not an inch from the side of her foot. As much as the huge noise of it, it's her recklessness that makes the shot utterly, instantly convincing. Jack, ears ringing, is moving fast for the door.

"I'm gone! Gone! I'm sorry, but I really don't—" Out the door now, he almost pauses on the porch to finish his protest, make a last plea for some kind of explanation, but seeing her eyes, he bolts for the sidewalk instead and hurries off, putting some space between himself and this sudden, mysterious agenda everyone seems to have for him.

A little fuckin bit of the Power. A little fuckin bit of the Glory. Cozzens and now Willy. Both men are speedsters, but they've *been* speedsters all along. Why should they turn delusional on him at the same time? And what are these delusions *about?* Word from Someone. An invitation to a party full of Power and Glory . . .

Why did he let Cozzens force that capful on him? His blood is buzzing through his veins. He finds a small, half-empty bar and applies a double bourbon and a beer to the fire within.

After a couple hours and a couple more drinks—he really does need to damp down this speed—Jack comes out calmer, but only slightly less buzzed. He decides on a stroll to help clear his head.

He likes the late-night streets, the buildings dark-windowed, with only the streetlights' gleam on their glass—but maybe he's been living too long on Graveyard Shift time. Two totally different cities share this ground, after all, and he's been haunting the Night half for many a month now.

The Night City is like a vast stage set, or like a theme-park on its down cycle, and misfits and wackos are its wakeful denizens . . . the sleepless damned, just crazed and alert enough to be poking around, feeling the lurking sense of *hoax* that pervades it all?

And isn't there something definitely sinister, something ominously phony, about this emptier, dead-of-night city? The vapor lamps drizzle their alien light on the asphalt, like skinny derricks that are sucking it out of the ground, but who's it for, this miles-wide bleed-out of anemic light?

Behold these perfectly ordinary streets and buildings. Can you find the optical illusion? Spot the cracks in the camouflage? Spy the Reality looming just behind it?

Soon those restless souls start thinking they just might poke their heads around the right corner, and . . . spot the Morlocks, the maintenance demons who are down stoking the furnaces and tending the machinery of the Carnival during the day, and who come up now for a smoke and a prowl. Drugged-out guys like Willy and Cozzens, Jack can almost understand their secret hope: to glimpse those Elementals, catch them crouched behind the plywood walls and phony windows, see their brute, misshapen shoulders hunched over their smoldering cheroots, see the glitter—when they turn and know themselves witnessed—of their inhuman eyes . . .

And what Willy and Marni and Cozzens are acting like, is that they've *met* one of those Elementals.

But why are they making *him* part of their fantasy? He's just had a woman aim a loaded gun at him. And that's what the *woman's* prepared to do. How might Willy or Cozzens come to express their unfathomable delusions, grim Cozzens with his death ticking away in him?

But, stitching its way through all these fears, Jack also feels a thread of curiosity. What the hell do these people believe is happening? Might happen? *Beat Death.* Go to a party for the Power and the Glory. It sounds like millennial Christianity, but none of these people are Jesus types.

He's got to completely stop *visiting* these people. From this moment on, let them whirl away on their own orbits. Somehow turn this meth into cash as fast as possible, and meanwhile have nothing further to do with any of them.

He reaches the hotel with only minutes to spare before midnight. It's Bill who buzzes him in.

"I'll be right there," Jack tells him passing. Bill gives a lazy wave of his Marlboro. His bruised eyes look so exhausted, so dark. Jack continues up to the second floor. He'll lay out DeeAnn's grams uncut from the bindle, a generous touch that should soothe that little short-out between him and Razz this evening.

At his knock, Razz's muted voice calls, "Come ahead!"

In Jack goes, and freezes at his first step. Razz sits on the bed with his back to Jack, his pants opened, winged out to either side. DeeAnn, mostly obscured, is on her knees in front of him.

Razz says to DeeAnn, "I keep *tellin* you you got to give longer strokes!" Then, looking back over his shoulder, looking unsurprised, says, "How you, man? 'Scuse us, didn't know it was you."

Jack has betrayed his shock, been sucker-punched. The pimp knows he's scored on him. Jack's rage kindles. "Razz, you just tore it. You just tore it wide open."

"Hey, man, we aint makin any money here!"

Jack shakes his head, delivering his final judgment, which, even as he speaks it, he changes. "Your rent has just doubled." He manages a stately exit and closes the door quietly.

Jack brings typewriter, manuscript, glass, and .38 into the cage. Bill remains on the couch, as if he means to hang out. Jack makes pleasant chatter, trying to calm himself, says his book's moving along, hopes the typing doesn't bother Bill and his wife late at night.

Bill's tired eyes give Jack's a bitter twinkle at the last remark. Almost as if Jack understands their solitary struggles in that apartment across the hall, their struggles so fierce in the dead of night.

VIII
Bedside Visitors

All day, old Chester Chase has lain curled on his bed. It's after midnight now, and he's hungry, but that doesn't seem terribly important, not as important as lying here, snug and secure, on his bed. As long as he's in here, he can't be locked out of here.

He's gotten up a few times during the day, for a drink from his sink. Has pissed there too, relieved to realize he doesn't have to go out even so long as it takes to visit a bathroom. Because this old room of his, each moment of it's precious now.

All day and deep into the night Chester has been trying to think about what he's going to do, but these thoughts keep slanting off into thoughts about what he has already done. He's lain here twenty-four hours, lost in his past, straying through the landscape of his years.

Remembering driving down to the City one night—he and Emily lived in Richmond then—a night when he was still, at forty, a shipyard worker who liked his Friday nights in a favorite bar with some beers and some buddies. He'd just dropped in to visit his kid brother Charles, Charles and Frances and their new-born baby, and was crossing the Bay Bridge into town, when it suddenly struck him, with perfect, final clarity, that he himself would never be a father.

Remembering when he first made love with Emily, Emily gone for sixteen years now. . . . Still only engaged, they did it on her parents' couch. Though her parents were away, the couch seemed less sinful, more provisional than one of the beds. Remembering how they both cried out in surprise and delight.

Remembering all those times he could have been kinder to Emily. All those nights at the bar he'd granted himself, thinking his hours of work had earned them, but what of all *her* hours he could have made less lonely, all those hours when they could have had closeness and sweetness together.

Remembering all the ships he worked on, with fantasies of seeing the places they'd been, places he'll never see after all. Remembering a couple women he had on the side, in his still-swaggering forties when he had stout, thick shoulders on him, and a deep, muscled chest.

His room's embrace, and his memories, have contained him through all these hours, but off and on he has also been unusually conscious of the entire building around him. As if his hunger has attenuated him, his sense of touch expands airily into every hallway, every room of the hotel, and the Hyperion's stirrings seem extraordinarily distinct. And all the while, beneath the ebbs and fluxes of its noise and movement, Chester has become aware of a deeper kind of stirring in the building's bones. This subtler movement has grown more insistent in the hours since nightfall darkened his airshaft window. It's a prowling, probing kind of movement that searches and sniffs its way: pads along, pauses, and again steals forward . . .

Chester is surprised, at first, to realize that he *understands* this presence, feels its intent, its personality. The prowler is dangerous, very dangerous, and yet somehow Chester knows that is not concerned with him. That its hunger is for those with more red blood in them, more hope and future. How strange this apparition is. How strange that he understands it. He sees that it's very important, very significant, this new awareness he has discovered, lying here on his bed. Solemnly, he recognizes that such metaphysical awareness comes to you near the end. That he may not live to suffer homelessness.

And suddenly he is aware that the dangerous visitor is very near. Is right outside his door.

His heart goes cold and smoky like dry ice. He was deceived. The presence sneers at him, mocks wordlessly the exemption he assumed. Almost, it articulates. Almost it brings its identity to birth within Chester's mind. And, in this almost-utterance of itself, Chester feels an ageless ridicule. He understands the thing outside his door is old as Earth, and murderous as Time.

Then . . . it is gone, as if it never was.

Was that simply Death out there, the way an old man feels it near the end? Chester does not think so.

At least—how strange it is this seems a blessing!—at least he's far too weak, his force burnt far too low, to move, to hope, or struggle for escape. Escape with what? All that remains of him are the things that he *was*.

He remembers when . . .

Britt watches Jack striding high, wide and handsome down Valencia Street. No hugging the shadows for a big guy like that, no scoping the blocks he enters, reading the recesses for unfriendlies. He's buzzed in, and enters with a thrust of the door—goes right up into that box of vipers. Britt shudders for him. She remembers his head reared back in climax, and the pale, unearthly limb that crushed his throat.

She's across the street, and a little ways down from the hotel on the steps of a small apartment building recessed between two larger ones, and deeply shadowed. A good perch, anywhere but here. This close to the hotel, she doesn't feel hidden enough by half. She should run. But she's here because of Jack and DeeAnn, their kindness. She can't explain their danger to them, and description seems like invocation. She can't do shit if something happens, but she can be here.

She freezes at footsteps on the sidewalk. The walker stops right in front of her steps, though facing the other way. T-shirted, brush-cut hair, Bettina Butch. She plucks the hardpack from her sleeve, snaps a kitchen match with her thumbnail, and fires up a smog. Britt's not sure she's been seen till Bettina, spouting smoke, says to the street, "Quit your job, Brittany?"

Britt blinks. Job? Oh. She means Jack. "Jack's a pretty sweet guy, really."

"Yeah. I think he's OK actually." Bettina keeps facing the street—a courtesy, Britt sees, not pinpointing her perch for other passers. Another plume of smoke. "I tried men for years, I mean I really tried. It took me forever to catch on. They really can't help it. They have to devour you, a bite at a time."

Britt feels exhausted. Her blankie is already threadbare. Are her nummies and vals losing their power for her? The thought is pure dread. She feels too bitter and tired to care what she says, what Bettina will think of her. "I didn't leave because of Jack. There's something dangerous in the hotel."

A long, slow spout of smoke. "No shit, Sherlock. You just noticed? You need to wake up, Brittany, you know what I mean? You need to keep your eyes a little wider open. Because what it's about is just what I said. Men devouring women."

Britt is bolt-upright. "You know about it?"

"Enough not to touch it, not even in talk."

"I understand that. But can't you just . . . ?"

"No."

Even this much lifts her heart. Someone else *knows*. Bettina checks the street in both directions, then lightly springs up the steps. "Take this."

It's a folded bill, a fifty. "Bettina, I—"

"It's just some help. Forget it."

"Thanks . . ." Her voice almost cracks. All this kindness suddenly.

"You should leave this neighborhood, shouldn't you?"

"Why don't you leave?"

"I don't have to worry. I stay away from men."

Britt watches her cross the street, light-footed and square-shouldered. Watches the Hyperion swallow her. This sympathy, following DeeAnn's, pulls new tears from Britt's eyes. She's going to deserve it. Stay right here all night.

She swallows more pills. That was cruel of Bettina, "eyes wider open." A dig at Britt's pill habit. A person's drugs are their business, that's the unwritten code. Her downs are her survival style. How else, without her blankie, can she make cozy beds out of concrete?

She's cold and scared. Hurry up, little pills. She pictures them on their tardy way through her body's chemistry, like tumbling asteroids in a space movie, slowly falling through the light-years . . .

Behind and above her at the top of the steps there's a light on in the front window of the downstairs apartment. It has curtains and a thick blind, but she can see a thin rim of lamplight outlining the blind.

Right there. That thin, square outline of light. That light means that someone is sitting in there, totally oblivious to Britt out here. Sitting in there just as Mom would be sitting in the living room every evening, with Brittany shut in her bedroom. Mom never to be approached after 8 P.M., propped in her La-Z-Boy in front of the tube, with her vodka tonic and her pills close at hand. Britt, lying in her bed, could hear the remote burble of the set—as remote to Mom herself as to Britt by 9:00 or so.

Years of such nights. It seems they filled Britt's childhood.

Ended it too, because that's just where Mom was—beyond that bright rectangle—the first night (Britt had just turned eleven) that Unka Doug climbed in through her bedroom window.

Unka Doug was a jolly, comical man, short and balding ("Thick in the middle and short on top," he would grin) with a single wet-combed lick of black hair isolated in the center of his forehead. He was, Mom said, a wonderful provider. A pharmacist, he provided Mom wonderfully that way too, Britt realized later. Mom would have found marriage reassuring, but she adjusted immediately to what was offered—the house paid off in her name, a healthy checking account, and an educated man for a warm, caring domestic partner. He was so entertaining, and so affectionate and fatherly to Brittany.

Britt, her Dad divorced and gone when she was two, loved being made much of, *noticed*—though at ten and three quarters it was a little embarrassing to play cowgirl and ride on Unka Doug's back, clowning for the new camera and albums he'd bought. But she blamed herself for the awkwardness, was anxiously grateful for a crack at having something like a father, who would make them complete in a way she knew they hadn't been.

Britt had few friends—because it was less trouble for Mom that way, no other moms to cultivate, no outings to clutter her restful weekends. But from the few friends she had, Britt gathered that dads had the power to distract moms from themselves, to command their attention, and liven them up.

Unka Doug was not really a Dad. That one reservation, his not marrying Mom, always hovered there, a subtle space around him. But he was such a complete companion to her, hugs and kisses and presents coming naturally to the man, that they seemed *nearly* married. He came home every night in time for dinner, and at first even watched TV with them afterwards. It seemed so much less spooky to watch it together like this, three against one, talking back to the actors, making game of the plots. He steadfastly insisted, though, that Brittany go early to bed, to stay sharp for school. And he himself, over the months, tended increasingly to withdraw after dinner to little homey repair tasks in his garage workshop, or to his and Mom's room with a book, or some business at the big desk where he handled all the bills. And soon enough, Mom was back in her groove, snoring in the glow of the tube.

But how Unka Doug filled the weekends and livened up the days! And Britt took all he offered, afraid to discourage his good will by any failure of enthusiasm. She squealed at piggy-back rides and tossings in the air and ticklings, not from pleasure (these contacts scared her a little) but to thank him for all he'd come to give them.

Then, at her eleventh birthday party, in the midst of all the laughter, he chortled confidentially in her ear, his breath tickly, "We'll play cowboys some more, just us, tonight. I'll climb in your window! But sshh! It's a secret!" He snickered, and she giggled back to show that she enjoyed the joke, thinking at the same time how strange the idea was.

All through bath and bedtime preparations she thought of this strange proposition, growing ever surer it was just a joke, until she was tucked in her bed in the dark and lay watching that thin, bright rectangle round her door, hearing the tube take on that sound of authority that said Mom was zonked even before she started snoring—that authoritative sound of being the only one in the room . . .

Then Britt grew a little more uneasy, thinking that Unka Doug did mean his whispered project after all, and she lay nervous awhile with her lamp on, trying to concentrate on Nancy Drew. But nothing happened, and she was asleep, dreaming of a huge dog, or bear perhaps, its huge heavy breathing arched darkly around her like a living building that roofed and walled her in . . . and then she woke up, and here was her window sliding up, and here was Unka Doug in his funny pajamas printed with teddy bears, wearing a kid's cowboy hat ten sizes too small comically perched on his baldness, with his little slick black forelock peeping comically out from under the brim. Here was Unka Doug making big comical shushing gestures with his finger across his lips, and climbing into her room with great vigor for all his chunky shortness.

And he was at her bedside, taking both her hands in his, pumping them up and down like merry-go-round horses, humming in a low voice, "*Giddyup. Giddyup, giddyup-whoa!—my po-o-o-ny girl!*"—one of their cowboy songs she rode on his back to.

He grinned her and grimaced her and funny-faced her though a series of their horsey-play routines—all done in whispers and murmurs:

"*Whoa,* cow-girl!"

" *Whoa,* Black Bart!"

"Bite the dust, pardner!"

" *You* bite the dust, Black Bart!"

"Ca-da *clop,* ca-da-*clop,* ca-da-*clop!*"

"Ca-da-*clump,* ca-da-*clump,* ca-da-*clump!*"

Britt giggled dutifully, in a whisper, doing her best to get into the game, but sensing at every moment that a different game was the goal of all this, a new and vaguely scary thing Unka Doug had in mind. She had a sense of recognition, of something always felt but not acknowledged, and now at last emerging. It was a . . . central emptiness in his eyes that never altered, no matter how he crinkled them up with his smiles.

And when she identified this unknown in the man, she felt that a frightening gulf yawned under this game of theirs, an empty place into which she felt instinctively afraid of falling.

Until at length, the game did become a kind of falling. This phase of the game was Frontwards Horsey, where Britt straddled dear old horsey Unka Doug's lap, with her back to him, and they jiggetied-joggetied, pony-girl, pony-girl, won't you be my po-o-o-ny-girl? Don't say no, here we go, off across the pla-iins! Giddyup, giddyup . . .

All in their pajamas, with nothing so stark in it that she could clearly tell what was happening, but with an under-rhythm to it, and a friction between her legs, that terrified her. The rhythm was like a drumbeat on that emptiness, emptiness, emptiness, that void just beneath them in their game, a void she could fall into, where she would be lost, with Unka Doug's empty eyes watching her tumble and tumble, and grow ever smaller, and vanish. And as the game approached its ending, Unka Doug's patter settled into a low, gritty chant: *Have a hunka unka, hunka unka, hunka unka* . . .

Those two years . . . Except for the final night, when the veil was torn for her, and her life was changed forever—except for that, how those long months deadened Britt, rubbed her away down there, between her legs. Since then, she's always found it easy to fuck for necessity's sake. This part of her, breached so long ago, is uninhabited, a rentable zone, a negotiable bond.

At last her chemical reinforcements are crashing into her desolate heart like big smothering pillows, silly-punching the fear from her, tilting and staggering the thoughts in her head.

The steps supporting her are already more supple than concrete— more yielding and responsive, more like a mother's arms. Britt's in bed at last, and a much better bed than the one she had in there across the street. All those people snoring unaware in their rented walls—*thin* walls, wormholed by the Emptiness, and the things that prowl in it.

Britt knows they're there, and they know she knows. They're sneering at her, taunting her with her own death, and her friends' deaths, because they love to taunt, to feed on your terror. That's what today has been about.

OK. OK then. Here she lies peaceful at last, wrapped in her blankie. And for what it's worth, here she will stay. Soon she'll be deeply zoned, but she will be *here*.

IX
In the Cage

Jack's typing up a storm. Dark, muscled Rackham has appeared, startling Lupinnia as much as the hounds have been doing, snarling behind
their bars. He startles her, but sets her bodice heaving too a bit. He takes
her pail of meat scraps, getting her into the game of teasing the hounds
with the scraps, bringing them to a baying frenzy, and then hurling the
meat through the bars. Lupe's flushed, her eyes bright.

Bill is still in the cage, but so mute that Jack can enter into his story
unhindered. He sneaks Bill a look. The manager is hunched there, Marlboro bannering from his fingers, his bruised-looking eyes fixed vacantly,
watching TV with the sound off. Perhaps he's afraid to enter his apartment. Afraid of the war that he's waging there with his wife.

It strikes Jack how few words he and Bill have exchanged through all
their months together. How much English does he really speak? When he
watches the TV, he never seems to care about the soundtrack.

Jack worries about his ultimatum to Razz. If he and DeeAnn move
out, there goes Bill's pocket money, three hundred a month off the books.
Or what if Razz decides to dig in and fight? Blackmails Jack by threaten-
ing to drop the dime on his little traffic of grams?

Jack has no choice but to play it tough. Razz knew he'd be dropping
off the product before going on shift, so that display of his was a calculated
affront. To keep the upper hand on Razz, you *can't* do less than bitch-slap
him for an insult like that. If Jack forgives it, it's like handing the man the
Hyperion's keys.

There is a harsh groan right in Jack's ear. He almost jumps out of his chair.

No. It's someone beyond the bars—at least a yard away. It's old, bent-in-half Mr. Cunningham, bowed in profile at the counter. His bristly neck tremors with the work of holding his head this high, just high enough for him to cant his profile up and meet Jack's eyes with one of his milky-blue own. He groans again. It's speech of course, but indecipherable, for all the effort he gives it.

". . . nnnyarrr-taaa . . ."

"I'm sorry, Mr. Cunningham. What are you saying?"

He tries again, with quavering prolongation. "Nnnnnya*aarrrrr*-taaaaa!"

"I don't quite . . ."

But a new struggle shakes the ancient, bent frame, while his glaucous eye stays fixed on Jack's, a rheumy moon too sick to rise more than a few inches above the counter's horizon. His shoulders shake in their shabby jacket, and his hand comes slowly into view. His gnarled fingers climb just high enough to plop a smudgy tract before the bars.

The old man groans a sigh, subsiding once more to his crouch. Turns himself around and creaks back the way he came. A long journey for his inching gait, and all those flights of stairs . . . Jack's amazed to be the object of such an arduous delivery.

He scoops up the little document. Now he'll get a look at what's hooked those Koreans at the Silver Dragon.

It's verse! It's . . . *strange* verse . . .

He stands rapt, reading, and then re-reading. He was sure it would be biblical snippets, apocalyptic trumpetings. But *this*. As he reads, he realizes that his jaw is hanging slightly ajar.

> *My ancient lust was to enslave the dead,*
> *And up the brittle ladders of their bones*
> *To climb to zeniths thick with stars bestrown,*

Against vast, cold Eternity to spread
My sinewy wings; to press my taloned tread
Upon the very pinnacle of Time.

But now it is quite otherwise I climb,
For, not long past, my lust did learn to know
Through living flesh a readier way to go
To oversoar the mortal pantomime.
Now I empower all those who will be mine
To imbibe a deathless vintage red as wine
And—ever unentombed—run wild at will,
And breach Time's very walls to seize their kill!

The sonnet has so involved and baffled Jack that he is not startled to find Bill at his shoulder, scanning as intently as he is. But surely such English as this has to be out of the man's reach.

"You understand this, Bill?"

"Yes." A tremor in the word. Bill understands something, because he looks stunned as his eyes scan the lines. His hand is half reached out, as if to test the words' reality with a touch.

"Here. You want it?"

"No!" Bill's hand recoils. "That yours."

"Well . . . what does it mean?"

"I don't know."

"But you just said—"

"That yours. You see yours. I see mine."

Jack stares at him, astonished. The tall, aristocratic Aryan is suddenly an unknown man, an utter stranger in this cage with him. . . . A stranger with terror in his eyes, and apparently hallucinating a wholly different text upon this page.

Jack makes a business of pouring himself a drink and sipping it, but is really just watching Bill, who has sat down on the couch again. His mahogany fingers work a smog from his pack, but then just hang there pinching it as he stares at the tube. Whatever he's seeing there fills him with amazement. Amazement that becomes, at length, acceptance. Bill stands up very slowly, as if he's on a different planet, where gravity's far greater. "Oh Jack," he says. His sketch of a smile seems borrowed from another man, long dead. "Never marry weeth a wooman!"

Jack watches him cross the hall and confront the door of his apartment. Will his hand ever reach that doorknob? At long last he goes in, with no backward glance.

I see mine. You see yours.

Well, Jack can't see Bill's message in these wild, ghoulish lines, but here by God—*forever unentombed*—must be some part of mad Cozzens's "word." And what about poor Willy's Power and Glory?—*to oversoar the mortal pantomime . . . run wild at will, and breach Time's very walls . . .*

Willy and Cozzens, both beseeching him tonight for something that, all at once, he has. Are those two wily street devils setting *Jack* up, or are they the dupes, and Jack the catspaw, of old Mr. Cannyharme?

Mr. *Cannyharme?* Where did that come from? Jack rather likes it, though. There's something villainous in the old man's frosty eye and stubbled jaw. And why do we always assume the very old are mellow and benign? Age can mantle malice as readily as mildness.

Of course Cunningham/Cannyharme's a catspaw himself, or a field worker. Someone far younger and more articulate produced these vigorous lines. But to what *end?* What kind of sect or cult gathers what kind of converts for what kind of *purpose*, with wacko metaphysical verses like these?

Jack's definitely in the Carnival now. Is he himself the Fool at the Fair? Willy and Cozzens could be a pair of shills just setting him up for the pitch, and now here's the pitch, and it's totally incomprehensible.

So far he's lost nothing by it, and he's been given maybe twenty K. And to judge by Bill (him too, yesterday!—*You got something for me?*) all the seekers do is look at the text and walk away. But why do they have to get the text from *Jack?*

Tomorrow he's going to call Willy, get him somewhere away from Marni. He'll use this poem, use Cozzens's crank, to leverage some explanation from that weasel. He shoves the tract into his pocket. The story behind verses like these must really be something. The whole scam is fascinating, truth be told.

The next scene of his story comes to him all of a piece. He starts typing furiously. His nostrils burn and his thoughts race as if he has just snorted anew. Good thing he took so little—this stuff seems to take forever to wear off.

One of the teased hounds, lunging at the door of his pen, jars loose the catch and erupts, indifferent if it be the meat-scrap or the girl's flesh that he tears. Rackham's caught off balance, his leap barely intercepts the brute in time, and his tall muscled frame is toppled by the hurtling carnivore. The girl screams and recoils from their rolling battle . . . till Rackham rises, gripping the mastiff's throat one-handed, holding its convulsing mass out straight-armed, and crushes its throat. The creature tremors and hangs slack. Rackham's eyes meet Lupinnia's then, showing her a blaze of savage triumph.

As Jack's fingers dance and the images stream, his imagination seems to be taking simultaneous, unrelated flights. As he writes he's also seeing strange aerial views of the San Francisco Bay by night—seeing black waters hammered silver with moonlight, seeing freeways threading black hills with arteries of light, seeing cities and streetscapes he never thought his memory contained, seeing the gem-strewn shorelines, the great bridges streaming with lights. The sensation is enrapturing. It's as if he's writing and flying at the same time. He types with eyes half-closed, keys clattering, and suddenly, something twitches powerfully inside his pocket, something like the muscled convulsion of some trapped animal—intimate, galvanizing. More than startled, Jack experiences a neural meltdown, the sensation of all his nerves liquefying and draining out of him through the soles of his feet.

He slumps in his chair, momentarily emptied by his fright, his right

hand pressing the pocket, feeling nothing between the fabric and his leg
. . . and a voice addresses him.

"I need to know where we at wit' the pack of smokes DeeAnn give
you."

Razz's face hangs at the bars. His face has the trick of freezing between utterances. The plump bud of his mouth, the old-ivory look of his
yellowish eyeballs . . . they radiate poise, completion. A finished mask.

Finding Jack slack and stunned, Razz croons, "You trippin?" His
face gets closer to the bars—a little carnivore nosing for paralysis in the
quarry, for opportunity. "Didn't you maybe space somethin of ours,
Homes? I mean, money has changed hands."

Jack sits, still almost empty of any reaction, except that he can feel his
heart has started beating again. He gazes fascinated at Razz's face, this
beautiful work of skin-art—a life-form, he feels, completely alien to his
own. This icon begins to breathe into Jack a vague excitement. He thinks
of Razz's face as a taxidermied trophy on a wall, and the thought causes
him to sprout a slow smile.

Jack makes his voice boomy and sly. "Ain' no space, Ace," he soothes.
"It just aint took place!" He rises, leans on the counter, his own face right
up to the bars, backing Razz off a notch. "You just gotta hold your mud,
stud," Jack continues, "'cause when my man can, it be in yo *han'*. But
now, if you *resent* your new *rent*, well I only deal with resi*dents*, so if you
decide you don't con*sent*, I be givin back what you *spent*. If you aint gonna
be stayin, don't wanna be payin, I give you *back* your Marlboro *pack*."

Jack listens to himself, burning all his bridges with this menacing little
man, but he relishes every rhyme. He feels larger than life, as if a ghostly
augmentation of his body has enveloped him. And Razz, as if in response
to this ectoplasmic brawn, has retreated yet another step without seeming
quite conscious of it.

A poised little rogue, though, is Razz. He holds Jack's stare and gives
him the tiniest little nod, and then turns and creaks softly away.

Not an atom of "yes" in that nod. All it said was, "I see."

Jack plops down onto the couch. How his thoughts are seething! A trancelike buzz engulfs him. His head drops back, his eyes close . . .

From a high place, like Jesus in the third temptation, he beholds again the City, and the glory of the bright-spangled Bay. All the jeweled hills stretching to the rim of sight, and the pearl-string bridges webbing them all together across the waters—how vividly he beholds them all!

He's the *owner* of all this grandeur, and its beauty sinks a thorn of sadness in his heart. For all its noble architecture, its stone and steel and globed light, it's still just a fucking Carnival, still just a gypsy camp of tents and booths. It's all as evanescent as seafoam, bubbling so briefly on the dark enduring bones of old Earth.

Someone—some resonant, grieving voice—is telling him: *Look at the millions swarm, living-till-losing their lives, millions on the heels of millions, while every moment, under their feet, yawns the gulf of Nonentity . . .*

This someone at Jack's side . . . his and Jack's eyes feast together on the Bay's bright galaxy. Jack can almost feel this other's emotion, a furtive, infra-red glow around the heart. It's no longer melancholy, though. His invisible companion's emotion has become something much sharper, livelier. It's glee. It's *appetite* that this Other feels now, and Jack has to admit that this whole prospect, this gorgeous spill of jewels, causes something like greed to thicken in his own throat.

What a playground, for those who run wild at will, prowling those lamplit lanes (is the thought Jack's own or his companion's?), coming and going as they please, feeding and rutting . . . theirs the power . . . theirs the glory . . . theirs the harvest eternal . . .

Somewhere, other voices groan and snarl, begin a harsh duet in an alien language, and to this accompaniment the jeweled city melts away, becomes a soft hellfire of nearer visions, as close as the walls around him. High-buttocked tarts strutting in neon-glazed nylons, needling death in their twitchy arms. Thugs killing children in cramped places crusted with old shit. Red-eyed hermits opening closet doors and furiously clubbing crouched shapes inside that lift stick-thin arms in chains to shield their heads . . . Pairs couple in the fire, yodeling joy, while with each thrust their torsos shrivel, spoiled spots blooming on their brows. Rookeries of gorgons perch on dumpster rims, too sweating-sick to fly, but racked with fecundity, groaning their newborns out on nests of trash . . .

Jack watches till the duet twists down to silence, and the visions burn out, and he himself is gone.

X
Now I Lay Me Down to Weep

In the misty morning, Britt crosses the rolling lawns of Dolores Park, leaving dark footprints in the dew. She's heading for the park's far side, where the streetcar stops after roaring out of its tunnel from Noe Valley. She can rest on a bench there till the sun has dried the grass and then take a proper nap out in the open.

As she nears the restrooms, she hears herself shrilly called from behind the bushes.

"Blade! Help me! Help me, Blade!"

Fat Sal's voice, but in a pitch of panic Britt has never heard her strike. There is a violent commotion of the shrubbery.

"Get away from her!" squeaks Britt, pulling her knife. Numb from downers, Britt's onrush is a sorry affair. Her run is a stagger, and she gasps for breath. She blunders into the bushes, knife high—and is seized from behind by steely arms and hugged against a tall wiry frame that is convulsing with laughter.

"Whoa!" crows Sal, spinning Britt around, shaking her. "You call that shit *runnin?*"

She breaks down and caws some more. Sal's grin is too wide for her narrow face. She's hook-nosed, her hair beaded back tight to her big, oblong, shapely skull.

"You bitch!" yelps Britt. "I almost *peed* myself!"

"Me too!" gasps Sal. "You looked like . . . you looked like someone in traction, duckin out on the hospital bill wit' the cast still on! You can't run for *shit!*"

Britt knows exactly what kind of kid Fat Sal must have been in school: a major bully, to be sure, but never in a thug-pack, always a loner. The kind that, if you were a loner too, might hijack your lunch one day, as a first step toward becoming friends. Exasperated, Britt shrugs Sal's hands off. "Why should I run? I don't *wanna* run. I wanna cop some Zs in the sun."

"Why should you *run?*" Sal shakes her head. "You hungry? Come on, have a bite."

They sit on a bench and have breakfast from her peacoat pockets: two little tubes of chocolate micro-donuts, a pack of Twinkies, a pint of half-and-half. They chew with gusto, but Sal's eyes begin to brood. "I'm not sayin you should *run,*" she erupts. "I'm sayin you should be *able* to run. You never hear of fight or flight? Either *one* needs some stren'th! You not in shape to do jack-shit."

"Fine! I *don't* do jack-shit, OK? You ever *see* me doing jack-shit? Did I ever *say* I could do jack-shit? So just back off!" Yet again, Britt has surprised herself with tears. It's like since yesterday she's been coming apart, melting . . .

"Hey, Blade. You a pillhead, OK? But you don't have to *stay* that way! You don't have to cower down *all* your life, an' die that way!"

"What the fuck are you saying? You've sold me pills!"

"The hell you say!" They're screeching now, in spite of the handful of commuters just down the embankment waiting for the streetcar, and in spite of the golf-capped, red-tasseled bag lady who has sat on the opposite bench and blinks at them gummily. "It's *Squash* sold you pills. An haven't I been kickin his ass about it all the time you known us?"

"But you stay with him! You're his *partner!*"

"Hey! Just cause my partner's fucked up doesn't mean I'm gonna give up on him without a fight! Whaddya know about it? Only one you takin care of is yourself!"

This perspective surprises Britt. Who else was she supposed to be taking care of? Wasn't it her job all along—just to survive?

"Look." Sal's quieter. The way she's controlling her temper makes

Britt uneasy. "You know why I'm talkin to you like this, don't you?"

Britt's heart is quickening. "Know what?" Britt fears what she'll say, and wants her to say it.

"You remember . . ." Sal's voice lowers. "You remember Demetrius, don't you?"

There it is. Still, Britt's reflex is concealment. "What about him?"

Sal's voice drops even lower. "What about him? You know better than I do. You looked right at it. I was too scared to raise my eyes." Silence ticks past. "You wanna tell me about it?" A quaver of fear there that Britt *will* tell her.

"I don't know! I mean I don't *understand* it, I don't know if it *feeds* off our talking about it. . . ." In all her seven years on the streets, she has never said a word about her enemy, the shaper of her life. Coming even this close dazes her.

"Listen, Brit'ny. Bettina talked to you, didn't she?" Sal is showing her something rare. She's showing Britt fear.

"Yes."

"Well, it's time to wake up. There's women been disappearing. A lot of us *know*, but not like you do. We talk about you—we baby you because of what you know, but you gotta wake up an' help us now."

"Women are disappearing . . . ?"

"It offers men some kind of deal, an' the price they pay is their women's lives."

A long silence. "Jesus. . . . But you know more than *I* do, Sal!"

"You've *seen* it!"

"It's different every time!"

They look at each other across the gulf this leaves between them: every time—all those long looks Britt has taken into its changing face.

Sal's eyes concede. "Just try to wake *up!* You got to help us find out what this is. We all got to help each other. You got to start bein strong. I've always got your back, sweetheart, you know that . . . it doesn't matter *how* shitty you run."

Both are startled by the bag lady in the red-tasseled golf cap. She is towering quite near them now, a gently swaying mass of rancid clothing. Her eyes are swollen so nearly shut, her gaze is just a gleam. "Only way to get by is to stay crazy, girls. That way, you don't suffer fearin it, an' when it comes, you're too gone to know."

She waddles slowly off down the path, her little cart's wheels creaking behind her.

When the grass is dry, Britt chooses a sunny spot. She's too upset now to hope for sleep. With a guilty thought for Sal, she pops a couple more nummies—just so she can get some of that deep rest that you can't get on stone steps.

It won't come. The sunlight comes through her shut lids, behind which she finds, not sleep, but her own past. Run, Sal says, you have to be *able* to run. Christ. Way back there, when her whole life could have been changed by it . . . if only she *had* run.

If only! If only she'd run away sooner from home. Not so much her fault, maybe, when she had just turned eleven . . . But after a year? After almost two?

Unka Doug, that sly, sleek rat, was so cunning, sensing her moods, adjusting the frequency of his violations with unerring intuition, and using Mom so skillfully too. At the moments when Britt was shakiest, he knew just how to turn up the volume on Mom's happiness, to stoke her enthusiasm for dear Unka Doug, that wonderful, thoughtful provider. He knew Mom's bliss was the best cage to contain her daughter in.

The gifts! And not just the gifts themselves, but his flair, his clever theatrics in the giving of them. The new Bronco with the huge pink ribbon around it that they all discovered out in the driveway after breakfast one Saturday, and which Unka Doug viewed with astonishment equal to theirs—till he burst into laughter, and Mom into ecstasies, hugging and smooching him.

Or what about the new entertainment center with the big-screen TV?

He brought Britt herself in on that little game. He hired two guys to bring it in at 10 P.M. one Sunday night—to bring it in silently, with much comical shushing and exaggerated tiptoeing, while Mom snored softly away right there in her La-Z-Boy. The whole thing installed, the big screen turned on, the old set whisked away.

Then, *voilà!* He and Britt woke Mom. Oh, her groggy transports then! Tears actually came to her eyes! But even back then, Britt detected the subtle mockery hidden in this gift, that display of Mom, slack-jawed and sprawled for those two strange men to see and grin at. And that taunt in it aimed at Britt too: *Old Mom will be extra comfy now when we play our little games, won't she, Cowgirl?*

Why didn't she run sooner? Earlier in her thirteenth year, at least, when the dark down began to grow on her pubes and in her armpits, sparse growths that wavered reed-like in the shower's runnels. She would have washed these tufts *off* if she could, realizing at some point that it was because they made her think of Unka Doug's little dab of forelock hair, his little rooster-comb peeking out from his cowboy hat when she joggled on his hot, stony lap, fear in her heart.

She should have run—but she lay low and held on. Nights when he'd just left her, other nights when he hadn't yet come but still might, she lay plunged into one of her Nancy Drew books, or later the Tolkiens, or listened to an all-night rock station turned low—anything would do to hide in, to fence out the surrounding silence and what moved in it.

Lying low. Ducking and covering. Just like Mom in her La-Z-Boy.

Until it was too late. That night, when Unka Doug climbed in through her window, the game culminated in something new and terrible. Somehow Unka Doug, through his bony prodding and stony poking, his sly, tinkering frictions through the layers of flannel, orchestrated in Britt's young loins an orgasmic commotion—a terrifying upheaval for the girl. For she was falling, falling as she'd always feared, and Unka Doug up there behind her, his flinty eyes glinting, was watching her fall. She was disintegrating, pouring away into the emptiness with only one witness: his cruel eyes like two icy moons, delighting in her annihilation.

Long after his comic departure, she lay staring at the window he'd left by. All the months of their strange play came clear to her now. His game's aim was to destroy her separate self. To possess her for a toy.

Still she did not run! Even then she might have escaped!

But the wideness of the world frightened her. The suburban darkness all around her was, she knew, a desert void of help, a wilderness of strangers' doors. Beyond were the Cities, where Mom had rarely taken her, and known to Britt mainly through video images: blizzards of light by night, and thronged with predators. This bed she lay on was the only personal ground she had, her only owned space.

As she lay there staring at the black square of that window, a chill began creeping through it into her room. At first she thought the chill was in herself—and it was, because her heart was still frostbitten by the terror Unka Doug had taught her. But it was also an actual cold, pouring in through that window, Unka Doug's little spiderhole—pouring through and licking her icily through her pajamas.

And a suspicion entered her: there were others besides Unka Doug, much *worse* than Unka Doug, just outside of that window, and now that Britt had fallen, now, on any night of their choosing, these others might come in and play with her too.

And *still* she didn't run, still lay there staring, because it was powerfully hypnotic, the way the window was changing, or rather, the way that square of darkness under the raised sash was changing. It was thickening into a denser kind of darkness, a squid's-ink kind she'd never seen, a smoky, roiling darkness alive with intricate movement, seething like a million ants in their hills or black maggots in their broken meat. Almost it seemed this darkness might pour toward her, as the icy cold was doing . . . and as a stench like the open grave was also doing. . . .

Then Britt sensed movement just outside the window—the push and probe of something swimming nearer through that darkness.

The window frame's lower left corner—just there she felt its approach. And when the sharp white tip of it thrust into view, sprouting a hand's length into her room and twisting there over her sill, a spearpoint of wet meat as white as the moon—when this pale tongue came tasting her air, Britt screamed without breath the strengthless yelp of a road-killed rabbit.

For all her cry's weakness, the intruder quivered and homed on it. *This* was the taste that the white tongue savored: her terror. It poured an arm's length farther in, and thick as an arm it was behind its tapered tip, and wet-slick, and segmented too, yes, each segment a bulging torus plumper than the preceding. Delicate little black jaws glinted and scissored at its tip . . . like nothing so much as a maggot it was, a maggot as big as a boa, which teasingly circled and swayed but always slid spiraling toward her, almost touching her bed now, in a moment to touch it and pour itself over her blankets—

Then Britt ran. At last. Leapt up and sprang for the door.

New tears scald her eyelids as she huddles recalling it under the warm sun. So bizarre, what she did. Plunged out into the hall, ran to Mom's La-Z-Boy, cowered down behind it. As if Mommy could save her from the Monster. Those days were long past, but still, ludicrously, she cowered there next to that sad, softly snoring shadow-protector.

For a measureless time, her enemy did its probing dance within her bedroom—she felt it in there, sinuously mocking her through the paper-thin walls, the cold sleet of its radiation, the absolute zero that it breathed, coming right through Mom's helpless mass. Even then she understood it. Knew it wasn't hunting her then, but claiming her, declaring her its prey. The hunt was to come and would last all her life.

She awoke on the rug as dawn grayed the windows. No going back to her room. Old clothes and shoes from the hall closet. All the cash from Mom's purse. The phial of Mom's pills too.

Britt learned that first time that she had a gift for streeting it. She tasted three weeks of escape before they picked her up. Unka Doug was long gone by then, the bank accounts emptied, address unknown, and Mom was already at work again, back at the bank, when Britt was returned.

Normalcy resumed. Dinner with Brittany, vodka and tonic. By eight, snugly tubed, by nine, catatonic, while Britt's reinstalled in her teddy-beared walls with her shelves full of dolls. . . . But Britt had already copped some street smarts. She took a tip from Mom and kept on pinching her pills. Sleep? No problem—as long as you gobble em.

She quickly mastered the art of pills because she faced it right there every night, that window, and she *could* not face it without a shield. Meanwhile, she worked incessantly on her running-away skills. Just after her fifteenth birthday, she achieved escape-velocity, and launched herself for good into the wide, interesting wilderness of San Francisco.

Only to learn, and relearn once or twice a year ever since, that the Window, having found her, would never leave her.

Britt can't stand it any more, this grief and regret. How could she have lain there all those long months, until she had taken the wound that will never heal? She's *never* escaped! She's had to stay paralyzed every day of her life just to get by.

She lurches to her feet. Stands swaying on the grass. Mid-afternoon. Quite a few joggers now, all along the far-flung rectangle of the park's perimeter. How can they make themselves *do* that? Strip to their skin and go chugging around like that, all-purpose but going nowhere, just around and around? Don't they know how stupid it looks?

But how stupid is her *life?* How much difference can it make to try out a new kind of stupid? Fuck it. She is scrolling up her heavy-laden coat, tears dripping off her face . . . tying the coat around her waist. Maybe Sal is looking on from somewhere. Show her smartass Britt can run when she feels like it.

She's got an ache in her legs already, just trotting to the perimeter path. She should start carefully, maybe with that stupid walk some of them are doing, arms pumping. . . . She hits the path and starts power-walking.

She's never felt more ridiculous. Another power-walker overtakes her before she's gone three strides—a spry old lady in lavender sweats. The only thing that keeps Britt going is that it would be too embarrassing to be seen starting up and then almost instantly stopping.

But the walk's just too ridiculous. She escalates it to a loose-jointed lope. Feels slightly less ridiculous like this, jogging, though in moments her sweat is streaming. She's chugging up toward the park's highest corner, up near where the Muni comes roaring out of its tunnel mouth.

Now a new and intense embarrassment looms before her: the embarrassment of *collapsing*—to be seen jogging less than a block and then taking a nose-dive from exhaustion. Astonishing, how she must fight for air! Just stay with it! You can't drop so soon! But doesn't breathing this hard cause heart attacks?

She rounds the high corner, and the long downhill begins. Now . . . it's not so bad, lofting her legs along, letting her breathe deeper. And she feels the good of all this sweat too, with a downhill breeze cooling her. Is she blending OK? Does she look as strange as she feels? She's totally faking this thing . . . but is beginning to suspect that faking it, if you stay with it, is more or less the same as *doing* it.

Gently the uphill recommences, along Seventeenth past the tennis courts. She perseveres, wondering if she can do the whole thing, go all the way around to her starting point.

Britt laps the park eight times. On her second circuit she's plucked at from behind. "Keep runnin, Blade, I'm just untyin your coat!" and grinning Sal flourishes the coat after her like one of those flags at a car race: "Vroom-vrooom!"

Eight times! She discovers she is spare and hard under her chemical sloth. Years of living on her legs have kept her lean. And she discovers adrenalin—not the terror kind, but the workout kind. A joy-inducing medicine. A purge for grief. The work of running becomes more smoothly circular, as if there's a wheel in her, and she can ride this wheel like a passenger, digging the view. Bright Frisbees are floating, dropping like hummingbirds to fingertips half the park away . . . a tennis player's eyes flash in her tanned face as she thwacks that fuzzy yellow sphere . . . cyclists crank stoically past, their inexorable calves flexing as they suck from little bird-feeder bottles. The whole park is one grand celebration of bodily movement! All these years, she could have been part of it!

Grinning, then, at Sal. "Can't run worth shit, huh?"

Sal returns her coat. "Not too shabby. You aint much for style, but I *knew* you had stamina."

There is a pause. Already the sun is beginning to decline, and the amber light raises the question of night. "I'm gonna crib right across the street from the hotel," Britt says. "There's no way I'm going inside again, but I'm not running away, OK? That's all I can say. So, how about a shower at your place?"

"Shit, you can wash your clothes too, since you finally got some honest sweat on em!"

XI
Of Passions and Pimps

Jack awakens in a rush. He has been half awake, buzzing people in for an indeterminate, cobwebby time, nodding hello to stair-climbing tenants who look like vaguely theromorphic shadows . . .

And then, suddenly, he is clear-eyed, spine straight and tingling. Is knocking on Elmer's door to bring him on shift, keen to get outside, to use his legs and see some City, see some early morning City with all its buildings half gold, half shadow in the slanting light.

Out he goes, at a stride that matches the tempo of his teeming imagination, and quickly puts the miles behind him. All the way to the top of Twin Peaks he walks, his head full of possible poems, and impossible poems, and story ideas, and even *bodice-ripper* story ideas that he can make *money* on. It's as if a surf of ideas has picked him up and lofted him here. He paces around on the flanks of the peaks and studies San Francisco's noble sweeps of hillsides all robed in intricate architecture, while *behind* his eyes unrolls a more than equal sweep of architected images, of supple sentences of chain-linked words, shining words.

It seems to Jack he's never in his life felt this alive. *If I had world enough, and time,* says the poet, but that's just how he feels! He *has* the world, and all the time it spins through, world without end to unfold his schemes in.

His pocket notebook is soon filled. He must get back to his typewriter and a nice stack of virgin paper. Downhill, he sets an even faster pace, deep in the buzz of his projects, trying out lines under his breath as he powers along.

And is almost home again before it strikes him. The thing that has gotten him so energized is a lurking, lingering, vibrant echo in the back of his mind. It is a chorus of words like silver trumpets thrilling his nerves, words he cannot recapture—not one of them—but whose electrifying grandeur still sparks along his spine. The cause of this energy is nothing less than that insane poem Mr. Cunningham gave him last night. How his brain hums with its resonance! Eagerly, he digs for it in his pocket.

In all his pockets . . . digs again . . . and again. The tract is in none of them. Nowhere.

A prickly sensation crosses his back. It's strange that he's lost it, yes. But it's even stranger—isn't it?—that some verse he's already forgotten should have set him humming like a powerline for the last three hours. Poetry acting like a potion? Of course, as a poet, his official position would be that verse *was* a drug, the best of them all, but he'd mean it metaphorically. This . . . this is literal. His imagination is resonating to the echoes of lost words.

It hits him that, of course, he's *been* drugged lately. Enough at least to have mishandled Razz pretty badly, verbally bitch-slapped the man at just that point when a frosty control was what was called for. And how fucked up was that, losing the verses that could have dissolved his obligation to Cozzens? He shouldn't have drunk so much last night, and he should never have let Cozzens make him snort that capful. He suddenly has a wad of potential cash that could mean his reunion with Erika. It is in the form of a very dangerous drug that he has no right to let any more of into his brain. He has ticklish business to accomplish here.

So. Before he can settle down to writing, he's got to go up and drop off to Razz and DeeAnn the product he owes them. Pissed as he is, he sees he has to salvage the status quo and will probably have to modify the rent penalty he's imposed. Bill and Phaasri are too near domestic disaster as it is to lose such a chunk from their budget. Then, when he's done what he can on that front, Jack can go up and get another tract for Cozzens from the old man.

He charges up the Hyperion's stairs. Elmer says from the cage, "Say, Jack. Yuh know, Brittany's moved outta twenty three."

Jack scarcely pauses, rushes on up to DeeAnn's floor. "Thanks, Elmer."

It's just as well, better really. He worries for the girl, but he's glad to be free of the guilt. Things are coming together for him, if he just starts proceeding a little more carefully and soberly. That uplifting, onrushing feeling of this morning still hasn't left him. His life is moving. Good things, changeful and bracing things, are going to start happening fast, once he's done a bit of repair work.

The halls are empty on the second floor—good if things should get testy. This delivery should at least defuse some of the tension with Razz.

DeeAnn's muffled voice answers his knock, and he enters.

Bent over the night table across the room from him, DeeAnn is honking lines from a mirror, presenting to him as she does so the little red triangle of her panty-crotch, as well as a goodly view of the bivalved moon of her buttocks overflowing that filmy bandage.

"*Snurrf!* Hi, Jack! *Snorrrf!* Wanna rail?" She partly turns, offering the straw, but pro that she is, has noted the focus of his attention and keeps it partly in view.

"No thanks," croaks debonair Jack. "Here's yours." Into the pan of her little plastic pocket scale he plops her bindle.

"Oooh! Great weight!" she laughs with a little wiggle. Instantly she's multi-tasking—her deft little hand chopping herself new lines, and her deft little behind twitching and switching with a deadly accuracy. Getting two steps nearer like this is stiffening Jack fast. Within seconds he finds himself in such an intense condition of sexual readiness that he cannot hide it, and has no will to turn away from her.

She honks a fat track of her new stash.

"I love taste-tests! *Snorrf!* Whoa! Who-o-a! You really talkin somethin besides *shit* here, Jack!" The black parody slightly surprises what's left of Jack's mind. "Now I have something for you," she continues, not straightening up, still swaying her hindquarters, her hands doing something out of sight. "Oh, Ja-a-ack?" Now she's holding up to one side a newly opened rubber. "You know I've always liked you, Jack. I mean strictly affection, not business."

The badger game. Razz will walk in any second. Even if he doesn't, even if she just tells him, this would be major leverage for the pimp. And even if DeeAnn didn't intend to tell, it would come out, whores are childish, apt to spill anything handy during domestic squabbles with their exploiters. Jack is weighing these sage thoughts with his pants puddled around his ankles, as he briskly dons the rubber. It scrolls down as easily as it might onto a sledgehammer's haft. DeeAnn peels down the little red triangle one-handed, as with the other hand she honks another line.

"*Snurrf!* Oh, naughty Jack! You're so *fat!* Easy at first! Yes . . . yes . . . I've always liked you, Jack, you're such a gentleman . . . tha-a-at's it . . . tha-a-a-at's it! Oh, my, you poor ba-a-a-a-by! So-o-o fat! *Snorrf!* . . . Oh, my! We're so *horny!* . . . Oh, my! . . . You poor ba-a-a-by! . . . Oh, my! . . . That's just right! . . . Oh, my! . . . That's just *excellent!* Oh, my! . . . That's just *perfect!* Oh, I think . . . Oh, I think . . . I *think* . . . I think I'm gonna come! . . . I mean . . . I mean . . . I think I really *am* gonna come! . . . Oh, my! . . . Oh, MY! . . . Oh, MYYY! OH, MYYYYY . . ."

Her rhythmic, rising monologue is like a rocket that Jack rides. Up, up her voice lifts his mind, stretches it taut the way the tent-pole stretches the tent. It's lift-off in a fast balloon—he sees Erika, a surprised look on her face, dwindling away below him on the plummeting earth. He's astonished by the greed swelling him, swelling him—what is he *after,* he marvels, surely not this cheerful, comic little tart, like a zeppelin his craving, his lust dwarfs her, he's mating with a Lilliputian . . . He bursts, and blows her to pieces.

When, a short time later, Jack shambles down the hall, he is urgent to get back out of the hotel before Razz might come back. He rages inwardly. He is the very pattern of an idiot! It's all the worse that DeeAnn seems to have taken a major liking to him. Can that have been acting? He knows he's as easy to fool as the next man that way, but her pleasure seemed so convincing. If he's any judge, she's basically good-natured, and she's not faking her friendliness at least. And that's bad. It means that this is going to come out to Razz, one way or another. By taunt, or hint, or accidental utterance. DeeAnn's a sweet kid, but like many hookers, she can't resist drama.

Meanwhile, what is happening to Jack's standards? His self-respect? Bad enough to exploit a self-crippled outcast like Britt. Much dumber to violate a business arrangement with a pro. Where has his brain gone? And immediately after that blow-up last night? He has just dug the grave of his whole arrangement. This triangle could really hurt him with Bill if it gets explosive. Jack will lie low and hope for inspiration, and in the meantime he'll get something constructive done. He'll stay out of the Hyperion at least till the late afternoon, by which time DeeAnn and Razz are usually gone. He grabs his workbook from his room on his way back down to the street.

At a payphone near the BART he taps out Willy's number. Jack will tell the Poet of the Streets that he's got the Invitation—the lost verses surely had that tenor. Then, with a new tract from the old man, he can get Willy to move the speed in bulk for him, to their mutual profit.

It's Marni who answers, and Jack instantly hangs up.

He'll go work in the Silver Dragon. Cunningham might come in while he's there, and save him a trip up to the old man's room.

He takes donuts and coffee to a corner table, and screws in his ear-plugs. He opens his notebook and, even with all his tensions, falls right in.

A sonnet he began a month ago is finished within half an hour. He adds three good pages to a sketch based on a shooting down at the May-fair he read about. Turning to *Master of the Hounds*, with deft strokes he blocks out a scene where Lupinnia is dusting the statuary in the long East Gallery of the manor, flushed with her exertions. Lord Darcy comes upon her at her work, and his first passion for her kindles . . .

Then, because inklings of memory are teasing him, he leaves Lupin-

nia for an attempt to reconstruct some of the lines from the lost tract.
Phrases flash before him. Writing these down, and struggling to piece out
connections between them, Jack at last arrives at a triplet of lines that he
believes forms part of a quatrain—its beginning or end he cannot tell:

> *Through these you may go where the galaxies sprawl*
> *And up through the starweb dance sprightly as spiders,*
> *And dart quick as rats through Time's ceilings and walls*

No added struggles can push his reconstruction any further. The
place is silent—the lunch crowd has come and gone—and for some time
he has been conscious of the Korean matriarch observing him from behind
her register. The place is near empty and she has little else to look at, but
when he smiles at her, she stares back even more intently.

And it strikes Jack. She too got a tract from the old man. Maybe it
was the same as his. Maybe she will show it to him.

He takes a loose sheet of paper and approaches her smiling. "Excuse
me. I work at the Hotel." (pointing) "Mr. Cunningham?" (bending, miming a cane and a severe stoop) "He gives *you*" (folding his page like a
tract, opening and closing it) "to *read*." (miming reading) "Can I *see*?"

Her face shows nothing through all this. Then she surprises him.
"Yes. You go." She points out her window to the Harvest Moon down
across Sixteenth. The teenagers are in there painting again. "You get
N-U." And to illustrate, she takes up one of the Dragon's own little half-
sheet take-home menus. "You," she says again. And points to herself.
"Not like."

Jack gets it. She wants to scope the competition, but is too resentful
and proud to ask them herself. What a bizarre errand! He realizes it was
pretty strange of him to ask to read her own personally solicited tract. He
smiles, though still not quite believing this transaction he's agreeing to.
"Deal. OK."

Every step of the way down to the Harvest Moon, he feels the unreality of this little mission he's undertaken. And isn't the strangest part of it

the woman's unsurprised acceptance of Jack's desire to read her tract, and her assumption that he'll go to this trouble to do it?

The paint-fumes he steps into are intense. Someone should tell these kids about water-based semigloss. Inside here and surrounded by it, he finds the tint is so bright that it seems to stain the air with a fine yellow mist. The new 'spoon's most important furnishings have arrived. The big steel counter-cum-steam table has been delivered, standing centered in the sizeable space, and behind it stands a huge black range that is still strapped to its hydraulic dollies. These megaliths are islanded on the empty white tile floor, and the frizzy-haired woman is sitting behind the counter, looking at a tiny portable TV.

It's so quiet the TV's faint murmur is distinct, as are the soft frictions of the kids' two paint-rollers rising, falling. All three of these people seem sunk in their own thoughts. Their eyes barely register Jack's entry.

"Hi!" His voice seems to boom. "Almost ready for business! Ah, you have your menu printed? Could I see your menu?" His sociability clutters the silence. The painters keep painting, but the girl's two little ponytails give a twitch, which might have been a nod toward the woman at the counter.

Jack goes over there. These fumes are really intense. It would be fair, in fact, to call them dizzying. In here for hours, these people are stoned too, beyond a doubt. The woman, without lifting her eyes from the TV, sets a take-out menu on the counter.

Jack draws near her. The paint's halation makes the space in here strange—the room's volume seems subtly to shrink and expand. The woman's eyes, behind remarkably thick lenses, are avid for that little TV screen, which looks no bigger than a postcard.

The tiny screen presents a remarkably clear image. It's clips of a football game that the woman seems to be devouring. Jack watches two opposed lines of helmeted, big-shouldered shapes collide. It's a spectacle he has always found pretty boring.

But look there! Is he *seeing* this? At the center of the impacting lines, a woman lies stark naked! Her head is engulfed to the shoulders by the jaws of a monstrous hound, while her loins are locked in coitus with a nude male. Only his laboring hips and thighs crest into view—the mêlée swallows all the rest of him and hides the beast that half devours her . . .

Less than two seconds of retinal stimulus, but searingly distinct. He thrusts his face down at the screen.

Just a scrimmage. And now another cut, some guy running out under a high pass . . .

Behind Jack, there is a concussion and a muffled cry. He whirls, swaying on his feet. The girl painter has kicked over a bucket, and though there's nothing but yellow in this room, it's a spill of bright scarlet that spreads its tongue across the dropcloth. Jack gropes a hand for support on the counter and blinks.

No. It's just more yellow paint. The girl is kneeling, mopping it up . . .

"Thanks," Jack croaks, and with the menu turns and lurches toward the door. He is no more regarded in his exit than at his entry.

He stands out on the sidewalk sucking air. Whoa. Actual hallucination. He realizes he's never had one before. As a college kid he smoked dope now and then, ate a few mushrooms too . . . and experienced only a somewhat more complicated visual field. His eyes have never before invented something from whole cloth, something that wasn't there. So brief it was, but so sharply drawn.

What did Cozzens put in that speed? It has to be that which is fritzing his wiring. It's suddenly so clear—how urgent it is that those five OZs leave Jack's possession as soon as possible. Get them and Cozzens out of his life, and Erika back into it. He's kept enough strange company.

The Dragon's matriarch's eyes are utterly black, like lambent tar. She looks straight into Jack's eyes and takes the menu without regarding it. And she hands him a tract. There are lines of big bold print on the outside, and a body of smaller text inside, and it's all in Korean characters.

He meets her eyes again. Is that . . . mockery he sees there? Or is she urging him to something, something she thinks he understands? Bill's odd

words come back to him: *You see yours, I see mine.* And he feels something more elusive in her. That she knows he too has been honored with
her master's words, and that she will no more explain anything than Bill
has, or Willy, or Cozzens.

He phones Willy again. No answer. The day is declining. He'll go up
to Cunningham's room and get another copy of *his* tract.

As he reaches the foot of the stairs to the third floor, he confronts Willy coming down them. Coleridge comes back to him:

His floating hair! His flashing eyes!

The Poet of the Streets looks half-gone in rapture. He stands staring
down at Jack for a moment before Jack's identity registers. Then an ironic
little smile sprouts within Willy's beard.

"Hey, Big Guy. I'm glad I ran into you. What I asked last night?
Forget it. I've been invited."

"To the party."

"Oh, yeah. To the Party. See, it turns out he has a use for more than
one wordsmith."

"*He* wants you for a wordsmith." Jack nods up toward Cunningham's
room.

Willy just stands smiling at him a moment. "Tell you what. Let's go
down to Mike's liquors. You buy us a bottle. I'll tell you a couple things."

The rush-hour traffic is loud, and Willy sets a pace that discourages
conversation. There's an energy coming off of him. He seems for the first
time in Jack's experience to be fully inflated with life, to be filled with the
joy of it. Jack's intercepted him coming down from Cunningham's, and
the man is transformed . . .

Across the street, Jack sees Brittany walking with Fat Sal. The girl
looks fresher, healthier somehow. It's good she's gone, he thinks. She still
has friends to watch out for her, and he is free of guilt.

They take Eighteenth down to Mission, and when they emerge from
Mike's with their flat of bourbon, Willy wants to stand in a doorway just

off the corner to drink it. "Take it in, Jack!" He sweeps his arm at the swarming boulevard. "I love the streets! It's all happening right out here! The living are dying! The dead are walking!"

They are standing almost kitty-corner to the Mayfair Hotel, that hooker-and-hypodermic haven. Jack notices a duo he happens to know by sight who are sitting on the bus-stop bench in front of the hotel. He's reminded of his stand-off with Razz. Jack was dumb from the start even to have an arrangement with a pimp. Pimps are all about face and standing. Just look at those guys. One is really big and muscled, has a waxed baldy—Be-bop? No, T-Bone. The other is Trinidad, some kind of Central American, tall and lanky, wearing a side-hang of stylized dreadlocks, and a purple beret perched slantwise. Look how they sprawl on that bench, filling it, owning it. Crowded buses wallow in and out of the traffic-stream, while little Latins and Asians, hugging bundles, stand all around the bench the pimps have claimed.

The two of them talk as if they're alone in the world, making broad, showy gestures, spouting long, slow plumes of cigarette smoke, their smiles flashing like blades: *here we are—our spot.* The spot itself never matters, only that they're muscling everyone else out of it.

Willy takes a pull and smacks his lips, and seems to be waiting till Jack has taken one too. When he has, Willy speaks.

"First thing, Jack. You're talking about *he*. But you should know damn well, it aint no old man we're dealing with. No! He's a lot more than that, Big Guy. And that's all I'll say about that—you have to learn the rest yourself, those are the rules. And now there's just one more thing I'm going to tell you, and that's about Marni."

"Yeah. Good. Tell me that. Because I didn't like looking up the snout of that pistol."

"She thinks there's . . . like a blood price on it. She thinks that to go to the Party, you have to pay with someone else's blood. She's wrong. Lemme get that clear between us. See, Jack, I *need* to go to that party. See, there's some people, still alive, that I am going to visit. And my reason is because, all my life since I met them and lived with them a while, all my life since then I've had to do this"—he takes another jolt of bourbon—"to live with my *memories* of them. Man, how I need to visit them when I have the Power, while they are still alive to feel what I'm gonna do to them! Now, I tell you all that, so you'll understand just what Marni means to me. Because as much as I want it, as much as I want the Power and the Glory, I'd take *death* before I'd see her hurt, before I'd *think* of seeing her hurt."

This is the most speech Jack has ever heard emerging from Willy's mouth, and among the strangest from anyone's, but he's distracted. Because Spruce little Razz, in his gunfighter hat with its crown-band of coins, has just walked up to the two bigger men on their royal bench. Jack, half listening, and sinking a little deeper back into the doorway, watches Razz, the small dog, greet the two larger predators with proper respect. He smiles a nice smile, shows a touch of self-deprecation in his body language, his forward tilt is almost a little bow there (not intruding, am I?). The big dogs take it regally, tolerant smiles, a grin traded between them, their slouches more expansive. Razz has permission to address them.

Jack looks distractedly at Willy, who's watching him with a half smile, not apparently surprised at the new focus of Jack's attention. "Pimping," says Willy. "I guess somebody's got to do it."

"You know anything about those two big ones?"

"You mean T-Bone and Trinidad?"

Jack jumps, because it's not Willy who asks this question. They both turn to confront the seamed face and half-bald head of Ron Ratchett, who has quietly joined them in the doorway. "That T-Bone's bad news," says Ron. "Gotta poke a that for me?"

And as Willy hands him the flat, Ron says to Jack, "I guess you know that little one—he's yours."

Razz is laying forth some detailed rap to his sprawling colleagues. Here and there he offers them an astutely raised brow (you understand what I'm sayin?), an earnest hand to his chest (I'm not shittin you here). The big dogs trade more smiles, keeping it plain that they're being entertained, but now and again T-Bone puts a question and weighs the reply with a smile more reflective (your petition may not be altogether lacking in interest . . .).

Jack struggles to get a grip on his own affairs. "Listen, Willy. You and I need to talk some biz."

"No more biz for me, Big Guy. I'm outta the biz. Tomorrow night I do the only biz I care about. So long, Jacko. I'll see you at the Party."

Distracted as he is, Jack is too slow to react, and Willy has turned and walked off. Jack almost goes after him. He can't turn five OZs in grams! He has to have help moving quantity.

Ron has just drained the flat and is giving him a wistful look. Jack might as well use this opportunity. "Tell me about those guys, Ron, and I'll buy you another one."

"OK. T-Bone. My last bit in City? Guy, not too fulla shit, told me T-Bone strangled two of his whores that were lookin at charges and were gonna dime him."

"Hey, every pimp puts stories like that out about himself. Usually bullshit, so they'll loom large."

"I dunno," says Ron. "Tweak that told me, one of those whores was his girlfriend. The story didn't make the tweak look good, so it sounded true to me." Ron's whipped out his narrow little blade-like comb and is stroking the crackly hair back from his half-bald dome. This grooming tells Jack that Ron is not quite as drunk as he needs to be. It's like the man's brain itches when he's too sober, and the comb is his scratcher.

"What about Trinidad?"

"I know zip about him, except I heard he likes little girls."

"What do you know about the little one with the hat?"

"Don't you know him? He lives in your hotel."

"I *know* that, Ron. That's why I'm asking what *you* know about him."

"Man, that was some righteous A and A, Jack! Almost gave me a glow!"

"All right." He gives Ron a five. "Come back out and talk to me."

While Ron's inside, Razz makes a courtly, ushering gesture toward the doors of El Vato Loco, two doors down from the Mayfair. It's a bar Jack doesn't frequent, from which wafts, if you pass on a Friday night, the very essence of Carnival: a mixed whiff of whiskey, pussy, and gunsmoke. At Razz's invitation, T-Bone and Trinidad trade a why-not smile and take their time rising and stretching. They cut a lazy course through the eddies of lesser beings and precede their host through the Loco's doors.

"OK," says Ron. He cracks the seal and hoists the flat. His throat does a deep double-wobble. He loudly sighs, and his eyes look fifty watts brighter. "*That* little we-be, that Razz, is a real snake, what I heard, man. Like when he was a kid practically, he leaned out of a car and capped a total random stranger, just to prove he was bad."

"That tweak tell you this?"

"*A* tweak, but a different one. Nice guy. No reason to lie I could see." Ron is at his most convincing like this, Jack realizes, right after getting that first half pint of the evening socked back. His eyes actually look shrewd.

"Yeah, but Ron, there's just *so* much bullshit floated in slam. They can't talk about anything without pumping it up."

Ron keeps talking, but it's just variations on what he's already said. It costs Jack yet another flat to get rid of him.

It's getting dark. Restless, Jack goes walking through the noise and the nightfall and the city's jewels a-kindling. His spirit is painfully divided. The poet in him is still revving, spinning off ideas, drinking in the city and its splendor. This half of him feels as bird-free and happy as he felt this morning. But the fear in him is the other half, a fear sharp-awake now and working. He can't trust his mouth, he can't trust his dick—it seems he can't even trust his eyes. And, as a result of his mouth and his dick problems, it now appears that he is facing a very real multi-pimp problem.

He can't do anything about that right now (though the thought of Bender's silenced Glock flits through his mind), but he can get this wretched drug of Cozzens's out of his life, because that, if anywhere, is where his problems started. He can try Cunningham again for another tract—pay Coz off with it and trade back the OZs for some cash if the biker wants to reward him. Yeah. That just might be worth trying.

Though Bill should be on for the seven-to-midnight shift, it's Elmer who buzzes him up. "No evening break?" Jack asks.

"Naw. Bill left a note. Said not to bother him. Said for you and me to split the evening shift for a while."

"Well, maybe I'll spell you for a few hours before my shift."

"Thanks, Jack."

Jack climbs the stairs. The hotel is near empty in the dinner hour, and the third floor has, as always, its air of deeper stillness—especially this remotest corner here, room 96. Mr. . . . . *Cannyharme's* residence. That name seems somehow even more right up here. The airshaft window is still open. Why doesn't more street noise filter in from the city-wide bustle of early evening? Silence flows in like a chill vapor under the lifted sash. Jack knocks on the door.

The impacts sound too echoey. Jack is nettled to feel slightly spooked by the sound. He knocks harder, and at the third blow the tongue rattles loose and the door creaks ajar. He pushes it open . . . and, for just an instant, is completely disoriented by what he sees.

Then he blinks, and is of course looking into a room that is just what it should be: dull brown walls, a back window overlooking the alley, a floor of worn linoleum, threadbare bedspread, nightstand, lamp, sink, desk—all so neatly in order that the room might be just cleaned and not yet rented.

He wants to step in, look around, but that's trespassing. Firmly he pulls the door to and turns away. He is shaken as before by that gruesome blip on the tiny TV screen. Yet this instant of strangeness is not quite so surely an hallucination. It was *so* brief, what he thought he saw, that as he walks slowly back downstairs, reconstructing it, he can't tell if he saw it. Or if his own imagination is creating it right now: the interior of a tiny shack; windowless; the walls are all gappy planks, and beyond those flimsy walls, black starry night is peeping through the gaps. *Cold* in there—cold inside and outside in there. In one corner stands a battered little worktable and chair, a typewriter on the table. Nothing else. And the glimpse sends a powerful sense of *déjà vu* through Jack. Because the tableau suggests to him all the similar places over his nomadic years—in attics, back corners of garages, sheds, basements, barns—where he spent his long solitary hours, writing.

XII
Midnight Meetings

Britt's on her steps. It must be way past midnight. She should be numbing into sleep by now, but the hotel across the street radiates an ugly energy, seems to glower like an evil giant. Through the window near the end of the hall she can see just a fragment of the pay phone in the cul-de-sac where she stood two nights ago and heard for the first time in eight years the hideous intimacy of that voice. The black Zs of the fire escapes shine with the mist, and it seems a kind of sick sweat, an unholy fever in the twisted iron. The building almost breathes, its exhalation touches her like frostbite, with a whiff of carrion.

The second window leftwards of the pay phone—it flashes, and its heavy frame whispers. Makes a square black mouth, out of which climbs a smallish black shape, which crouches on the fire escape. Britt can see the bright reflective rims of running shoes under the hunkered-down silhouette, which rises, darts forward, crouches again, and releases something.

Down swings the fire escape ladder to the sidewalk. The smallish shape descends it. Dark jeans, dark sweater, black hair tucked under a watchcap. Just a bit of her dusky neck showing under the streetlight, and Britt knows it is Aarti, the manager's daughter. That's the manager's suite she's come out of, of course. . . .

The girl sends the ladder back up with a little toss, turns, and makes a diagonal across Valencia straight toward Britt's perch. Britt feels some slight pique—has fancied she was pretty discreetly perched here in her shadow. The girl stops at the foot of the steps.

"Brittany? Do you remember me? Aarti? Can I come up there with you?" The voice is shy but quavery with emotion. Its speech is that of a complete little American schoolgirl, except for a delicate trace of foreignness in the way she enunciates all three vowels of the name: *Brittany.*

"Yes. Yes, Aarti." Britt's flustered. Saying the girl's name seems instantly to link them. Up the steps she comes like a shot, sits down and shoves herself, her wiry little body against Britt's side. Britt puts an arm around Aarti's shoulders, and now the girl's youth, and her terror, are right in Britt's face. She can smell coconut shampoo from the black hair that escapes the child's watchcap, smell that Indian spice on her too—is it saffron? The whites of the girl's eyes are stark in her dark face. "Brittany . . . Brittany, did you come out here . . . because there's something in the hotel?"

There's no backing off from this. *This* is the twelve-year-old girl Britt herself *should* have been, when she first confronted Unka Doug in her bed and intuited what he was. Look how boldly this little monkey has gotten up, geared up, climbed out, and *run.* Britt does not doubt that Aarti has seen the enemy in some form.

"Yes. There is something very dangerous in there."

Convulsively, Aarti hugs herself under Britt's arm and says in a desperate little whine, "Brittany. *Brittany?* It's in there with my mom and dad!"

"Look Aarti. Look, sweetie. Sit still, OK? Get down here so I can keep you warm."

She arranges Aarti between her legs on the step below. "Sit on your watchcap to keep your butt insulated. I'll keep your head warm." Britt opens her field jacket and wings it around the skinny shoulders. It's good to offer the girl this comfort, but it's also good to hold her so the girl can't look into her face, because Britt can find no heart for comforting the child. Her own heart is a stone of fear, and she has no hope to offer—only this cold comfort: "You're not crazy, Aarti. It's real. It's there. It comes in different ways. What happened?"

"I didn't see it with them. I wasn't in there with them, in their bedroom. . . . They're *fighting* in there, night after night, a terrible fighting.

They were fighting and—it came in there with them. I felt it come in there with them, there on the other side of my wall. . . ."

"Go on. Get it out."

"I was in bed and I was like petting the wall. I pet it when they're fighting in there, like to calm them *do-o-own . . .*" Sudden hard tears break out of her. Britt hugs her harder and is amazed that it seems to help, that the girl groans out some sobs and tears and seems to rest for a moment. "My wall has these bumpy patterns on it." Britt nods. An embossed tin wainscotting, with many layers of paint on it, survives in parts of the hotel. "I was stroking it and I thought it was working, their voices changed in there, but then I could hear that was because it wasn't just my mom and dad. Their voices were different because they were talking to someone else, and just then all those bumpy little things started squirming like *bugs* under my fingers.

"I screamed, but my mom and dad didn't hear, they kept right on talking, and something, something like *inside* my head laughed at me."

"It knows us," says Britt. "It plays with us."

"What does it *do?* What does it *want?*"

"I don't know," says Britt too quickly. Then more firmly, "I don't know."

Aarti's little frame goes a bit stiller in Britt's arms. She senses Britt is hiding things, but wants it that way for the moment and settles deeper in her embrace.

They sit thus for a moment, till Britt breathes, "Shhhh."

Footsteps approaching from the right, scarier because the tread might almost be stealthy. A womanly shape appears below them, a cascade of shadowy hair down her jacket-back. Apparently unaware of them, she's looking at the Hyperion. A full-bodied woman, scowling at the hotel, offering them a severe little slice of profile.

Aarti betrays them with the shift of a shoe sole on stone. The woman spins violently, plucks something bright from the back of her jeans . . . and then tucks it away again behind her.

"You scared the shit outta me. You. You're Brittany? Jack Hale's friend? Sal said you'd be here somewhere. Who's that?"

"This is Aarti. Her mom and dad manage the hotel."

The woman comes several steps up, till she's eye-level with Aarti. She has a smooth oval face, not as dark as the girl's, but with a gloss that limns it in the shadow. A stern face, with black, glittery, prying eyes. "Why are you out here like this? Did you *see* something in there?"

Britt hugs the girl and answers for her. "Yes, she did. Just tonight. She came right out to me . . . for help." She can't, in her desolation, keep the irony out of the last two words.

"My name's Marni. I've been talking to Sal about you. Sal says this and Sal says that, says you understand this thing, that she wants you involved, but *I* tell Sal she doesn't know shit. *Her* man's not in it, not yet. But Jack Hale is in it, whether he knows it or not, and my man's in it an' *knows* it, and that thing is *awake* in there. You should both get right out of the city. Take this."

Again cash! A slim packet of fifties. And a phone number. "Call a cab tonight and get a motel. I'd take you, but my man is in deep shit and I've got to get back. Call me tomorrow."

"I have to stay here!" This from Aarti, rigid now in Britt's arms. "I have to be close if they need my help!"

"Your *help?*"

"We're gonna watch here tonight, Marni," says Britt, though intimidated by this stern, emphatic woman.

Marni snorts but relents. Looks at the Hyperion. "I came here to gauge it. Thought I might go in. No way will I go in. Or even touch its door. Listen, is Aarti your name?"

"Yes."

"Listen, Aarti. Tomorrow night, I think something's going to happen with my man, and I'm gonna do something that might help your mom and dad. I'm gonna 'front the thing that's in there with them now. But just in the meantime, you have to—"

"I can't leave! They might call for my help!"

"I know. I'm gonna leave you here the rest of the night. Are you *alert* here, Brittany? You really looking out for this girl?"

Are you on pills? And she is, of course. "I'm looking out for her."

"OK then. And you *call* me in the morning."

"OK, we will." And Britt is glad of it. A bully, but a protector.

When Marni is gone, Britt says, "We shouldn't talk about it Aarti—it gives it strength. We just have to be here. It's all we can do right now."

"Yes, Brittany."

"We just listen, and if we can, we sleep."

"OK."

The mists have thickened almost to fog. The hotel's façade is bland and blank. Something sinister has receded. A feeling of peaceful solitude on the empty street replaces it.

"Brittany?" The girl sounding drowsy already.

"Mmm?"

"Are you a drug addict? My mom says you are."

Oh, this stings! "No, I'm not. I used to be, but not any more. Now listen. Tomorrow, when the sun's up and your mom and dad are safe again, I'll teach you how to street a little. And when your mom and dad have rested, we'll call them. And, if we have to, we'll call Marni. We'll walk around the city. I'll show you some nice green places we can hang, with good views."

Aarti is softly snoring. Britt has performed her first lullaby, and it's worked like a charm.

A frightening flood of light falls on the huddled pair them, and Britt hears the grille opening behind them. She looks up. It's a gaunt little old lady with a twisted, stern-looking face. Her hair is a dark unnatural red; she is hawk-nosed and seems to be trembling with rage at finding street-trash defiling her property. A long glare. And without a word she turns back inside.

She's going to call the police. Britt's body is stupid, it seems—she's not moving. She dreads awakening the girl, hating to traumatize her with this new alarm. Yet if the police come, the girl will be returned to the Hyperion, to her apartment where the enemy prowls.

The old woman is back, with something bulky under one arm. Pain-fully slow, she's easing herself down the steps . . . unfurling a blanket! Draping it over both of them! Is offering a stiff arthritic hand, two dollar bills in it as wrinkled as herself!

"Wait!" squeaks Britt. She unlimbers, without waking Aarti, Marni's packet—gives the woman two fifties. "Here. Please," she croaks. "We have more." She grins crookedly to signify a joke: "Rent."

The woman's own smile is crooked—Britt realizes that her face is slightly paralyzed on one side. "'Ank you, 'ear," she says. Hobbles herself back up, shuts the grille, and kills the porchlight.

Without awakening the girl, Britt gets them well cocooned with enough blanket under both their butts, developing some serious warmth. Britt feels herself slipping into sleep—but then hears a distant scuff of feet, a sketch of low voices.

Waits . . . coming more awake as indications of two large males grow clearer. Leans harder into the shadow, hugging Aarti perfectly still. There they are across the street. She's seen them both around the neighborhood. Dangerous guys. They're slowing. . . . The bigger one presses the bell of the Hyperion. She can't quite make out their conversation. They are buzzed in.

She had been toiling there for perhaps an hour, her earnest exertions put-ting a rosy flush on her face, when there strode into the gallery the Master of the manor, the impetuous, haarmsome young Lord Darcy.

Jack curses, backs up and x's out *haarmsome*, types *handsome* above, then sits back with a sigh. The street door's death-rattle makes him jump.

He thumbs the buzzer. Some random visitant. No tenants due for hours. In the bubble mirror: someone big with a cueball head climbs into view.

Here we go.

The head sprouts full-size from the stairwell. T-Bone, bigger than shit. He advances to the cage with a back-tilted stroll, high and wide. Jack finds himself standing at the bars. He has a sensation of falling, while at the same time conscious that he is presenting a perfectly impassive exterior.

"Evenin. Can I get a room?"

"'Fraid we can't he'p you. We full." Jack finds he is not exactly inside himself. He seems to hang a foot behind and above his body, detachedly fascinated by how he's playing this. The touch of black parody in his words is upping the ante right out of the gate, since the man (a white guy himself) is a wannabe black. T-Bone has a lot more chest and shoulder than Jack, is probably ten years younger, and his face presents an unnerving simplicity: eyes, ears, nostrils combine into a single sense-organ with a single focus—the detection of weakness, advantage, leverage. A slight droop of T-Bone's lids acknowledges the insult.

"Well, if I can't get a room"—smiling T-Bone hunkers more intimately toward the bars—"then it's my understandin that I can get my hat blocked here, get some pussy, you know?" Between the bars he gives Jack a little conspiratorial twinkle.

What is Jack going to answer? His right hand is reaching under the counter, has taken hold of his little .38, keeps it down there in a nice comfy grip. T-Bone stiffens slightly, noting the movement. Jack raises his eyebrows at T-Bone in honest bafflement.

"Gosh," he says, "I'm at a loss for words here. I mean, I thought a guy like you would have all the female attention he needs already. Isn't that the *point* of your line of work?"

T-Bone takes a small step back, not quite hiding his surprise at how fast this is moving. He stands half smiling, weighing Jack.

Just then, from the manager's suite, Phaasri utters a muted, gibbering wail, followed by a dogged snarl from Bill. Their ghastly duet has begun.

It restores T-Bone's aplomb. Such noises—or what the pimp takes them to be—are home ground, are stock-in-trade to him. With a little smile, he references what they're both hearing. "I tell you what it is, Homes. I'm a special kinda pimp. I'm a Management Pimp, dig? I'm official Pimp Protection for this whole neighborhood. Now you runnin a pimp right here, you runnin our fren' Razz, and the way things be workin is, that you owe me my district Pimp Protection Fee for this pimp you be runnin in my district. You understand what I'm sayin?"

The sounds from Bill's suite are almost inhuman. What are they *doing* in there? Christ, their little *girl* is in there! The cold fury that fills Jack brings his hand up with the .38 and aims it at T-Bone's chest. His words come smoothly. They seem to resonate in lungs slightly larger than his own, as if that larger self behind him has stepped forward and become him. "If you think I won't blow your pus-sucking heart right out through your spine, you are one seriously retarded pimp. Take your ass out of my hotel right"—and he thumbs back the hammer—"now."

He feels his finger putting that first half-ounce on the trigger, feels a high, righteous *longing* to squeeze off a fat little .38 slug and punch a nice hole in this black slaver's ticket. He feels the impulse rising in him, and T-Bone feels him feeling it and is moving toward the stairs now, hands palm-out, very definitely surprised at how fast the game is moving.

"Hey, I'm goin, Homes! This is your crib, I don't need to intrude in another man's crib." He's halfway down to the stairs' turning now and pauses, his eyes just above floor level. "Thing is, you gotta go outside some time. An out on the street, see, we *all* got roscoes, an' we can *all* be blowin holes with em, an' *you're* ass aint—"

Jack fires, aiming as precisely as he can for the cueball head. T-Bone ducks just in time. His quickness and nothing more has just saved Jack from murder. The enormous noise leaves an enormous, astonished silence that Jack stands there in, amid dense gunsmoke, watching the pimp shrink quickly in the mirror down to the vestibule, where a second miniature, Trinidad, appears—sneaked in under cover of T-Bone's entrance! Backup. The two of them thrust out into the street, and the door shuts behind them.

No room doors open. The shot thunder has no effect. Amazingly, the ghastly duet in the manager's suite has not faltered. It's as if the shot has thundered only in Jack's world, is exclusively his. What has he *done?* What has he *started?*

XIII
New Friends

Far past midnight now, Chester Chase lies curled on his side. For three full days and nights he's eaten nothing. Hunger, he finds, the farther you go into it, is an airborne sensation. The stomach's emptiness expands and fills the body. There's an ache, an anxiety to it, but these are somehow outside the emptiness, a thin envelope of craving and unease that, if you lie really still, just disappears for long stretches, and only that buoyant void remains.

Then, floating like this, your thoughts really unfold. Meeting no resistance, they no longer cut and stab with regret and remorse. They just are. The memories unscroll and you think yes, that's who I was . . . that's who we were . . . that's what I did . . . that's what I failed to do . . . that's what I lost forever.

And your surroundings unfold too, so vivid in your detachment. You float . . . you accept . . . you allow . . . and the others in their beds, sleeping or not sleeping, find their way to you and seep into your watchful void. He hears the faintest, driest weeping—or rather, the sound enters those oversized ears on that old man down there on Chester's bed, ears like flabby flowerpots sprouting white weeds. The weeping is coming from Karl Cabron, just next door. Shouldn't he still be working at that all-night dirty bookstore? Maybe he got laid off. Or maybe his tears are about that daughter he has, the one who will never talk to him, never see him again. A shy, kind little guy is Karl. He gave Chester that copy of *Bra Busters* a few years back, just a gift out of the blue, must have had to work up his nerve, a shy guy like that. That was the last time Chester ever jerked off, mainly to see if he could still do it. Christ, what a lot of work! He felt kind of proud he could still pull it off, but knew it was the last time and wasn't sorry either, another burden lifted.

Farther away, two people are struggling in their own darkness. Rage and terror and greed maul the pair of them, like a surf hammering them on ragged rocks. Their agony is in crescendo: surely they can't sustain it much longer. That's Bill and his wife. How many nights have they gone through this? What monsters haunt their Hindu brains? Perhaps their devils are different from ours, thinks Chester.

Something else is in there with the manager and his wife.

Something cold and sinewy coils around them in their struggles. . . .

There is the doorbell, and Jack buzzing someone up, but Chester is riveted by that icy presence, that muscled darkness that enfolds the manager and his wretched wife in their agony, because, just as his thought touches this presence, the presence feels the touch of Chester's thought, and touches *back*.

And for long suspended seconds, that presence pauses and *listens* to the old heart hammering in Chester's ribs, hammering in that old man down on the bed there with his bony legs tenting the blanket.

An enormous noise, a gunshot, erupts, but Chester scarcely registers it, because it is followed by the *uncoiling* of that sinewy darkness from the tangled bodies of the manager and his wife. It uncoils from them, and it begins silkenly to pour, like smoke, toward Chester himself.

Its approach sends a delicate bulge through the air, like a bow-wave, and Chester knows that this is the same mocking visitor who came to his door last night.

And hovers now, just outside his door again. How can it have chosen him? How can it be concerned with Chester's little bloodless shred of life? Float . . . accept . . . allow. Chester clings to his emptiness, hugs the void of his hunger. He feels the utter frailty of his being, his life a bubble of thought, in a bubble of tired skin and bone, inside a frail box of wood and plaster.

Hello in there . . .

Allow and acknowledge. That's what it wants. Acknowledge that the desolation he confronted on the empty street two nights ago, under the indifferent stars, is not the worst thing that the universe holds for people. Mere death on some empty street at some final moment is not the worst thing.

Acknowledge that the universe has spawned more than stars, that it's also spawned spirits, beings built of itself, of the only materials that endure: the cold and the dark. Gods. There are gods, and this is one here, taunting Chester's lesser being, which is made of heat and light.

> *Hello in there.*
> *Time to prepare.*
> *You and I must go somewhere.*

The strange rhymed words originate right in the center of Chester's floating mind.

But not just floating. . . . For it begins to seem as if he quivers to a kind of gravitation, a sidewards tug on his hovering self.

Gently, insistently, something is tugging the spirituous roots of Chester's soul from their frail grip on his body down there.

Yes. He is beginning to drift—a sentient knot of atmosphere—toward the wall. And it seems that invisible tendrils of body-memory cling to his soul as it drifts, misty wisps of limbs, a smoky ribcage with a phantom heart whispering inside it.

Is this Death? This Something that is *with* him now? That is tugging him away, as it murmurs again in his mind:

> *Faster, Chester! Chase, make haste!*
> *Let's go where they rest and fester,*
> *The hustlers finished with the race.*
> *All lie low now, slow with faster—*
> *Let's fly down and scope the place!*

Is this Death's voice, this sneering jollity? But isn't Chester's body still breathing, down there on the bed? See the stir under his shirt? His ribs' slow rise and fall?

Chester impacts the wall, and though he's frailer than smoke, he pierces it, experiences chalky plaster and splintery laths, dense dusty studs and then laths again and plaster, and he's next door, there's Karl Cabron below him, a folded lump under blankets, his seamed profile sunk in the pillow like a clenched fist desperately gripping sleep.

Karl quickly slipping past, the next wall is more quickly pierced, its textures combing Chester's phantom nerves. In the next room a breathing darkness, a shrouded shape rank with sleep, the next wall a blink of passage, and then, in a bath of light, he passes over Jack hunched in the cage, sitting as if paralyzed in a stench of gunsmoke. Then come the hotel's outer wall and the cold iron bones of the fire escape, and Chester plunges into the open air, the drench of night mist.

Evicted! In a way he never dreamed of dreading! He is houseless and fleshless, a soul in tow. *Is* this Death? And if it isn't, then wouldn't it be better for him if it *were?* He's gliding fast now, the buildings pouring past, the street a black river beneath, Chester himself part of a river of wet air, a streaming clot of sensation and terror.

> *Upsy-downsy, in and out,*
> *Let's see what this town's about!*
> *Chester, what are you afraid of?*
> *Let's see what this city's made of!*

He plunges like a crashing jet, through asphalt's petrochemical fudge, through gravel and earth, piercing thin shells of metal and concrete for brief baths in water, sewage, natural gas, more earth, earth the most frightening stuff of all, its grip so smothering, can't breathe in this stuff! And the realization that he *isn't* breathing is more frightening still.

Earth, earth, stone, earth, roots, grass, air again, air!

Sky. Up into the sky now—oh, much better, this! He's erupted from a high hillside. Beneath him, vast pavements of rooftops softly spangled with streetlamps pour down toward the Bay. He is angling downwards too, toward a freeway flanked by stands of great trees. Chester recognizes this neighborhood: Colma, Cemetery City.

Slowing, he descends among those towering trees, their moonshadows scented with eucalyptus and cedar and pine. Now he's gliding no faster than a bird, zigging and zagging whimsically, sinking toward wide spreads of lawn that are studded with tombstones.

It is Death that has him, Death beyond doubt. This is it.

> *Look where they moulder and crumble away—*
> *How rank-and-file orderly is their array!*
> *An army of underlings, mine to control.*
> *Let's do some recruiting. Come down! Lend a soul!*

And Chester is plunging toward a fresh-looking headstone, plunging through sod, through earth, through metal. . . .

And Chester has a solid body again, a dead-still body in a box, a body in a nice suit but clothed, within that suit, in a rotten garment shrunken to the bone. If Chester's terror had any leverage at its disposal, this coffin and the ton of earth atop it would explode into the moonlight—but Chester's terror is the tenant of unmoving meat laced with formaldehyde.

Except . . . there is something faintly alive within his ghastly envelope. Chester encounters a subtle stir, tendrils of misty memory lurking through the cadaver's parched terrain. Chester encounters scents he's never known, snatches of music he's never heard, the glimpse of some cobbled street in some Mediterranean town he's never seen, the terror of clutching a rifle and hugging the sand under whistling bullets in a desert war he's never fought. The corpse's spirit, in shreds and patches, begins to adhere to the bones Chester lies in. Those bones stir, and give the faintest shudder.

I bid thee to a banquet, lich!
This is an invitation which
Thou'lt not refuse. Bestir thee then!
I'll come for thee—thou knowest when!

Chester is snatched upwards, airwards, and hovers in the sky, but not for long he knows, for now he understands that this is not Death that has him, but something else, making use of the life still left in him, using him like a taper to rekindle dead candles. He understands this clearly just before, again, he plunges, into another grave. . . .

Chester's return to his room, hours later, is incredibly swift, a delirium of textures and streaming air. His will, his mere power to *feel,* seems all but burnt out of him.

Until he's back on his bed, back in his body. Chester finds feeling aplenty then. He finds an agony in his chest and a numbness through his left arm and shoulder. Has he had a stroke? A heart attack, while untethered to himself? Is, after all this, Death itself at hand?

XIV
Jack in the Archives

"Jack! Hullo! You got people buzzin to come up. Jack?"

Jack's eyes open grainily to the face of Elmer, to his swollen eyes behind the thick smeared lenses, and his white rooster-tail of hair half dangling in his face, disheveled by his interrupted sleep. With his gnarled old hand he reaches across Jack and hits the street buzzer, seeing that Jack is still not fully awake.

"Thanks," Jack croaks. His throat feels rusted shut. He takes up the half-cup of cold coffee from the desk. The swallow makes him shudder, spiked with bourbon as it is. The returning night-shifters climbing up look pissed. How long were they waiting? "It's OK now, Elmer. Thanks. I got it covered."

But Elmer drops onto the couch and runs his knob-jointed fingers back through his hair. "Bill an his wife sure have been goin at it, haven't they?"

Jack looks at him. It's not like the vague, evasive Elmer he knows to broach a discussion like this. "Yeah, they have. What's eating them?"

It's strange to be asking it of this bony-chested old Midwesterner in his undershirt. Elmer doesn't volunteer his thoughts on things. And so he surprises the hell out of Jack when he says, "Wull, you know Mr. Cunningham up in ninety-six? I think it has somethin ta do with *him*."

"And why do you think that?"

"I think yuh know as much about that as *I* do, Jack."

"I don't know much." It's disorienting, after a year's acquaintance, to be speaking to an alert stranger whose existence he never suspected. "I know Bill was . . . strongly affected by a leaflet Mr. Cunningham gave me."

Elmer nods slowly. His lens-warped eyes are no easier to read than they ever were, except that Jack now feels far more sharply seen by them. "I got business of my own with Mr. Cunningham. Least I think I do. But yuh know, Jack, there's been one thing I been wantin ta do an' can't, cuz my eyes are so poor, an' that's go down an' look in the hotel records an' see what I can find out about him. He's been here quite some time, I believe."

Jack sits there, trying to read those smeared eyes. "Do you mind telling me what business you think you might have with him?"

"I don't feel I'm free to say just now, Jack. But you wanna know about him too, doncha? Let's make a trade. I'll take the cage now to midnight, straight through. You go down there an' see what you can find out."

"OK. I'll take a shower, wake up, and go down."

Down in the foyer, in the wall to the left of the street door, is another stout door, which opens into the ground floor of the Hyperion. Jack unlocks the beefy deadbolt. He pulls the door open, steps into dusty darkness, and flips a wall-switch. A sprinkling of clamp-lights freckles the wide gloom.

The whole floor is a wall-less wilderness of posts and rafters, filled with the old furniture and abandoned baggage of the hotel's past generations. The lightbulbs reveal little islands of it here and there, a sprawling archaeology of furnishings. Here are half-collapsed Stonehenges of box-springs and headboards and mattresses and tilted, frameless doors; there are dusty ziggurats of stacked chairs and desks. Beyond loom the broad-shouldered sarcophagi of old wardrobes and refrigerators; and everywhere, sown through the grander junk, the smaller building-blocks are irregularly stacked—suitcases, trunks, cardboard boxes.

Watching his shadowy step, he goes fifteen yards into this wilderness to the little stand of cabinets and files, with its own clamp lights arrayed above a rickety table and chair. Jack turns on the lamps and takes his seat at the table. Now he's in a good bubble of bright wattage, the shadows pushed back on all sides. The hotel "records" surround him, a disorderly thicket of filing cabinets and boxes. He must keep track of where he starts and eliminate each box and cabinet systematically. He creates a clear space for restacking what he has gone through and begins. Is surprised to realize how fascinating he finds the prospect of this search.

He wades into an utter lack of system. A drawer labeled Accounts holds only boxes of canceled checks. Another, labeled Taxes, holds a rat's nest of utility bills and repair bills going back to the late '70s. Jack keeps sifting, scanning, restacking, setting aside. The time unspools as he works, no shred of payoff but an undeniable excitement in the task. The shadows that surround his isle of light feel pregnant with discovery.

He comes to a blond oak cabinet, a piece of decidedly older vintage. The top drawer is empty. In the middle drawer, pliers, screwdrivers, snarled extension cords, old pencils, scabby glue bottles. In the bottom drawer are cigar boxes. In these boxes are papers—elderly, dry pages, faintly mottled like the backs of old hands.

They prove to be mostly business letters, in the vigorous pica of thunderous old Royals and Underwoods, from the era when typists wore arm-garters and visors. A glance at the letters' dates shows he has struck the early years of the 1930s. That's bordering on *too* far back. True, Cunningham could easily be in his nineties. But why would he have been here as a young man? Jack sifts and studies the correspondence, savoring the style and diction of a bygone era.

The business letters are addressed to one Amos Vickers. They are communications from carpenters, electricians, painters, plumbers, referencing now-quaint technology and ludicrously low prices. A lot of renovation and repair going on here. Vickers begins to look like a new owner who is engaged in fixing the place up. And then Jack experiences that tingle of a historian's confirmation when he comes upon a suite of personal letters, written by a Miss Dorothy O'Dowd in elegant cursive.

Miss O'Dowd, in the course of three successive epistles, reiterates her regrets that her late father Colonel O'Dowd's "last illness," "tragic decline," "fatal affliction" has left his records in "a shambles," "terrible confusion," "hopeless disorder," and that in consequence the requested wiring diagram of the Hyperion, and next, the name of the plumber who made certain baffling modifications in the hotel's hot water lines, and finally, the names of the bank agents who disburse the rental payments for a few of the older, long-term tenants—all these data requested by Mr. Vickers are, alas, not to be found.

In each letter Miss O'Dowd earnestly hopes that Mr. Vickers will, his current puzzle solved, begin at last "to enjoy to the fullest your new captaincy of the noble old Hyperion."

From these letters, and stray details from the various renovating contractors' reports, Jack gathers the hotel's history in broad strokes. It flourished under O'Dowd a decade before and perhaps two decades after the turn of the twentieth century. By the '30s, the inventory of Vickers's repairs suggests it was far past its prime, though still respectable enough to warrant renewal. He seems to have bought it in 1930, and to have been grappling with the renovation and modernization for most of the next three years.

Jack toils through the correspondence with a growing sense of detachment. It all concerns the owner's dealings with the outer world, not with the lodgers themselves. No ledgers, no budgets, no logs, no record of life inside the hotel.

Then, an interesting glimpse of the tenantry. It is a thankful letter from Stuttgart that, in spiky, almost unreadable handwriting and stilted English, blesses Vickers for "the vigor of his researches" in finding out the connections of a genteel German woman, a tenant of the Hyperion already mature when she first took her room at the close of the Great War, and who has, in the decade since, grown helpless with senility and amnesia. Fräulein Rotblatt's conveyance back to Stuttgart is vowed, and a grateful remittance, which apparently accompanied the letter, is alluded to.

Jack finds it poignant—a ghost from the Jazz Age, stranded in a hotel room on the eve of the Great Depression. Vickers seems to have been a decent man. The vigor of his researches . . .

After this, nothing but more contractors' correspondence, a desert of plasterers' projections and plumbers' estimates. He's almost finished the cigar boxes' contents, has still not found material dated later than 1933.

A short, typewritten letter from a legal firm greets Jack's eye. In its second brief paragraph there is a Dutch-looking name that makes Jack's nape prickle and stir.

The letter is dated 22 October 1932, letterheaded Horace and Maplethorpe, Attorneys at Law. The writer, though, has signed an illegible something that resembles neither of these names. Some junior partner. An ancient stain obscures the letter's last sentence, but everything else is perfectly clear.

> Mr. Vickers:
>
> We are appalled to discover ourselves long in arrears to you. The enclosed draught, we hope, makes ample reparation.
>
> We were ignorant of your acquisition of the Hyperion.
>
> Our excellent and most valued client, Mister Connyng Van Haarme—himself slow to learn of the change—belatedly conveyed to us this circumstance.
>
> In our ignorance, we have continued to make our quarterly deposits in Colonel O'Dowd's account. Henceforth they will come to you. Accept our apologies and our thanks for your patience.
>
> (illegible concluding sentence)
>
> (signed illegibly)

Mr. Connyng Van Haarme. Connyng Haarme. Who-o-a. Jack tingles to find how his imagination has anticipated this discovery. The coincidence itself convinces him, despite the improbable stretch of years involved. So here is the old man in his youth—here is a young *Cannyharme's* first footprint in the annals of the Hyperion. Has the guy stayed here continuously? Been here more than seventy years? Dutch, by the name. Jack sees the old man's milky blue eye, hovering just above the counter under the cage bars. An eye with the chilly North Atlantic in it. Dutch . . .

Horace and Maplethorpe are letterheaded a San Francisco firm, but here and there in the brief text Jack is sure he sees the diction of a cultivated foreigner's acquired English, suggesting the firm was European in the first instance. The letter is short and sweet, the writer seeming confident the new owner will have no desire for renegotiation of terms. The accompanying payment was undoubtedly a handsome one.

Apparently Vickers was over two years in possession without payment. That strikes Jack oddly. Conceivably Cannyharme had no English in his youth—indeed, how much does he speak even now?—but why would two years pass before he "learned of the change" from Vickers? And why would Vickers wait so long without payment? Was he just . . . letting it go?

The cigar boxes hold no further clue, but curiosity burns in him now. He's going to find more. He knows he is.

Cabinets, boxes, more cabinets encircle him, and he plows through them steadily, forgetting the passage of time. So much of it is rubbish, old magazines and newspapers baled over a decade ago and still awaiting recycling, yellowed stationery, rat's-nests of receipts stowed away by junior-grade Patels preceding Bill through the past two decades. Jack sifts it all.

At first glance it's just more debris: a box full of old paperbacks. Then, when he rummages through it, he finds a letter postmarked July something 1974, folded back into its torn-open envelope and rubber-banded to a notepad with some faded ball-point scrawlings on it.

The letter proves to be a half-literate plea, addressed to a certain "Jimmy Baby" and scrawlingly signed by "Chanel."

> Dear Jimmy Baby
>
> I tole you Iv *change* now hony! I relly have! That time that make you so mad I have to much to drank swetee an' that is relly all it was!
>
> You now I love you an' you my ensperation an' I don't drank so much inny more at all now an' if you lemme move back in I now I can be maken you so happy an' you now I maken you cum so good!
>
> We hav it so good together swetee I now that man jus some lokul trash I don't even member his name I dint even liken his lovin not lik yours an' he coont even git it up!
>
> Whynt you come to the phone win I call?
>
> Your Chanel

The envelope is addressed to Jimmy Clark at the Hyperion, no room number. This, the number of paperbacks, and the box's inclusion in the hotel records cache make it seem likely that Jimmy Baby was one of Jack's forbears, an ancestral clerk in the cage. By his paperbacks, Jimmy seems to have liked John D. MacDonald, so he can't have been a total idiot. Jack sets himself to decipher the ballpoint scrawl on the notepad, tangled though this is.

It soon appears this is the work of a man a good deal more educated than the woman writing to him. Jack realizes that what he has here are two different drafts of a letter of reply to Chanel. Jack painstakingly copies out into his own notebook both drafts:

Chanel

It's still hard to forgive you going home with that clown—I don't care how drunk you were. On the other hand, we did have some good times together. Part of me wants you to move back in as if you'd never betrayed me, but my pride has a really hard time with that.

I guess I need you to give me some proof that you really have changed. Next Saturday night I'm going to a Banquet with some friends of mine you haven't met. I'm inviting you as my date, but I want you to show up decently dressed and sober, and if the evening goes well

Dear Chanel

It's still hard to forgive your infidelity, but the booze can make fools of us all from time to time, I guess. You really hurt me when you betrayed me, but your letter has made me realize I still have a lot of tender feelings for you.

But my pride has been wounded, and I'm afraid to trust you. I think it will help me if we meet like on a first date, like we were still new lovers. I'm invited to a Banquet this Saturday night. Why don't you meet me there? It's out in the Avenues. Meet me at eight at the Sons of

Jack is very unsure of the last three words of the second version. "The Sons of" is the best he can do. Their scrawled incoherence, though, gives him a strong writerly hunch that this was the version Jimmy Baby went with—that he broke off the draft so hastily because he had made up his mind about it and turned directly to writing the fair copy he was going to send her.

The more Jack weighs them, the more interesting he finds these alternate versions. Jimmy Baby is trying out strategies. First he tries the stern voice. Chanel, you've been very bad. Against my better judgment, I'll take you to this banquet—it'll be like a qualifying exam for your reestablishment in the Hyperion.

The second draft is much more forgiving. Jimmy tries the can't-stop-loving-you voice. The banquet will be like a first date, an attempt to recapture that honeymoon feeling.

It's really quite intriguing, this little fossil of a lover's spat. One way or another, Jimmy Baby wants Chanel to come to that banquet next Saturday. Out in the Avenues, at the Sons of . . .

Fascinating. On the face of it, Jimmy had gotten over his pique at her, decided it would be nice to be fucking her again, and was trying out which footing to take her back on, which persona to use, sweet or stern. But why a banquet? Why an organized dinner in the midst of a crowd? If he wanted to make a ceremony of their reunion, why not something one-on-one—a restaurant, with maybe a motel handy to it? Jack imagines Chanel sprawled on a motel bed, dusky on white sheets, big melon breasts, soft, practiced lips. He feels a moment of comradeship for Jimmy Baby, his long-past predecessor in the cage—hopes Jimmy got what he wanted from Chanel.

What was that?

He has sensed a delicate shifting far back in the shadows. A whisper . . .

Jack rises—plucks a clamplight from its purchase and holds it up like a torch. The light washes out against boxes and bedsteads, drawerless dressers and frameless doors.

A stirring? All he sees now is the shift of shadows his own nervous hand is casting. The only whisper he hears is his own startled blood rumoring in his ears.

He replaces the light and sternly resumes his work. And as he sifts and sorts and stacks, he stays aware of the darkness surrounding him. The shadows, like a single taut fabric, stretch and strain as if something is at work under their dark garment, something whose breathing he can almost hear.

Drawer after drawer of trash and irrelevance. More bundled newspapers. Shoeboxes full of more canceled checks. Old calendars baled by rotten rubberbands that break at the touch. Then, from the next-to-last box, emerges an old three-ring binder of blue plastic. There's a whole packet of lined paper inside it, but only the first few sheets are written on—covered with a crudely blocked handwriting in black ballpoint.

Jack smiles as he begins to skim, recognizing what this is. All that paper, and just these first few pages with their dated entries (the first July 3, 1957), all the rest still virgin, though aged now, and stained round the holes with rust from the rings. This is obviously a specimen of that classic literary genre, the Aborted Journal. To judge by the childish handwriting, it's the legacy of some simple man, resolutely embarking on a sustained undertaking, only to be exhausted by the effort in four pages, and quit— renouncing the witness stand, and closing the binder forever.

And then Jack spies a pair of numerals embedded in one of the little thickets of handwriting: *rm 96*.

A sharper scan of the pages. The number recurs in other entries.

A prickling sensation moves up his spine and into the hair on the nape of his neck.

Here, at the very last, may be just what he has been looking for . . . and yet he feels a powerful reluctance to read these crudely written lines.

The reading in any case will not be easy. The childish penmanship is made even more obscure by misspellings of dyslexic proportions. Jack is lucky to have spent all those months grading papers, honing his unscrambling skills. He begins to untangle the narrative from the garbled text.

July 3 1957

I hope you can reed this ok Mr Kelleher an you reeliz Im *trine* to slove the prolemb so hers my log wch I hopp is what you meen by a *daylee re-*

card. Tonite I stade at the dekse til 9 to catch rm 96 coming down. He com down an I caym out an stant infront him. He cant see in front cuze he so *bint.* I stant infront him an tolt him exsifickly to mayk his cheks to American Hospitality Inc. I given him the payper you wroten it on. He given *me* a payper. It was a Pome on it. I doe not get it. Its a strayng Pome!

July 5 1957

Mr Kellihur I red yr knote an I wayded for rm 96 agan an I stanted infront him agan but I was very pulite an I tolt him his chks *haff* to be wroten out to America Hosplitaty Inc!! I thanck he shuk his hed yes but waddif hes deff?? I cant tel cuze he cant harley talk rite he gruntses and gorwls lik a dog so I cant untersand if he heers wat I sade or not. Enywaze I given him a paypur agan wch Id wroten on it Amercian Hosplitaity esedera agan an he gaven me a payper agan with a Pome on it a difernt Pome but so strayng lik the 1ˢᵗ Pome I red. I red the Pomes agan but I stil dint get them.

July 7

Mr Kellahur I thanck I hav bin gotten invorelved in somthink bad. Rm 96 cayme down yisturdaye it was the midil of the day but ther was nobudy around. He taked to me but not with words he taked lik with gruntses lik a *woof* but sum how I cd *untersand* him he was enviding me up to rm 96. He sayde he had mor Pomes to reed me his Pomes our so strayng Mr Kullihor I cudnt get them but I *liket* them

I wint up to his rm lik he sayde. His rm is so big insyde Mr K!! It dint even sem pocible it cd be so big insyde that rm he has

He reeded me Pomes out lowd his voyse lik a dogs and his words lik the gruntses and gorwls of a meen smart dog.

I lik Pomes Mr K! I dint never now I lik Pomes but I do lik his Pomes

Thin he given me some salzanpouters. He sade they wer majik an now I thanck I have gotting invorveled in sum thinck bad cuze after he given me them he red me more Pomes an I cd untersant them todully!

July 10

Mr K I aplogyize I dint finich that last port so many thincks ben hapend-ing. I wish I cd ixplayn them al but me an rm 63 Mis Doyle are levving the Hypernion

Im sory but Mis Doyle an me hav gotting deply envorveled thes last feew days and she ben taking the salzinpowters with me an ben lissning to Pomes with me in rm 96. Mis Doyl is a very swete wormen Mr K an she an I ar getting encaged an we all ar goyne to go to a big bankwit to sali-brate.

Im sory Im quidding but I fond a job sudingly that pays to good to refewse. So Im so sorey but gdby.

We haff to porvide for are fewcher

Peter McM

Having at last negotiated this syllabic wilderness, Jack sits stunned. These materials—their apparent age, their every detail—are completely convincing. But how can Jack *believe* that the old man's near-terminal de-formity was *just the same* fifty years ago? There is a loathsome physical *unreality* to the very notion. At the same time, this odd little stack of evi-dence he's extracted seems so authentic. The Vickers correspondence alone—it just couldn't be hoaxed. His writer's ear tells him the letters have the voice and idiom of the '30s, not to mention the paper, the postmarks.

And this box of Jimmy Baby's books here. When he takes everything out, there are things he missed before: a comb, a broken wind-up Timex, a half-smoked pack of Marlboros (no cancer warning on that one), some ballpoint pens. It looks like someone cleared out Jimmy's drawer in the Cage *for* him. Chanel's letter was rubber-banded to Jimmy's practice drafts, but would the writer himself have kept these scrawled rehearsals? Jimmy's departure from the hotel, then, came soon after writing that letter. *Sudingly.* Last known destination, a Bankwit.

Peter McM's *Salzanpouters* nags at Jack. An idle memory comes to him, the phrase "saltes and Powders" from some horror fiction he has read somewhere. He cannot for the life of him recall the author, but Peter

McM's half-century-old reference to what might have been a powered drug sends a delicate movement up his back: a second intuition that Cozzens is not only Cannyharme's *suitor* for divine intervention, but perhaps also a partner in gaining converts.

Jack struggles for clarity. This has to be a scam, doesn't it? Look how Elmer sent him on this quest. Elmer's been here a long time himself, if Jack's not mistaken. What if he's a part of whatever shell-game it is that Cannyharme's running? The point of these records would be to give that game an authenticity, a scary reality: a quasi-magical cult that has been running for half a century. And if that's true, of course, then anyone who has gone *this* far to propagate belief has already crossed a scary line—is dead set on capturing believers.

But what could they be after? What could they *want* from their believers?

Well, so far anyway, Jack's lost nothing to the game, he is still showing a net gain in the form of the speed's potential cash value. The thing is, it could mean more danger than profit, without Willy to buy it in quantity from him. Jack knows a couple people he just might sell Bender's Glock to, though. He should liquidate some of the crank that way. And till he has sold the gun, there'd be some kind of comfort in having a class piece in his possession, with those pimps he's antagonized. Not that any kind of gunplay can be a way out of that problem—did he really shoot at that big cueball-headed one? Oh, man—this isn't a movie he's in, its life. Suppose, though, he goes to Cozzens—a man Jack's sure pulls major weight out on the street—and asks him for some help? Gives the biker back all or most of his speed, trade it in for this more urgent favor?

It's worth a try. It's already mid-afternoon. He'll go up and see Bender. Then go see Cozzens.

As he's putting the Horace and Maplethorpe letter into the stack he will take upstairs, the grease-stain that obscures its last line catches the light at an angle that reveals the ghost of typing underneath it.

Jack shifts his seat, and begins tipping the letter this way and that against the light. Bingo. He has found the angle at which the obscured line is perfectly decipherable:

> . . . In our ignorance, we have continued to make our quarterly deposits in Colonel O'Dowd's account. Henceforth they will come to you. Accept our apologies and our thanks for your patience.
>
> *Because our client's extreme age and deformity make it difficult for him to communicate, we are doubly grateful for your forbearance and your faith in ultimate restitution.*

Extreme age and deformity. Eighty years ago.

XV
A Trip through the Moon

Perhaps it surprises Elmer, the almost hostile look Jack gives him when he trudges back upstairs. "We can talk tonight," Jack says. There's an unmistakable hoax being run on him, and he's got damn little reason to think Elmer's not part of it.

He goes into his room. He shoves Cozzens's packet into one of his pockets and his little pocket scale into the other. His fingertips detect, crumpled against the pocket's bottom seam, a piece of paper.

And what he extracts and smooths out is Cannyharme's missing tract. Here are the lost verses in their crude black print. He's been even more stoned than he realized. He'd searched his pockets repeatedly. Perhaps it is the lingering effect of Cozzens's product.

It's odd that only two or three lines here seem familiar to him. But the grotesque tone of it, and the strange ghoulish imagery, are recognizable enough.

> *Where the lich in the loam has lain mouldering long,*
> *And the maggoty minutes gnaw meat off his bones,*
> *There Time is a monster that mows down the throng*
> *Of once-have-been, gone-again, featureless drones.*
>
> *And that lich's coffin to me was a door*
> *Through which I went nosing Eternity's spoor.*
>
> *But the living dead's doorways, once opened, gape wider.*
> *Through these you may go where the galaxies sprawl,*

And up through the starweb, dance sprightly as spiders,
And dart quick as rats through Time's ceilings and walls.

There we go feasting and rutting at will,
And Time is a wine we imbibe when we kill!

There, by God, is Cozzens's pitch, all right. Time is just what he is quickly running out of. Jack is deeply relieved to have regained this piece of leverage. Whatever scam is being run on Cozzens, it's made him truly desperate for some word. In exchange for the tract, the giant biker could be one bad ally against T-Bone.

Bender opens at once to Jack's knock. "Expecting me?" Jack laughs.

Bender hesitates slightly. There's a brief look, almost of dislike, in his gray eyes. He smiles bleakly. "I knew it was an offer you couldn't refuse."

"Actually," Jack says when the door's shut and he's unfolding his little scale on Bender's desk, "I'd like to make *you* an offer." He smiles. "Why give up your nice piece? For fifteen hundred I'll give you an ounce you could step on by half."

"I'm cash-poor, Jack. The Glock's all I have to offer."

He surprises himself with this offer. Is he getting so nervous that he wants to cut and run? Cash out the stash quick?

On impulse Jack asks, "You've been here a long time. What do you know about old Cannyharme up in ninety-six? Check this out. He gave it to me."

As he proffers the tract, Bender turns his head aside and thrusts Jack's hand away. "Keep that to yourself. I don't want to know anything about it."

Jack stares at him. Bender stares back, mouth compressed, defiant.

"You must know something?"

Bender looks cornered—and then he looks amused. "You've got that exactly wrong. You're *letting* him show you. I *refuse* to see. I'm a lot more careful than you are, Jack."

"And just what is it you're being careful *of?*"

"It's a big world—you know that, don't you? It's a big universe.

You're an educated man, so you do grasp just how big a universe it is, don't you? And in so big a universe, do you know what freedom is? Freedom is *boundaries.* Sharp, clear boundaries you never cross, because on the other side of those boundaries is that big universe, and its prevailing temperature is absolute zero. And that's all I'm going to say about it. So. Are we going to do business?"

"Yeah. Sure."

"Then let me suggest you go get a jacket or sport coat. You can put on the rig and we can see how well the whole thing hides."

And it hides very well. Surprising how the pistol's heft—so elongated with the suppressor attached—hugs Jack's torso so trimly under the jacket.

He wears it as he weighs out Bender's half-OZ. The residue in Cozzens's packet seems scarcely dented. How much has the mad biker actually given him? The excess is a measure of his . . . what? Worship? Reverence? His awe of that bent old man. Bender's strange silence, and his stranger fervor . . . a measure of his *fear* of that same crippled figure?

When Jack comes back downstairs, Elmer waves a note at him from the bars of the cage. "I think it was one a them girls from the Mayfair dropped this off, Jack."

He unfolds two words childishly written:

bang bang

He looks at Elmer. He feels at sea in this rising tide of developments, of unanswered questions surrounding him. "Tell me something, Elmer. Why did you get me to go down and look into the old man, and why don't you tell me *your* business with him?"

"Wull . . . I guess because you don't know enough yet, Jack."

"You expect I'm gonna know more?"

"Yep. I gotta feelin you're gonna . . ." The goggle-eyed old-rooster face, the folksy white peckerwood hair—he could be a guy from a Faulkner story. . . .

Jack stares in silence. "I'll be back by midnight, if nothing happens to me." The man's face gives him nothing back.

In his room Jack takes a healthy shot of Old AA, thinking of the Mission streets he's about to walk through to see the mad biker Cozzens. This old Mystical Carnival is getting to be too real for fun any more. To hell with the poetry here, if all it's going to do is get him shot.

He considers keeping the coat and the gun on his walk—and instantly sees that as a bad move, a cracking under stress. No one's going to cap him in broad daylight, and if he walks around terrified of it they've already whipped his ass.

No. He's going to walk right down there, right past the Mayfair. He pours another shot and swallows it more savoringly. He puts the Glock in his drawer, but keeps on the coat and the rig. It feels right, like a promise of his counter-attack if it comes to be called for.

Out on the street, under an already declining sun, he feels a pleasure in that empty little gun-nest under his arm, its secret counter-threat to his enemies. He feels armed by his insouciance and thinks that, after all, it would not be so reckless to be actually packing the Glock, because in the Carnival the right touch of recklessness is the best disguise. He pauses, lingering at the intersection in front of the Mayfair Hotel. Then crosses the street slowly and lingers over there, in full view from the Mayfair's windows. Let *pimps* send little pussified *notes*. Here stands Jack Hale in the flesh to front them.

Continuing on his way across the Mission, the phantom gun enlarges him and makes him suave and easy. On the badder streets the ghostly Glock is sensed, he thinks—he passes the cholos on their porch steps, or clustered near the liquor stores, and never hears a single sneer, or murmur, in his wake.

The sun's not far from setting when he climbs up Cozzens's knoll at last. There's a big, glossy black van parked in front of the house. It strikes a doubly discordant note. There's *never* anything parked there. Plus which, the van's freshly store-bought look is totally out of character for Cozzens.

Traffic grumbles on all sides of this knoll, but these few weathered Victorians seem to exist in their own bubble of isolation, their own silence.

They look somehow more sinister in daylight . . . and Cozzens's front porch looks different. A narrow path has been cleared through the junk that crowds the porch, and the front door (like Willy and Marni's) stands slightly ajar.

Jack climbs the steps, threads through stacked wicker furniture furred with dust. He maneuvers amidst planting boxes with dry plugs of soil still in them and the jutting brown bones of dead stems, and boxes of newspapers, and boxes and boxes of beer bottles. . . . He pokes his face in the doorway, into cool dimness and the smell of dust.

"Cozzens? You upstairs?"

And hears, after a beat, a dull voice inside. He pulls at the door, then has to pull harder, till warped wood gives with a grunt.

Ahead, beyond a short hall, is a gloomy parlor jammed with furniture, and a big shape sits amidst it. It's Cozzens, looking not at Jack, but at something nearer to him, within the parlor.

"Coz? Can I come in?"

"Hey, Ace. Come in and take a load off." Still not looking at Jack, voice weary or preoccupied.

What looks to be furniture from all over the house jams the parlor—not just couches, armchairs, and ottomans, but kitchen chairs, writing desks, wardrobes, and breakfronts—all old-fashioned stuff, the gloom and the dust hovering over it like an exhalation.

But there's an open patch of worn carpet at the room's center, where Cozzens slumps on a couch. Jack sits across from him in a high-backed armchair.

Even in this curtained dimness, the lesions on the biker's face are stark. They seem to smolder like embers. He eyes Jack remotely, somewhere deeper inside himself than Jack has yet seen him. Has been sitting with his death, here in this defunct house. He says, "My grandmother raised me in this house, Slick." His face is somber, a mournful note in his cave-bear voice. "Old Gran, a real lady, straight as a pine, steel in her spine, grit in her guts, and spit in her eye."

The monster is grieving. The fiend confronts his coffin and is, it seems, penitent before his end.

"It was just about when I hit high school that Gran had her strokes, an' after the last one I took care of *her,* see, like she'd done for me for so many years. I fed her, cleaned her, changed her sheets. I got her outta bed an' dressed her up every morning an' set her up in that chair you're sittin in. She liked to sit there during the day and look out the window. I never failed her. I just wanted to, like, *give back* something where I had received so much. An' all through high school, right up till I went into the service, I'd bring my dates here to meet her on weekend nights. On those nights I dressed her in her church best, the hat with the little veil and so on, an' I'd put her makeup on like she used to do herself before church, little lipstick, little powder on her poor old paralyzed face, an' I'd put her Bible on her lap because she wanted no mistake about her faith, nosiree. And then, when I had her set up the way I knew she liked, I'd take my dates and I'd hump 'em six ways from Sunday across every stick of furniture in the room."

Now with the punchline comes a big, mad sunburst grin. This grin gives Jack's heart a powerful jolt. Cozzens's teeth have been, just detectably, *sharpened.* The corners of the incisors are filed off, like little sword points, and the canines are more dagger-tipped. It's a subtle but frightening alteration seen in full when he grins.

"See, she couldn't even close her eyes, Ace—not the left one anyway. I had to put drops in it for her all the time and like a wet bandage when I was gone, but I was glad to do it, anything Gran needed of course, but especially that. She couldn't close it, an' she couldn't turn away, an' I gave her an eyeful all night long. And man, every time she'd get so worked up wanting to kill me that a little rope of spit would start hanging off her mouth, get longer an' longer the longer I performed. I figure it was me that killed her without even touching her, or at least I like to think so. It was a disappointment when I found her stone cold in bed, because I always wanted her to go right in the middle of one of my shows.

"Would you mind getting outta that chair, Ace, an' sittin over there in that one?"

Jack is more than glad to get his ass out of the seat of so many memories. As soon as he's resettled, Cozzens reaches behind his couch and plucks up a twelve-gauge that is sawed off almost to the pump, levels it at Gran's chair, and—

WHACK

—annihilates Jack's hearing. He thunders out two more shots, these less audible to deafened Jack, but still making him flinch from the spray of splinters and stuffing. The chair is demolished, its crooked bones slumped in the ringing silence. Jack sits blinking, waiting for whatever comes next, thinking of firing on T-Bone last night, thinking that gunfire is suddenly becoming a part of his life.

Cozzens lays the twelve-gauge aside. "From that day, Slick, I made my own way, an' I've had a full an' wonderful career. I M-fuckin-P'd two tours in Saigon, man! Military Police! An' R-an-R'ed in Bangkok! I've had *every* kinda chicken God ever made. And I've run kitchens all over California, Texas, Mexico—I've cranked mega-mils in hard cash! I've taken the falls, done the walls, got out an' gone back an' done it all again! I have had one fuckin wonderful life!"

Cozzens rises, takes a step toward Jack. "I've been more blessed than most, Chief. Old Gran liked to tell me that, and so it proved, so it proved." The biker looms right in front of him. Jack must look up steeply from his chair to meet those mad yellow eyes—until, suddenly, Cozzens drops to his knees on the carpet, and there are those tawny eyes straight on, and not a foot away. He clasps his huge hands before his chest, those hands just a short snatch away from Jack's throat.

"Can you hear me here, Chief?" Oh, yes, Jack nods, he can even feel the vibration of the softly growled question, can smell the giant through the gunpowder stench: a musk-and-motor-oil smell, laced with a scent of spoiled meat. "Because I tell you now I don't intend my life to stop. I'm no fucking way done living. So I'm beggin you here, Chief. See?" The sinews are stark in his prayerfully clasped hands. "I'm humbly beggin you. You got some *word* from him for me?"

How glad Jack is that he has something to offer! There is a horrible undertone here of Cozzens *proposing*—Cozzens as his nightmare suitor. "I have this," Jack says quickly, fumbling it out of his pocket. "This is a paper from Mr. Cunningham, I don't know if—"

"No!" Cozzens has pulled his hands away from the offered tract. "Hold it up so I can see it, I don't want to touch it, hold it up so I can *read* it!"

The fierce face scans the leaflet, lips parted from those sharpened teeth. The face morphs into a mask of relief and joy. *Tears* fill those bestial eyes, and his fangs are bared in a pathetic, crumpled smile of gratitude. He raises his eyes and his prayerful hands toward the ceiling. "Thank you, Master!" His voice is cracked with feeling. "Thank you! Oh, thank you!"

And, suddenly light, Cozzens's great mass rises. He lifts his arms in a touchdown gesture and does a slow pirouette on the carpet. "Thank you! Thank you, old one! Thank you!" Growing ever merrier as he turns. Beaming at Jack now. "You're my main man, Jack-o! Whatever you want, you got it!"

Jack stands, relieved to be freed from the chair he's been boxed into. "Well, you know, Coz, I'm glad you say that. The thing is, I've got kind of a *situation* at my hotel."

"Do tell! Siddown, siddown! Run it by me—run it by old Cozzens!" The biker sits back on the couch, his posture regally at ease, a man whose ship has just come in.

Jack—perched now on an ottoman—runs it down. The biker, as he listens, occasionally parodies a counsellor—steeples his fingers, strokes his beard, nods owlishly. An irrepressible humor hums in the giant. The man seems so genuinely happy.

At the conclusion of the tale, he nods gravely, then breaks out another sunburst grin of savage teeth. "It's amazing, Ace, the coincidence here. I *know* these players of yours! That little Razz? Mmmm, what a cutie! I've admired him for a long time: a miniature pimp, perfect in every detail!

And check this out: Your man T-Bone? And Trini, his pal? We've done mucho biz! I don't think this problem is gonna *be* a problem. I'm not sayin they're sweetie pies like that Razz, but I see some room for maneuver here. I'll be in touch, couple days at the most, and meantime don't sweat it. And bring me whatever you get, right? Toot sweet! Go in peace, Chief! Go in peace! Oh, wait—just one more thing. Sit still and let me look into your eyes—just humor me a sec."

Jack blinks as smiling Cozzens leans down, his great troll's face filling Jack's sight. Cozzens lifts his palm and blows. White dust gusts into Jack's face. His startled inhalation sucks in fire, his eyes and nostrils and lips taste fire. "What the fuck?" Jack has leapt to his feet, is—too late— wildly sweeping the dust from his face. Cozzens stands back, palms raised placatingly. "I apologize, Ace. It's the old one's orders, the only thing he insists on. It's an eye-opener. You know the crank you've been doing? It's like those candy-ass henna tattoos—it wears off. But this stuff's like a *real* tat. From now on, you'll be able to *see* what's bein offered. The choice is still totally yours. He wants it to be! He needs it to be! But from now on you'll *see* what you're choosing. Meantime, I'm at your service. I'll talk to T-Bone this very P.M. Just stay outta the hood till dark, an' I'll have the situation chilled! Go in peace, Chief!"

It's been dark for hours when at length Jack walks back into the neighbor-hood. The neon signs are a raucous jazz of colors jubilating over the traf-fic's roar. The sidewalks are streaming with people. Belatedly, he realizes that it's a Saturday night.

He's walked the city for hours, testing his senses against the ogre's claim that they have been altered. The drug feels like meth and nothing more, and he has been drinking the edge off it as he walks. Not only have they been manipulating him with *Pomes* and *Saltzanpouters*, not only have they been playing him all along and he too obtuse to see it, but they feel such confidence that they've *declared* their game. Their indifference to his know-ing stokes his rage. While he's sure that any strange drug will have shown itself by now, that the crank in the face was a trick, like hypnotic suggestion, he can't *know* this, and the uncertainty keeps his anger simmering.

Passing an alley mouth, he sees, just beyond a dumpster, a skinny little Latina hooker—heavy lipstick, micro skirt—squatting with her panties pulled down past her knees, and shaking a bottle of Coke corked by her thumb. She tucks it up herself and jets in the foam—a quick douche. Her face during this operation is unconsciously lovely, brows intent with the athletic demands of the task, eyes inward, her garish young mouth thoughtful.

Jack walks on, feeling he's possessed her life in that glimpse. The next time she blinks she'll be thirty, slack skin on bone, the Death in her veins, or will be a face-busted abuser's prey, sinking fast in fat and booze. And the next time she blinks she'll be dead, blown off Carnival Street by the evening breeze like a crumpled popcorn bag. Time the Reaper towers like a giant over this glittery underworld, stands knee-deep in the crowds with his scythe. . . .

Here come three of Time's fools, three gaunt, grimed shapes. Local needle-freaks, vaguely familiar, maybe just coming from needle-exchange up at the Free Clinic. Jack begins to tingle with an inspiration. He's been totally passive, predictable all along. They've put crank in his pockets, put it right in his nose. He's got over fifteen K's worth in his pocket right now.

"'Scuse me, guys! Listen, I'm not a cop or anything. You mind my asking, are you guys junkies, or tweaks?"

The tallest one is clearly their leader, still sporting more than half his teeth. He notices Jack's hand slipping into his pocket and tilts his head cagily. "Depends."

"Well, this is crank, several OZs. It's yours free if you want it—I just decided to put down."

And he leaves the pale packet on the filthy palm, six eyes beaming incredulously down on it—leaves it there and walks on by.

How do you like *that,* you crooked old charlatan?

An eye-opener indeed! Because he can see now so plainly—he's got to call Erika *now*. Added dollars will avail nothing against added delay. For when at last her heart has turned away, the biggest down payment won't matter. He's been fooling himself, been hiding from his fear that Erika's already lost to him. He thanks the old man for opening his eyes indeed. He feels free and strong.

He's just crossed Mission and stops in his tracks. Half a block ahead, just this side of the Free Clinic, there is a perimeter of yellow tape jutting out onto the sidewalk. It fences in black debris that has spilled from a doorway. That fire-gutted ruin there—is that the Harvest Moon? He advances slowly. By god, it is! And he recalls that, as he left the neighborhood this afternoon, he heard a distant storm of sirens.

A skinhead he slightly knows is pumping toward him, apparently another guy with clean needles from the clinic. "Fuckin *fire*, man!" is his explanation. "Like three people toasted! Fuckin fire, just this afternoon, man! Three fuckin people toasted to death!" He goes pumping on his way.

Jack approaches the tape barrier. It must have been a raging blaze to have made this great black hole he faces. The would-be 'spoon is now an inky cavern breathing cold, wet ashes in his face. The interior is a black tangle—all the laths of ceilings and walls have fallen like jackstraws in bristly heaps. The glass doors have been smashed inward, but the windows remain, so densely sooted they are more like walls, their half-circle of lettering still legible, though cooked away to a ghostly residue. *HARVEST MOON*

Jack feels a kind of touch on the back of his neck, a tingle of *déjà vu*. He looks around. And there, diagonally across 17th Street, is the intent little matriarch, watching him from the window of the Silver Dragon.

My god, is this what Cannyharme is selling? Arson and murder? And is he perhaps stringing along guys like Cozzens and Willy to do the dirty work for him?

It seems to Jack she sees his thought and mocks it, so legible across the streaming glare of traffic the contempt in her face! It mocks him with scarcely the stir of a muscle. It says to him: *you are afraid to know.*

Jack must be on guard. He is, OK, still pretty fucking buzzed, truth be told. But he is sure that he really *feels* her thoughts. Saying to him that he doesn't dare go into the burned-out Moon, because he doesn't *dare* find out.

Though the street swarms, the sidewalks are oddly empty. Jack ducks under the tape, crosses the gritty litter on the sidewalk ... and steps through the twisted metal door frames. Into ashy shadow. Inside, he's unseen from the street.

It's *big* in here. The collapse of the beams and plaster from ceiling and walls seems to have doubled the room's volume. The floor is a landscape of charred laths all silky and brittle underfoot, or springy where they're interlaced, and heaped in spiky dunes round the big shapes of the steam table and the range. He takes a couple steps deeper inside.

The ash smells like the rank fur of a sleeping beast. There's a forest smell too, an innocent wilderness scent of wet night. He looks back at the street door. Amazing how distant it seems. Amazing too how long it already seems that he has been in here.

Is this Cozzens's eye-opener messing with his brain after all? He realizes it doesn't matter! He thinks: *good*. Bring it on! Toe to toe now, you crooked old dog, and then watch me laugh at you, and walk!

And it occurs to him, as long as he's in here, that there is something in fact that he would very much like to look for. That little TV. That strange blip of cannibalism he saw on it ... Suppose it was a plant, a video. What if the people here were accomplices before they became victims? Accomplices of the old man's to mess with Jack's head?

He begins to pick his way toward the lath-heaped steamtable-cum-counter. Beyond it is the big range, similarly heaped. On all sides the charred studs of the walls, and above, the rafters—they all look so remote. The space in here ... is off. Is much too big. He turns and once more looks behind him. The doorway is impossibly far away! So distant! And framed in the doorway's square, the busy street beyond looks flat and fake, like a video with the sound on low.

A blink and a headshake dispel the vision, but almost at once it comes seeping back into his peripheral vision. OK. Bring it on, then, and resumes his careful advance through the tangle. The charcoal is velvety to his fingertips, while little nails in the laths bite him sharply. The pain a reminder that three people have been incinerated here. The agony of such an end! Are their shriveled ghosts still here? How distant do the charred walls loom to *their* vaporized eyes, these walls their universe now?

At last (how long has it taken?) here is the counter. Just enough light sifts in from the street to sketch its outlines. Nothing. Perhaps down in the shelves behind. He picks his way around, growing keener on this search. Crouching carefully, he sees a shape on a shelf curtained by debris. He begins clearing, the little nails biting his hands. He opens enough space for him to crouch down, and grope inside the shelves. . . .

And here it is! Here is the tiny TV, perched on the topmost shelf, where a ghostly drift of light from the street puts a dull sheen on its screen. The thing is perfectly intact! And not only is it perfectly intact. More than that! The thing is turned on! Incredible though it seems, he's really seeing this. Two reddish glints of light show on the screen, and there's audio too. He gets down on his knees, leaning as close as he can . . . and the screen goes dark.

He's lost visual, but the audio gets stronger, the hissing, staticky noise becomes more pronounced, with a sputtering, crackling undertone. He shifts his knees, meaning to pick the thing up as gently as possible, and his movement *restores* the red lights to the screen, while the crackly hiss rises to a sharper level.

A smell, too, enters the air, a foul greasy stench. And in the floor Jack begins to feel a gritty vibration. It dawns on him then: the red lights on the screen are not a transmission, but a *reflection* of some source behind him, which is also the source of the sound he hears, and of the stench even now growing thicker in his nostrils.

He turns and looks behind him.

The big range, not three yards away, has shed its cocoon of debris, and all its burners are blazing, their flames fanned out under an array of smoking, sizzling, bubbling pots and pans, while the whole range—still strapped on its wheeled hydraulic jacks—is beginning to move toward him, burnt wood splintering and crunching under its rumbly, slow advance.

Jack takes off like a sprinter, forgetting he is on his knees. His legs are instantly entangled, and he is clawing, floundering, thrashing—everything but *moving*—from the spot he's on, while the blue glare of the burners shows him the entire feast a-cooking on the range: arched ribs snap and spit in frying pans; overlarge soup bones jut from steaming kettles; and on the griddle, amid scorched fingers that swell and split like sausages, a frizzy-haired head fries on her neck-stump, hair shriveling away in the heat, thick glasses grease-fogged and cracked.

He flounders forward on his belly like a big lizard, the debris deepening under him, nails snagging him everywhere. The range looms less than a yard from him, a black cliff crowned with smoke and flame. He digs with the balls of his feet, tucks his head, and thrusts himself through a crude forward somersault that almost breaks his neck and leaves him sprawled on his back, his back now snagged in a dozen new places as he struggles to sit up.

Is sitting up, because the range is swinging broadside behind him and lifting the mass of debris like the wave of earth before a bulldozer, heaping it higher and higher, and tilting Jack more and more upright as it thrusts him forward, bulldozing him toward the wall of charred studs just ahead. He tears his shoulders free, has almost freed his legs to run, when the range surges powerfully, the frying head bannering smoke. He'll be crushed against the wall—

Except that, suddenly, the wall's studs are way too far apart, and there is nothing in the spaces between those studs but deep night and thick stars, dense fields of stars in black abyss. It's like beholding a galaxy through a giant jail's bars . . .

With a splintery roar that sounds almost like surf, the wave of laths pitches him forward. Grabbing for the studs to save himself, his fingertips miss them on either side and, arms spread like a diver's, he plunges out into the starry void.

And is standing, slumped exhaustedly against a bright white wall in a very small room. He looks around. He is in a spotlessly clean room, and not three feet in front of him an astonished-looking man sits, staring at him.

The man is dying, his naked knees mere knobs of bone, his Auschwitz shoulders tenting his empty-looking flannel shirt. His breathing, even in his amazement, is shallow and careful, each breath coaxing the air into his frail lungs.

"I'm terribly sorry," Jack says, thickly, with what feels like someone else's tongue. Sorry about the man's death, he means. Then he catches sight of the mirror above the sink and beholds his own blackened apparition, a wild-haired shape of soot with mad-bright eyes. "I can't explain," he tells the man. "I'm just terribly sorry." He thrusts out of the bathroom, but closes the door gently and finds himself in a hallway. One of the doorways he passes reveals an examining room. He is in the Free Clinic, next door to the Harvest Moon—the hall opens out ahead into the waiting room he has glimpsed often enough walking past outside—folding chairs on a scuffed varnished floor, a few street types in the chairs.

He walks straight out through the waiting room, not yet sure enough he is actually here—and then sure he *is* from the open-mouthed stares he draws, even from these outcasts, these bandana-ed, tattooed strays.

He walks out to the sidewalk and down the sidewalk a few yards to the juncture of the two buildings, and stands—in the shadowiest spot he can find—staring up at it. Two four-story buildings, their concrete walls abutting, but distinct. There, through the Moon's black maw, he went in. There, from the clinic's lit entry, he came out. The two structures must have a communicating door. But through two outer walls? They don't build like that. Not here, not anywhere.

Through the traffic noise behind him a brief, harsh sound touches Jack between the shoulder blades. A low sound, and not close, yet he instantly knows it's aimed at him.

Mr. Cannyharme is coming toward him, on a diagonal across the middle of the street. Straight through the traffic he hobbles and totters, not pausing once, yet somehow his each trembly step finds an aperture in the traffic. No one brakes, no horns sound, the cars roar purposefully past, but random gaps between them embrace each creaky foot of his advance.

Suddenly the old man is climbing the curb in front of him, and Jack is wondering what he has really seen. Hasn't he in fact just seen something very different? Seen the old man drop to all fours and lope through the traffic, huge tongue lolling like a great gray wolf's, his pale eyes so sure of the path they never flicker from their fix on Jack's own?

The last steps of Cannyharme's approach dispel this vision. He can scarcely lift his eyes to Jack's, and the strain of doing so sends a tremor along his bowed spine. He's groaning as he inches forward, his crooked hand beckoning, such sore deformity in the gesture that Jack's unwilling legs concede a step toward him, and another.

Cannyharme pokes a confiding knuckle in Jack's ribs. The dense strength in that little jab surprises him.

"Nnnn*yarrr*taa!" says the old man. A glee as sharp as a rat's bite glints from the rheumy eye. "Nnnn *YARRRR*taaaa!"

The old man is done. He sighs, sags back down, turns, and creaks away up the sidewalk.

This time Jack gets it. It's a single word, that long groan, and the word is *immortal.* And whatever else the meaning of the wild, drug-spawned dream Jack's just been through, that room where it ended was a demonstration of immortality's alternative.

XVI
Reminiscences

B ritt and Aarti have spent the day together—much of it sleeping in the sun on the grass of Dolores Park, and the rest of it walking around the city, Britt pointing out, as to a small apprentice vagabond, all her little routes and havens, all the little tricks and techniques essential to a streeter's life. A phone call to Marni, when night had fallen, directed them here.

They're out on the bayside patio of the Mission Rock Café. Dinosaurian cargo cranes unload a freighter docked downshore of them, arc-lights blooming around the work as night falls on the Bay. The City's all lights now too, and the Bay Bridge, a river of headlights, marches titanically across the water to Treasure Island and beyond. The girls are on the bench by the patio's railing, Britt with an arm around Aarti against the growing chill. That freighter's black hull looks ten stories high, and the Bridge's piers twenty higher still. Britt feels desolated by the brutal vastness of the world—all stone and steel, all cruel heights and abysses. Is it really just people controlling all this colossal machinery, just pint-sized men and women? Where do they get the courage? A few yards downshore of the patio is a series of corpse-piers, skeletons missing half their planks. Perched here and there on them, lone fishermen sit with their lines in the water. These people are more on Britt's pathetic scale. She picks her way among the world's big bones, staying low and sticking to the waste areas, finding little perches—and now she has this girl to look out for.

At least tonight they have a protector. Marni's behind the bar inside—easily spotted through the window because her billowing Hawaiian shirt is a riot of color. It's all macaws, palm trees, pineapples, seashells, monkeys in screaming colors. It hides her big breasts, probably still hides that pistol too in the back of her belt, but it is definitely not a hideaway shirt. It's an up-yours-buddy shirt. She and the blue-collar crowd she's serving seem to get along fine.

"Brittany?"

"Yeah, hon?"

"Brittany . . ." Britt knows what's coming before the kid gets it out. "I'm so *afraid.*"

Britt hugs her a little tighter, but her own fear is coming up fast, along with exhaustion and resentment. What does this kid *want* from her? All day long, Britt hasn't popped one pill. And now, getting on for eleven P.M., all she craves is a bit of a blankie to wrap around her cowardly heart. Surely, for the deep of night, she has a right to that much.

But the kid can't let it go. "I want to help them, but I'm too much of a coward to help them. I'm too afraid to go back there." Her voice is wavering and she's spilling tears, but she's still holding on, not letting the sobs break out. To the shame of craving her pills as the child weeps, Britt adds a new shame: that the child weeps for those she loves, and all her life Britt has only wept for herself. She remembers what Sal said, about looking out for someone else.

"Come on, Aarti. It's time for some dinner. It'll make us feel stronger."

In a booth upstairs the waitress takes their order (on Marni's tab) and Britt plans a break to the bathroom, to sneak some nummies.

"When I was little, in Calcutta . . ."

Britt sees amazement in the girl's face. And she understands the girl's going to tell something she's never told before. "Tell me, Aarti."

"I was very little." That charming precision of the girl's t's—Bri*tt*any, Calcu*tt*a, li*t*dle. It's the only touch of an accent she has. "My mom took me marketing one day, a very hot day. The streets were really crowded, and I got separated from her. I remember . . . I remember there was something I had to go see. I didn't know how I knew about it, I just knew I had to go see it. It was something down by the river, just a few streets away. I was so

... *excited.* I started walking as fast as I could to get to this thing." The girl's eyes are back in the past. She trembles as she talks, an engine of fear pumping this up from inside her. Her brows knit, intent on getting this out.

"I got to the river, to where there were all these little docks, a few boats tied up there but a trashy place, garbage everywhere, and no people anywhere around, and that was strange, that was a little scary because all the other streets were swarming. And I was also getting scared because there was a *smell.* The whole place stank, but this smell was coming right from where I was going, from this little like dock where I had to go out and look down in the river for this thing that I *had* to see. And it didn't matter how I was getting scared. I went right out onto that dock and looked down.

"It was floating in the water down there between the pilings. It was a *man* floating there, a man with a cloud for a head. A man all fat and swelled up, floating like a blimp, and his clothes were just like rags and strings floating around him.

"And that's what he had for a head. It was all his *skin* floating around in a cloud. And in this cloud, I saw his *eyes,* looking out at me. And I knew he had tricked me, this thing had *tricked* me into coming here to see it, so it could tell me what it wanted to tell me. It told me with its eyes that no matter where I went, someday it was going to find me again and take me down into the water where *it* lived."

Telling the story calms her some. She's described their powerlessness, and for a moment it frees them both. Britt cups her hand round the back of Aarti's neck. "I just call it the enemy. The enemy wants to terrify you. But it's been trying on me for eight years, and it hasn't been able to do *jack-shit* to me." (Except drive my whole life underground, under bushes, under bridges, into numbness, into loneliness . . .)

The waitress sets the meal down. Britt wolfs cheeseburgers, not nummies, and stays in the booth with the girl after eating, settling into the cushiony seats with her.

Marni wakes them at her shift's end. Seems to study Britt's eyes for drugs, then leads them gruffly out to the street, to her battered old white Volvo. They rocket up Sixteenth, Marni stern-faced and silent gripping the wheel. It's good to be in a car, insulated, the blocks slipping easily past. And there's comfort in the company of this woman warrior in her wild, gaudy shirt, until her silence has lasted almost all the way across the Mission and Britt is beginning to feel that Marni too is afraid, is struggling to form a plan.

She pulls up to the curb in a residential block and kills the engine. "That's my place." She nods at the corner house across the street. The curtained front windows are lit and a stripe of light shows the front door slightly ajar. In the corner window a figure is silhouetted, sitting straight, as if at some task.

"It's getting late," Marni says, but doesn't look as if she means to move. "I have to get back in there with him as soon as I've dropped you off, but I wanted you to know where it is . . . when you come back from where I'm sending you."

"Marni," pipes Aarti, "we can't go away, we can't leave my—"

"Shhh." Britt pats her leg. "Let's listen to Marni first."

Marni is looking at the silhouette. "That poor, sad asshole. He thinks he can cut a deal. He thinks if he chooses just the right words, makes just the right pitch, he can get his own special deal, that it won't cost him"— she glances down at Aarti beside her—"won't cost him the full price. He takes that poetry shit of his very seriously. He's pitiful. Working all the time on his fucking *prayer,* thinking *words* make any difference at all, *ever* make any difference at all."

Britt's amazed to see her quickly scrub tears from her eyes. Then she grabs a wrinkled pack of cigarettes from the dash, fumbles angrily for a lighter in the glove box. Some awkwardness there, getting the smog out and lit, the smoke only an occasional prop, Britt guesses, a steadier.

"He was fucked with the joint," says Marni. "Just a kid; they fucked him hollow. I'm the only person in the world who ever gave a shit about him, ever tried to look out for him. I could just take off right now. Run hard and far, and never look back, and save my ass. But the thing is, see,

I—don't—run—away. I fight back. I used to hurt myself, but now I fight back. I hurt *them.*

"See, I was messed with too. Plenty. But you know what I did? When I was fifteen? Just after I turned fifteen, my big brother decided it was *his* turn to start in on me. My dad was in the bag around the clock by then, so my badass brother decides it's safe to take a turn, so he pins me in my bed before I wake up one morning." Marni blows a plume of smoke, smiling a bitter, savoring little smile. "Then he goes into the *shower.* To wash me off him, right?

"I didn't even have to decide. I heard that shower, and I ran to my dad's room. I knew just where that sick asshole kept his pistol, right under that greasy pillow his head was on. Like it was safe there, like he wasn't just a sack of booze you could lift right out of the way like I did. I took that piece and man, did it feel good!

"I went and stood in front of the bathroom door. I knew what was coming. I was totally sure of what was going to happen, and it gave me . . . such peace! The shower turns off, I hear him toweling off, getting into his jeans, even hear him buckling his belt. The door opens, and there he is with all his ugly muscles, no shirt on. I aim that piece right at his heart and *wham,* put one right into him."

Now Marni's really smiling, the first real smile Britt has seen on her. The woman's beauty is startling. "But I *missed,* see? Amazing. From three feet away I missed. I missed his heart, and just blew the shit out of his shoulder! It knocks him on his ass, blood all over the door frame.

"Man, he's raging and thrashing and groaning, madder'n shit, but now he can't *do* anything to me, his big ugly muscles can't make any difference between us any more. I lean over him with a big smile and say to him, 'Hi, Manny! Here I am! Come on!' And I blow the shit out of the other shoulder!"

Sudden sadness for Marni fills Britt, watching the woman still exulting, still warming her hands at that little moment of justice so long ago. Britt understands. Marni's afraid of what might happen tonight, in that house over there, and she wants someone else to know of her long-ago victory. Maybe Marni is realizing the same, because her smile is fading, her reminiscence grows brisker.

"I looped his belt around his neck to drag him—only way I could move that ox. Dragged him into my dad's bedroom over those funky, splintery floors we had and man, he started helping me with his feet to keep from strangling. Tied him to the leg of my dad's bed. Told him if the belt was uncomfortable he could just reach up an' loosen it. Ha! Then I went in to take a shower and wash *him* off.

"When I was all the way to Fargo and my bus just ready to pull out, I called the Reservation pigs and told them where they could pick up a rapist that needed some medical attention."

She fires up another smog. "I left there with that Colt, and I have never been without a gun since. I'm staying here, and I'm fighting. That's who I am, a stayer, and a fighter. That poor sonofabitch in there hasn't had a happy minute in his life that didn't come from me, and I'm gonna save his ass in spite of him. But you two are not staying."

"My mom and—"

"Be quiet!" Then Marni tries to amend her harshness. "Hey. There's nothing you can do tonight. Something's going to be settled here, before the sun comes up. After that . . . I'll make sure to get you back. Here's some more money, and here's the motel's address, and my phone number. For right now, I'll bring you somewhere safe. The time's getting near I have to be back up here with him."

Not another word from Marni as she drives them down to Van Ness and Market. She's afraid; Britt has no doubt of it now. Afraid of the fight that's coming. Collecting herself. Gathering her will.

She doesn't pull away from the curb till they're inside Zim's Restaurant down on Market.

They watch her go. Britt gropes for something to soothe them, to build their confidence. "Hot fudge sundaes," she tells Aarti. "I've got room for one—what about you?"

XVII
There Have to Be Angels

Since dawn, Chester's whole left side has been paralyzed. Through the long hours that have followed, he has moved toward a kind of peace. If he only surrenders—does not struggle to cry out, to strike the wall, to drag himself off the bed—if he only lies still and accepts, then, weak with fasting as he is, he can achieve an intermittent unconsciousness. He must just lie still, find hunger's floating trance once more, and then maybe he can pass like that, can slip into death, make his exit without torment. Will thirst, perhaps, be a torture near the end? Not if he is already deep enough in hunger, not if merciful coma closes on him pretty soon. And after that, the unfelt end. . . .

But as night has drawn on and darkness fills his airshaft window, fear begins to pulse in him. Slowly at first, as slow as his crippled heartbeat, a groundnote of apprehension. The night deepens, and human movement dies out of the building, and then his fear begins flaring, comes like sudden rat-noise in the walls, climbing his back (the feeling half of it) with little claws, and up his nape, and across his scalp.

Then Chester's fear becomes terror, this terror a bigger beast astir within the building, a swift scuttling weight along the floors, up and down the walls. The Hyperion's big old bones begin to groan and mutter.

When it seizes him—brutal and swift as the shark seizing the swimmer's legs—it's almost a mercy. No mocking rhymes murmur this time in his mind. An icy presence engulfs him, plucks him out of his body, and thrusts him, in a blur of speed, through walls and rooms and walls, and out into the midnight air.

How has he ever thought his little room was a habitation and a shelter? In it he lay half-evicted from his very body, and now his own death is his new and terrifying co-tenant. And now, again, he is evicted, his soul is in tow through the empty night.

His bodiless odyssey repeats itself, but at terrifying speed, plunging him through mist, through pavement, through plumbing, through the sticky, rocky flesh of under-earth, then erupting through grass, up into mist again, arcing out high from the hillside over suburban slopes measled with the sparse lights of midnight. There is an added terror tonight in the *silence* of his captor—Chester has been snatched up like an implement by that malignant being, which does not spare him even the thought to mock him.

He is arrowing down to the ranks of tall trees that shelter the graveyards, accelerating toward the tomb-studded lawn, meteoric now as one grave looms huge . . . and he is hurtled through its earth.

He collides vaporously, a puff of smoke blown into a box, and coheres within the coffin's occupant, within the bone-bowl of the occupant's skull. Then, nasty-sly, his master's voice is heard at last.

> *Let reanimation start!*
> *The butting skull's the bulky part.*
> *So let it, Chester, lead the way,*
> *And ram your passage through the clay.*

The skull leaps while Chester is still but a foggy commotion within it. It impacts with the coffin. Stiff metal gives an earth-muffled groan, bulges, cracks, and sunders. The cranium, like a slo-mo fist, drives a sinus up through the stubborn soil.

> *From its rack, unjoint each bone*
> *To climb the rathole one by one,*
> *Each rib and radial, ulna, femur,*
> *Scuttle limber as a lemur!*
> *What rags of flesh that may remain,*
> *Worm after in a snaky train!*

Chester pops into starlight, his aircraft the empty-windowed skull in its leathern mask, and then feels beneath him the impacts of the following frame, the upsurge of bones rejoining beneath him. Now the skull crowns the skeleton's shaky scaffolding, and tatters of skin and sinew begin to bind and bandage it. Now Chester has dangling arms and hands, rag-and-bone hands, the skin-rags beginning to prickle with fragments of tactile memory. . . .

The memories are not his own, but those of the dead man he tenants. They trickle into his consciousness like strays to a shelter. Memories of a sun-warmed kitten stroked, of a loved breast gripped almost too hard, of fingertips picking foxtails from an itchy sock, of a gripped handsaw burring through soft wood. . . . He has legs and feet down there too, strings of muscle that remember treading concrete's unforgiving hardness, remember the weary work of shifty sand dunes climbed, and the silvery feel of scissoring in the bright blue chlorinated water of a public pool . . . while his remnants of ears now remember the summer clamor of a hundred kids splashing and squealing . . .

> *Captain Chester! Ten-shun!*
> *Pull yourself together, man!*

Chester struggles to obey. A chaotic tremor goes through his borrowed body, and he brings it to a swaying straightness. Here and there the night breeze gusts right through the body, erasing the memory-traces of its vanished life. Then the breeze pauses, and their softer whisper returns: the odd, in-drag feel of a first graduation robe skirting the ankles, the exultant burst of back-muscle smacking an outside pitch past the center fielder. . . . Terrified Chester exerts his cloudy will again, and his truant corpse stands straighter.

> *Let us stroll down to the bus-stop, old buddy!*
> *No one will squawk that you're smelly and muddy.*
> *It's your own private coach, and your fare is pre-paid,*

And no one will notice you're slightly decayed.
Give them the signal, Ches! Lead the parade!

Only now does Chester grasp, as his cervical vertebrae creak and he scans the field, that in the stone-studded acres stand other shapes, dozens of crooked, crumpled shadows like himself, are teetering here and there, while the towering eucalypti shudder and whisper in the breeze above them: *Yes . . . Yesss.*

Give them the signal? Chester gropes for the memory of his own arms, recalls bringing his right arm up with a rivet gun in it. Exerts that memory. Up comes the corpse's creaking arm and waves those others forward. The gesture almost topples the corpse, and toppling, Chester stumbles into a walk, a scarecrow's totter.

Down the gently sloping grass they move, tilting, teetering, drunken-footed. They look scarcely more animate than the tombstones they trudge through, so feebly propelled by will that their slow march seems almost accidental. The breeze that does not sieve right through their gappy frames contributes to their swaying, while the great starlit trees acclaim them in whispers: *Yes . . . Yesss.*

Is Chester dead after all? Is death just this? Dancing in a graveyard to a gamesome demon's will? Ahead, a boxy shape squats on a ribbon of pavement: a big, squarish old yellow bus with a jutting hood, the kind he remembers from school days. He remembers that high first step they have, and as he approaches the gaping door of the bus, he gathers his corpse for the effort—and feels his cadaver take sudden strength, reach up and grip the little chromed banister. It is the corpse itself that mounts into the stepwell, climbing with its own will.

Chester has only a glimpse of the driver, a shadow poised behind the wheel. He has great bug-jaws like barbed scythes jutting from no human head, but a bug-head that is eyed with black-diamond knobs in which every hunger glitters, but no spark of pity, eyes that know Chester to his core within the borrowed lich he rides.

Deep in the bus he goes and drops into a seat. He has no lids to seal the eyeholes he looks from as the other beings of bone and mold drop into their seats around him, with impacts light as rustling leaves.

The motor purrs to life with the sound of a dreaming beast in a deep lair. The graveyard begins to flow past the windows, the rippling trees proclaiming their passage with soft applause. Those trees are beautiful— tall, slow waterfalls of starlit leaves. Dear Christ, what Chester would give to be up there in the air with them, up there in the world of living things!

And as he thinks this, he is plucked up and out, pierces metal, sees the bus roof shrinking beneath him. He rises, rises, rises . . . till he hangs high in that air he longed for, high above the rippling trees.

> *I'm so sorry, Chester—it seems you're in trouble.*
> *Your body is ailing, poor man!*
> *You'd better get back to your meat on the double—*
> *I fervently pray that you can!*

And Chester is adrift, is utterly alone, a wisp of mind in a sea of atmosphere. Not possessed, not propelled, but simply left hanging in the air. The absence of his captor is as terrifying as its presence was. There is the bus, far below, gathering speed down the highway, while he floats, powerless to move. Will the next gust of wind shred him to atoms? Blow him out like a candle?

Gone are all thoughts of easeful death, of trance and painless passage. The death he faces now is too stark to be borne, this lonely annihilation in the empty air, a bodiless knot of longing unraveling while the whole earth rolls on beneath it. He must regain his body, however crippled. He must have limbs to claw for help, must have a throat to cry from: somebody, help me here, I'm dying!

But he cannot move. If he had those limbs of his, half paralyzed though they are, he could *drag* himself at least, move inch by painful inch along that sidewalk down there, down that street where a Target outlet,

half a mile away, hoists its red neon bull's-eye. His limbless will longs to
arrow him to it, strike that bull's-eye, advance!

But . . . has that bull's-eye grown fractionally larger? Yes—the graveyard has displaced itself slightly below him, and he hangs above the trees
of its northern border. He focuses his desire on that target, desperately
wills it larger, nearer.

And slowly, slowly, it grows. He pours his longing toward those red
circles and—so gradually!—their circumference swells, like ripples
through an almost-frozen medium. Till, at length, they loom large as a
sun, they engulf him as he passes through them and beyond. He hangs
above the building's roof. He has swum the atmosphere! Flown, through
his will alone!

His exultation is such he fears it will swell him like a nova and dis-
perse his substance. Not purely a victim after all! Not merely a ghost on a
demon's leash!

Focus, Chester! This skill's not mastered yet. It works more simply,
swiftly than this, it has to! There, half a mile farther on, is the orange and
white of a Taco Bell sign. Pour your will, your longing into a beam, a
beam straight and pure as a laser, right into that little brightness.

It is such labor at first. It seems he drags the city out from under him,
landmark by landmark, hauling its concrete hugeness away beneath him,
one block at a time. Until he realizes that the immense inertia he is struggling against is in himself, is the clutter of his fear and grief and bitterness.
Realizes that if he quiets down to his will alone, his pure intent, he can
move without struggle, can *glide.*

Mission Street begins to flow under him, its empty asphalt his stream
channel, his desire the stream. A lonely car moves under him now and
then, outdistancing him at first, then keeping pace, then dropping behind.
There is Army Street passing under him. Almost home!

Then a fearsome turbulence batters him. He veers and plunges,
brings his crippled movement up again just inches short of pavement,
wobbles drunkenly airborne. An invisible sleet of terror is blasting him,

whittling his will to a feeble thread that he follows like a buffeted balloon. He understands what is happening. His body, just a few blocks away now, is dying.

The discipline Chester has learned on his lonely flight is fraying away to nothing. The demon's parting mockery echoes in him. The monster has released him to extinction, would possess him still if his life had more than a few dozen heartbeats left to it. He is still a victim, a plaything, and shortly, a corpse, a corpse not borrowed, but his own.

He is already almost nothing. Apart from his useless terror, his will to fly is all he is. So fly then, fly past his death. If it wants him, let it catch him.

His will, regathered to a point of flame, thrusts him forward. His terror trails behind, a bulky baggage, a panicked mob of all the ephemeral selves he has been, all of them crying: *Death! We're dying! Oh, Death!* While the resolute flamepoint, Chester's core, burns its way forward in spite of that cloudy anchor of despair.

The hotel is blocks behind him now, that body of his back there in its box beginning to convulse now, its old heart fumbling its beat, the lungs locking up and heaving for air that can't be had. Now Chester's flame burns thinner, the fuel it springs from turning cold and stony. His will's wick is short, with only a dollop of wax pooled in the bottom of the socket. He glides above Market Street, slowing, slowing, still unyielding but thinned to a wisp now, a tendril melting into air. . . .

A plate glass window, full of light and color. Two figures just inside it. A final landmark in a world of landmarks all about to vanish. Go for that, Chester, till there is nothing to go for, and no more going at all.

Two girls at a table. He knows them both. Sweet kids. Harmless young lives. A last touch of life with the last of his own. Company at the end. He chooses the older one, and dives through the glass.

Britt is paying for their sundaes. Their waitress takes her money. In an orange uniform with a gaudy corsage, she's an older woman with a gray curled perm and bright lipstick. Her mouth is faintly clenched with disapproval of this girl and young woman, dressed like hooligans, out on their own in the dead of night. Britt likes her disapproval. What if Mom had been like this woman? Someone who would scowl at the mere idea of swallowing pills and sipping vodka tonics?

As she turns from the register, Britt experiences a light, swift sensation. It is like an airy impact against her back, right between her shoulders, more delicate than a puff of breeze. Then, in her chest, there is a tingle that melts away. . . .

This must be the effect of going so long without pills. She feels cold and raw and scared all over. If she is getting nervier, it's just as well they're going to find a motel. The luxury of a door to lock against the world, just for one night anyway . . . And here's their cab at the curb outside.

There is something subtly unpleasant about the vehicle, something about the oil-smooth way it glides to the curb, and, when they step outside to meet it, something about the oily purr of its engine. Britt hates being bare of her blankie! The world is so raw! She glances back through the window. Their waitress watches them from behind the counter. Is her face less stern, a little anxious for them, maybe? Britt's scared and exhausted. She shepherds Aarti into the back seat and pulls the door shut.

"Lombard," she says through the grille, though the driver is pulling away as if he already knew. A short man with shiny black hair is all she can make out. His photo is all but obliterated.

It's the small hours. Empty Van Ness is smooth sailing, but they seem to be going so slowly. The sidewalks slip past at a normal speed, but through the windshield the broad boulevard pours tardily toward them. Block after block slides under them, rising and falling, before the driver speaks, without turning around.

"Hey, you girls know why a cab driver is like a whore?" Britt finds herself already braced for something like this. The grainy intimacy of the man's voice is as scary as the obscenity. They don't answer. "Because," he chuckles, "you pay him and he gives you a *ride*. You pay him, and he takes you to places you never dreamed of."

Britt's heart thuds through a silence. "I don't like you talking like that in front of this little girl here," she says. This sounds so weak! Then somewhere she finds some anger, and it helps. "I don't like you talking like that *at all.*"

"Hey." Grainy chuckle. "Just a joke. A joke on myself, right?" He turns them his profile, gives them half a friendly grin. The only hair his forehead sports is islanded between two wings of baldness, an oily little black forelock.

It's not him. It's not Unka Doug. Look—darker skin, a bigger, Arab-looking nose, it's not him, no. But Britt's stomach is still falling, falling . . . waiting for impact, and she yelps, "Right here! Let us out right here!"

"This isn't a motel. There's motels in these next few blocks here, let's cruise em a little . . ."

Something's happening in Britt. She feels . . . an anger in her arms and legs. Her arms seem to remember . . . driving iron into steel with a big heavy hydraulic tool. Her shoulders seem to recall brute leverage in their sinews. And suddenly, all the adrenalin in her body is going for it. She drives the heel of her hand straight-arm against the mesh behind the driver's head, and his head snaps forward. The car accelerates mightily, then swerves with a screech to the curb.

Undaunted, the dark man smiles at them as they climb out. "It doesn't matter where you stay. You know that, don't you? No charge, girlies."

They stand on the sidewalk till the cab is out of sight, Britt almost shaking with rage and fear. She has her arm around Aarti's shoulders, but it's the girl who's calming her, holding to her waist.

"What did he mean, Brittany?"

"I don't *know.* Maybe nothing. Maybe he's just some random asshole. . . ."

They find the address Marni gave them, a block off the main drag. The clerk's actually sitting the desk at this hour, reading a newspaper, a scrawny old guy with red-rimmed, spiteful eyes. She thinks of looking elsewhere, but feels too urgent to get them both indoors.

Their room is small and shabby, but the door seems strong and the lock stout. They shower together so that Britt can wash Aarti's hair—she senses the girl still takes comfort in this attention from her mother. Aarti is soothed by the gentle operation, and perhaps she weeps a little under the camouflage of the streaming water. When they are showered, they dress for the street—Britt lends the girl clean underwear and socks, and they set her things washing in the sink.

They lie on the bed, street-ready save for their shoes. "We can doze off now," Britt soothes. "We're ready to hit the pavement at a moment's notice, so it's safe to rest."

After a time, the girl says shyly, "You know, Brittany, I have been thinking. We know there are demons. You and me know there are demons. But if demons are real, then there have to be angels too, don't there?"

"I sure hope so." There falls a silence between them . . . that becomes sleep. Then sleep, still in darkness, is broken by a booming knock at their door.

Britt gestures to the girl to get behind her. She takes out her Buck and confronts the door.

The knock is repeated, three measured impacts.

"Who is it?"

The knock is repeated. Britt pulls the door open and recoils from it, crouched, knife up.

It's Marni!

No. It's a different woman, but in the same outlandish, riotous Hawaiian shirt—exactly the same, it seems. This woman is also full-bodied . . . but she is much older, more massive than Marni, with a cloud of frosty hair, and a darker face, set like stone.

"Come with me." Her voice is patchy, more than half a whisper. They see, beyond her, another cab, this one very battered and scuffed-looking. The woman stands stonily enduring their stares. The room's feeble ceiling bulb throws more shadow than light on her, but they see a face that is almost a Laplander's—flat-cheeked, stoically fixed, with dull black eyes. There seems to be a chill around her, as if her Arctic origin still clings to her.

Trust her? It's the shirt that tips the scales with Britt. It's unbuttoned, and under it the bulky body is sheathed in something like leather or hide, as scuffed and battered-looking as the taxi behind her, but that shirt has exactly the pattern of Marni's. Britt will take it as a sign.

"OK . . ."

The woman's gait, as they follow her to the cab, has a weighty roll, like a bear crossing open ground. When they are shut up in the cab behind her, her aura of cold fills the vehicle with a smell of icy spaces, of storm-scoured stone. The engine makes a remote, gusty noise, like wind heard outside of some isolated habitation.

Britt begins, "Do you know where—"

"I know."

Van Ness is even more desolate. The blinking signals seem like some coded message left by a dead civilization for its rediscoverers. The cab's speed makes this aura of abandonment even stronger. They sweep through intersections as if cross-traffic, cops, were things of the distant past.

As they cross Market and swing onto Mission Aarti asks, "How"— then pauses—"how will you help my mom and dad?"—her voice a quaver at the end.

The ice-cloud head never turns. "What can be done for them, I will do." They pull up to the curb in front of the Hyperion. "You will walk behind me, and behind me you will both remain. Swear it!" Still she has not turned her head.

"We swear."

"Walk behind me." The woman does not touch the bell. She lays her palm against the door, and it opens. They climb the crackly stair treads . . . and two flights up, there's Jack in the cage. He looks so haggard, scarcely capable of motion, slumped beside his typewriter as he watches them through the bars with half-conscious eyes.

The woman in Marni's shirt plants herself before the door of Aarti's apartment.

"Behind me," she says, still not looking back at them. "Get ye low to the floor, and do nothing, say nothing."

She lifts her fist and smites the door, three booming impacts, though their echoes sound dwarfed, like drumbeats on an open plain.

Silence within.

Then, from far away in that interior emptiness, a faint clatter echoes, like someone crossing a talus slope and causing a shift of stony rubble just barely audible in alpine quiet.

The woman presses one hand against the door and holds it there, and the door subtly changes under her hand, looks denser, more massive and ancient. A centuried door that will groan when it opens. The tread within quickens. Rock rattles, earth reports padded paws. It seems the tread of a four-legged thing, a massive beast advancing at a trot. "Hold fast," hisses the woman. "Be silent."

Now the sound of claws is staccato on some broad stone floor, the brute hastening down some corridor through high architected spaces . . . and suddenly it stands panting just beyond the door, from which now leak tendrils of a vile, searing cold.

The doorknob twitches. The woman withdraws her hand, straightens, stands like a bulwark. The door swings inward.

Haloed in white vapor, in a roiling smoke of ice crystals, Bill Patel stands at the threshold, naked except for a pair of filthy shorts. His posture is a cringe, as if from the cold that wreathes him, but his eyes blaze hot from a face that has darkened to the congested color of a bruise.

"Come forth!" booms the woman.

Bill twists where he stands, as if the command tears him. Aarti, on her knees, has thrust out her arms toward him, but at a touch from the woman she pulls her clenched fists back against her chest.

"Come forth!"

But the gaunt, battered man stands with feet rooted, while the rest of him shudders like a dark flame in its corona of fog—as if the cold consumes him—while from the tangle of his hair his wild eyes flash, seeking his daughter's eyes around the barrier of the woman's body.

"Come forth!" Now the voice is thunder. "Break the grip of the ghoul!"

His arms reach for his daughter and then recoil, a gesture of self-repressed longing—as Aarti's answering outreach is.

"She is denied you! Break the grip of the ghoul!" Something inhuman in the woman's voice has drawn Britt's eyes up to her face. Britt's legs turn to water and drop her to her knees. For the woman's face, under her stormy hair, is no face at all now, but a winter-scoured skull with empty sockets black as caves, while, with her utterance, a shriveled scrap of leather, a mummy's tongue, flickers between her tombstone teeth.

Bill thrusts out his hands—warding, renouncing. "No! Take her! Save her. Aaartiii!" And he cries out something in Hindi, the girl sobbing now, her eyes only for her father.

"Daddy! Daddy!"

But Bill is straining to reach something, groping for something he's desperate to find. It's the edge of the door he grips at last. With a last wild look of grief at Aarti, he hauls at the door as if it weighed a ton, strains every sinew, and thrusts it, booming, shut.

With icy hands the woman pulls them to their feet, her face a human one once more—at least, in its rigidity, a bearable human mask. "He is lost to you, young one, and so is your mother. Now you must flee the house of the ghoul. Flee!" And she wheels ponderously and leads their flight down the stairs, then pauses halfway down, looking up at them, and says with a parting intonation, "But avenge her! Return when you are prepared, and avenge your mother!" Then she wheels again and rushes down.

They scramble to follow her, but she's already made the turning, her bright raiment billowing behind her. When they reach the turning themselves, she is gone, though the street door has made no sound.

She leaves one token behind—the shirt, puddled at the foot of the stairs. They rush down as if it's vital to retrieve this scrap of brightness, but already it is liquefying, is a little pool of melting colors . . . and is gone, drained away through the floor.

There is no cab outside. Emptiness and night rule the streets. Drained and aching, the girls limp to Dolores Park, where Britt finds them a covert in the bushes. She lies holding the child, who shudders with her tears for a while. When her soft snores begin, Britt's eyes close, and she too falls asleep.

XVIII
Tales the Keyboard Told

Is Jack really seeing this? A big, shaggy woman in a dazzling shirt, pounding on Bill's door, with Brittany and Aarti crouching behind her. Bill, almost naked, his face looking as if he's living a nightmare. Confused shouting. Then the door slamming. The girls rushing back down the stairs, out of the building. . . .

When *did* Jack come on shift? Not a trace of memory. His body is slumped and slack. No idea how long he's been like this, sitting at his typewriter, tranced out in his chair. The clock says five to three.

He remembers the Harvest Moon, all right. Remembers—just as sharply as if it really happened—toppling toward that skeletal burnt wall, hands desperately reaching for purchase to either side, finding none, *falling* . . . falling into space, into absolute zero . . .

Wherever he's been, he's full awake now, his heart racing. He ducks out into his room for clues to his last eight or nine hours. There are his soot-black clothes, heaped on the floor under the sink. There his soot-smudged towel. His Glock, tucked back in its shoulder rig, lies on his bed.

It's the dead of night. Where has he *been?*

Back in the cage he finds three-quarters of a dense page sprouting from his typewriter. He has no recollection of typing it, but finds what's unmistakably his own note-taking style. It appears Kitty, a clever little slut of a maid who has beguiled honest Lupinnia into friendship, has led them out for a countryside ride on a pair of hijacked mares from Lord Darcy's stables. They hear the commotion of the hunt ahead—a fox-killing cavalry riot that includes both Lord Darcy and Rackham, the Master of the

Hounds. And it is a leaderless pack of hounds that ambushes the two young women in a quiet little valley. . . .

The brutes' human masters are not in evidence, the beasts bring down the girls' mounts, and both the horse and Kitty are torn to scarlet fragments, while Lupe huddles cowering, surrounded, on the grass. A cry from Rackham stills the tumult. Lupe looks up to see, from opposite sides of the Vale, Rackham and Lord Darcy simultaneously approaching. Rackham, the pack opening before him, reaches her first, a lustful fire in his eyes. She cries out with ambiguous alarm at the carnal mayhem he plainly intends her. He seizes her, stuns her, rips bodice and gown asunder, and begins to plunder her. She tilts back her head and solicits succor from Darcy, striding toward her from behind, but Darcy's body is changing as he comes, his shoulders swell huge, hatch all dense with fur from his fragmenting clothes. He drops to all fours on massive paws, is, as he nears, a titanic hound, huge-jawed.

Where has he been? What was he *thinking* there? This is a bodice ripper he's writing here. He's in the wrong genre!

Who has been writing this? Who else is inside him?

And dazed Jack, digesting this . . . realizes that a terrible silence has congealed around him. The air is like cold jelly. He cocks his ear and feels a gelatinous vibration. He is hearing an utterly empty building. He's back in the cryogenic warehouse—room upon roomful of nothing that moves.

Except that . . .

Except that far, far away in the labyrinth, there is in fact just the faintest stir, a remote presence that has just begun to move.

. . . Isn't there?

Yes. He does detect it. He would have it otherwise, would far rather believe that dainty, distant crepitation was just the sinew of old timber settling, or the chalky friction of rat claws on plaster. . . . But it isn't.

But it isn't. It refuses to be that. It delicately insists, each time an iota nearer: it is a mincing imprint of balanced, muscled weight on crackly runner.

Well, so what?

So what is it that he doesn't want to see approaching, is suddenly so terrified of seeing, as it leisurely, discreetly comes, even now to the head of the stairs four flights above.

They've got him panicked, Jack admits it. He senses, knows that some new hallucination is coming to him, some new impossibility that will appear so real, so dire, it will be like enduring the reality. They're still one jump ahead of him, they've tricked him into this, he's going to see and feel this shit unless he gets up, now, books it straight down to the street, and straight away. Now. Then the whole sick ploy will be wasted, he'll escape, calm down, regain the upper hand.

But instead, bitten by anger, Jack begins to type. It's intentional gibberish, mere noise-making. Because he chooses to claim his rightful space here. He chooses to proclaim his defiance. Neither pimp nor voodoo-working charlatan will dislodge him. No old con-man, no matter how canny, is going to chase him out into the street.

/6\\…thr..%\$/:rou `|
@%!gha!] {ll'''79the&9(hu& ^ %m + = _an% |s-t/ock
(., <yar005 = @4"dsyouhav0#!etrod

His industrious fingers clutter the silence, though the clatter of his keys does not quite obliterate—here and there—the stealthy, padded pressures on the risers, coming down. He types on desperately, striking keys at random. This cage, right here, is Jack Hale's chosen roost, his last chance to make something of his ambitions. If he bolts, he will surrender something vital to his manipulators, will yield them an edge for ever after.

*…11 `w8?/her*8 = !eyour/\ /)5 = be,?'",:stial*6 ^ %\$!!*

His eyes cling to his fingers, to the type bars darting like snakes, to the sheet of nonsense sprouting from his platen, because, through the latticework of all his noise, he still hears that delicate tread. It's come down one whole flight, come down half another, and now, as it still comes, he begins to hear a faint clicking in the tread, a clicking like claws . . .

. . . w% ^ 7cr?335"'aw/?"[{kno0)((?wwor=-
_dsm+*/?`iththa**&%57titis|?-\$#*

His eyes cling to his machine and his hands storm through line after line, banging the carriage back, trying to annihilate it with his racket, that tread that *will* not be concealed, that soft, clawed tread that's started down the third flight now, that tread which—now so near—is definitely not a biped's, definitely more *multiple* than a biped's.

*+=citesto&/>/,<tryth))9'3?eirwi<<~!6970ngsy"!oust@#3/?-
=erverfe?5%6^wII9!1/}
iftu0)637"ptoth7. . . {77eplan|||?enwh ^..>>ereIe. . .11{{xis**&75t!*

Still his eyes cling to his dancing hands but—treacherous eyes!—their peripheral vision reports (he will not look at it) a shape now stepping down to the landing, a long, low, slinking shape (he will not look), a shape lower than the banister but long, moving daintily down past the banister-posts.

He *will* not look, but still his eyes, edge-on, declare too much, show him a dense-shouldered, high-haunched, jut-muzzled quadruped easing down, inching down, *pausing* now, pausing and posing behind the banister-posts just at eye-level with Jack behind his bars.

Waiting there. For Jack's acknowledgment.

Jack's fingers have stopped. This is ground zero. Jack shows some balls now, or he hits the street and, sooner or later, joins the homeless for good. To hold this post of his, he is required to meet, eye to eye, every intruder in the dead of night. It is the night clerk's job.

So. Each behind his bars of wood, of iron, meets the other's eyes.

Pale timberwolf eyes Jack sees, of a brute so mightily jawed that his great shoulders seem too slight to bear that head. Hugely sexed and hugely tongued, the monster is balanced fore and aft by these pendant obscenities. The furred sheath of his penis knocks gently between his stark-tendoned, back-jointed legs. His tongue hangs more restlessly, probing and tasting the air, a white, segmented tube, a monstrous maggot.

It is the eyes, though, that most electrify, orbs as cold as glaciers, wormy with unspeakable delight. That complicity, that *knowingness* shining from that pre-human skull, makes the world shift beneath Jack's chair, yanks the whole globe out from under him and hangs it elsewhere, outside of time and all its laws. . . .

This beholding—it appears it's all the monster wants of Jack. It seems to nod, and pads down the rest of the steps to the manager's door. It hoists its muzzle with a conjuring flicker of its verminous tongue. The door gapes softly open, and the monster passes inside.

"She said they were lost to you, but we don't know what that *means*. We don't know who *she* was."

The sun is almost two hours up. At Dunkin Donuts they have warmed the park's chill out of their bones. They're walking to Marni's place. Aarti is trying to act calm, but Britt sees the whites of her eyes flash as ugly fears cycle through her young head. Britt sees her anew, coming down that fire escape two nights ago. So brave, and still such a child.

"She was wearing Marni's shirt. She was on our side, Brittany. What's a ghoul?"

"I don't know."

"How do you spell it?"

"I don't know." Damned well knowing both. "Aarti. We don't know anything for sure. We have to be calm. We have to find out. We have to be brave."

That sequence has a sinister echo in Britt's own ears. What must it feel like, losing your parents when you're twelve? Britt's mom was already gone, almost as long-gone as her dad. This graceful little thing at her side is losing so much more.

Here is Marni's block. They are standing just about where Marni parked last night. Now that Britt's looking right at it, she feels far more fear in that house than hope or help.

"So," she quavers, "you wait out here for me."

When the girl begins to protest, Britt grips her shoulders. "Show me I can trust you, OK? Stay right here."

She crosses the street. The house with all its plantings is lovely in the sunlight, its front door still slightly ajar, but an unreal silence envelops it like a glass bell.

As she draws near the porch steps, the city around her sounds miles away. The porch planks creak under her slight weight, a desolate sound. The shadow slot between the front door and its frame leaks out a breath of emptiness.

But what she senses just beyond that door . . . isn't quite emptiness, actually. Isn't there, in fact, far inside, a murmur, too tenuous to be voices? And a scent too? A faint scent, but strange.

"Marni? It's me. Brittany. I'm coming in, OK?"

She pulls open the door and takes one careful step inside. Before her is a seriously littered living room, empty of people. The scent is stronger here. It's coppery, and it makes her uneasy. Her ears confirm that murmur—something very faint and inanimate, farther back in the house. Maybe it's the hum of some appliance.

But Britt advances another step into the room and calls again. "Marni?"

As if her voice has summoned him, Britt discovers that there *is* someone in the room after all. He was there all along, of course, and she missed him because he sat so still. He is seated just about where she saw him silhouetted in the corner window last night—seated at a desk in front of a big typewriter that is surrounded by litter on all sides. A sheet of type-covered paper protrudes from the machine.

The labor of typing this page must have been exhausting, because the writer, a skinny little man with cloudy gray hair and beard, is slouched back so abandonedly in his chair. Head lolled back, mouth gaping, he looks utterly sacked out. There is a little glittery, twisty cloud of flies hanging above the man. Britt takes a quick further step into the room, and then her eyes have seized the whole picture.

Below the man's gaping mouth a second bloody mouth gapes still more widely. Sliced meat its lips, and gore its pendant spittle, hanging in crusty drapes down both the man's shoulders. There is a straight-razor lying in the black puddle below one of his dangling hands.

That typed sheet . . . A testament, a last testament.

Somewhere behind her, deeper in the house, a voice sounds. It is a soft, crumbly voice, intimate, inhuman. *"Here,"* it says. Britt turns, knees going weak.

"Heeere!" The voice, so teasing, drifts out from around the turn of that hall. Why is Britt going *toward* it? Stepping slowly between clothes-heaped chairs—she has no thought of calling Marni's name, knows this is not Marni's voice she's walking toward, knows too that toward it is where she does not want to walk.

Her galloping heart has a will of its own, though, and her legs are moving in spite of her.

The hallway is short, with two doors opening off of it, and it's empty except for something lying at the foot of the farther door, a bright metallic thing, with a dark, sticky root hanging off of it.

Her heart is so insistent now, filling with grief before she quite understands why. Its beating drives her forward against her will. She kneels beside this thing.

It is Marni's revolver, and its dark root is her hand, torn off at the wrist, the dusky fingers still clutching the grip.

When Britt kneels down and touches that hand, she understands suddenly that her body is not obeying her alone, that it is moved by something else that is less afraid than she is. And when she touches that cold, clenched hand, it is undoubtedly her own terror and grief she feels, but it is not exactly her fingers that loosen those others—stubborn as frost-hardened twigs—and which, at last, free, and grip the gun.

Her hand seems to know the feel of this gun, and is pleased with it, not *quite* her hand, but so be it. With her sleeve she drags the tears from her eyes. The trigger feels so reassuring to the middle pad of her index finger.

Behind the door before which she kneels, a buzzing syllable, strong now, is teasingly protracted:

"*Heeeeeeeere!*"

Now she's rising, gripping the doorknob, holding the gun by her ear, muzzle ceilingwards.

She pulls open the door.

A blizzard of flashing blue particles, sliver-winged, fills the room solid, and at this blizzard's core she sees—as through a heavy cloud—a bed, and sprawled on it, a vaguely human outline within the storm.

At once the turmoil condenses, contracting to a savage shape, a huge hound whose flesh is flies, whose lifted, leering muzzle and lolling tongue are flies, whose canny, mocking emerald eye is a vortex of flies. Regal and rampant in posture, the brute poses astride the meat that was Marni. Britt raises the pistol and fires straight into its head.

The detonation deafens her. The fly-shape explodes, is a blizzard once more, boils out onto her, batters her like furious hail. "Fuck you!" she screams. "Fuck you!" Whirls and runs.

Across the living room in three bounds—wait! She swerves left and snatches the sheet from the dead man's typewriter, springs out on the porch, and shoulders the door home behind her. It clicks shut with a crunch of crushed flies, and a gust of them has emerged with her. But out here in the sunlight, they are . . . just flies, wandering off into the open air.

Across the street stands Aarti, staring goggle-eyed. Britt looks down at her own hands—a crumpled sheet of paper in one and a beefy bright pistol in the other. She shoves them both into her pockets and stands staring back at the girl. In the house behind her, their only protector is a red rag doll. Grief and a helpless rage shake her. Brave Marni, the ghoul's toy. She stumbles down the steps and toward the girl.

*　　*　　*

It's late in the day. Traffic is loud outside. Jack lies fully clothed on his bed. Has he actually slept? There's no sense of awakening, no sense of sleep's darkness behind him. He's just suddenly here, and it's hours later. This is just as it was when he came onto shift—there he was in the cage. Now here he is out of it with no memory of coming off.

But oh, Christ, he well remembers what he saw in between!

They've got him blanking in and out, Cannyharme and his cohorts. They've got him switching on and off, so is it any wonder they've got him hallucinating? Because that was, *obviously,* what happened last night.

Oh, the old man has him running now, no point denying—has his heart pounding now, has him trance-writing! Is changing his novel for him, turning *Mistress of the Hounds* inside out! This old fucker is *baad,* is not to be shrugged off, but it's essential to keep a grip here on the key point: these visions Cannyharme's giving him are only that, *visions,* and they can only last as long as the doctored shit that Cozzens blew into his face does. Once he detoxes *that* from his system, everything will be fine, everything will be normal. He just has to ride out the storm that he's brought on himself with his recklessness and his mercenary impulses.

He finds that his notebook and a typed sheet of paper are lying on the bed beside him. Propping himself up against the headboard, he finds that his pen, too, is on his lap. What was he working on here?

The page is gibberish . . . is what he was typing while—while that crank-phantom was "creeping" down the stairs. And in the notebook, here's a line written in his own hand across the top of the page:

Through all the human stockyards you have trod

He looks again at the typed gibberish and quickly sees that this line is what results if, in his first two lines of nonsense, he crosses out all but the letters and then adjusts their spacing.

Something cold starts crawling down his back. The gibberish stirs, like a pond with a big, unexpected 'gator in it, but he gets up and takes the papers to his desk, turns on the lamp, and sits down to the task, extracting just the letters from these lines of frenzy-tangled symbols. At once the work yields fascination, in equal measure with fear.

All the letters link—re-spaced—into a perfectly coherent stream of words. Of *verse*. As he distills this poem from his intended chaos, printing it in his notebook, his fingers remember how wildly they worked to produce this page, to make mere noise, not meaning. It is with awe he sees the unintended lines emerge.

He makes a final fair copy, painstakingly neat, his hand half-consciously enjoying the writerly delight of a final draft. He reads it aloud, as he would a just-finished piece of his own.

> *Through all the human stockyards you have trod*
> *Where your bestial brethren broil and bleed,*
> *Beseeching brute Predominance, their God,*
> *To grant them scope to blunder, bray, and breed—*
>
> *Here you have wandered, haunted by a will*
> *To weave from words a world more rare and bright,*
> *Outreaching Death, to shed its radiance still,*
> *When you have sunk to dust and endless night.*
>
> *But I, who lay so long entombed below*
> *That abattoir by your brutes tenanted*
> *(O how their hooves did teach my soul to know*
> *the living deaths by which they're tormented!)*
>
> *I who now long have walked among that herd,*
> *I am unroofed by Time! The eons sprawl*
> *Like open fields I pillage undeterred!*
> *My feet outrace the centuries' slow crawl!*
> *Know, wordsmith, that it is my wish to shower*
> *This grandeur, this forever, this deathless power*
> *On your rare kind that strive for vaster views—*
> *You hard and hungry ones whom the Abyss*
> *Excites to try their wings. You sterner few*
> *I lift up to the plane where I exist,*
> *To serve as my immortal retinue!*

Here then, by God, is the Pitch. And it has come to Jack through his own unknowing hands, words metered and measured—for all their madness—to a whisker. Jack has written a lot of verse during his career, but he did not compose these verses. Someone else did, using his fingers while he thought *he* was using them to write gibberish.

Visions are one thing—and potent visions they have been, to be sure! But still, just visions: cannibal feasts smoking on stoves, disappearing walls, fields of stars, monsters in the night that wink and pass on . . . And at the end of the day, the senses are always fools and can be had.

But this. This is intimate. This is his own nerves and muscles at work.

Jack goes to his window, moving with a slightly formal air, as if he's a visitor here and this is a window he's looking out of for the first time. . . .

Heavy traffic. The sky just going gold. Flashing brake lights. On the sidewalk across the street, a tall lean kid stands nonchalantly on a skateboard as it saunters past. And just below Jack, in the window of an idling bus, there's another, much smaller kid, hemmed close to the bus window by his wide mom. The kid looks up at Jack with innocent interest, while Jack looks back at him, as at a being on another planet.

The thing about believing what's been happening, about even *considering* believing what's been happening, believing that some true sorcery is now at work around him, on him, in him . . . would be the *loneliness* of it. Crossing that line. Deciding that monsters and wizards truly walk at men's sides. After crossing that line of belief, what real company could you find in the world? What face could you face and be known by? You'd belong to the Night City then, having peeked behind the scenery and *seen* the Morlocks. Monstrous Cozzens, crazy Willy—such would be your only compatriots then.

But Jack's *been* alone all his life. Wasn't that what Erika was always telling him? That even though they were together, he lived by himself? And wasn't she right?

Admit it—he'd come here to the underworld, just to find this. A miracle, some kind of magic, something to cash in on and take back to Erika in reparation. Would it be perverse, then, to turn away from Revelation when at last it comes? But on the other hand . . . on the other hand . . . no way! He would be insane even to *consider* believing *any* of this shit!

Jack experiences a panicked recoil, similar to the sensation of falling in sleep. Is he actually knuckling under this scam, tranced by the biker's spiked crystal?

He's got to get out of this dump. He's got to take the air and clear his mind.

XIX
Conflict Resolution

Hey, Jack." Elmer says this from the cage as Jack strides out of the compound. Its intonation is just folksy greeting, but something in it makes Jack stop and turn. Surprising how clearly the old rooster's lens-swollen eyes say: *You've seen something. What?*

Jack *wants* to tell what he's seen, but not to someone in Cannyharme's camp. Did the man innocently send him down to the files? No. Those bulgy eyes know the dark outline of what was down there. Does he know without being *part* of it? What are the odds? Everywhere Jack turns, people are part of it!

The pay phone rings harshly. It makes Jack jump a little, but not Elmer. Jack snatches it up. "Hyperion."

"Hey, Chief. Great news: your pimp problem is solved."

"Whoa. Well, I'm really—"

"It's solved but not *done* till we have a meeting. Tonight—why waste time? Down in your basement floor at the hotel there at nine?"

"What kind of meeting?"

"I got an' agenda. You be down there at nine tonight, and I'll come by. Capeesh?"

"Yeah, but—"

"This is a *just do it* kinda thing, Ace. Be down there and listen for my knock." And Cozzens hangs up.

Jack looks down from the street window at the heavy traffic in the dusk, letting this new development reverberate. Cozzens can handle T-Bone and Trini, but meeting in a big, dark basement sets visceral alarms ringing in him.

Why assume that the twisted giant *needs* him past this point and doesn't have something going on with the pimps? Just because he acts like it? He's seen the giant's need for communication from the old man. And Cozzens *has* expected the messages to come through him. But still. Damn.

He's not going in there unarmed. He's not going to shoot anybody, but if he *has* his Glock, that'll guarantee that he won't have to use it. No way is he going in there without it. So he has to get used to wearing it. He'll take it out for a stroll till it's time for the meeting.

He turns back toward his room to get the gun and rig, and finds Elmer staring at him from behind the bars. "Find out anything, Jack?"

Jack lets that hang, frankly studying Elmer's face. "I found out a lot. Some of it I think you already know."

"I know what's down there. What else have you found out?"

"I'm not sure I wanna tell you."

"Looks like you trust me just enough to tell me you don't trust me. That's better'n nothin, I guess." Elmer offers nothing more.

"Well . . . maybe we'll talk when I've thought things over." Jack goes back to his room to dress for the street.

Down on Valencia, in his sport coat, with his secret wand of fire strapped beneath it, Jack just stands on the streaming sidewalk a while, feeling his hidden surplus mass, the brutal leverage he can now exert on anyone who passes. A number 33 bus pulls up to the curb, and the door gasps open. Impulsively, Jack follows its waiting boarders up into the vehicle's fluorescent belly. Eventually the tidal shift of passengers installs him in a window seat, and Jack finds himself well pleased to sit there and ride for hours, watching the streets stream by, watching the tide of faces coil around him.

At some point he takes the page of verses out and peruses them. They must have inserted the sheet into his typewriter while he was passed out. What lengths they go to for his persuasion! Whatever the hell they want it to lead to, it's plain that they want Jack himself unharmed. Why persuade someone you're just going to trash?

Phrases from the page begin to take on a poignancy in the crowded transport:

This grandeur, this forever . . . I am unroofed by Time . . . immortal retinue . . .

—and meanwhile all these tired people climbing onto and off of the bus. They're short-timers, every one. They buy their ride and stand here in the light for a while, and at the end they get off and step carefully back down into the dark. . . .

Whatever Cannyharme is selling this line for, Jack clearly sees why it sells.

The girls, as the dusk darkens, move down Clement Street. Past noodle shops and dim-sum joints, through a brisk pre-dinner bustle of people, they are moving slower than those around them, tired with their day's long walking—down and up the great highway, around the bluffs below the Legion of Honor, over to the Park, back through the Avenues. They've watched the surf and the great trees blowing in the wind, and from the cliffs watched the Golden Gate standing ankle-deep in the steel-gray sea . . . and nowhere have they found escape from the death they've discovered, nor from the deaths they fear will befall, or have befallen, Aarti's parents.

Chester Chase sees all that Brittany sees, and a great deal more as well. He sees how the girls are *seen* by those they pass. Chester hovers like the bubble of a level at the center of Britt's awareness. A few miles away, the slack old bodily vehicle that his soul, for so long, called "home" is now scrap, a festering weight on stained sheets.

But what a vehicle, what a habitation, is this Brittany! To Chester, she is like a house of stained glass, with all the world's radiance pouring in through the panes of her senses.

And with all the sights and scents and sounds comes the touch of other senses that possess her as she passes through them. The impacts of these alien attentions are to Chester two-way paths of pure energy, out of which he flows, quick as thought, and knows their sources.

The aproned cook, from the window, scans the pair and decides he wouldn't mind using their bodies in tandem, if he could tie them up first. At the register his wife, knowing her husband's mind, sends a pitying, protective wish their way.

A handsome, lean young lad with grey eyes, skateboarding, likes them and does a grinder along the curb to entertain them as they pass.

A black cop in his cruiser pegs them for streeters, thinks he might roust them to get the younger, darker one—already at such risk—out of the older white one's clutches, then reads the white one's face a little better, sees protective determination for the smaller one, thinks he'll pull over and talk to them, maybe slip them a twenty, but in the end just glides past.

A villainous, ear-torn, one-eyed alley cat under a parked car lustfully considers the pair. He scents their endangerment, the horror and harm hovering at their shoulders. They are marked prey, and he craves to join in their despoliation. But, bound in this feline shape, he is very soon to die under the wheel of a pickup truck—a death his reconstituted body is to suffer a dozen times more before his punishment is done—but unrepentant still, he glowers and lusts.

Conversely, an infant pushed in a boat-shaped stroller by her jogging dad beholds the girls haloed by a golden corona of radiance. A thrill goes down the tiny, prescient child's spine, and she claps her chubby hands and gurgles with joy at the sight of these two slight goddesses.

An old street veteran, toothless and seamed, sees the white flash of Aarti's smile at the infant, and thinks nostalgically how fine and fearless it was to have teeth like that in one's jaws.

Trapped inside the bricks of an old building's corner, a monstrous, immortal entity tastes the aura of doom that surrounds the girls. Its spider-shape ripples and tenses to spring, to devour a competitor's prize, but it is condemned to its imprisonment until the next great earthquake strikes. . . .

A tiny old witch, eking an hour's worth of warmth and society from a dollar's worth of green tea, sees them from a restaurant window. She recognizes their danger and searches for a sheltering spell to cast their way, but their tender youth distracts her mind to thoughts of her own orphaned girlhood, two hundred years ago, on the cobbled streets of Providence. Her eyes fill with wistful tears for all three of them, and her chance to aid them slips past.

Britt's body is a marvelous glove that Chester grips the world with. He feels himself to be so quick and strong and coherent here, a flame on the wick of the young woman's spine.

Could he fly free of her and remain this coherent?

Terror surrounds the thought. He remembers his bodiless crawl through the midnight air. But willing it, daring it—could he? Survive like that? Perhaps even be in his element then, a tentacled awareness free-floating in an inexhaustible new world?

The thing is, childless old Chester has a kind of daughter now. Two daughters. He can tell they need him, and as long as they do, he realizes that he needs them.

"I want to read it again," says Britt. "Let's sit here."

The bus stop bench is in a glass shelter, one of whose panels, impacted by some furious fist or foot in the empty night, is a network of cracks. Britt takes out the typed sheet from her pocket. A nearby streetlight makes the page just legible under the darkening sky.

They've read it once before, earlier this afternoon, after miles of walking to deaden their grief, and after finding greenery and sunshine to read it in, on the slopes above the Sutro Baths. Now they struggle with the lines in a cold pale light that makes the web of cracks in the bus shelter glint silver like knife blades that menace them. Britt has told Aarti only that she found both Marni and her man dead. Her private knowledge, that the author of these lines slit his own throat, adds for her an aura of defeat and hopelessness to their incomprehensibility:

> *Harm-hound, whose throat is a smoking tomb! Whose icy eyes are scythes that mow down souls!*
>
> *Harm-hound, whose greed is forever, and forever after! Whose sneer is a sepulchre where the dead die again and again and again!*

Whoremonger, whose male bitches are the wasted and twisted and emptied and strayed! Seducer, whose tongue is the wordless Worm Eternal! Whose tomb-breath whispers the bargain of life everlasting!

Dire-dog, before whom I've crouched lowly! King Cur, whose henchmen must hump and haul ass, popping sweat through eternity attending his comings and goings! Must follow him fleetly, scuttling on inhuman paws!

Your feast is the slain-in-spirit, served to you by the heartless-in-hunger! Your slaves pant after you, scouring the junkyards of souls for the bleeding and blinded!

Harm-hound, I spurn you! Despise you! Dire-dog, I mock you! I know you! If you were a god at the outset, then you were a hunchbacked, tomb-thieving cur of a god, a dirt-licking jackal, and no speech ever came out of your bone-crushing jaws!

Sly, social-climbing brute! How is it you've licked and slavered your way—you clod-nosing hustler, all dead meat's Minion with the hanging tongue!—how is it you've nosed your way out of the bone-vaults? How is it you've managed to plunder the godly arsenal of speech?

But I know. I know how it is you have words now. How it is you have sick, slick seductive verses that nestle like mink-smooth warm vermin in a sick man's heart!

But oh, how is it I have done this? How is it I have betrayed my Love to you, and her poor flesh does even now the death-dance for my lonely greed?

Out! Out! Out! Out! Out!

"How . . ." Aarti has been reading with her, and her voice is as thin as a spiderweb. "How did he die?"

"I don't know. I couldn't be sure." It's not a convincing lie. All it does is make Aarti sure that however he died, its cause was horribly obvious. The girl's eyes fill with tears and seem to see only a wasteland of fear around them. There have to be angels, but where are they now?

Britt gropes for something hopeful in the mad lines. "Someone has to betray you, see? A man close to you has to betray you to it."

And when Aarti breaks down weeping, Britt winces at the memory of the child's father twisting in the icy fog. "They can't help it, sweetie! They're trapped, they're hooked somehow. Look at this man, Marni's man, how sorry he was! Their wills aren't their own, you understand? I'm so sorry, so sorry . . ." She hugs her there on the bench, her eyes looking out over the child's nestled head, looking at the cracks in their shelter. All walls are as frail as air. The walls of poor Marni's house? No help at all to her.

Britt feels Aarti against her ribs, choking and shuddering out the loss that she will have to weep again and again over the years. The child's hopelessness helps Britt to find a stubbornness in herself. Listen, we're going to head back to the Mission. We're going to find some of my friends. We're going to get some help and we're going to go back and see your mom and dad again. We don't know anything, yet—don't really *know*. Come on, it'll feel better if we're moving."

They buy a couple hot pork buns and gobble them down as they walk. It's almost full dark now. The neons' colors seem cruel, a festive mockery of their danger. Britt struggles with her fear, but she feels so nakedly *here*, no fuzzy space inside to slide herself into. Not a molecule left in her bloodstream of nummie or val—that's what this is. She's stone cold straight now, naked down to her nerves. Frightening.

"Come on, Aarti. Let's cut over to Geary now. We'll take a bus." She grips the girl like a life-preserver and turns them down a long, dim-lit block. Geary's bright river of traffic can be seen pouring past its farther end.

From porch steps halfway down the block, four youths, in baggies and backwards caps, watch the girls approach. Chester is aware of them before Britt, feeling their attention fix on his daughters. The boys' aura is a vague static of hormones—anger, anxiety, yearning; all these boys are looking for material to enhance their status in one another's eyes. The tallest one, who steps down first to intercept the girls on the sidewalk, is a slightly more serious matter. He crackles with a sharper energy, and Chester detects that he is unknowingly in love with one of the other boys and craves especially to loom large and fierce for his beloved.

"Yo, sweet stuff—hold up. Hold up!"

"No, thanks." Britt is already steering smoothly around him, but the youth sidesteps and blocks them again. A Latino youth, handsome, but his left eye slightly walled. His sense of deformity about this is aggravated by his buried shame at his love of the other boy. This kid is dangerous. A red streak of violence fills the rift in his heart and masks it from him.

"Hey, you don' need to go. Take it *slow!*"

"Excuse us, please, we're kinda busy right now." Chester can hear how scared Britt's voice sounds. Distracted by unearthly dangers, the girl's street skills have deserted her for the moment, and when she sidesteps again her movement is hesitant, inviting persistence. The youth blocks her a third time.

"You don' wanna be dissin me."

Chester melts into Britt's muscles, is straightening her wrist, bringing her shoulder back and her elbow up, shifting the ball of her right foot a half step behind, then putting her whole back into a straight right to the youth's nose. Chester, a bit wild in his youth, is perfectly at home with planting a punch on a taller opponent.

It lands with squishy impact, maybe forty pounds of the girl's slight mass delivered straight to the schnozz. It tips the youth straight off his feet.

Her perfect delivery of this blow at first astonishes, and then galvanizes Britt. She grabs Aarti's hand and they start off running. Now Chester recoils from his intrusion, a guilty wraith amidst her senses, watching the dark block stream past them. Irresponsible of him! Putting her in the same kind of scrape he put himself in when he was young—but *he* was a thick-shouldered one-ninety. These girls don't have that much weight *between* them, and what if the boys chase them now? This wasn't like last night, nor like this afternoon, when they faced an assault from their Enemy himself.

The boys are chasing—the punched-out kid furious in the lead, the others laughing as they follow, their trailing mockery stoking the leader's fire. Will Britt beat them to Geary down there, where there are lights, traffic, witnesses?

"They're chasing us, Brittany!"

"Faster! . . . cut across . . . get to Geary . . . lots of people!" Britt in fact has no faith in safety through witnesses—she knows people turn and slide past other people's trouble double quick—but something else buoys her: the powerful way she's running now, and all this strength she's coming up with. The power of that punch she threw! And the perfect way she threw it! She feels that she *is* running toward help, help from herself, from this wild surprising Brittany she's turned into.

They round the corner onto Geary, headlights flowing past them now, vapor lamps bathing them. Britt stops Aarti, and they turn and stand.

"Brittany! Why are we—?"

"It's OK. They've got no right to drive us, this is a public sidewalk!" She scarcely knows what she is saying, is planting her feet the way they were when she threw that punch, and bringing up her fists the way she's seen fighters hold them on TV. "We've got embarrassment on our side!" she crows. "Four big punks against two little females!"

But as the youths round the corner, the lead kid's face all smeared with red, their onrush seems about to trample the girls. "Get behind me!" Britt shouts, hoists her fists higher—and feels an amazing potency flow up her back and into her arms. Here's that power again!

The blood-smeared boy hesitates, feeling his pack falter behind him, and it seems to waken him to his surroundings: himself advancing on a girl a foot shorter than he is, and a second girl *two* feet shorter than he is . . . He comes within a yard of them, boiling with frustration. He's clenching and unclenching his fists.

Nearby, the thunk of a car door. The rearmost youths catch it first. Here comes a young black cop.

"Good evening, gentlemen. Do we have a problem here?"

"She punched him out!" complains one—the charge hangs there a moment, then all three burst into quickly muffled laughter. Now young Bloodynose is the image of misery. At last he bethinks himself of his smeared snout and starts wiping it on his jacket sleeve.

"Really," says the cop. His eyes linger on Brittany, who only now remembers to lower her fists. "That true?"

"He wouldn't get out of our way!" Britt's voice is breaking with anger. This sounds wrong; she should explain it better. The cop's face seems to be struggling with something. He looks at Aarti and it breaks out a little: a smile. "Are you OK, miss?"

"Yes! Brittany is taking care of me. She lives in my dad's hotel, the—"

The cop has lifted his hand to stop her, bends closer and tells her, "Say it in my ear, miss." Britt nods to her, understanding that the cop, if he can't detain these kids, doesn't want them knowing where to go to harass the girls.

"The Hyperion . . ." Murmuring the name makes Aarti's face go grave. She seemed ready to pour out their whole plight to this sudden protector, but is remembering now those dark walls and her parents' mortal struggle within them.

The cop digs some bills out of his pocket and gives them to Britt. "See that bus?" He points to the nearest of several crowded busses laboring along Geary from the west. "Cross the street there and get right on it."

"Thank you, sir." The cop is moved to see tears come to Britt's eyes. He pats her shoulder.

"You're doing a good job of looking out for your little friend, but you've got to steer clear of trouble, OK?" He hears, in the muted talk of the youths behind him, the word *faggot*. He had a beloved gay elder brother, recently dead of AIDS. He rises and turns sternly to the pack, going to kick ass and take names, but already he hears a squawk from his patrol car's radio, the code urgent, a domestic violence call nearby . . .

The girls just make the bus and thrust themselves up into the yellow-lit interior, tucking themselves through the standing crowd, gripping a pole. Their big boat wallows out into heavy traffic. A hundred strangers here, shoulder to shoulder, all mute, rocking with the vehicle's stops and starts. Every face Britt sees is a carefully closed door. Not an angel in sight. Steer clear of trouble.

"Look, Brittany."

Back where Britt made her stand, the patrol car's door is shutting, the car speeding off, and the four youths are sprinting across Geary on a lucky light. They hit the bus stop just in time to get on a bus just one block back from the girls' vehicle, and in a moment are wallowing along in pursuit.

Chester can focus them clearly. It's the punched kid who burns for the girls. The others are tied to this one, used to his giving them games to play. And their quarry fascinates them. They've never seen someone so large punched out by someone so small. Throughout their childhoods of watching the weak and solitary getting mauled by the stronger and more numerous, they've never seen a marked victim *win* like this. It arouses in them a sneaking admiration, a buried longing for justice in the world. And, of course, the humor of their red-nosed leader's mishap keeps flickering among them. A volatile mix of motives among the four.

Chester is ready for much more serious situations than this one. He is perfectly aware of what Britt has forgotten, of the weighty object in one of her jacket pockets. In this instance, if they are cornered, he need only display it, but even for this he must choose the moment carefully. He appreciates now how very sparing he must be of any direct intervention. And not just because he has gotten them into this pickle. Because the girl has her own fate to steer through, must learn her own inner reserves.

"Aarti, look." An express passes their pursuer and drops in behind them. "That'll screen us. We get off quick at Divisadero there, duck away in the crowd."

But the express bus rolls on when the girls' bus pulls up and they jump off. The boys spot them instantly and jump off not far behind.

"Isn't that DeeAnn?"

It is. A little way up Divisidero from the bus stop, DeeAnn sits in the front seat of a white Caddy convertible. A ride! DeeAnn will help them! "Come on, Aarti. We hit the sidewalk running."

They try to keep the crowd of people getting off between them and their pursuers as they start to sprint up the sidewalk.

"DeeAnn! DeeAnn!" The little hooker turns and brightly waves.

"Brandy! Hi! And that's Bill's little girl, isn't it? Hey!"

"DeeAnn, let us in, drive us away, please! Some punks are after us. Please."

"Get in, guys!"

They pile into the front seat beside her, but she doesn't slide behind the wheel, though the keys are in the ignition. She touches the controls and brings the roof up over them. Hits buttons that raise all the windows and lock all the doors.

"DeeAnn, we should really get away."

"Don't worry, Brandy, we're OK like this."

Here come the boys, red-nose first, hammering on the Caddy's roof. "Hey, you bitch-ho! Come outta there!"

Helplessly Britt looks to DeeAnn again. "Just don't worry, Brandy!"

And suddenly red-nose's friends recoil, and red-nose himself levitates, with a startled expression, and flies backward through the air. A big man with a waxed baldy towers over them. "You beatin on our *ride?* You get your bitch asses gone!"

The youths retreat. While Britt and Aarti are still goggling, the driver's side door opens and slams. Razz has slid behind the wheel and is firing up the engine. The big bald guy gets in the back behind Razz—they feel his mass settle even the big Caddy's frame—and an instant later another big shape slides into the back behind the three females. Razz hits the button that locks all the doors again, and the Caddy roars out into the traffic-stream, while the three females turn as one. Streetlights strobe across the faces and wide-looming shoulders of two very large men, the nearer one narrow-faced and long-jawed with a fall of braids down his gaunt left cheek. He has dreamy eyes that the taut lids seem too small for, eyes that linger particularly on Aarti, though they scan both her and Britt with the same pleased speculation.

"What that trash want?" Razz is asking DeeAnn, and DeeAnn is asking Britt, "You guys OK, Brandy?"

Breathless Aarti pipes up. "Her name is *Brittany.* Those guys were hassling us and Brittany punched one right in the *nose* and knocked him right on his *ass* and then a policeman put us on a bus but they got on another bus and started following us!"

Britt senses that the girl's excitement is partly staged, that Aarti is covering her fear that they are in a probably worse situation than their last one. The air in the Caddy is thick with male collusion, lots of eye contact going on via the rearview between Razz and the two men in the back.

Razz says, "Really! No lie, Brit-uh-ny? I know you bad! I know you ready to slice an' dice widdat blade of yours! An hey I'm *down* widdit! I *respect* that!" His eyes play this ironic praise to that rearview. Britt—as the headlights and streetlights pour past, traffic heavy but fast down Divisadero—is getting scareder by the second. She doesn't like how long DeeAnn has stayed quiet, doesn't like the way Razz is checking all his words with the two big unknowns in the back seat. Across DeeAnn, she tries to catch Razz's eyes with her own.

"Razz? DeeAnn? We really do thank you for your help, but can you let us out up here, anyplace along up here? We've got somebody we have to see, somebody's expecting us and we're already late."

Why does that sound like such an obvious lie, that there's somebody expecting them? She feels a big hand gently crushing the seat-back behind her head. "You don't wanna be runnin off on us? Where you have to be?" The gaunt, braided one. A sweetish, burnt smell wafts off him when he leans close like this, as if he has come from some strange rite or sacrifice. His murmur, like an intimately aimed touch on Aarti's neck, makes the child shiver against Britt's side.

Britt turns, meets his tight-lidded caramel eyes just inches away. They are full of a joyless irony. Anything she might do or say is meaningless. All she sees in those eyes are the things he is remotely considering doing to her and (less remotely) to Aarti.

And Razz, checking the rearview for his cue from the biggest one, the bald one, leans around DeeAnn to add, "We just saved your boodies, girl. Ainchoo grateful?"

"Hey, really, we are grateful, it's just—"

But Razz, not attending, has just whipped a sharp left through a No Left Turn, clearing on rushing headlights by less than a yard, and plunging up a cross street, a darker and narrower one. "Hey, guys," pipes Dee-Ann. "Let's just drop em off so I can get to work. I wanna get tricking!" Her carefully casual tone, the way she says "guys," scares Britt. The tough little hooker is in a changed power situation. Neither she nor her pimp are calling the shots in this car. She's groping for footing.

"You girls got all this business." It's the big bald one, leaning close in his turn, his deep voice rumbly-velvety, his tone slyly amused. "But you don't *realize* it's all jus nickel an' dime, see? Now we helped you out, an' we gonna be helpin you out some more, big time, see?"

"Truth," chimes Razz. "Gonna make all three of you some major money." All three. DeeAnn bagged up with the accidental prey, suddenly not a player at all in this car. Right here is where DeeAnn should start talking Razz some trash, telling him she was the moneymaker. But her voice is still careful, and Britt gets scareder with every word. "I don't have time for this. Get us down to the Whizburger. We're missin trick rush hour."

"See there? See the per*spec*tive you got?" The back of the seat crackles as the huge fingers of the man renew their grip. "What you missing is nickles an' *dimes,* DeeAnn! What you losin is chump-change! Now we just gonna stop by my crib up here for a little while, an' we're gonna run the whole thing down to you."

And Razz is throwing another turn, and an even darker side street of the Fillmore is slipping past their windows. Big shabby Victorians loom shoulder-to-shoulder, dark-windowed; the few cars parked here look like victims, one wheelless up on blocks, another with its side windows smashed in. The Caddy is moments from one quick dive down into a driveway, a garage door that will open by remote and shut behind them. Just moments from being boxed and locked.

"We want out right now," squeaks Britt. Her voice appalls her. It is a pathetic, weak noise, like a last prayer raised to an absent god. She feels Aarti cringe against her side, catching the terror from her.

"We get out at my crib," purrs the man pleasantly. "It's totally Uptown, real plush. We got everything down there."

Chester is just about to intervene when Britt's hand goes into one of her jacket's big side pockets and touches just what Chester himself has in mind. The girl is growing up fast! He is proud of his newfound daughter.

Her hand touches it . . . but is paralyzed by the touch. The pistol's murderous strength puts a spell on her fingers, a spell of fear. Her fingers don't quite dare. Now Chester need only meddle a little bit.

The terrifying feel of the gun against her palm changes to something else—familiarity. Her grip intimately *knows* this dense and polished weight, and she's doing what comes naturally, is drawing it out smoothly, as if she knows what she's doing, is tilting its muzzle back over her shoulder, as she does so thumbing the hammer back, feeling its snugness in the web of her thumb, cocking the hammer with a meaty click. The sound causes a powerful recoil in the back seat, but she does not look to see if the man will be hit as she squeezes off a round without the least pause. A liquid pulse of thunder jolts her arm.

Deafening, the mere noise an annihilation! But still she does not pause, cocks and fires again, this shot tilted toward the second man, directly behind her. The Caddy's braked with a screech none of them can hear, as she cocks a third time, jams the muzzle against the side of Razz's face, and screams, "Unlock the door! Unlock the fucking door!"

She thrusts the door open and she and Aarti pile out, pulling a gust of thick gunsmoke out after them. They stand there a moment, as stunned-seeming as the four people in the car, smoke billowing from the gaping door. The first to regain her wits is DeeAnn. She leans out, grips the door, and pulls it shut, flashing them a wink just before it closes. The girls turn and sprint back toward the lights of Divisadero.

XX
Pimp Productions Inc.

"God-*damn!*" laughs T-Bone. "People be *shootin* at me lately! Seems like some kinda new fad!"

Razz is steering them down Sixteenth, the Caddy already slipping over the border of the Mission. "Man!" he yelps. "Two fuckin holes in my *roof!* I can't believe this shit!"

"You need a new ride anyway, Razz-Matazz! You need you a SUV, not these Yesterday wheels. A white Caddy—I don't wanna hurt your feelins, but you lookin sorrier'n shit in this rig, Homes. I'm ashamed to have any of my associates see me in it, aint that right Trini?"

But Trinidad is focused on DeeAnn. "You ready to work, *Dee*-Ann?" The sneer in his voice is like a prod between her shoulders. She's the only remaining representative of the females who have defied him. "You lookin tense, *Dee*-Ann. You see that Razz Matazz? You skanky old lady lookin *tense.* She so tense she be tellin us what to *do* with those two little bitches we had!"

There's the briefest pause before she lashes back, but she has to hang tough or they'll eat her alive. "Hey asshole, I'm twenny-three! *You* call me old cause you're short-eyes for schoolgirls, *Trini*dad!"

This yields another, slightly longer pause. A pause in which DeeAnn waits to learn if her gamble of showing some 'tude is going to work, or if these goons Razz is flirting with are going to yank her chain and do her some hurt. A pause in which Razz himself seems to wait for the same answer, his uneasy eye corner flicking to the rearview to scope T-Bone's big dark moon of a face.

T-Bone grins, and it seems as if he just has to chuckle. "Let's let this good ho get back to *work,* Homes! She wants to be kickin some, let her get to it. You might as well have that chump-change too!"

So everybody relaxes. Razz steers for Eighteenth, is free to do his standard pimp riff now. "God *damn* you, DeeAnn! Will you *stop* messin widdat Brandy bitch? Last time she whip a shank in my face, an' now I got two fuckin holes in the roof of our ride!"

"Hey, Razz, it's you guys panicked her, what can I say? She's a sweet kid if you don't threaten to fuckin *kidnap* her!"

They bat it back and forth until, shortly, they've pulled up to the curb on South Van Ness just kitty-corner to the Whizburger. The men sit back and watch DeeAnn as she gets out and takes her switchy, glittery little butt across the street, her raccoon eyes radaring left and right for possibles. The pimps' eyes stay on her, all absently making a professional assessment that does not find the little hooker wanting, while T-Bone says, "You should leg it on over to the Hyperion, Trini. Stop by the hotel for your piece, I'm strapped already. Don't go in till nine, an' go in frosty. I'll be right nearby, scopin your back. Phone me."

Trinidad gets out and leans at the window to give Razz a long, weighty look, making sure the junior pimp has taken in the homicidal overtones of these instructions. Then he crosses the street in his turn, but angling away from the Whizburger, heading up toward the Mayfair. T-Bone and Razz remain, watching DeeAnn go to work. T-Bone explains, "Your man Jack, I told you the fucker tried to cap me in the *head?* An you remember I told our *backer* about it? That Cozzens. Well, the three of us are gonna take care of Mr. Jack toot sweet. We takin care of you here, Tazz my man. Now what about you? You gonna pony up? You got her up for tomorrow night?"

DeeAnn is leaning prettily at one of the order windows, has made a contact already, a Latino man in a 49ers jacket. The man, after some quick conversation, has ordered a coffee—is paying with a hundred he won't get change for. The counter girl shoves across a coffee and (invisibly) a key to the utility room round back of the building. DeeAnn wanders away with the key, saunters aimlessly round to the rear of the building. 49ers jacket sits at one of the outside tables, trying to act absorbed in sipping his coffee.

"She bitchin about it," says Razz, keeping his eyes on the john. "Say she aint sure about no *group* work." T-Bone, scenting defection, leans over the back seat, folding his arms under his chin. The two of them watch the john stand up, shit can his coffee, and, none too casually, head round to the back of the building in his turn.

"She's not pullin no train," says T-Bone, his tone mild. "That aint the story. Story is she be doin a group shoot . . . only be workin one or two dudes at a time for the camera. You told her that, right?" He aims a pleasant, almost uninterested sidelong gaze at Razz.

"Yeah, I told her that."

They return to gazing at Whizburger for a moment, as if they can see DeeAnn on the job back in that utility room, making short work of the john's C-note amid the mops and brooms and the chill perfume of Clorox and ammonia.

"You know, Tazz my man, I think *you* the holdup here, am I right? You feelin doubts, you not right in your *mind* about it." At Razz's protest, T-bone lifts a calming hand. "Naw, naw, just wait now an' listen up. I'm not gonna talk hard to you. I'm not gonna remind you this was *your* idea, that *you* brought it to *us*, wastin her cause she free-fuckin behind your back. And I'm not gonna *remind* you that you now have two serious associates that have committed their time and their labor to the project. And I'm *also* not gonna remind you that we, your two associates, have taken this snuff flick idea seriously, and have hooked you up with a backer who is himself a serious dude, who has already put his money into the project, and who on top of that is about to give us some very *substantial* assistance with this little *Jack Hale* business, which you were *also* instrumental in bringing us into. You understand what I'm sayin? I'm not gonna remind you about *any* of that."

"Hey, T-Bone, please, man. It just that she—"

"Shhhhh! Shhhhhhh. Just hold up an' hear me out, Tazz-man, cause what I'm *tryin* to *share* is part of the bigger picture. It's somethin you need to grasp for your *own* sake, for the sake of your *career*." The faintest hint of a growl has entered the big man's voice. Razz nods, contrite. Pays devout attention.

"Razz, you got to ask yourself what a ho really *is?* What is the *essence* of a ho? A *ho,* bottom line, is someone that threw herself away a long time ago, and the deal she got with her pimp, bottom line, is always the same deal: I'm trash, I'm already thrown away, so you use me any way you want. Bottom line, Razz, every time. And all a pimp is, a *good* pimp, mind you, is a man that takes *on* the responsibility to dispose of that ho! You put them to use, give em a crib, give their lives some structure, make you both some money, but the *point* of it all is they yours to dispose of . . . an' they *want* you to. They *dependin* on you to do it. They want *out,* my friend, an' that's why they live like they do. They all of 'em want *out,* even if they won't admit it to themselves.

"You think I never put down one of mine? Or Trini, one of his? Course, I got to say just between us, Razz-man, that Trinidad . . . well the dude's unstable. You see that sometimes with a short-eyes. That Trini, though"—an indulgent chuckle—"he be takin a little girl like we had in the car here an, well . . . My *own* philosophy is, what's the point? Why add pain to a painful world? Now, your DeeAnn aint gonna go cruel an' un*usual.* Just a cap to the head, *whack,* clean an' quick. Like Cozzens was sayin, this aint no splatter snuff flick, it's an *art* snuff flick, an' it's gonna make bow-koo bucks. DeeAnn's just gonna reach her natural fulfillment, an' she aint gonna suffer.

"So I want you to be at peace, Razzman—at peace widdit."

Supple, powerful T-Bone has gripped Razz's shoulders and turned him face to face, twisted rather painfully at the waist, but Razz tries to look, accepting, nodding earnestly at the big man. "Because you *owe* us here, man. We got you the connection" (the connection with Cozzens, in fact, with strange timeliness, simply dropped in their laps, but no need for

Razz to know it) "an we got you lined up for ten K out the door. You got it all started, got us all obligated, by offerin the meat, an' by god, you gonna *deliver* the meat. Am I right?"

"Hey, T-Bone, it's *down.* Down *solid.* I'm sorry you even think you need to mention it! We there, all systems, tomorrow night!"

"That's my Razz-man talkin! 'Nuff said. Well, it's time for me to stroll on over to your hotel. We takin care of you already here. A couple hours, your Mr. Jack problem will be history."

The big car rocks, yielding up T-Bone's weight. He pauses beside the car and then leans down to the window. "Man, those bullet holes do make your ride look funky! You gotta get you an SUV, Homes—honestly."

The girls stride on down Divisadero, ears ringing, bodies adrenalized. Aarti makes a fist. They will go straight into the Hyperion, straight up to her door. They will pound and shout, and they will fire the gun into the floor until Daddy will *have* to open, they will *demand* that he bring Mommy out, that he *explain* what is going on. . . .

But then they cross Haight Street, beyond which Divisadero climbs through a darker, hilly stretch, and as they trudge up the slope Britt glances behind them. Three blocks back, four lanky figures are jiving along.

"Hurry up, Aarti. Maybe they won't spot us before we get on the other side of this hill."

But as they reach its crest they see the distant figures register their identity and begin to run. The girls take off. Out here the pistol seems worse than useless, a ticket to jail if merely brandished, let alone used. They are running full out, lungs toiling. Divisadero climbs and dips, climbs and dips, and as they struggle up each new grade, muscles burning, the boys gain on them.

But here is the long downslope to Market, beyond which Divisadero becomes the swarming Castro, all bright-lit shops and crowded sidewalks. The light turns against the girls as they reach Market, but they plunge across anyway, rousing a din of horns and screeching tires, and drawing so much notice that the boys, almost on them, pile to a halt at the curb and wait glowering for the next light.

The girls are in the crowd now, Britt threading them through a screen of statuesque males, leaving a series of "Excuse *yous!*" in their wake. They make a cross street, sprint outright to the next, hook down that . . . and, ducking in a doorway, scan the path they've come. Minutes pass, and no pursuers materialize.

"Look!" hisses Aarti. "Brittany, look!" She's pointing directly across the street, to a coffee-and-donut place called *Oh, Mary's*. The well-lit interior is empty except for a single occupant, a small black man in a loud Hawaiian shirt. *The* shirt.

The girls find themselves crossing the street as if pulled by a magnet. The little man, seated over a coffee and donut, is gazing back in their direction, but as they gain the opposite curb they see his gaze is vague, luminous, and a world away. He is very black, with amber eyes and wide, sculpted lips. His scalp is shaved, except at the very back, where a long braided ponytail hangs. He absently strokes this braid as the girls draw near the window.

His big honey-brown eyes seem to focus now, to find them. He begins to smile, and then his face contracts into a pout of indignation, seeing something beyond them. He rises from his chair and comes swishing purposefully toward the street door, causing the girls to turn—and to confront red-nose and his pals, crossing the street right for them.

"Yo, ho! Where you think you gonna *go?*" But just as they mount the curb, the little man in the blazing Hawaiian shirt steps out, steps between.

"You stop right *there!*" he tells the youths. Amazingly, their feet freeze in such sharp unison, they all stand swaying for balance. "What do you think you're doing, dogging these sweet girls like this? I'm telling you right now to be *gone!*"

The boys seem to have no voices. They stand giving one another you-believe-this-shit looks, but no words come out of them. The graceful little man plants his slender arms akimbo, looking very displeased. "Do you hear me? Do you see me? I'm telling you to be *gone! Now!*"

All four of them blink, and turn, and go. Britt and Aarti stand staring after them.

"You poor girls!" flutes their savior. "You must be starving! You must be exhausted! You come in here right this minute an' have some nice coffee an' donuts!"

A wave of strange warmth exudes from the little man—both Britt and Aarti have to wipe sudden tears of gratitude and relief from their eyes as they follow him inside. They step into the scents of cinnamon and sugar and cocoa, like a wonderful blanket of safety enfolding them. He seats them at the window, whose glass seems to work a subtle transformation on the street outside. Its colors grow richer, like a friendly carnival. The passing people, all clothed with bright style, flash smiles. The neons are jewels and the shopfronts all grottos of treasure.

"I'm Skip," says the little man from behind the counter, where he bustles up a basket of donuts and mugs of steaming coffee. He sits beside them and watches them dig in. "And you are, little one?"

"I'm Aarti. That's Brittany."

Skip seems to find their names delicious. He crumbles a bit of plain cake donut into his stirred coffee and watches the golden crumbs melt into its slow swirl. "I don't quite know you yet, my dears." His voice is a melodious alto. "I know you're in trouble, in very serious trouble, but I don't know just how."

"You don't understand it?" Britt has blurted this in surprise, then fears it rings like disappointment. Skip smiles at her, smiles vaguely out the window.

"I've been very ill, dear. I've only just now . . . pulled myself together. I'm with you, don't worry. I just need time. I'm getting more with you, as we sit together like this. . . ." His profile is very African, the nose broad with drooping septum, the cheeks like polished ebony, an exquisite face. His smile has a poised fullness to it, like a singer's about to sing. He turns to Britt suddenly. "You have a friend with you, don't you?"

Confused, the girls look at each other. "We had a friend," falters Britt, "who was trying to help us. But she—"

"No, dear, I don't mean that. You have a friend with you right now, very close to you." Skip's head is cocked, as if he's listening to Britt, though Britt can find nothing to say. Then he pats her arm. "Never mind, sweetheart. You eat up now, eat everything right up."

They feast, watching the festival outside. Every bite of the donuts is first-bite delicious—they wolf them and wolf them with unflagging pleasure. When at last they are filled, it is safety as well as satiety they feel. The sweet meal wraps them in a sense of bedtime-and-storybook security.

Skip's voice has a bedtime-story croon to it. "You two are gonna come up to my nice little apartment upstairs now, gonna have a nice shower, get into beddy-bye all snug, an' sleep to your heart's content. And tomorrow . . . tomorrow I'm gonna tell you what you have to do."

XXI
An Invitation to a Banquet

Nine o'clock. It seems to take Elmer forever to buzz Jack in. Jack calls up the stairs, "I'm workin in the basement a while, Elmer." He goes to the storage-floor door.

Why meet down here? He just doesn't like it. His Glock now feels ridiculous. *Shoot* somebody? Here in the real world? Lose his next couple decades in prison? Lose his last chance at a real life?

Cozzens is clearly Jack's only choice if he's going to solve his pimp problem. Who else *could* help him, even if willing? Whatever else Cozzens is, he's *bad.* Jack unlocks the door, clicks on the lights . . . and steps into the shadow-floor. Standing here, he feels just how flimsy, after all, it could be—his assumption that Cozzens does not want him harmed.

The street doorbell is pushed. Afraid it's Cozzens, not wanting to face him just yet, Jack closes the basement door behind him. Someone is buzzed in, thuds past and on up the stairs.

Jack stands looking at the jigsaw of light and dark flung by the light bulbs, thinning out to dark in the floor's deeps. He feels again that the dark is a taut-stretched fabric, that an ice-cold grief stirs beneath it, and a rage with the grief. A phrase from Poe comes back to him.

> *Flapping from out their condor wings*
> *Invisible woe!*

That's the feeling that stirs in these shadows: woe without end, and an undying, watchful malice. His brain feels . . . crumbly at the edges.

The street door sounds again. It's buzzed open. A double tread approaches the basement door. There comes a knock, and he opens to the knock.

And as he opens, the door erupts. Cozzens's hugeness lifts him like a wave, slams his back against the wall. The sawed-off shotgun's barrel is thrust against his throat. Paralyzed, Jack hears the ogre say, "Shut the door, man. Call Bone and tell him it's party time."

And Trinidad steps in, shuts and bolts the door. "You fucked up, Jacko," Cozzens leers. "You trusted me!"

The lanky pimp, after looking warily around the vast basement, tucks away an automatic and plucks out a cell phone. "Hurry up," barks Cozzens.

"Yo, Bone? It's down. Come on."

"All right," says Cozzens. "Drag that mattress over here, Trini, and let's get this chicken wired down."

As Trinidad turns where he points, Cozzens whirls. Jack is unpinned so suddenly he falls, and falling, glimpses the punch the biker launches, but only hears its impact against the side of Trini's face.

"Take out your piece, Ace," the ogre is saying, as Jack regains his feet, "and you hold him right *here!*" with that word slamming Trinidad's back against the same wall where Jack was pinned. "Stick the suppressor in his mouth and snug it in his tonsils and keep his head pinned right back against that stud."

Trinidad's half-slack jaw lets the suppressor in, but then his eyes clear and widen in fear as he's pinned in place, his lips an O around the silencer. "Now you lock your arm, Chief, that's it, and you pop him quick if he even twitches. He came here to buttfuck you and then kill you, you read me? Straight truth. Just keep him pinned."

The street bell sounds again, and Cozzens stands ready at the door. Someone is buzzed in, steps approach, there's a knock.

The biker half opens the door, makes a show of looking out cautiously, then breaks into a grin. "Hey, Bone! Welcome to the lo-o-o-ve connection!"—stepping back in a bow that brings his right hand up behind him.

As T-Bone steps inside, Cozzens hooks that right up into his diaphragm with his whole great mass behind it. The big pimp folds and falls like cement sacks.

"Just keep Trini pinned, Ace, while I make Bone comfy." Cozzens relocks the door. As he handcuffs T-Bone's wrists behind him he whistles "Whistle While You Work." The wrists secured, with a nylon cord he anchors the chain of the cuffs to one of the floor joists above, jacking T-Bone's arms so high behind him that the man struggles to his feet though still doubled over in agony.

Then Cozzens comes back over to Jack—and there is the shotgun muzzle again, this time rammed into the back of Jack's neck.

"Now listen hard, Chief. These two men had their nasty little hearts set on fuckin you and then killin you, and now they'll have em set on killin me if they ever walk outta here. You see how I've come all the way out on a limb to solve your problem the only way it *can* be solved with meatballs like these? But I don't put blood on my hands for anybody unless they match my ante. I don't need you any more, Ace, I'm gonna get what I want, so you can believe me when I tell you this: if you don't pop Trinidad right now, I'm gonna blow your head right offa your neck. Right *now.*"

Jack feels perfectly transparent. He's a bubble poised between two contact points with Impossibility: there is his Glock's contact with Trinidad, which means Murder, and the shotgun's contact with his neck, which means Death. It seems he can feel the warmth of Trinidad's spit radiating right through the pistol and into his hand, while the shotgun muzzle against his nape is a big cold cave whose breath numbs his hope. Cozzens's desire for Trinidad's death pours into Jack from behind, and suddenly Jack's own desire for the same thing floods forward into his Glock. Look at this pimp's bug's eyes, soulless as wet black rocks. These eyes have overlooked the writhings of how many victims, have sucked up the suffering of how many powerless strays twisting and crying under his cruel invasion? These eyes have savored the plundering, the pain of his prey, and would have savored Jack's own plundering (*but will Cozzens really kill you?*), his pain (*don't you have a choice here?*), his death.

It's the power in Jack's hand that tips the scale, becomes an imperative. He squeezes the trigger. The 'nine, doubly silenced, bucks and says *phhhtt.* Trinidad's head slams back and his eyes are pulled back, recoil and flatten into their sockets, trying to follow the blown brain out.

Jack snatches his gun out of the corpse's mouth, wipes the suppressor with desperate loathing on his pants leg. He hasn't felt the shotgun leave his neck, but it's gone now. He turns, knowing just what he'll see, and sees it: Cozzens's fanged, mocking grin.

"From don't-know-shit college boy," leers Cozzens, "presto change-o! You know some shit now, don't you, Jacko? Had your cherry popped! Check it out. Get the afterglow! Savor the moment!"

And by God, Jack does know some shit now, knows he has jumped into an abyss and is falling, still falling, will never stop falling from this moment on. What has he done? What has he *done?*

The dead man slumps there, a jumble of knees and elbows, a smell of shit wafting up from him. Jack discovers he has just blown a huge hole in *himself,* and that the Void breathes through that hole, forever and ever. For the first time in his life Jack Hale knows he will die, knows it right down to his bones. It stuns him. He thought he *knew.* All those years of wise self-admonitions: seize the day, you won't live forever, no man knows his hour, life is short. All lies, all posturing, all smoke blown up his own ass. But *now* he knows. Now.

"I got ten K." It's a choked, rusty little voice. T-Bone's voice.

"Hey, Bone!" beams Cozzens. "You're breathin again! Good man. I was afraid I'd stopped your clock there."

"... got ten K," rasps the eerie voice. "Quo of smack. Top grade. Yours. Take you to it. Leave town."

"What're you sayin, Bone? You say you're gonna give me ten K and a quo of smack if I leave town?"

T-Bone starts shaking his head, shaking his whole strung-up body, in his urgency to correct this misunderstanding.

Cozzens laughs. "Oh, I get it. You're gonna give me ten K and a quo of smack an' then *you'll* leave town." The bald head nods vigorously. "Well . . ." The biker strokes his beard consideringly. "That's an' interesting offer, I guess, if you're just talking about the side dishes, the trimmings. But where's the *beef*? Where's the real *meat* of this proposition? What about immortal life? You're offering me immortal life too, aren't you?"

T-Bone just looks at him.

"I didn't hear you, Bone. Cause if you're *not* offerin me immortal life, well, I'm afraid I'm gonna have to take a pass."

T-Bone has given up speaking, just hangs there working on breathing, looking up at the ogre. "I guess I can take that for a no, hey, Bone? Oh well, don't worry. I'm not gonna do you ugly like Jack did Trini. I'm gonna leave you totally handsome, except maybe for your tongue hangin out."

T-Bone can't struggle much without breaking his arms. Cozzens snugs the noose of another nylon rope around his neck, threads the free end over another joist, and pulls it powerfully. T-Bone leans forward at the limit of his crackling, back-stretched arms and commences the grueling labor of strangling.

Jack stands watching. He is in an alien, transformed world. He now inhabits an exit-less Carlsbad Caverns of terrors new and strange. This is what *is,* and he stands numbly, humbly watching it.

T-Bone shits himself, shudders, and dies.

It is done. Cozzens releases the rope. He gives Jack a friendly, thoughtful smile. "You oughta tuck that away, Ace. Lend a hand. We gotta tidy up. Look." He pulls from the back of his belt two tight scrolls of plastic and unfurls one. "Ta-*da!* Body bags!"

Jack spreads the bags open, Cozzens lays the bodies in and zips them shut. There is something steadying, almost domestic in this task: two workmates finishing a job. Jack's the apprentice, while Cozzens *lives* in this cavern of death, is the master of its terrible wonders. "It aint murder,

Chief," Cozzens tells him as they work. "You were forced." A merry glance here, a knowledge that Jack's own will in the last instant had kindled to the killing. "I lied, of course. I still need you. I couldn't have shot you. But how could you know that?

"Not murder then, but still a mess that you don't need anyone else messin with. There's brains on that wall, and a slug somewhere. Still, who's gonna know? Your manager's got the only other key, and where he is now, he don't give a shit about it. Come on. Take Trini on your shoulder an' follow me."

Cozzens shoulders T-Bone and leads them back through the depths of the storage floor. Jack finds his following tread is sure, despite Trinidad's weight and the darkness. This is right, this is urgent, making the corpses disappear. These are the first necessary steps on the path out of this nightmare.

The shadows feel busier than ever around them. The entombed furniture seems to creak under its shrouds of dusty darkness. The cavern stirs with sentience . . . empathy.

Cozzens opens the door to the alley behind the hotel. A big glossy black van stands there with its side door open. They set the bodies inside. They close the hotel door, slide the van door shut, and climb into the front seats. It's all so efficient, so neat. Here they are in this gorgeous black Soul Ferry, ready to hustle the dead off this world without a trace.

"A bitchin ride, no?" Cozzens slips into gear and eases the van down the alley. "I'm a man of many wheels, Jacko. Hell, tomorrow night I'll be drivin a fuckin *bus,* you believe that? Drivin guests to a banquet. In fact, you're invited to it. Lemme tell you about it—no, don't say anything. Just chill, get calm while we take a little ride and I run it down to you."

They're cruising down Mission now. Jack watches the Carnival flow past. He finds he feels at home here in a new way, because he has actually stepped through one of those mysterious doors he has always felt were to be found here. Has stepped through and is an Insider now. Here he is, ferrying a pair of dead Carnival predators to their just reward.

"First, you'll know some of the people there. Your friend Razz is my date. He doesn't know it, see. He thinks he's takin his little twist, Dee-Ann, to star in a snuff flick! He thinks it's a video shoot he's goin to. It was his own idea—the bitch must've done something to piss him off." A sharp grin at Jack here. "Oh, that Razz! I think I'm in lo-o-o-ove, Jacko. A perfect micro-pimp with a little pint-size brain on him. He pitched this snuff flick idea to our friends back there, and they took the front money he gave em—it was just a joke to them. Weren't they surprised when I looked em up, said I heard on the vine there was a snuff flick cooking, hauled out some bread an' said I wanted in. We all had a meeting. They thought they were in pimp heaven when they took my cash and I threw in *your* ass as an extra bonus. The rest is history.

"Now the thing about this banquet is that nothing's changed, Jacko. You're on a totally free-will basis here. You're wanted—*He* wants you—for a witness. You don't have to participate in any way. It's just show and tell. He wants you to know what his offer means. No strings, no obligation to buy. Now you've got a messy little involvement here"—a tilt of his head back at the bagged bodies—"an involvement that's going to vanish without a trace, as long as you show up at the banquet. Hell, *I'm* gonna vanish without a trace then."

"I thought I was on a totally free-will basis, Cozzens."

"Hey, you just come to look! No strings, man, no compulsion of any kind. He wants volunteers, volunteers *only*. But they got to *know* what's being offered. That's the only compulsory thing. You're some kinda poet, right? An adventurer of the mind? So if you're worth your salt, if you're a *real* poet, man, how can you turn away from the only *real* miracle you're ever going to see?"

"What . . . just tell me. What's the miracle?"

"Hey, going on faith to find out is the price of admission to every miracle there ever was. Don't you know that about miracles? Grow some guts, Ace. You gotta step up to the brink and look in!"

They have meandered their way back up to Valencia. Cozzens pulls to the curb not far from the hotel. "Tomorrow night around ten. The Sons of Holland Hall out in the Avenues. Just be there, man. You won't be sorry."

Jack finds he is reluctant to leave the vehicle. Away from his ogre guide, he will be alone with what he has done tonight. He takes the poem from his pocket, unfolds it. "Do you want to—"

Cozzens glances calmly at it, grins his fanged grin. "Naw, Jacko. I've got my Word. That one's just for you."

Jack steps onto the curb. The madman tips him a wave and roars off, his ebony chariot floating majestically up the street.

Jack starts walking. It seems that if he doesn't, he'll freeze to this spot, will be standing here at dawn, and the dawn after that. . . . He heads for anywhere but the hotel. Starts walking, it doesn't matter where.

Ron Ratchett, lithe as a panther, tireless as a wolf, is striding down the midnight sidewalk. He can't remember ever having walked like this in his life, with such power and purpose. He can't even remember starting out on this walk.

The last he recalls, it was a couple hours past dark and he was settling down into a doorway, well sloshed but not as sloshed as he wanted to get. It was up on Guerrero somewhere, just off Sixteenth, he thinks. He remembers wedging some newspaper between his skinny butt and the gritty cement of the step, remembers sucking the last corner of bourbon out of his little flat. And why was he in a doorway in the first place? Oh, yeah— because Dixon, the night clerk, would be sure to demand his rent, two days late, while Mohammed, the day clerk, was a more understanding guy and would let him go up and see a friend who was likely to front Ron his rent on the promise of Ron's next packet of food stamps.

All this comes back to him so clearly because man, *Ron* is clear now. He's striding like a decathlete, he's running a full sweat, his lungs are pumping cold night air. Ron has heard tell of an aerobic rush. This must be what they were talking about.

But this has to be a dream. Doesn't it? One of those just-like-reality dreams? Because he *can't* move like this, doesn't have the muscle or stamina for it. And he has no reason to do it, nowhere to *get* to in this kind of hurry. It has to be a dream.

Except that everything is just too clear, too steady. There are no sudden shifts of scene. His legs eat up the sidewalk one square at a time, he can see each brick of the walls he passes, each window and doorway distinct. The dream-time is definite, too—a past-midnight emptiness everywhere, but before 2 A.M. because there's an open bar, a neon Coors sign in the window, one of its O's dark, a faint jukebox noise inside growing louder, then dwindling behind him.

It's kind of a gas, really, like flying on his legs, like being some superhuman android in a space flick. On the best day of his life he couldn't even run as fast, nor as long, as he's striding right now.

It just goes on and on. Dreams don't do that, do they? Just go on and on without flickering, wavering? Because where's the story? What's the dream about?

Uh-oh. Suddenly there's a story developing. A block ahead, two big dark shapes step out from the corner and stand on the sidewalk directly in his line of travel. Big shapes. One in a watch cap, one in a baseball cap. Lazy postures, legs spread, big shoulders. Gonna-fuck-with-you stances. It's a dream then, a nightmare, because if it *wasn't* a dream he'd be angling off right now, booking it across the street. Not powering right on toward them, as if they weren't even there.

"Hey! Hold up a second!"

"Where you goin? Slow down!"

Parked cars to the left, wall to the right, Ron's in a chute, funneled right down into them. It's time, *past* time, to spin and sprint back the way he came—the fuck is he doing? He's starting to sprint *toward* them!

Everything in the next three seconds is incredibly vivid. He can see the little slump of startlement in their shoulders, see their high school reflexes kick in as they crouch to brace and block him, because it's just Ron Ratchett here, five-nine and weighing a booze-leached one-forty tops. Can see all this as he leaps, launches a soaring, heel-first Bruce Lee head-kick, plants it square on the left one's forehead and snaps his neck, rides his body down to the sidewalk, does a jump-spin and plants a side-kick in the right one's knee, feeling that joint snap like a celery stick and bringing the guy low enough for a hard, straight throat-punch, feeling his knuckles crush the larynx right back against the spine. The thug gets down on the sidewalk then, gets right into the hard labor of strangling all by himself.

Ron is stupefied and, after a second, ecstatic—now this is a *dream!*—but his superhero hands never pause. He flips the dead one over, finds the wallet in his back pocket, extracts the guy's wad—three wrinkled ones—and pockets it. He turns to the other guy, who's still dying, breaks his neck with another side-kick to quiet him down, and rips him off—a whole five on this guy, folded into his coin pocket. Then he strides on down the sidewalk without a backward glance.

Man, this is some top-quality dreaming! Total solidity, and total wish-fulfillment, with that invincible feeling of *running* reality instead of being stuck inside it. It's like he's watching himself in a movie, but from *inside* himself. It's incredibly cool. Already he dreads the moment of waking up, of shrinking back down to a dirty, cold, sick-livered drunk shivering on a gritty step. If only he'd had the money for a fifth yesterday! Give this vision some staying power. As it is, the world will come back any moment now—*he* will come back, huddled in the ugly gray dawn.

But it does go on, block after block his body strides as if it were all sinew and spring steel, while a soreness and exhaustion begin to accumulate in his limbs, a nimbus of pain that envelops his apparent invincibility. And soon the sheer accumulation of time and the unflagging clarity of the city around him begin to work a revelation in Ron. His body is actually moving, and he is not moving it. Crouched inside, like a cat gone to sleep in a car and waking to find it in motion, he grows tense with terror, increasingly sure he *is* awake.

Stop walking.

He can't.

Shout for help.

He can't.

But suddenly he's slowing down, moving more quietly. There's a man on the sidewalk ahead, going in the same direction. Ron is falling into step behind, matching his pace, hanging a block back from the guy.

The guy turns a corner under a streetlight and Ron glimpses his profile. It's Jack Hale, kind of far from his stomping grounds around the Hyperion, but a welcome sight: guy's helped Ron to a drink now and then, is a decent dude.

But Ron can't call out to him, can't do a fucking thing but what he's being *made* to do, which seems to be to follow Jack, stalk him. Could Jack be headed for the Tip Top? It's a place Ron's known him to frequent, and is just a couple blocks over from here. If Ron is supposed to follow Jack, maybe that's where they'll both end up.

No. It seems Ron is not going to follow him any farther. Ron has stopped and just stands staring as Jack turns the corner up ahead. And now Ron is turning to the brick wall beside him, reaching out and laying his hands on it . . .

And has leapt up and started *climbing* the wall, straight *up* the wall! Climbing as fast and steady as if he were running on all fours over level ground. By God, he is dreaming after all, of course he is, has to be. And terrifying though these dream-sensations are—the cold abrasion of brick under footsoles and palms, the sidewalk and streetlights dwindling beneath him three stories, four stories, five stories below—frightening though these are, he feels a deep relief that this wild vivid dream *is* a dream, has to be, past all doubting now, however much like cold reality it feels. He's not possessed by some monster or spirit or demon. He's just hard and fast asleep somewhere, curled up safe and sound, and brain-surfing.

Now it's the rooftops of course, he's sprinting across the tar-and-gravel, shoe-soles crunching, leaping over the parapets separating buildings, not even pausing, smooth as an athlete (of course) and now charging right to the brink of the next street over, and—

Whoa!

—scuttling *down* this wall on all fours, face first, like a lizard or a bug! Man, what a nightmare! What a rush! His face just plunging toward the sidewalk, its squares growing bigger, bigger . . . till he flips outward, lands on his feet, turns, takes three steps leftward, and steps into the Tip Top Cocktail Lounge.

Ron stands there blinking at Rick, the bartender. His nerves are so blenderized by astonishment he experiences a kind of calm. His body too is acting calm. He steps up and takes a stool at the bar, as nonchalant as if he has just arrived by cab. He's the only customer at this late hour. "Hey, Rick. Busy night." Ron doesn't say this—but his face and his voice do.

Rick shrugs. "Always Happy Hour at the Top. What's your poison, Ron?"

"Well, bourbon, draft beer back." He pays with the dream money that he took from the dream thugs that he killed with his superhero dream-moves.

This part of the dream is a perfect match for what Ron would do in reality. He knocks back the bourbon and half of the beer. The tastes are as real as real. Someone walks in, and Ron turns. "Hey, Jack! What a coincidence!"

"Hey, Ron, we meet again. Hi, Rick—gimme a draft."

Ron's eyes fix on Jack's hand going into his pocket for his money. A moment after Jack's hand comes out with the bills, Ron feels a strange bodily qualm, a phantom extrusion from himself, and something else sprouts out of Jack's pocket—a folded piece of paper, which falls to the floor.

Ron smoothly leans down and picks it up, unfolds it, and sits scanning it. Lines of typing. Ron on the inside can't make anything of them. But when Jack notices him reading, then does a double-take and recognizes the paper, Ron says, "You dropped this, man, and man, this *is* a coincidence. You know I got this same crazy like poem? An old man gave it to me on the street, this weird bent-over old fart. It was like printed on this little pamphlet thingie, and there was an invitation to a dinner, like a whaddyacallit—a banquet."

"No shit. Did you go?"

"Free food an' booze, man? Are you serious? Fuckin-A I went! It was at this like big funky auditorium out in the Avenues. I'll tell you, the food tasted like shit, but the booze was primo. But it was all a big come-on. It was like a wacko religious trip."

Ron sits listening to himself saying all this. It's so strange. You talk in dreams, but you sort of feel what you're saying. It might not make any sense when you wake up, but while you're saying it you're into it, you believe it. This isn't like that. He feels like a handpuppet with someone working his mouth and his voicebox and the expressions on his face.

"So what was their pitch? What'd they want from you?"

"Fuck if I could make it out, man! All their gobbledygook. I mean this thing here, do *you* get what it's saying? But it was spooky, I'll tellya that. All these guys in suits, and that creepy old man, all these white tablecloths an' shitty food, and a band playing and all these people dancing this old-timey dancing. I stayed with the punch and got hammered. I do remember leavin, though. This guy, like the biker from hell, man, he came to my table an' asked if I was going to join the team. Now I was toasted, but there was this weird vibe about the whole thing, Jack. I *sensed* it, an' I didn't want any part of it, you know? So I told him no thanks. An he said, well, no hard feelings, but you can't stay any more, the door's over there. So I strapped my legs on an' booked. I wasn't walking too straight, but I found that door. Woke up in the park next morning. I mean, what *is* this shit about? *Immortal retinue*—what's that *mean?*"

"You got me, Ray. I can't figure it out either."

"So did they invite you to a banquet?"

"Matter of fact they did."

"Well, if you go, eat beforehand. Their punch is primo, but their cookin sucks."

Jack nods thoughtfully. "You're kinda nursing that beer. You want another bump and back? I'm gonna split."

"Well hey, thanks, Jack."

"G'night Jack," Rick says. And to Ron, setting him up, says, "You gotta drink an' run, man. Closin time."

To this, Ron doesn't answer. Sips his bourbon. Sips his beer. Rick stacks the last of his glasses and after a few minutes says, "Come on, man, I'm beat here. Throw it back an' walk, wouldja?"

"Sure, Rick. Say, could you break this twenty for me?" He stands up and reaches into his pocket, as if he's got something in there. When Rick comes over to him, Ray shoots out both hands, seizes Rick's head, and with one sharp wrench snaps his neck. Then he vaults over the bar, tucking Rick down out of sight, and starts examining the bottles.

He selects a full quart of Smirnoff's hundred-and-one proof, uncaps it, and begins to chug it down.

Ron no longer has even a shred of hope that this is a dream. That booze is too real, spine-freezingly real. He chugs the whole quart, straight to empty, and though it nearly suffocates him to go so long without breathing, this doesn't seem to faze whoever is working his arm and his throat. He drops the empty bottle and, even as he stands gasping for air, his hands are calmly selecting another quart of the same fine product. He uncaps this, sockets it in his lips, tilts it up, and starts chugging away again.

Again, as his chest heaves for air, the freezing fluid chuckles down his slavishly laboring throat. The muscles in his legs are growing numb. When he drops the second empty, his gut roils and heaves to chuck it all back up, but the peristaltic muscles refuse to budge.

His legs are going dead beneath him, and he dimly discovers that it's something *inside* them that is holding him vertical, something alien at the core of his numbed-out, fading arms that keeps them moving, reaching for a third bottle, breaking its seal, tilting it up. Not a dream at all, he knows as he hoists and chugs. He is a bubble of terror in a cold caustic river of booze, his body itself a bottle now, as inflexibly upright as glass, rigidly retaining its quart and a half of pure ethanol. His eyes move helplessly to the Budweiser clock on the wall. When the minute hand joins the hour hand on the two, he begins to go blind.

He feels something leave him then, an almost impalpable bigness sprouting from his trunk and limbs. In the growing dimness a complex shadow molts off his collapsing, toppling shape. Sharp multiple feet rattle briefly across the floor, receding. Now Ray is slumped across Rick's corpse. No vomiting now. His spinal cord is frozen. His heart stops beating.

XXII
Knock, and the Door Shall Be Opened

Fresh and hot from the laundromat across the street," Skip says, wakening the girls in a sun-drenched little bedroom. He sets down the basket of their clothes. They rise and dress in warm laundry. "You go downstairs, dear," Skip tells Aarti. "Your cocoa an' donuts are set out for you. Britt'ny an' I will be right down."

Skip hands Britt her laundered street-coat. "I put everything from your pockets on this table here." Stands smiling at her with luminous eyes. Britt's glance darts guiltily to her baggie of pills, but it's the revolver Skip touches. "You won't need this today, Brittany. It's not the right kind of weapon for what you'll have to fight." Now he does touch the pills. "An what about these, dear? Should I get rid of them for you?"

"Yes." Her heart is still racing from the words *weapon* and *fight*—they make her cowardly part want to snatch back the pills. But Skip's face, so delicately carved, strikes her like a new idea she can't quite get her mind around. His beauty feels like an invitation to her stronger part. "Yes," she says more firmly.

They have their breakfast at a window table. Out the window, the sunlight falls like honey on the streets and buildings. The sky is an aching, absolute blue, except to the east there, where a dark bar of storm-wrack transects the horizon.

"Light!" Skip says. "It's everything." He stirs his coffee, pinches off a crumb of golden donut, and sprinkles it in. The gold crumbs tumble melting into the slow black swirl. There is a small, amazing beauty in those melting golden crumbs, so poignant it gives Britt a lump in her throat and tears in her eyes. The tears seem to blind her, for when she looks up at Skip, he's not there at all.

But she blinks, and there he is, smiling. "There's a billion billion stars, pumpin out light in all directions, like music. And light is immortal, see? It thins out through the dark, but not one spark of it ever dies. Whatever it touches it bounces back off and goes on. All the light you get, and use, you're giving right back to everything around you, and everything around you is givin it back to you. *Time without end.* An you two sweeties are *brim*-ful of light!

"Now *you*"—he pinches Aarti's cheek—"you're going to stay right here today where you're nice an' safe. Help me keep shop."

"You don't seem to have any customers."

"I never do, sweetie, but we'll have fun. Meanwhile Britt'ny's going to see your mom an' dad."

"But I—"

"Tell her, Britt'ny, that you *have* to do it."

Her heart starts racing. She's been cornered. "I *will* help them, honey. You remember . . . what you said about angels?" She turns her eyes to Skip, whose face, in just that moment, seems sad and forgetful. But he smiles when he strokes Aarti's shoulder. "Just relax here till I come back."

Out on the sidewalk, Skip is unhurried and seems to be listening or looking for something as they walk. "Looks like a little storm comin," he says. Half the sky above the Bay is roofed by stormcloud. The distinctness of the front gives it an aura of portent, the declaration of some mighty will. Sharp gusts of wind barge down these still sun-drenched streets, flaring people's shirts, tugging their hair. "Oh, good," says Skip, responding to something Britt has missed. "It's over here."

Down a deserted side-street, he brings them to an alley of dumpsters.

Three derelicts are nested on a litter of cardboard against the wall. Only one seems awake, sitting with his back to the bricks. He looks up dazedly at Skip. He wears broken boots and dun-colored rags. His slack jaw shows a wide gap in his lower teeth.

"Listen to me," Skip tells him. "Your death has found you. But I can help you save your life."

"How?" There is a note of irony in the croaked question.

"You're sitting on a weapon right now. Stand up and we'll find it."

The man nods thoughtfully. Clears his throat. "Death's coming. If I sit here, it'll find me."

"That's right."

"So what's the problem?"

Skip nods understandingly. "Will you let *us* find the weapon?"

"Happy to help." He struggles to his feet, a big man once, but now just big bones. He presents them his litter-bed with a woozy bow. Skip begins peeling away cardboard and newspaper.

"What are we looking for?" asks Britt.

"I'll know when I find it, dear."

Almost down to the asphalt, amid wood scraps and sheetrock shards, Skip's hands seize something. "Here it is," he says. It's a foot-long piece of thick pipe with a rust-clogged elbow-joint on one end of it. "Try it. Feel the weight of it."

Britt grips it and flexes her wrist. Dense mass. The thought comes to her, like a whisper in her ear, that it could splinter a door with a good swing. She begins to grasp what is expected of her. A cold gust of wind shoulders them, and the light turns gray. The cloud-wrack has slid across the Castro.

They replace the cardboard bed, and the man lies back down. Skip ushers Britt along the street a ways and stops. A chill spatter of rain blows across them. "Take it an' grip it like you're going to use it. Good. Now when you're at the door, *before* you break it in, you take *this* out." Skip digs into his pocket. Magic talismans leap to Britt's mind—cloaks of invisibility, impenetrable shields.

Skip produces an almost used-up roll of duct tape. "You grip your weapon like that, an' you tape your fist to it tight as you can. Whatever happens, don't lose your weapon."

"But what am I—?"

"You just bear down, tighten up, and fight your way all the way *in* there. Then I'll help you know what to bring back out."

"But what—?"

An icy rain comes crashing down. Skip reaches out and touches her cheek. "Do it, girl. Go right now, an' do it."

Britt heads for the Mission. The pipe in her coat knocks her thigh, and the rain drenches her head. She takes out a bandana and binds her head in thinking not of the rain but of a struggle ahead. And like the rain, reality pounds her. She is ridiculous. She's a skulking street-rat. Why did she give up her fucking pills? Why is she walking *toward* the *Hyperion*?

Every street she turns down seems emptier than the last, as if the rain is washing mankind away. The hissing cars grow scarcer, and the few pedestrians she sees are just vanishing around corners a block away. The rain's cold, skinny fingers slip through her collar and down her back.

Here's Valencia, and there's the Hyperion, that ugly snake-box, right across the street. Amazingly, Valencia is empty as far as she can see in both directions through the clattering spray of the rain. But just as she angles across, one lone cab comes cruising past, driven by a slick-haired man with an oily black fore-tuft. He gives her a wink.

She freezes mid-street . . . and two heartbeats later advances in rage. She thumbs the Hyperion's bell like an assailant's eye.

Yet her feet slow as she climbs the stairs. The air in here is thick as some vile molasses with dread.

It's Elmer in the cage. It once occurred to Britt that he was less blind than he looked, that maybe he could sense what else inhabited this building. Though she holds his gaze as she goes to the door of the Patels' apartment, she cannot speak to him, feels light-years away.

Confronted, that door fills her with more than terror. Her own ugliness and deformity stun her. She's no avenger. She's a stunted skulker, a bush-rat, a pillhead. Behind this door is what has done this to her, has stunted her into this creep's shape.

She pulls the tape with her teeth, and it shrieks off the roll. She binds her hand to the butt of her steel club . . . And *smites* the door . . . and *again* . . . and *again*—each time with more perfect wrath, and with more of her tough, street-lean little body behind it. The heavy wood cracks, cries out in pain . . . until it stands ajar, splintered round the lock.

Britt grips the knob with her left hand. It is searingly cold, and her fingers freeze to it. The knob twists itself and the door hauls her inside so powerfully she is dragged off her feet, is pitched into darkness, and is falling, black void beneath her, how deep?—and is impacting knees and elbows and ribs against concrete as she tumbles and comes, bruised, to rest on all fours in a fog-wet alley.

She stands. Far behind her sounds the boom of a closing door, but it makes no sense here, because there is nothing here but trash-littered alley. The fog is tendrilling round a streetlamp whose light falls just ahead of Britt, falls across Britt's girlhood bed. There's her old bed there, next to a brick wall. Right above her bed there's a window in the wall, and looking out of it, his elbows on the sill, is good old Unka Doug.

Unka Doug is out of costume tonight. No jammies and tiny cowboy hat. Instead, a foul stained undershirt, and for headgear the top half of a wolf's head. His greasy black forelock juts below the fangs, just where the beast's tongue would be. He's grinning and sticking his own tongue out at Britt, though it's far too fat, too white for a man's tongue, is a maggot as big as a cucumber, twisting and questing, its tiny black jaws nibbling air.

It's not Britt herself who raises the pipe, not exactly. But when the pipe hoists itself, her will pours into it, her heart exults, and it's Britt herself who leaps up onto the bed, pipe high for the first killing sweep—

And plunges straight into darkness and emptiness. She is falling, falling blind. She hugs her sanity tight, draws her knees to her chest, tucks her head . . .

And crashes onto her side, is tumbling down an incline, still in darkness but still armed, retaining both her weapon and her will to use it.

She comes to rest. Shakily stands. At last she's in an apartment, or in its dim-lit hall. But it's a hall far too wide, too high-ceilinged, and the gloomy living room at its end is much too distant. She's suddenly half-sized, her stature shrunk to a little girl's. From the living room, where she sees a curtained window and a couch, odors come wafting: dust, a dirty-kitchen smell of grease, a frighteningly strong menstrual whiff, and an Arctic tang, a scent of ice and stone. It takes all her strength not to turn and run. Then she finds a bit more, and advances a step . . .

And is in the apartment itself, much too suddenly. She stands before the couch and understands that smell of spoiled blood. The couch is one black crust of blood, and more blood blackly crusts the carpet at her feet. She lifts her gaze, and hallucination ripples through the room. The walls show skeletal patches of studs with starred black gulfs between, the ceiling here and there a tomb-roof of soil and veined stone. . . .

She fixes her eye on none of this, knows these terrors for a prelude on-ly. She waits for the thing she will have to fight.

A delicate, stealthing sound. . . . It's a light, scratchy noise like dry grass disturbed. Her eyes are drawn to the doorless frame that opens into the kitchen. On the dirty linoleum in there she can see two big black trashbags, bulgingly full, with something yellow hanging like a tongue from the mouth of one of them.

Again there comes that scratchy stir. It does come from the kitchen, but not from its floor. From the kitchen ceiling.

Britt brandishes her weapon. "Come on," she says softly.

Scuttle-scritch, scuttle-scritch—it has crossed the kitchen ceiling and paused just within the door frame.

And from under the top of the frame, two slender somethings sprout, frail things tickling the air. Black jointed twigs. Antennae.

With a scramble it pours past the frame and onto the living-room ceil-ing, human arms first, bug-body after, the upside-down face man-eyed but jawed with barbed sickles that click twice before it launches, diving down on her.

Her foot slips in the blood-crust as she swings her pipe to meet it. Her fall lowers the weapon's arc so that the pipe nests with a crunching smack between the jaws that were aimed at her midriff. Her attacker, near twice her size, falls into convulsions atop her, and it tears her with the kick of its tarsal claws. She is striking, clubbing, feeling a wet crunch greet her blows, feeling cold ichor spatter from wounds. Scrambling in slickness, she throws her weight on the heaving abdomen and hammers. Her blows find bug-legs that snap. Her blows find the head, and find it again. . . .

Too spent to strike again, she stands and staggers back.

Both its jaws are broken, one of its eyes a jellied hole. It drags itself in a helpless circle, seeking only escape.

Then there is speech in her mind, intruding thoughts.

"It can't die. It can't hunt. Eternal hunger for it now. Let it go."

The monster falls still at these words and turns its single eye to her, an infinitely sad brown eye. Aarti's father's. That eye delivers to hers an unutterable message of grief and regret. Then the monster thrusts its hands through the carpet, the floorboards, and pulls and tears a great hole in the carpentry, diving into an under-darkness all spangled with stars. She stands by the small chasm, which gives of a breath of interstellar cold, and is given further thoughts, to which she says, "I will."

She untapes her club, pockets it, opens her Buck.

In the kitchen, she lifts the yellow dangler from one of the swollen trashbags. It is the bloodstained sleeve of a nightgown. She slices off this sleeve and pockets it. She takes hold of the first bag, her eyes flinching from its contents, and gathers its mouth into a hasty knot. What a sodden weight it has! It juts with a jumble of protrusions that prod her ankles as she drags it across the living room. She is too terrified to shed the tears she feels. She drags the black weight of sorrow to that starry hole and drops it through, and goes back for the second one and drops it after.

The hallway is quite small, actually. Here is the broken front door not three steps away. . . .

Just a few steps out the door and she is at the head of the stairs. She turns a searching look to Elmer, watching her through the bars just as she left him. Is it grief or joy she sees there in the coarse, runnelled mask of age, in the bleared, tumescent eyes?

She plunges down, eager for the open air. Bursts out the street-door, finds the rain still pounding down, but the streets are all full of splashy traffic. Ah, this freshness! She has fought! She has spilled the inhuman blood of the enemy!

XXIII
Stepping Out

Razz is listening to some rap as he drives his Caddy down to meet Cozzens at the Skyscraper Bar. Cozzens has cash for him, but that won't make sitting down with the big goon any easier. The rain dribbling through his bullet-holed roof seriously chaps his ass. And he's not sure what rap station he's stumbled on, but this is starting to sound like some whacked-*out* group. He turns up the volume. What are they *saying?*

> *Arise and advance! To the banquet unending you're bidden on soul fire to dine!*
> *Oh, you god-summoned vagabond, no longer doomed to end sod-cumbered rag-and-bone, taste of this wine!*
> *The stars are our lanterns, while plenteous skulls furnish flagons abrim with the blood of our kine!*

Later for this shit. He kills the sound, but then he can once again hear the rain dripping on his upholstery. That whacked-out pillhead bitch! *Brandy's* the one he'd really like to snuff. But he's got to stay cool, got to be frosty to meet Cozzens.

What he hates about Cozzens is how the goon's eyes are always laughing about something he's not putting on the table between you. And the way he jumped on the idea of this snuff flick—Razz's inspiration. It's jerked Razz much farther ahead than he was ready to *be* with the project. Once DeeAnn let him know she'd banged Jack, Razz floated the idea to his two colleagues, basically just to impress them, promote a little backup against that asshole Jack. The next *day* they're telling him this connection of theirs wants to bankroll the flick.

They all met in Bone's crib where Razz, as soon as he laid eyes on this Cozzens, wanted nothing to do with him, but where was the room to back out? Goon put 2K each in their hands! "Security deposit." Got Bone and Trini seriously behind the project. Razz was just on the phone to him, and the goon said the pair of them were down the peninsula right now picking up the cams and lights and sound equipment. And *tonight* they're all going to meet at some hall and shoot the flick, and cap his ho DeeAnn's ass! Like a mark, is how Razz feels, and his leaking roof seems to emphasize it. Like he's the chump getting swindled out of his property, one of the best moneymakers in the hood. He's going to make 10K, but what about the future of his business?

The Skyscraper Bar is a gloomy little place. Two old farts, the bartender a third, are at the TV end of the bar watching a fight. Cozzens is the only other patron, a mass of deeper shadow filling half of a corner booth. Razz can make out, between the huge leather shoulders and the wild black hair, only a pale slice of cheekbones and forehead, and the glints of eyes. The giant cries jovially, "Innkeeper! Crank up the volume, and a JD and water back for my bud here!"

The old fart in his paunchy apron is quick to obey. Pumped up, the ringside voiceover is as frenetic as the punches the two Latin lightweights are trading. Razz slides into the booth, feeling like he's slipping into the Black Lagoon with the Creature.

The bartender brings the drinks and Cozzens fans him three fifties. "For yourself and your friends there. Hope that's not too loud for you."

"No! Thanks."

"Erasmus-Matasmus," growls the biker. "This *is* a pleasure."

How does the guy know Razz's name? *Erasmus.* Gramma hung that on him, Gramma a schoolteacher, his only parent, the righteous tyrant of his boyhood. Hissed from this white animal's mouth (there seems to be something not quite right with his teeth), the name hits Razz surprisingly hard, seems to knock him back into that undersized fourteen-year-old crack-clocker he once was, so desperate to loom larger on the streets of Hunter's Point, who finally cut his rep—on a Friday night down along

Third Street—by capping some random bitch in the head from the window of Jamal Jones's old yellow Mustang. But from that night on, he cribbed with homies, never stayed another night at Gramma's, her and her *humanists*. He called her, just once, a few years later, told her he'd grown up, was a *humanist* now, into *human resources,* and hung up on her.

And now, this goon Cozzens is calling him Erasmus and steering him toward a kill that he doesn't really *want* to do, and holding out . . . more cash! Razz counts ten thousand-dollar bills! The money looks gaudy, magical.

Cozzens leans closer. "Another ten K tonight after the shoot. Give her what you want of this to get her motivation up. 'S all yours in the end." The man is like a beast. His eyes blaze. His hair and beard, so wild, seem to merge with the surrounding shadow like smoke. There are these like bruises . . . two, three of them on his face. Razz realizes what they are, and the man sees him realize it.

"You trippin on my lesions? I don't mind. They say a leopard can't change his spots? Two days ago I had five of these suckers, all bigger. Whaddya think that means, Chief?"

"I dunno, man." This animal is too close. Leaves no room around him to breathe in, to turn and run . . . not that Razz really wants to run. A total of eighteen K in his hand tonight. So the guy's a deep-end wacko, is dying—who else would risk making snuff flicks?

"Here's one thing that it means, Ace. It means is my backer is Big League." (There *is* something wrong with his teeth: they're *sharp*.) "Now Bone and Trini are bad, and I am way badder than both of them together. But if you back out now, forget about *us,* because my backer is truly One With Whom You Do Not Fuck. But hey! I know you'll show tonight, so 'nuff said! Now look here. I believe skag's your bag? Well, you never had it like this. Uncut, so be reeel careful! Just a smidgin!"

Razz feels a glow of illumination from the snow-white bindle Coz lays in his hand. He doesn't like strangers knowing he enjoys a bit of smack. People start labeling you a junkie. But *this* bindle . . . this bindle whispers hallelujah to his palm.

"I'm outta here, Ace. You wouldn't believe the details a producer-director's gotta deal with!"

"I just need to axe you—what about Jack Hale?"

"We had a party set up for him last night, but then we had a better idea. We invited him to the shoot. He thinks he's gonna be one of the stars—an he *is*."

At the door of his room, Razz faces the hardest thing he has to do: spending the rest of the day with DeeAnn, knowing what's coming and hiding it from her. She's very sharp about finding things out from him. But she's been on a long run, so maybe she's sacked out and catching up like she does every three days or so—sacked out at least until dark.

He enters the room with endless precaution against noise.

Praise Jesus, as Gramma would say. She's sprawled naked on the bed, snoring.

Quiet as smoke, Razz settles in the armchair and assembles the paraphernalia of peace. Spoon, lighter, spike. He doesn't need to tie off, is proud of his tight muscles and good snaky veins—what real junkie would have veins like this? Is some slick exec sipping brandy in his penthouse an alcoholic?

When it hits the mainline, he slumps back, filled with awe. *Whoa!* It's like the ink from those squids in nature flicks, but snow-white ink, pure light billowing through his brain. He hasn't pulled the spike out yet—who cares? Time for that, all the time in the world. He studies DeeAnn.

Predictably, she's showered just before crashing, her hair in damp spikes on the back of her neck . . . Line her out when she wakes up, bullshit her a couple hours, then at the hall he'll have help with her. She's easy to manage, really. A little sweet talk, a little anger, a little bullshit. Easy to manage because she *wants* to be used, be used up. Bone has it right: she wants out of herself. Someone with no respect for themself is dead already. Look at all the time and work he's put in to looking out for her, *showing* her respect, trying to *teach* her respect for herself. He's done what he can, but it hasn't worked. She's still just a whore . . .

As good as admitted she free-fucked Jack Hale.

Last night, after drinking with Ron, Jack found a seat in the Terminal Building and dozed out the small hours, hearing, whenever he started awake, the comforting echo of buses braking or groaning out the echoey ramps.

And while he rested there, reassured by his perch at the City's exit, feeling but one step away from complete escape, he sifted again these last few days of marvels and terrors in his mind, reconstructing the details, trying to hold the nightmares up to the light . . . until once again he dozed.

At 9 A.M. he left the building and walked to his bank. Came back to his seat in the Terminal with 16K in his pocket. He sat more securely then. Had some more sleep. Went for a wash-up in the restroom. Sat back down and consumed coffee and a donut amid the echoes and the bustle.

Then slept again.

He's awakened by a change of the light pouring in the big Terminal window. A rainstorm is sliding across the sky. Headlights come on in the dimness brought on by the downpour. Headlights come on. Rush hour's not far off, and the city is alive with traffic.

Jack has weighed his situation and finds he is hopeful. His recent visions loom no less wild, his recent acts no less insane. But the limits of his present danger have grown clearer. Coz can't rat him on a killing that bloodied the goon's own hands. He manufactured that whole nightmare in the basement for leverage to force Jack to the banquet. Jack's present danger lies at the Sons of Holland Hall. And there, tonight, Cannyharme is going to be playing for Jack's *mind.*

And if Jack has learned anything, it's that the old fiend can break his mind if Jack lets him. The powers of hallucination the old dog commands are awesome and fully deserve the name of sorcery, whatever strange pharmacology lies behind them. . . .

But the biker hasn't lied. Once Jack's *seen,* the choice will be his.

Cannyharme insists that his converts choose, for with that choice, he *has* their minds. Poor Ron Ratchett had too little left to be made captive—it seemed they'd had better luck with simple, sober Peter McM. But good old Jack Hale, professional imaginer, is different meat. They've *had* him. Twice they've stripped the walls off his world and hung him in the void.

But now he knows, and as an imaginer, he is better armed. Nothing will pass his lips or nostrils while he is at that banquet.

He is calm and watches the beautiful turmoil of the city's rush-hour. The rain tapers down, sunset bleeds through a narrow seam in the west, and the cloud-wrack is underlit, a wild and wooly upside-down landscape hustling along on the wind. The traffic, like scoured gems, rivers between walls of windows flashing orange and gold.

The world's beauty has brought him clarity and resolution. Better than resolution, excitement. Whatever means they're using on him, his adversaries are sorcerers of ingenuity, and this scam of theirs *is,* in its intricacy, a kind of miracle. He has to face their finale, if only to redeem the dupe's part he has played thus far. He dare not underestimate them. Whatever they deploy will test his senses and his wits to their limits. But if he doesn't face their test, he will never be completely his own man again. They've foxed him into *killing.* If he flees them unfaced, just leaves them that victory, he leaves them with himself. He gets up and sets out for a walk.

Out on the sidewalks, his excitement grows. Erika is gone forever. It's all so starkly, sadly plain now. Was gone two years ago. He finds that the Jack who clung to her love has been flayed off him. He's a harder, wiser man who sees that safety may be gone forever from his life. Sees that he now has to face the intricate work of finding a wiser path, to a realer goal. Skinned is how he feels, and wearing now a fresher skin he can feel the world with. Exulting in the shove of the wind, Jack feels he could ride it all over the world, feather-light, like an indestructible tumbleweed, an untethered spirit. The poets are right. Freedom *is* having nothing to lose. And therefore, everything to gain.

And whatever else comes out of the Banquet, think of the fucking *story* he'll have!

He begins trending west. There's time enough he can meander his way to the Avenues, arrive keen and fresh, wind-sharpened.

As he's waiting for the light to cross Valencia, he sees Bettina, Karl Cabron, and Rich Rasp standing in front of the Hyperion, all looking right at him. He waves. They return the salute absently, staring at him.

The rain grows gusty, becomes more wind than water. He feels he could walk like this forever, through a world of endless luster. . . .

He's going through the Castro. He passes the boarded-up window of a defunct shop. The plywood flutters with the tatters of posters and stickers, and his eye is caught by an intact sheet of typescript, stapled all around its rim. He leans to scan it, and then settles to read it, and then reads it again.

Harm-hound, whose throat is a smoking tomb! Whose icy eyes are scythes that mow down souls! Harm-hound whose greed is forever, and forever after! . . .

Harm-hound. Cannyharme. Something from Joyce crosses Jack's mind . . . that God is a shout in the streets. The amazement is not that this city is so full of desperate, isolated, hallucinating souls, but that the old villain has recruited so many of them to his monstrous church!

"You noticed that poem too?" Jack starts. At his side there's a small, graceful black guy in a loud Hawaiian shirt, a basket of laundry under one arm. "It gives me the chills."

"It is creepy," Jack says. "And the writing's not bad. The guy writes like Ginsberg."

"Yes. That one of his about Moloch . . ." The little man has a sweet alto voice, a bit sad. "You know the part that creeps me? I don't know why. These lines right here."

Jack leans close and re-reads them.

Sly, social-climbing cur! Your crooked bite on bone and your grin of greed were all the speech there was from your jackal-face then! How is it you've licked and slavered your way—clod-nosing hustler, all dead meat's minion with the hanging tongue!—how is it you've nosed your way up from the bonevaults? How is it you've managed to plunder the godly arsenal of speech?

When Jack turns from the page, the guy is gone—is already across the street, stepping into that laundromat.

There *is* a chill to these lines. They call to his mind, for no reason he can discover, that moment he opened Cannyharme's door and saw, for just an instant, that strange bare room with the gappy walls and endless night outside them. . . .

So. What next? Before he gets to the Banquet, will he meet some guy in a sandwich sign with a new poem on it in twenty-point type? If he's sinking to hell, it's definitely to a poet's Inferno. It's damn well where he should be. It's the Carnival. He's got a party to go to.

The wind feels full of danger, and of promise.

Skip comes upstairs with Britt's newly washed coat and jeans. The girls lie on the bed. Full of donuts and cocoa, the girls have been told to take a nap. They are talking softly, but not far from dozing off. "Aarti," Skip says, "I want you to push back your sleeve, hold your arm out, an' close your eyes. I want to try something on you, but you have to promise not to peek."

"OK."

When the child's bared arm is extended, Skip takes something from his pocket—the bloodstained scrap of sleeve Britt has brought back. He slips the fragment on the slender forearm. The girl smiles and shivers. The sleeve melts into her skin and is gone. Aarti's eyes fly open, startled. She looks at her arm, brings her hand up wonderingly to her face, touches her cheek in the cherishing way a mother would stroke her child. Shivers at her own touch and tears jump from her eyes.

Skip wraps his arms around her. "You mom's OK now, sweetie. She's with you now, and she'll always be in you, loving you, and you'll always remember her."

The girl weeps against his rainbow chest.

XXIV
Arise and Advance! To the Banquet Unending You're Bidden

Full dark, with the clouds blown ragged by a rising wind. Gullies and canyons of stars peek from black chasms. Cozzens, his empty bus overarching the City on 101, savors this view.

"Thought you'd steal all this from me, eh Worm?" he bellows, grinning. He's talking to his AIDS. He circles thumb and forefinger, and gives a painful flick of his fingernail to one of the dwindling lesions on his brow. "Eh?" Happiness is like a hungry lion in his heart, rearing up roaring. He will eat this windy sky, this City. He will gorge on it in an endless feast of light and air.

Engines, wheels, he loves them in every form. He delights in this jouncy crate of a bus he is driving. It is World War II vintage, wearing a faded old coat of schoolbus yellow, with *Sons of Holland Society* black-lettered on both sides. Cozzens finds it hilarious to be shambling down the streets in this big rattling eyesore. Amazing what this world full of fools can stare at, rolling right down their streets, and not see. The gods themselves, bigger than shit, can pull right up to peoples' houses, like the trash truck—can toss these morons right in the compactor while they all stand staring, not seeing a thing!

But Cozzens has seen, for as long as he can remember. He has always known that if you want to keep your life, you've got to consume other lives, the only fuel that can keep that magic burning. Magic isn't stirred up from dried bats and powders. The only ju-ju that can feed it is the single miracle these fools have in them, their living souls. Cozzens lived so long thinking he alone knew, till at last he found Him. Thank you, Master! Oh, thank you!

But this is some heavy shit ahead of Cozzens now. The Joy is at hand, but he has to step through the Abyss to reach it. He's about to meet the Troops, hang with the Guys. He's going to have to face the eternity in their eyes.

He turns onto Sixteenth. His first pickup is just a mile off now, down along the bayside. He can handle this. To firm his nerve up, he tries to decide the hairiest thing he ever did—what took the most balls. It had to be walking into that motel room in Compton a few years back, carrying those sacks of groceries.

Two big bags of brewskis and snacks for the four armed guys waiting for him in the motel room. Four *edgy* armed guys who didn't trust him an inch, one with an AK, one with a sawed-off twelve-gauge (the same one Cozzens now owns), and all four with their pieces in their hands the second he opened the door.

He jollied the guy with the Beretta into taking the bags, and as he took them Cozzens extended the short-nose .357 that one bag had concealed and capped the AK guy in the face, at the same time yanking the guy who'd taken the bags between himself and the twelve-gauge's first wad of double-ought, and then capped the twelve-gauge guy—also in the face—over the bag-guy's shoulder, sending the twelve's second wad up into the ceiling, then turned as a nine-millimeter slug whisked his forehead and another snagged through his shirt and, dropping to his knees, capped the nine guy twice center-mass, and then stepped back from the bag guy, who was swaying with half his waist blown away but not yet technically dead, and capped him in the back of the head.

Whoosh! Four armed hard-rocks, four seconds, five slugs, and four guys so dead that not even a leg was twitching.

Cozzens can do this.

He crosses railroad tracks, rolls under the great Stonehenge of an overpass, and steers down the spur off Third that hooks past Mission

Rock Café and runs along weedy lots on the left, with derelict vehicles parked here and there, the Bay on the right, and rotting corpse-piers jutting out into it.

Any time now, as he crawls along in first, the bus itself will begin to teach him his pick-up route. He sits calm and chill. Out on those bony cadavers of piers, lone shapes here and there are perched, fishing, just as every poor mortal soul perches on the collapsing span of its life. Look up there—the mighty arc of the Bay Bridge, a star-hung colossus, mocks these mortal piers, little, collapsing bridges to nowhere except the black water.

"My feet are on the One Bridge!" roars Cozzens, unable, in his terror and his savage joy, to contain that bellowed triumph.

And in the next instant, the bus's wheel asserts its will against his hands and pulls them over to the weedy curb. With that one brute movement of the wheel, Cozzens feels his life mesh cogs with the machinery of immortality. Here we go. Stay frosty.

He scans the weedy lot for movement. Then detects a stir in a big faded tour bus sitting on four flats down along the curb. There is a slight vibration of the boxy chassis . . . then another more decided tremor . . . and then the door bursts open.

Nothing follows for several long heartbeats . . . until a rattle of small trash comes jouncing down the step-well: an empty sardine can, stained paper cups, a greasy slide of wrinkly newspapers. . . .

Next something big, a *mummy,* slides out. No—a rag-and-scarf-wrapped derelict still half inserted in a tattered sleeping bag. He hits the pavement and lies struggling in his envelope, as weak and dazed as a winter caterpillar.

Steady now, Cozzens. It's coming.

The wino rises straight in the air, does a lively kicking jig—shedding his bag, whipping scarves and old towels from around his shoulders—and stands poised there amid the sprawl of cast-off rags. He faces Cozzens's bus and bows. A deep, comic bow, though the wino's face is slack and uncomprehending, alarm just beginning to dawn there. He lifts one arm and cocks the other, in the posture of a man about to waltz . . .

And waltzes, advancing on the bus in stately three-step turns—invisible partner, mute music, but with grand ballroom style, he comes sweeping leftward, rightward . . .

And stands before the bus's open door, and bows again.

Now the moment is at hand. An Arctic cold whelms up the stepwell from this smeared and ragged figure. His face is a mask of disbelief and fear, but behind *his* eyes burn *other* eyes, merciless faceted gems. Those eyes' possessor moves his puppet up the steps.

The passenger pauses, shrouded in its own icy atmosphere, and looks down at Cozzens. The greedy glitter of his deeper eyes, scintillas of starlight, hang in a black abyss that he contains.

And Cozzens finds a voice to answer that look. Casually, "Hey, bro."

The wino's inner eyes grow fierce, then faint. The wino steps briskly to the back of the bus and takes a seat. It has begun.

The wheel gives a tug and, tardily, stunned Cozzens slips the brake and treads the gas. The bus wheels itself out and hums on down the desolate roadway.

The steering wheel is his commander now. He works the brake, and the gas, and the door.

A mile or so down they pull over behind a lone bag lady pushing a shopping cart. She straightens, turns, and waves. Wrestles her overcoat off a sweatered bulk too bent and stiff, it seems, to do what she does next—a full-out, elbow-pumping, butt-thrusting Funky Chicken, all the way to the bus door.

And when she looms near and shows Cozzens the eyes behind her eyes, he steps again into those abysses.

"All aboard, Ace."

Along Sixth, a near-dead she-junky, forearms like dirty sticks, stands on point when they pull up, does a series of classic ballet moves up into the bus. In the Castro, a big older drunk, gap-toothed, reaches behind himself, grabs his own belt and collar, and gives himself a bum's rush up the stepwell. Meeting each, Cozzens enters more boldly the wastelands of the eyes of his brothers-to-be. The Boys are having fun, as Boys will do. Cozzens, once he's across, will have fun too.

Another bag lady polkas up the curb on Duboce. Outside the projects near Valencia, a battered pillhead stands swaying beside an acned junky cholo—these two, in file, goosestep into the bus. As the girl passes him, Cozzens yields to a wild impulse—snags the pillhead's arm as her master turns her away, yanks her back, and 'fronts those eyes again. "Hey, bro," Cozzens growls, "Whaddya know? You get ready, Hoss, cause I *am* comin across, an' I'm gonna be the stud duck of the whole fuckin platoon!"

He sits braced, eye to eye, waiting for what the Immortal will do in retaliation.

Which is nothing. He simply turns his prey again and walks her to a seat.

Nothing. Except that when Cozzens hits the gas again, he is driving over the moon, the bus a windowless, motorless fossil floating like a recon ship just half a click above the lunar surface. His hands on the wheel are bleached white puzzles of carpals and phalanges. The only skin on his scoured skull is the absolute vacuum, as seas of dust and ragged anvils of stone slide under in absolute silence. The sunlight, a pure lethal blaze savaging a vast cinder and finding not a single atom left in it to burn, creates, in lieu of smoke, vast shadows black as ink and sharply edged as razors. Cozzens, always resolved to get first to the worst, struggles to spit out his terror in words of defiance. He has no tongue, of course. Even the clashing of his tombstoned jaws produces no sound.

His eyes, though—what a miracle they seem! His eyes are crystal seas that deepest space can't freeze, seas to sink the stars themselves in.

He has no air to flesh nor tongue to shape it with, so he thinks his defiance, shouting in his mind: "Fuck you! So what? It's a ride like no other. You scope it all, and the scoping never ends! Make room, because I *am* coming over."

His defiance breaks the spell. Flesh and noise and seething San Francisco surround him again. He calls out cheerfully over his shoulder, glancing up in the mirror at the shadowy troop that sit behind him. "Always gotta fuck with the new guy, right?"

At length the bus is almost full of dazed, immobile ragamuffins. Their possessors permit their faces no betrayal of their terror. Some, perhaps, accustomed to mental fugue, feel no alarm at this strange passage. The bus is deep in the Avenues, near the Hall, and Cozzens is surprised to feel it tug curbward for another pickup. A tall figure, striding along the sidewalk.

"Jack Hale!" shouts Cozzens as the door gasps open. "I'll be dipped in shit! Climb on. Come sit in front here with me!" He can see Jack is far from pleased, but the man climbs with a show of cheerfulness. Sitting, he scans the passengers with surprise. "So this is . . . this is an actual banquet we're going to? A fancy dinner?"

"Fit for the gods, Chief. A tastebud orgy. And gala too—a band, waiters, dancing! But the Sons of Holland aren't just about kicks! No! We have a social conscience too. Heart. The Banquet's an' outreach, right? To those less fortunate. We pick em up curbside, and at the Hall we sit em down for a nice hot meal!"

Jack nods skeptically. He's wary, but you can see he really has no inkling of who he's riding with. Pathetic—one of the many Born Blind. Sits at his typewriter thinking he's hot shit. And *He,* the old one, seems to think Hale *is* hot shit! Cozzens struggles bitterly with that. It galls him to envy a fool like Jack Hale.

But he grins. "Hey, Chief, look happy. *They're* ready to party—get with the program!"

DeeAnn, riding shotgun in the Caddy, devours a Marlboro as she watches the Park stream past. She's totally tricked out: black micro, tight white bodice, mascaraed and eyelashed like an houri, and her ticker is tricking happily along on the crystal she chopped for her brekkie when Razz woke her an hour ago.

Old Razz has a spoon or so in him, she judges. Look how he drives there, in his fully laid-back mode, his gunfighter hat cocked forward. Razz worries her tonight. It's not just that he's banged some smack. For some reason, tonight, she just doesn't trust him.

Her body's in top form, her professional ambitions are fully aroused by the 3K advance she's got tucked in her purse right now. She's ready to work.

But her smarts won't let go of her doubts. The advance itself is worrisome. When has Razz ever fronted her anything? Take his cut is all he's ever done. That's been just fine with her, of course—she loves treating her pretty manchild, buying his cute pimpclothes for him. She loves pampering him, tickling him out of his tantrums, and usually she trusts him. Trusts not his judgment or goodwill, but his predictability, the known limits of his mistreatment.

It's that sense of predictability that's missing from this little expedition. Razz could never dish out this much cash to her unless someone smarter than him had put it in his hand. Being a man, Razz's top priority is the swath he cuts among other men—she knows how he craves to loom large. He handed her the cash, ultra-cool, saying, "'S our advance from the dudes producing the flick."

The key question here, as DeeAnn sees it, is how *much* smarter than Razz these unknown dudes are. Because if you know how to manipulate Razz's pride, you can make him do almost anything and persuade him it's his own inspiration.

To do a multiple trick for a porn film, some reasonably sized daisy chain, DeeAnn's up for that, with the added 3K after the fact—finds it exciting even, putting all those moves on record for a bunch of strangers to beat off to. It would be cool, being celebrated by hundreds, even thousands of people she would never meet.

But to get tricked into some back room to pull a train, to get hit by a Mack truck of hostile men—that would be nowhere close to cool. From what she's heard, without a name, you can feature in a run-of-the-mill stiffener and maybe walk off with a couple K after the work is done. This larger, fronted money murmurs risk to her, hints a kinkier flick, where it's OK if the whore gets hurt.

With growing irritation she studies Razz's polished profile. Mr. Chill here, a knowing droop to his eyelids, one hand elegantly draped on the steering wheel. If she roughs up his ego a little she might shake something loose.

"So!" she says brightly. "How's that spoonful feel? You're just up to the eyebrows in cool, aren't you, sweetie? You must have banged a major wad of smack before you woke me up, hey?" And watches him, smiling, for his answer. She knows all Razz's G-spots for anger. She waits for whatever he's hiding under his blanket of skag to pop squawking out of him.

A couple slow beats and some definite twitching of Razz's lips there, but otherwise he's poised. "I mean, I know you're not a junkie *yet,* sweetie," DeeAnn tenderly persists, "but it *worries* me, all this smack you're banging lately. Somebody give it to you?"

Razz slowly smiles, but she knows she's scoring: his smile is crimped around the edges. But his answer is patience itself. "DeeAnn. Honey. You the bag callin the bindle black here. You take your own shit, but you hear me callin you tweak? We goin' to *party,* so we get partied up. You honk, I bang—what's the problem?"

"Well, there *is* a problem, sugar." Keeping her tone all lovey-dovey, planting a good one now. "It's about our whole partnership here, sweetie. You're my representative, my backup, that's what I pay you for, right?" She pauses, wanting this one to quiver in the bull's-eye a moment. They've had some major fights over this definition of their arrangement, him *work-ing* for her. But he impresses her. Just barely, he hangs onto the smile, gives his head a little world-weary shake. Silent and long-suffering.

"The problem is," she goes on, and her own anger is chafing now, her fluty tone getting harder to hold onto, "that I'm paying you to protect me, but if you set me up gigs when you're skagged to the gills, it might turn out those gigs aren't what we think they are. We might be hooking me up with some rough trade, see? And we don't want me to get hurt, right? I know we don't want that, right?"

Now Razz looks angry. "How can you even *think* that, DeeAnn? Don't you know I love you? Haven't I pr*ooo*ved my love to you a thousand times? You hurtin me here, girl. You *dissin* me! I don't deserve that kinda shit from you!"

DeeAnn is now *very* impressed. Razz does have, now and then, his genuine moments, and this could very well be one of them. But no. With Razz, she has perfect pitch for a false note, and he's just struck one. The Razz she knows, however stoned, would be far angrier at the crack that he worked for *her* than at the suggestion that he didn't have her best interests at heart. So this anger is faked.

So Razz is playing her now, is calculating all his reactions. Razz tonight is a Razz she hasn't met before.

OK. If she's right, then it's sad. It's creepy, but OK. She has her little .38 in her purse. She has her wits about her. If worse does come to worst, she knows how to dodge, how to run—and how to shoot, too.

"There it is, baby! Now does that look rough-trade to you?"

XXV
You Have Heard the Words:
You Know How It Is Done

T he Hall itself does not look upscale. It is a big old box of shabby
stucco with a little parking lot in front, where the only thing parked
is an old yellow bus. But brilliant light pours out of the wide-flung front
doors—light, and a lovely stream of suave jazz—and four white-coated
valets, or waiters, carnations in their buttonholes, flank the doorway, and
tip them a bow in unison as the Caddy pulls into the lot.

It's reassuring, even intriguing. DeeAnn gets no skulking, backroom
vibes from this display of elegance as they approach the door. The jazz is
the kind you hear in old movies, played by guys with oily little fingernail
moustaches. Beyond the valets you can see people dancing—a lot of people—on polished floors, amid a surround of white-draped tables. . . . One
of the valets steps forward to meet them, a skinny, dour-faced man with
vague, slightly elsewhere eyes and an aura of potent aftershave. He has a
very formal manner too. He sweeps one hand at the door, beckons them
with the other, and leads them up the steps.

Leads them into a warm, perfumey gust of music and voices, into a
large banquet hall full of a surprising number of people. Couples are dancing center-floor to a four-piece band perched up on a little bandstand. The
band too wear white coats and carnations and, yes, a slick little Thirties
stash on the sax guy. Other white-coats serve punch from a table with a
snowy tablecloth. The dining tables, just as whitely draped, form an L that
brackets two sides of the dance floor.

Their valet leads Razz and DeeAnn to the shorter leg of this L. Here the central table looms higher than all the others and is backed by a great fan or trellis of foliage and flowers. The occupant of that chair, toward whom they seem to be headed, seems to have his knees on his seat, because his whole upper body rests on the tabletop on his planted elbows.

"Hey," she tells Razz, "it's that old guy from upstairs! Mr. Cannyharme!"

Definitely him, but Mr. Cunningham looks very different tonight. His eyes are so sharp, following the dancers. His forward-thrust posture makes his jaw more pronounced. It's a *big* jaw he's got there—she hasn't noticed before because he's always so bent over. His smile is a wraparound grin. That's the most different thing about him, he's so delighted, so alive. Taking in the whole party, utterly enthused, leaning on the table as if he wants to launch himself out into the happy crowd. If he had a tail, he would be wagging it.

Though Razz tries to hide it, DeeAnn can see he's at least as surprised by this setup as she is. And indeed. What kind of porn could you shoot here?

The man brings them before Mr. Cunningham's table. He beams and nods at them and commands their valet with a look to take them across the dance floor to the punch table. The man leads them along the outskirts of the dancers. DeeAnn realizes half the dancers are street people. Nod-outs and burnouts and bag ladies! They're all dancing so well, she didn't notice at first. And they are all—hes and shes alike—partnered with well-dressed men. Well dressed and also *oddly* dressed here and there. Like that one in the bowtie and the old-fashioned suit, or that one wearing, what is that, an old-time smoking jacket?

She and Razz sip punch and watch the dancers. The punch is a rosy, ice-cold brew with an ethereal taste she can't identify, and it races her brain. Each sip is tastier than the last, and the dancers seem more comical by the moment.

"Is this, like, for *charity?*" she asks the guy ladling punch. He has black Thirties hair that shines as if it's painted on, and deep gaunt eyes that stare at her. "Charity," he says, seeming more to echo than to answer her.

It's really surprising that some of those derelicts can *move* like that, they're in such bent or bony shape. Razz, iced though he is, can't hide his disbelief. It tickles DeeAnn, though her own ass is involved here somehow, to see Mr. Cool so nakedly disoriented. . . .

Her eye snags on a familiar shape seated near the table of honor. "Hey, Razz, look. There's Jack Hale! And who's that big grizzly next to Mr. Cunningham? He's waving us over—you know him?"

Both Jack's and the stranger's presence seem to mean something to Razz—he looks a little less baffled. "He's like our cameraman," says Razz, leading them toward the beckoner. DeeAnn's getting uneasy. She's baffled, but reassured by Jack's being here. Him she trusts. But that other guy. Her quick eye for the flow of power among men has already told her that this huge, hairy figure is the bigger brain she suspected, the one running Razz and bankrolling him. The goon has those eyes that look at you and seem to be merry about something you've got no clue to. It's a look she watches out for in men. When you meet it, you get far away, fast. She wants to catch Jack's eye, but he hasn't seen her, is turned talking to two guys beside him.

Well, this is quaint, kindly old Mr. Cunningham's party. It's obvious—that fan of flowers behind him makes his high seat like a throne. How bad could things get with that old sweetie presiding?

Jack is fascinated. This whole scene is improbable, yet weirdly plausible too. A big fraternity prank from some early Forties movie. Say, fellas! It's time for Sigma Chi's hilarious annual Bum's Ball. We round up a bunch of hoboes, hire a hall, and set up a whole swank shindig, band and all!

All these men—and there are many mature ones among them—have the vigor of youth, and there's a prankish anachronism in the dress of some. When they bustled forward to greet the passengers that Cozzens was off-loading from the bus, merriment and irony were in their eyes. With what urbanity they greeted the smeared and tattered band! And the homeless chimed in on cue! Bag ladies curtseyed and simpered and took offered elbows. Gaunt winos returned manly hand-grips and shoulder-thwacks, displayed gapped grins, and ambled, chatting, up the steps. And now, look at them dance. The band sways dreamily rendering "It Had to Be You," the white-jackets tender trays of punch with courtly bows, and all the grimed vagabonds trip it on the light fantastic toe, the men like the women each partnered with a well-groomed host. Are these *real* street people? They all have the beat, have the moves. They could be extras in a movie.

Which of course they *are*. He's come braced for illusion. But what could be the *point* of this one?

He scans the festivity, this little machine of merriment they've set in motion. It surrounds him like a bubble of light and melody. And then . . . he begins to hear something *outside* the bubble. A massive something containing it, detected now and then through thin spots in the hubbub.

It's silence. An abyss of silence absolute, stretching for light-years in all directions. Utter silence is what this noisy bubble floats in.

He knew he would have fear to grapple with, and here it comes. His eyes go to Cannyharme. How the old villain kings it there, comfy in his doglike repose on planted elbows, freed of the toil of standing upright. His hoarfrost whiskers bristle and glow, and there's a bestial vigor in the jut of his jaw. His icy eyes are just drinking it all in—and shoot a look straight into Jack's. The old man winks and looks away.

We've seen what we've seen, eh Jack? says that wink.

Yes, we have. So bring it on, you crooked old con.

Cozzens, at Cannyharme's side, turns Jack a look. He lifts a hand and makes a drinking waggle, nodding to where a white-coat offers Jack a tray across his table. Jack smiles a demur, unpockets the flat of Jack Daniel's he picked up on his walk, and displays his preference for it. So much the better, if the con to come depends on Jack's ingesting anything at all of theirs tonight.

Two youngish banqueters approach the empty places to his left. They reach out their hands in turn. Their grips are powerful. Their smiles . . . have that touch of irony.

"John James."

"Jack Hale."

"Peter McMann."

"Pleased to meet you."

John takes the seat next to his, a trim guy in white shirt and slacks with a moderate Jewish 'fro. He has an ascetic, educated look. Peter is a bony-faced redhead, hair in a peckerwood DA, wearing a sport shirt with racecars on it. Despite his backwoods face, his greeting is as smooth as John's. Jack has the feeling he's met these guys. . . .

Then the connection dawns. Johnny Baby. Peter McM.

Of course! These two are good, dressed in character for the Fifties, the Seventies, even their faces just right somehow.

"A wonderful party, isn't it?" offers John. "Just look at them dance."

"Yes," says Jack. "You boys really know how to cut a rug." Giving the man some of his irony back. John looks at him blandly. "You know, John," Jack adds playfully, "I've got this hunch that you're a writer. I'm one myself, so call it my writer's intuition."

"I know you're a writer." He smiles. "I think your first romance shows exceptional talent. And your talent is greatly admired around here, Jack."

"I appreciate it. But what about you? Do you like to write *letters,* for instance?"

"It's been a long time since I've written a letter." John's smile is merely polite, but something hidden in his eyes seems to take a secret pleasure in Jack's question. "It's funny how you can just get out of the habit."

Peter leans forward. "I always hated writing of any kind, Jack. It was such hard work for me." Again his urbane smile is dissonant with his rube looks.

"I must insist, though," urges John, "that your talent is prized very highly here. Your way with words is *particularly* prized."

The band, concluding "Face the Music and Dance," is rising to a bright crescendo. John rises from his seat. "Excuse me, gentlemen. That's my cue."

He takes his position at the microphone. The old man tilts him a grin and a nod, and John begins to adjust the mike. The band hits a high closing note, and the dancers swirl to a stop with a final flourish of bag-lady coattails and swinging neckties.

And there again, in the instant before his voice takes over from the music, is that enormous silence around them all. . . .

John booms, "Welcome, dear friends, to the Sons of Holland Banquet! Once again we join for fellowship and festivity, for communion and conviviality, to renew and reaffirm the noble principles that we cherish in common, to do honor to our beloved Founder—"

A gesture here at Mr. Cannyharme, and a roar from the assembly so decided that it seems to come from a single throat.

"—our most righteous and revered Founder, and to do honor as well to the new members who tonight make entry into our ancient ranks!"

Another roar and a thunder of palms. Those already seated along the L of tables rise in their places to join the applause.

"Thank you, my friends! And now we come to a special moment, one that gives us all such a special pleasure." John's voice is the consummate Banquet Speaker's, a ringmaster's melodrama, a toastmaster's aplomb, but there's a fundamental coldness to it too, and between each syllable there echoes that silence. "Please put your hands together once again and join me in welcoming our newcomers to the Hall, all our invited guests for the evening!"

More thunder. Out on the dance floor men are bowing to their derelict partners. Before the hubbub has died the band strikes up a gliding, ironic rendition of "Jeepers Creepers," which provides a sly, mellow background to John's last announcement.

"At this juncture, we are going to ask those honored guests of ours to take this opportunity to freshen up for our banquet repast. The guest facilities are just through those doors, past the kitchen. Allow us now to escort you to where we can remove your wraps, spruce you up, and prepare you for a truly lovely meal!"

The punch table has been carried off through the double doors into the kitchen, and white-jackets flank these same doors, bowing the derelicts through The band pumps on, and the members out on the floor spread to fill its vacancy. All stand talking with great animation, setting up a real party roar.

"Hey, Chief, found a friend of yours here." Cozzens stands at Jack's side, presenting DeeAnn. "She can take Peter's chair; he needs to be near the mike anyway. And her date, E*ra*smus, is sittin with me. Sit down, my dear."

When she's done so, Cozzens presses a wad of bills into her hand. "Lemme put you in the picture, honey. You're not working tonight, not at all. That's three K—just pocket it, enjoy your dinner, and thanks for coming. See, we had to fool Razz a bit, a friendly deception. He doesn't know this is a surprise party for *him,* get it? Just leave your man to us—he's in good hands. Say, Pete—you mind snakin these folks a drink and introducing them around a little?"

Peter McM beckons a white-jacket. When Jack declines, DeeAnn elbows him. "Try it, Jack! It's delicious!"—and quaffs her cup.

"My colleagues," says Peter, "really do want to meet you, Jack. I just can't tell you how our Founder appreciates someone with a way with words. We all really envy you!"

He leads them down the rank of tables, and they meet some of the other brethren of the Sons of Holland.

Meet a portly gentleman in a vest and suit—watchfob looping down the vest—that's definitely Edwardian. Mr. Max Maplethorpe.

Meet the lean, balding man beside him—small wire spectacles, arm-garters on a snowy white shirt with an old-fashioned collar. Mr. Walter Horace.

Meet a younger-looking man with slick '20s hair, the outgoing smile of an agent or commercial traveler from the same decade—this one stands up to shake with DeeAnn. "I am completely charmed, miss. I am Oswald Luddick. And a pleasure meeting *you*, Mr. Hale." Hearing the man's name, Jack can now, with his mind's eye, read a signature that was previously indecipherable.

"Is it possible, Oswald, that you have from time to time written correspondence for Messrs. Horace and Maplethorpe?"

Jack sees in his eyes that familiar remote amusement. "What is the lowly composition of correspondence," says Luddick, "compared to the kind of poetry, of metaphysical music, that someone of your talents can produce?"

"I'm surprised you know my poetry. I could never publish it."

"Good verse, once achieved, is heard and remembered by the angels."

"Are you an angel, Mr. Luddick?"

An indulgent smile. "I cannot claim that, Mr. Hale."

As Peter ushers them on, it bothers Jack that these bit players evade elaborating on their concocted identities. Shouldn't they be doing the opposite? Or is this somehow more effective . . . more disorienting?

They meet Anthony Braggio, in suspenders and a dress shirt, vigorous white hair in a Little Italy cut. Mr. Alfred Lazar, a dusky Semite dressed like an undertaker. Mr. Sherman Elvis, a business-suited guy with brawny hands and a pleasantly skeptical redneck face. Meet others, all distinct in region, class, period, yet all the same underneath, all watching Jack and DeeAnn from the same place.

"Friends!" booms John from the microphone. "That pleasant time is at hand to take our seats together and tuck into the wonderful meal we've prepared for tonight. Shall we find our seats, gentlemen?"

The band swerves into "Smoke Gets in Your Eyes," picking up the volume a little. The people on the floor begin ambling toward their seats, while others of the brotherhood, emerging two and three at a time from the kitchen doors (funny, he didn't notice them going in there), likewise begin moving toward the tables. White-jackets next emerge, pushing carts.

They begin ladling soup into the diners' bowls.

Jack has no trouble abstaining from this offering. It's not just the sharp, bitter scent of the soup, but the server's after-shave that comes wafting up with it, harsh and antiseptic. DeeAnn, though, who can spend half an hour crumbling a donut into coffee and then leave the sludge untasted, seems ravenous tonight and scoops the soup right up. Its aroma, faintly recalling Vick's Vapo-Rub on his chest as a kid, makes Jack a little dizzy. . . . He snaps a sharp look at the big floral trellis behind Cannyharme. Just flowers, big blooms, and leafy sprigs. From the edge of his eye, he thought for an instant they were something else. . . .

All down the tables, spoons clink and conversation rumbles, the intimate rhythm of table talk rises. The laughter becomes more localized, the voices trading off rather than conjoining. The hubbub sounds so precisely right it seems generic, synthesized.

Frontal vision, and stay focused. Already they're contriving to tug at his senses.

"Man, that's tasty!" DeeAnn is nudging his arm. "You don't want yours?"

"No. Take it."

And she does. Jack looks along the tables. All the seats are full. So what about the guests? Where are they going to sit when they're spruced up?

The band pauses and then launches, much louder, into "Beginning to See the Light." John booms from the microphone, "And now, friends, buckle on your appetites. Remember we don't want to hurt our chef's feelings!"

The talk quickens, gusts of hilarity erupting. There's something much more convincing about these voices, an avid undertone. Jack hears the sound of wheels approaching from the depths of the kitchen.

He hears them, in fact, far too clearly, with the talk and the music so loud. As if those wheels are echoing in the great outer silence that the talk and the music are masking, though that talk grows even fiercer as the wheels approach. The wheels, he can tell, are the casters on heavy carts, but they make a crackly sound that's wrong for the polished floors of this place. Incredible how loud they are, through the uproar and the music.

And here comes the feast! Emerging on carts from the kitchen, broad carts heaped with steaming entrees, two white-coats pushing each cart, the carts fanning out as they emerge to advance in a wide front, steam billowing off them, the wheels grinding and crunching unbearably across the flawlessly smooth floor. Astonishing how distinct and what a torment their noise is, because the assembly's voices have now risen to a fury, are all wails and snarls and guttural shouts, and the band's unearthly din seems woven of shrieks and groans and brutal blows.

Here comes the fuming feast, all bright with grease and sauces, gaudy with garnishes! The carts' wheels sound like tank-treads on rubble. The waft of the cookery is like the smoke of a holocaust. Astonishing, too, how well the white-coats guide these carts! For the white-coats have neither eyes in their sockets nor flesh on their stark-toothed skulls nor skin on the bony puzzles of their hands.

Here comes the gorgeous feast, and there are no two ways to see it, not any more. Only one way to see it, no blinking it away. That busload of invited guests—they have joined the party after all! Their heads, baked plump and hairless, crown platters, neck-stumps nested in sausage-fried fingers. Swollen red loaves of lung-pudding drip brain-gray sauce. Calves and thighs are the neatly butchered roasts, eyed with sawn bone at both ends. Broiled forearms heap trays like drumsticks, toes and knuckles peep from purple stews where eyeballs bob, rib-racks barbecued on the spine arch up like roofless temple-pillars, the burnt craters left by erupted souls.

"Mmmm!" enthuses DeeAnn, leaning close to Jack. "This really *is* a banquet!"

Roast! Huge drumsticks! Unbelievable ribs! This trick has turned into such a bonanza that DeeAnn marvels at her fears of coming here. She's just tucked an added 3K in her purse, she doesn't have to fuck anybody, and now she's feasting on this incredible meal! As her mom would have said, she must be living right.

But all this a surprise party for Razz? With all this money, all this show in it? The idea is more than bizarre. How could someone like Razz arouse this kind of appreciation? Face it, Razz is not outgoing. He's the King Cool type. His only friends are people he wants to impress, wants to cop status from, like that T-Bone, another character to stay far away from. She glances over at Razz, seated there at Mr. Cunningham's high table. Razz is like her, not a big eater, but look at him chewing away, his always guarded face relaxed a little, looking younger, tripping on the tastiness of it all. And he really does seem to be a focus here. That big grizzly is standing by his chair, sharing some joke with him, both of them chuckling . . . is calling a waiter for something more to load on Razz's plate. Kindly old Mr. Cunningham is grinning down on them, catches Razz's eye, and actually gives him a wink.

Well, he's obviously made some connections he hasn't told her about, and they definitely succeeded in surprising him. Porn shoot! Razz really believed it. The crowd *is* all men, but none of their attention is on her, she can sense it. Whatever this party is about, it's not her. If anyone, it's Razz that all eyes keep flicking toward, Razz and his new goon friend. It's kind of neat, DeeAnn thinks, to be off-duty like this, to be the one on the sidelines for a change. That grizzly is someone to be feared, she trusts her instinct there, but he's Razz's problem tonight, not hers—just as those occasional scary tricks Razz has sent her in to were her problems, not his. This is how Razz feels all the time, isn't it? Standing by, not personally on the hook, and getting cash for it! All this fuckless cash in her purse feels so festive! It's as if Razz, obviously without knowing about it, has for the first time contrived a really special treat for her. This gala party, so uptown, with such a grand, triumphant feeling . . . These sausages are heavenly! So crisp and succulent at the same time!

But . . . all this for *Razz?* She's always taken a secret pleasure in devoting herself to someone who—be honest—most people just plain dislike. Is there something she's missed in him all along? There's an air of importance, of power in this room, all these vigorous, vital men like knights somehow, as if the hilts of broadswords jutted invisibly from behind their shoulders. . . .

She drains her refilled cup—each draft tastes better than the last, refreshing her tastebuds for the next juicy forkfuls. This is what they call clearing the palate, this is *cuisine*. Such a pecky eater all her life, she understands for the first time the thrill of recreational gorging. It's not just the rich tastes, it's the feeling of victory. All this food is yours, like tribute laid before you, and you consume it recklessly, laughing like a conqueror.

Look at that old man! Not a poor, bent thing, not tonight, not in this posture. He looks like a relaxing lion. All strength he seems, with glee in his eyes. He's *sexy!* He's not eating. It's the feast itself he's feasting on.

Jack here is another one not eating. She's noticed him cutting and slicing and forking his food around on the plate, but he hasn't put anything in his mouth. His plate is filling up with bite-size cuts around the rim and bare bones in the middle. He's totally intent on it too, as if it's vitally important, cutting little slice after little slice. . . .

Hands of bone take Jack's plate. He looks into the crusty tunnels of the white-coat's sockets, at the tufted scraps of scalp on skullbone, the dirt-packed crevices of lipless teeth. The lich's silence is like a hole in the uproar around them, its stark truth of bone punctures the noise-mask of the party and lets eternity leak in. The cadaver loads his plate and replaces it before him with a little bow, an ironic tilt of the skull.

Good evening. I'm Long Dead. I'll be your waiter tonight.

Jack discovers that his terror is containable, that his body already knew this moment was coming; and though his nerves have melted down and drained right out of him, his frame sits straight, he's hanging tough, his jaw refusing to unhinge and scream. He knew, knew at the core, that it could be this bad. After what he saw on the staircase two nights ago.

He knew. He's sitting upright. He's not screaming. But can he *move?* Can he move even one muscle? If he can't, his paralysis is their victory. Defy it. Does he have some balls on him? *Act.*

His will is Mission Control. Its signals cross a hundred million miles of emptiness and reach his body, a Martian orbiter. The robot arms respond, the robot hands and fingers . . . take up his flat of Old AA, uncap it, hoist it . . . and he drinks.

Don't stop moving now! By whatever psychoactive sorcery contrived, this alien landscape, this smoking mountain of cannibal cuisine, must be engaged, defied. He takes up his knife and fork.

Let's see. Is this thing here really a broiled, juice-dribbling forearm? Let's see. . . .

At the first thrust of his tines into softness, the first stroke of his blade through succulence, the noise around him surges up into a hellish din. The voices of the assembled Sons of Holland become the coughs, grunts, and throaty frictions of carnivores—big ones—gorging. And the music becomes a torture-chamber riot of banshee wails and dungeoned moans and the clanking, clashing gears of rack and wheel.

He cuts the slice, forks it aside, begins cutting another. Steadier and steadier his hands grow. While all hell howls around him, grimly he dissects the horror, poring like a surgeon over each detail: the tiny glinting ends of cross-cut muscle-fibers, the delicate diamond pattern of human epidermis still discernible in the shrunken skin-shards along the roast's rim. He mines every inch of the meat-scape—

. . . fork and slice, fork and slice . . .

—while his terror whispers that this is only a prelude, that there's something more to come: Cozzens is going to kill that fucking Death in him.

. . . fork and slice, fork and slice, fork and slice . . .

The band crescendos, wails a fanfare. John booms from the microphone. "Your attention, gentlemen. Brothers, your attention! That magical moment has come!"

. . . fork and slice fork and slice fork and slice . . .

"That moment when we welcome into our ancient order a new member! Brothers, I give you Sly Cozzens and his charming, most *honored* guest, Erasmus!"

A roar from the assembly, and the big room goes pitch dark. A spotlight illuminates the dance floor. Jack lays down his silverware. This is the Beholding that he owes. What's coming now, once endured, will free him.

The band erupts: "It Had to Be You." Two shapes move, dancing, into the spotlight. Cozzens, with Razz gripped like a waltz partner. Cozzens is leading and Razz, powerfully embraced, is following—cannot help but follow, for his feet are off the floor, his one arm held outthrust by Cozzens's iron strength, and his other arm back-bent and pressed across his spine, his small ribs crushed to Cozzens's huge ones. His legs kick as the pair whirl waltzing amidst a zoo of acclamation from the dark assembly—kick, then suddenly desist at a coercive pressure and hang obedient as he is swept round and round through a grandiose ballroom parody that the mad band derides with gibbers and squeaks and flatulent glissandos.

In the darkness all along the tables, as if they were a midnight shoreline, a tide of movement boils. The hall was an illusion. This darkness masks an abyss on every side, where furious energies roll in. The tables shake, chairs are splintered, big shapes jostle up and down the line.

Panic seizes Jack at last and lifts him to his feet. It is time to be gone, *gone* from this unhallowed assembly.

As he's pulling DeeAnn up from her chair, the spotlight broadens and the turbulent assembly roars at Cannyharme revealed. Attendants help him shed his coat, his trousers while the trellis writhes behind him, a blood-red macramé of lopped limbs struggling to free themselves. . . .

"Now DeeAnn! Now! Run!"

She obeys balkily, as if coming out of some kind of stupor. On the dance floor, Cozzens gives Razz a ballroom fling, gripping one of his arms and snapping him like a whip with a sharp report of breaking bone. He slams him face-down to the floor. Cannyharme, disrobed, is the muscled beast revealed once before, huge-tongued, huge-sexed, and poised to leap down from his dais.

DeeAnn seems to waken at last. "Don't look back!" Jack howls in her ear and hauls her after him, plunging through the dark in the remembered direction of the door.

DeeAnn can't believe it. What a night of surprises! Razz spinning out into the spotlight, actually *dancing* with that grizzly. And the moves Razz has got, slick and fancy, like Fred Astaire. Who'd dream a guy like Razz could move like that, the coattails of his black leather trenchcoat even flaring a little like Astaire's long tails? Could *Razz* have a gay side? It's almost easier to believe that than it is to believe he has this sense of *humor.* Because it's hilarious. What a wild night out Razz is showing her!

Then Jack seizes her arm, and she almost pisses with startlement. Get out? Now? She's stunned for a moment, but in that moment she finds the whole feeling of the hall has changed around her. It sounds like a riot going on, furniture is crashing, men are howling, the band's not making music but an insane racket . . . and the *smell* in this place! How could she have missed it? It reeks! Like rot, like shit, like garbage!

Then she and Jack are running. Big shapes are turmoiling, chairs splintering, the floor quaking with violent impacts, yet amazingly she and Jack collide with nothing, the chaos seeming to part before and close again behind them.

Until they collide with four white-jackets whose coats shed a dim luminescence that limns the doors they block. "Excuse us, Mr. Hale," says the biggest. "Will your guest be so kind as to wait for you out in the parking lot? Miss, here's the key to your car, Erasmus wanted you to have it. Wait out there just a moment, and Mr. Hale will join you."

Jack gives her one wild look, but then nods. "Just for a minute," he tells her.

The white-jackets part and bow, and out she goes double-quick. A real lady, mom used to say, always knows when to leave a party.

One of Jack's shoulders is numb, where the white-jacketed cadaver had gripped it with naked bones. A whisper comes from the lipless thing, a murmur directly within Jack's mind.

"You can only leave if you look."

Here's the toll. He has to pay it to get out of this nightmare. He has to do it. But eyes are so intimate! Things can barge into your eyes, straight through your mind and into your heart forever. Jack's heart mutely asks for mercy, but there is no mercy in this room. This is the hall of the harm-hound and his minions, where mercy is howled to scorn and terror is torn asunder like the wolf-caught hare.

Until Jack Hale goes through with this, there is no turning back.

He turns to face his only exit, the spotlit dance floor.

There, centered in the pool of light, Razz sprawls all but obscured by Cozzens, who covers him in coitus, while the monstrous hound looms above his head, baying a note of triumph that pierces the din of the seething shadow riot.

Razz screams, and rutting Cozzens lifts his twisted face and bellows from his corded throat, "Accept my offering, Master! Receive me in your service!"

As Razz lifts his head to scream again, the hound engulfs both scream and head, and mighty teeth sunder the living meat, and the Hound aims a polar eye directly at Jack's own and winks.

The sharp crunch of bone lifts the hall's pandemonium to frenzy. The shadows explode into inhuman shapes. Shoulders swell and spread like wings, bulging flanks sprout limbs grotesquely jointed—but it's spotlit Cozzens's transformation that engulfs Jack's mind. The giant's back fans wider, black leather shredding with the stretch, while his head rolls in agony as his jaws expand and branch in wide black thorny arcs. Jawed like a giant stag-beetle, his face has stretched into a gem-eyed carapace. Heaving up on spike-legged haunches, the thing that was Cozzens flourishes its baroque jaws in the light, like two ornate arms raised in hallelujah, then twists around and dives straight through the floor.

The whole assembly is plunging through the floor, the walls, the ceiling melting away, as the immortal hound, left alone in the light, lifts his ensanguined muzzle and laughs with a sound like a crowbar breaking into a crypt.

The doors gape open before Jack. The white-jackets step aside. But one detains him as he rushes out. "You have heard the words. You know how it is done. The choice is yours."

XXVI
Rendezvous at the Hyperion

Past midnight, Britt and Aarti are dressed for the street, sipping cocoa with Skip at a window table. Out of a silence Britt asks, "But how *can* we live there? In the *Hyperion?*"

"By taking no shit—by fighting back," Skip smiles. "By keeping an upright heart and helping your friends, like you're going to do now. They can't touch you then."

A trio of street people trudge past, the wind buffeting their rags—not the first they've seen since sitting here. "They're restless," Skip says. "They feel it without knowin it. The Old One's in a party mood. His pack is on the prowl. . . ."

"Will you stay at the hotel with us, Skip?" Aarti blurts this out, perhaps foreknowing the answer, as Britt does. And the moment the girl has asked it, all Oh, Mary's lights go out. They sit looking from darkness at a street that seems a world away, otherwhere and otherwhen.

"You know about the solar wind, darling?" asks Skip. He is a silhouette beside them. His voice is gentle and seems to come from farther away. "Well, I'm sorry, ladies, but it just blows me away." He chuckles—a sad, thoughtful sound, like someone softly putting things away in another room. "My light's got a will of its own, sweetheart, and it has to go with the solar wind. But you'll see some of me again, and some of me is never going to leave you. Look there."

Two figures are approaching on the sidewalk, one massive, and one lean. Britt's on her feet. "That's Sal and Squash."

"Well, let's go talk to them," says Skip softly.

The girls step out to the sidewalk. "Yo, Blade," says Sal. "We gotta get back to your hotel—it's coming down." And then, to Aarti, "What's *this?* What have we *here?* Is this Little Blade? You come right here, you pretty little thing!" And Sal wraps Aarti in a serious, full-money's-worth hug, shutting her eyes and smiling like a happy python. Then, still hugging, she flashes a fierce look at huge, impassive Squash. "You big fool! I *want* one o' these! Get you a goddamn straight job, fool! Just look at her!" And she advances blushing Aarti—though with her arms still around the girl's shoulders—for Squash's closer inspection. He leans down and carefully offers Aarti a hand that is half the size of her head.

"Hi, Little Blade. I'm Squash." Like one of those stone Olmec heads, he has a rounded cliff of a face, serene. The pencil-line stash curving down round his mouth is its only flourish.

She extends her hand to be gently engulfed. "I'm Aarti"—but you can hear something tentative in her voice, hear her thinking that Little Blade sounds pretty cool. Squash's thin stash flexes ever so slightly, a regular upheaval of humor for him.

"I dunno," he rumbles to Sal. "I guess somethin like Aarti Little Blade here would be worth drivin a bus for."

"You girls hear that?" Sal caws. "You *witnesses.* Well, what you waitin on, Squash? You the muscle here, walk us on down! Time's wastin!"

"Wait," says Britt, and turns for some last reassurance from Skip. But Skip isn't there. Oh, Mary's itself isn't there, not the way it was a moment ago. A locked grille masks the door. Plywood tattered with torn flyers masks the window they were just looking out of.

Sal touches her shoulder. "You not alone, Blade. And now there's two friends of yours we gotta try to help. OK?"

DeeAnn has the white Caddy idling. She revs the engine as Jack bursts from the hall. She rockets them out of the lot, talking as fast as she's driving.

"What the hell was going *on* in there? I mean, everything was so tasty and then suddenly it *stank* to high heaven! I mean, how did Razz get us involved in something like this—did you see him *dancing* like that? I never dreamed he knew how to *do* that! What was going *on* there? What were *you* doing there?"

Jack's collecting himself. He answers her second-to-last question. "It's like a club. That was the initiation ceremony . . ."

"Are *you* in this club?"

"I was invited, but I decided not to join."

"Well, let him dance with that crowd if he wants, but he can walk home because there's no way I'm goin back *there* for him."

Let him dance. Walk home. Razz has done his dancing. Won't be walking anywhere.

If all that really happened. Did it really happen? Isn't it nothing more than the wildest brain-bubble he's ever been drugged into? Aerosol hallucinogens?

How can it have happened? How can it have been real? Look around. Houses. Streets. Signals. A burger wrapper windblown down a sidewalk . . . The dull old world, block after block of it. Immortal monsters devouring human sacrifices have no place in this world.

It's a big universe. The choice is yours. Both true, thank God! As for what he chooses? He chooses to grab his manuscript, his Olympia, pick up his wonderfully portable career and take it elsewhere. So many beautiful Elsewheres in this big beautiful world! Elsewhere, drugs—however exotic— will wear out of his system. Elsewhere, this indelible nightmare will shrink into . . . a story. Elsewhere, it will become an ordinary stack of typed pages.

DeeAnn, meanwhile, has not ceased to motormouth. ". . . and the food was great, I just pigged out! And the money! I mean, like six K just tonight, and not to *do* anything, I mean what kinda club *is* this that throws around money like that?"

"It's one that really wants new members, but exactly what *for,* I don't know. They never really explained that to me."

They're gliding up Lincoln, the Park streaming past on their left, and as the streetlights strobe over them, DeeAnn looks incredibly vivid, gesturing as she talks as much with her micro-skirted thighs as with her hands. His terror, he finds, has left his nerves raw and alive. Left him lustful. It strikes him that the quickest and readiest way out of town is the car he's sitting in right now, and in the female company he is enjoying at this very moment.

DeeAnn has caught the shift of his attention. Laughs. "Listen to me blabbing!" She drives smiling, rocking one thigh more slowly, rhythmically now.

"Look, DeeAnn. You wonder about those people back there, and you *should*. That big guy Razz was dancing with? He was giving me OZs of free crank. Just like all that cash for you. And with guys like that, there's no free lunch. I don't know what they're after, but I do know that guy is *very* dangerous. What I'm telling you is, I'm leaving town tonight, and you should come with me, at least for a while."

"Jack! Are you proposing? What are you thi-i-inking, Ja-a-a-ack?" Oh, her merry little houri's eyes! That teasing rocking of her thighs!

"Hey, we really could have some fun together. But first—no shit here—we should drive this car right out of here. Stop for our stuff and get gone, within the hour."

"Hmmmm. Is it me or my car that you want?" Still smiling.

"Both!" he laughs. "But I'm not after your money. I've got more cash than you do, and this is all on me." He knows she'll do it. Jack Hale, the indestructible human tumbleweed! Amazing, the levity he feels, so recently emerged from the Ninth Circle. So how real could it have been? It's already blowing off of him like smoke.

"I guess I *wouldn't* mind a little vacation," croons DeeAnn. "I know a good hotel in Santa Barbara." A teasing smile. "I might give Razz a call in a few days, see if he's got his shit straightened out."

"Maybe you won't *want* to." Jack waggles his eyebrows. "But whatever you choose, it's all my treat. We'll do the town. Thing is, we can't hang around there. Run in, grab our stuff, and go."

"Whatever you sa-a-ay, J-a-a-ack." Rocking her thigh. He can tell she plans to sack him once they're in the hotel, but he's going to disappoint her. How glad he will be to put the Hyperion—and the bloody dark of its ground floor—behind him forever.

She hooks up Stanyan and down Haight. Though the wind is gusting, there's a lot of street folk on the sidewalk. They're more clustered than usual and seem to confer. Bearded mouths murmur, and watch-capped, hair-flanked faces flick sharp glances left and right.

He feels the car jostled by something like a wind *within* the wind, a current more concentrated, more sinewy than air, pouring past them. He sees, or thinks he sees, all the shopfronts, the barred windows and grilled doorways, ripple in this wind, as if they were all one painted canvas backdrop. Jack suddenly, achingly feels his years, feels the long loneliness of his artist's ambition, a loneliness he lived in even when he had Erika. All the streets he's walked down, all the panoramas he's stared at with his longing for insight, for glory. Those sunsets, those seascapes, those cityscapes—canvas backdrops all of them, cunningly painted to look like Revelation. Another decade or two and he himself will be so thinned away he will be little more than another painted figure on the canvas, shuddering to the winds of eternity.

"Pull over to this liquor store, would you?"

It's a tiny old store with creaky wooden floors. Jack has to wait behind the sole other customer, a shrunken little crone in a filthy trenchcoat, her trembling fingers almost too gnarled to count her nickels, dimes and pennies onto the counter. The owner, short and blocky, doesn't seem impatient. As he watches her fingers, he strokes his thinning hair back—only one slick tuft left on the forehead—with an indescribable little smile of complacency, like a cat washing itself.

Across her palsied head, he lifts his eyes to Jack's and gives him a merry wink. Then he says to the woman, "You know what you're lovin' uncle thinks, Moms? He thinks you can just put your money back in your pocket and take this as a little present." Another wink at Jack as he sets a pint of Night Train on the counter.

The woman gives a moan of acknowledgment and begins putting the coins back in her pocket. Stroking his hair, the man smiles on this equally slow process. At last she takes the bottle, hesitates, and then extends it to the man, a plea in her posture. He angles her a look of comic reproach, then takes the bottle and cracks the seal of the cap for her, muscle flashing in his meaty forearm. She takes it gratefully in her incapable hands and creaks out. The man says to Jack, "Babes! You gotta love em."

Jack laughs in spite of himself. The man is so easy, none of that careful reserve of a liquor clerk late at night in an iffy neighborhood. "What's your pleasure?" he asks.

"A half pint of Jack Daniel's."

The bottle looks bright and beautiful on the counter. The man lifts a preventing palm at the sight of Jack's money. "No, I think I'm on a roll here. That's a present. I'm in a holiday mood."

"Holiday?"

"I'm celebrating how good it is to be alive."

Jack gets a little thrill from the way the guy says *alive*. That old wino, only technically alive, throws it into sharp relief. "Well, hey, that's very kind of you."

"Kindness has nothing to do with it. We're talking *joy* here."

DeeAnn accepts a drink before she pulls out, her little tits peaking her tight top as she hoists it. Alive is just how this makes him feel. They've got wheels, money, and strenuous things to do in some faraway bed. He gathers DeeAnn feels the same. She gives him back the bottle and roars from the curb as if they've got a purpose.

She slants him a smile. "The way you're looking at me, Jack. You sure you don't want to come up to my room? Help me . . . get packed?"

Squash doesn't look as if he's moving fast, but the others are striding to keep up with him. The last clouds have been blown west, and the stars are incredibly brilliant, as if they were coals this wind is fanning brighter. The constellations out-blaze the city lights.

Here's the Hyperion. That Britt has fought here, won here, doesn't calm her hammering heart. That was day, this is night—and a night when the enemy owns the city. Nothing can be more dangerous than going through those doors and up those stairs. It helps that allies await them on the sidewalk. Bettina Butch. Old Karl Cabron. It doesn't help that Britt is carrying the only weapon they can use—that only she can use it.

They stand in a little ring, looking at one another. The wind moves among them like everything unspoken that unites them. Bettina glances at the others and says to Britt, "If they go in, there's nothing we can do for them. Can we—help *you*?"

"I think . . ." She doesn't think, she *knows*. "I think I have to do it by myself."

"Guys." Karl Cabron is always faint-voiced. "You know Chester? Next door to me? I think something's wrong." They stare at him.

"Wrong how?" asks Sal. A big white Caddy swings onto the empty street and arrows to the curb. Jack and DeeAnn jump out. So vivid they look, faces glowing, eyes flashing. Jack's greeting is hectic. "Hey, guys! Hey, Brittany! You disappeared on us! Are you OK?"

"Jack, DeeAnn . . ."

"Hi, Brandy! You sweeties all right? You were great with that gun! I was so proud of you!" Both she and Jack are elsewhere, both of them urgent to go inside, oblivious to the fear in their friends' faces.

"You need anything?" Jack asks Britt. "You OK for money? I'm sorry, but we're just ducking in and out of here. Let me give you—"

"*Don't* go inside, Jack! That's what we're here to tell you. Don't even go inside for a minute, neither one of you. Just leave as you are—get back in your car and drive away."

"What? What are you saying? We *are* leaving, but we've gotta get our *stuff*."

"You *know* why, Jack. Don't go back in here."

His eyes go doubtful. "What do you know about what I *know*? Are you all suddenly my counselors?"

"Jack," says Squash, "we can't stop you. You just got to believe us, man. Don't go in there. Just *go*."

He scans them all. Britt sees him almost trust, then sees the glint of doubt he quickly masks. "Listen, I'm grateful—truly I am. I know there's . . . a situation here. I'm well aware. But I've got a hundred pages of *manuscript* up there! No *way* do I abandon that much work!"

XXVII
This Grandeur, This Forever,
This Deathless Power . . .

Jack and DeeAnn trot up the stairs and into the smell of death. "Jesus, Elmer," says Jack. Elmer, behind his bars, tilts his head down the hall, where one of the room doors gapes open. "Chester Chase is in there, Jack. I think he passed away a day or two ago—'s been dead a couple days now. I was just gonna call the cops, but I thought I'd wait for you."

"Oh, no! Oh, man! Look, Elmer, will you handle this? Will you hold off calling a few minutes? We're in a hurry and we can't get involved. We've gotta get away—it's a personal emergency."

Elmer nods vigorously. "Sure, Jack. It's a sad thing, but it's pretty much routine."

"God bless you!" To DeeAnn, "Hurry and pack." She goes upstairs, and Jack dives into the compound, into his room. In two minutes he returns to the hall with his Olympia and his stout little satchel of clothes and pages. It appears Brittany has followed him and DeeAnn in. She sits on the steps up to the next floor, looking at him.

"Jack," says Elmer, beckoning him to the bars, beckoning him closer with a glance at Britt. He murmurs, "I was down in the storage. Saw something there I think you might've left. I'm not gonna say anything about it—I'm not gonna *know* anything about it—you understand me?" And Jack nods, numb with sudden fear. "But I think you might wanna take care of it before you go."

"Thank you, Elmer! Thank you! I'll be right back up." He leaves his belongings in front of the cage and rushes down the stairs. It must be a shell from the Glock, or a bloodstain. There's dust down there, rags. Obliterate it fast—smudge it, disguise it. . . . He keys open the storage door and shuts it behind him before switching on the lights.

Not two yards from his face, dead Trini and T-Bone dangle from a ceiling-beam. The corpses fill the shadowy space like giants. Under a nearby bulb, the back of Trini's skull is a half-black lunar crater. T-Bone's noose-canted head is a sphere swollen to bursting. His turgid, jutting tongue, black and inert, recalls to Jack a very different tongue, white and seeking.

Oh, dear God. Elmer has set him up! It's time to flat-out run.

As he shuts and locks the door behind him, he hears sirens come whooping onto Valencia . . . and whoop to a stop just outside the door.

He's got to go up, get to a back window, and out through the alley. He pounds up the stairs—and stands frozen a few yards in front of the cage. Elmer sits aiming Jack's own .38 at him through the bars.

On the counter in front of him is Jack's shoulder rig and Jack's Glock with the suppressor screwed on. More sirens are converging down on the street. Radio-squawk is heard: people on the sidewalk being questioned.

"I've reported you by name already, Chief," says Elmer, but not with Elmer's voice, with a sly grizzly growl Jack knows too well. "Said I found those bodies down below, found a bullet-hole in the wall, found this weapon in your room. Said I didn't know if you were in the building, but that you might be in any one a the rooms."

The street buzzer howls, and there is a hammering on the door. The glittery eyes that were Elmer's ignore it, hold Jack's. "I can stall em. Delay em down here. You got just enough time to put this kinda trouble behind you forever, Ace. Only one direction you can run in now."

Jack bounds up the stairs to the second floor and sprints for the rear of the building. DeeAnn's room has a window over the alley.

Britt slowly stands. She is trembling. She faces the man behind the bars, the width of the hall between them.

"Whaddya think, little bitch?" asks Elmer in his new voice. "Should I hit the buzzer now? They're gonna break in that door pretty quick. Should I give him another sixty seconds?"

"You see this?" shrieks Brittany, drawing the pipe from her pocket. It produces, in the captured Elmer's face, a blankness, a pause. "This has the blood of your stinking kind on it!"

And she hurls the pipe, end over end. It tumbles flawlessly between the bars and strikes Elmer's forehead, making his captor flinch. A shadowy mass sprouts upward from Elmer's head and shoulders. Tenuous barbed jaws, like great antlers, rise from him, and in that instant of displacement Elmer's face becomes his own again. With fierce facility he seizes up the Glock, swings the suppressor up to his brow, and squeezes the trigger.

Cops know that determined suicides with semi-automatics can put more than one slug through their own skulls. Elmer sends three angling up through his forehead, and now the monstrous immortal hauls itself out, a giant erupting from a small man's back, his jaws wildly clashing with pain. Where his clustered eyes were are only weeping holes of ruptured black plasm.

The blinded monster tumbles thrashing around the cage, clawing as if in search of sight within a dark eternity, and, finding its way by feel, drags itself at last through a corner of the ceiling.

This isn't happening. This isn't fucking happening. Oh, please, please let the alley be clear. The BART station's just half a block away. He has enough cash in his pocket to start anew somewhere. Buy some ID . . .

He slips into DeeAnn's room and locks the door behind him. She's bent alluringly over her packing—has foreseen this scenario and is posed for it, in fact.

"Are we really in a *total* hurry Ja-a-ack? Hmmm?"

He rushes to the alley window and looks down.

Two squad cars, three or four uniforms, a couple of tough-looking suits peering in through the jimmied back door to the storage floor.

A steel door rumbles shut in Jack's heart.

Down there is the end of his life. Is, at best, more than a decade in prison. Down there is a vile, impoverished future when freedom does come again, when he steps back out on these mean streets, a defeated heart in an aged, aching frame. Down there, a few years farther on, is an unnoticed death like Chester's, lying days dead on a stained bed. . . .

DeeAnn, still smilingly packing, puts more derriere in the work, showing him the silken terrain of her little underside. She is here and now. Why shouldn't he plunge into her? Where else is there that he can go? Why not have at least that pleasure, if all this misery is to follow?

Unless.

Unless, when he enters DeeAnn, he enters a doorway, and his feet are set upon a bridge, and he walks across into *another* world.

He doesn't believe it for a moment.

He doesn't believe it, but his *spine* believes it. His body, cringing from those dark years in a cage, is tingling, aching for that doorway. His hands are unbuckling his belt, unlatching that doorway. His sex is stiffening for that doorway, like a tree limb branching toward the light.

"Jack! I thought we didn't have ti-i-ime! You naughty man! Oh dear, let me help you . . ."

They are mounting the bed on all fours, are merging doggie-style. This little cell of a room—how high in the night sky it seems to be! The walls seem thin, and a vast windblown blackness surrounds them.

They couple . . . couple . . . couple—and with each thrust, it seems to Jack that a layer of this dire box of a world is peeled off of him. This high place they mate in grows windier, wilder, the blaze of stars winking through the gappy walls. He is *traveling!* He moves along an unretraceable path! The skepticism that he wrapped himself for comfort in—that thin garment of doubts—is tearing, shredding, blowing off of him.

And as he is flayed of doubt, with terror he acknowledges the words he must now speak, the murder he must now commit. They are a thousand stories high now up in the wild night air. He sees her profiled under him, her brow intent on coming, her eyes fixed on the dark in front of her, seeking her private destination.

Forgive me, DeeAnn. You're already aimed for wreck and ruin. A hooker's years will be short, disaster multiplying on her. I'm sorry! Sorry! But I can't stay here. I can't rot my last years of life out in prison.

"Master!" he hoarsely cries. "Accept my offering! Accept me in your service!"

This is a kind of brutal mercy, isn't it? Surely it is a mercy to her! As they gallop more wildly toward their conclusion, how her groans are echoing! How huge their noise, a clattering thunder, as if they are engulfed in an enormous engine, and as she cries out he hears her cries echo in that engine-maw, in the jaws of the world-machine that munches women raw and swallows the fruit of their wombs, the colossal engine of entropy, bestridden by the Ghoul-God. As his climax starts to tear his body into fragments, shreds and shards snatched away by the wild night wind, he sees again her profile under him, locked in her private rapture, blind to the fanged machine which—*now!*—with a spray of blood, coffins her in darkness.

Jack's old flesh is blowing off his bones. He is pouring away in a glowing smoke as the walls are whipped away in the snatching winds. He hangs, a light-year high, amid the stars, his old life draining out of him with his seed's effusion, his bones and muscles melting, branching into a new shape, a new understanding. . . .

Fat Sal is riding shotgun in her Yellow cab, and Britt is at the wheel, getting some unofficial cabdriver training from her testy mentor. Sal is something of a novice herself, only two months on the job, but she is one passionate—even abusive—instructor.

"Don't signal those lane-changes, fool! Just slide over an *take* it. You signal, you let em know what you doin, they hurry up to block you out! . . . Now slide *into* that yellow, don't slow *down* for a yellow, you crazy? That's it! Roll through an' *whip* that left, they see you comin they *got* to stop for you! All right now, punch it some! You got a green up there! Get *to* it an' get *through* it! . . . OK, that was a much better yellow, just remember the law says if you even got one *inch* of your bumper into the intersection while it still yellow, you good to go! OK now, swing up here an' let's do some more *freeway.*"

Britt executes all these instructions completely unflustered. She's getting as good at filtering out Sal's passion as she's getting at driving itself. Driving! It's magic. It's sorcery! To wing through the world like this, to see all that tricky sidewalk she's known so well, full of traps, alleyways, doormouths, lounging lowlifes—to see it just streaming past is wonderful.

Of course, put Britt on the pavement now, and she can jog ten miles of it at a nice steady clip—and throw a good punch too, if that's ever called for. But that just makes it feel better to be at the wheel of this little rocketship, makes it feel more earned. She's a natural at this, and who would have believed it?

"We should get back to the Mission, Sal. I've got to get Aarti from school."

"Well, you're *drivin,* girl! Get off on Bayshore. You need me to turn the *wheel* for you?"

They are cruising up Army when Britt sees someone ahead. Sal explodes, "What you doin? You not pickin up *fares* yet, *I'll* tell you when you start. . . ."

Her voice trails off as they approach this fare, Britt gliding to the curb in a bus zone where he sits on the bench, one hand half lifted to flag them. He's a white-haired old man in a screaming-bright Hawaiian shirt, shabby slacks, and worn loafers. The two women sit in the idling taxi looking at his face, their lips slightly parted, lost for a moment, trying to understand how the old man's eyes, bright under the bushy brows, are *doing* that, are telling them so many strange things that they can almost understand.

"Hi, Chester," Britt calls, with a slight quaver. "You want a ride? No charge?" Not a peep out of Sal at her saying this. In fact, there are the faintest beginnings of a smile on Sal's mouth as she stares at this man.

He smiles and stands. The brilliant shirt dangles past gauntness in his midsection, but heavy shoulders and arms stretch it widthwise. A strong man in his youth and somehow, though at least in his seventies, not exactly old now. All that space in his eyes. The way that his smile seems to say that his face is a little joke, just between the three of them.

He gets in, and his nearness there behind her gives Britt a thrill of remembered sensations, of her arm pile-driving an ugly face from her path, of her right hand wielding thunderbolts. . . .

She pulls back into traffic. The question—where do you want to go?—dies in her throat. A different one comes out. "Do you know . . . Skip?"

"Yes. We met."

"Are you . . . staying here?"

"I'll be hanging around for a little while."

She gathers herself and blurts out the hard question, with an orphan's sadness in it. "Why can't you stay here for good?"

There is a pause before he answers. The cab seems to flow through the traffic without her agency, the way her life will flow through its years ahead. "Do you girls know about the solar wind? When you get to my point in life, that solar wind . . . well, it just starts to recruit you. It's got a thousand other worlds it wants to blow you to, and you've seen too much, felt too much, not to go to them. To add yourself to all the rest. You understand? It's like light. It heads out in all directions as fast as it can. It can't do otherwise."

She finds his eyes in the rearview. "Are you . . . still Chester?"

"Mostly, still." His reflected eyes still smile, but the gulf of space in them has grown. Britt knows she's had all the answers allotted her, but, heart thudding, she tries for one more:

"Can we win?"

Scary voids now, those eyes in his silence, until a faint rim of humor glints round them. "I don't know. Keep kicking ass on them, maybe we'll find out."

And the back seat is empty.

*   *   *

Plump, brown Ramdass Patel, a distant cousin of Bill Patel and an employee of those same loftier Patels that Bill worked for, sits in the cage thinking that of the four different hotels he has managed for them, this Hyperion is by far the best.

"Hey, Ram!"

"Hi, Rich!"

The tenants are a pleasant, steady lot, most of them employed, going out to their jobs, coming back some nights with a whiff of beer about them, or, as with Rich Rasp there, various drugs in them, an aura of artificial energy. And there's the usual—

"Hi, Ram. Say, did Terry go out?"

"He said he was going to the store, Sherry. He said to just wait in his room for him."

—the usual number of completely lost souls, like Sherry Shambles here, poor girl, with her bubbly breathing and her sick face, and her pal Terry, always reeking of *kif,* both on the dole but peaceable, themselves the only people they will ever hurt.

Yes. Sitting in the cage on an early spring evening, Ram Patel very much approves of the Hyperion. The last one he worked, in the Tenderloin, was squalid and dangerous. The Hyperion offers shelter, privacy, and peace.

The door of the manager's suite opens and out come Brittany and Aarti, in sweats and running shoes. Ram, though very fond of both girls, can never repress an impulse of disapproval when he sees them heading out to run in the park (it's almost dark!) and, after that, go to a kung-fu class (to practice kicking and punching like savages!). They sense his disapproval, too, and tease him about it. Here they come smiling to the bars. Aarti takes a wide-legged stance, scowls fiercely, and pumps out three straight-arm punches:

"Hah! Hah! Hah!" Then presents him with a solemn bow. Ram has to smile. American culture. These girls must reach their womanhood by the paths it offers.

"Good evening, ladies. Did Aarti do her homework, Brittany?"

"*And* two pages of extra credit. Can we bring something back for you,

Ram? Something to drink with dinner? We're making spaghetti."

Ah. Ram loves their spaghetti. "Well, perhaps some root beer, thank you."

A couple hours later, they have dinner in the manager's suite, for which Fat Sal drops in to join them. Ram, initially uneasy with raucous Sal and her huge bus-driver husband, is comfortable with both now, recognizing their love for the girls. Aarti recites some of her French homework for them as they eat, and Brittany, who is learning it through helping Aarti, follows suit. Sal tells them some of her recent experiences driving cab— really most amusing, if somewhat improper. She has imparted enough of her relish for this occupation to have Brittany half-persuaded to quit clerking at the bookstore where she works and try it herself, further grounds for unvoiced disapproval from Ram. The bookstore is nearby, and safe. But driving cab all over the city, a young woman!

Well, he trusts Brittany. A sober, vital girl. Cast adrift from her family so young, like so many of these poor Americans, she has achieved such alertness, such compassion for one of her years. And her tenderness for Aarti is nothing less than providential. Poor Aarti! Both her parents vanished! No one could have given the orphan the comfort she now enjoys but the loving elder sister that Brittany has become to her.

Sitting in the apartment with them, Ram admires the walls the girls have freshly painted, the floors they've recarpeted. He felt some initial irritation at being denied his own room here, but that is quite gone. A manager, of course, properly resides *in* the manager's suite, and a man who assumes what amount to fatherly responsibilities should properly reside *with* his charges, so that no casual domestic opportunity to share his wisdom and guidance with them might be lost.

He has them at mealtimes, though, and has come to feel it fitting they should discover that they can themselves make a new home to replace the homes they've lost. And they *are* at home here. They often patrol the halls— that's their own humorous term for it—like little managers themselves, pay visits to some of the rooms, tour all the floors, chatting with the tenants they meet.

After dinner, Ram returns to his last few hours in the cage. He ponders, not for the first time, the mysterious generosity of the Higher Patels in creating this arrangement for the girls. He has direct experience of some of the hell-holes they own, and they have always shown the sharpest eye for profit, but here they have decreed this compassionate protectorate for the orphan and her friend. The rich and powerful must always remain inscrutable to a man like himself, Ram supposes, a poor man patiently grinding away at his correspondence courses for a contractor's license.

Meanwhile they have provided quite adequately for Ram himself as well. He has for the first time a decent salary. He has the pleasure of protecting the girls, and a generally pleasant body of tenants. He possesses the sizeable room, here in the staff compound, of the vanished night clerk (what was *happening* in that wild week?—four staff vanished, one a suicide, and a tenant deceased in his bed!), and it's a perfectly comfortable room, with a window onto the street from which he likes to watch the traffic flow from time to time.

Although . . . perhaps it's not a *perfectly* comfortable room. There is nothing definite about it that he could complain of, at least not coherently complain of. It's just . . . an *unquiet* room. It's not noise from the halls; that doesn't reach him there. It's not noise from the street; the windows shut snugly, there are good curtains, and he's as well insulated from the street noise as the manager's suite is.

The problem is perhaps the walls themselves, and the ceiling and floor. There is some restless infirmity deep in the aging carpentry of the room. A shifting, a murmuring, a creaky whispering . . . when Ram's deep in his studies at his desk late at night, his ears will prick to these sourceless stirrings, and an odd unease will tingle in him. And now and again he has been awakened in his bed in the deep of night by the same dream of hearing a faint, irregular clatter, a sound of hesitant, solitary labor right there in the room with him.

In an hour it will be time for Ram to waken Leroy for his graveyard shift. He stretches and rubs his eyes. It's only late at night when he experiences these admittedly tenuous disturbances, only late at night, when everyone is liable to feel unquiet sensations, that he is less than happy here at the Hyperion. One of the tenants who makes him a bit uneasy tends to come out then too. In fact, here he comes now. . . .

Though the old man's tread is quiet, Ram detects his approach long before he totters past the bars. Ram is a man of experience and observation. He knows that an old man is not necessarily a venerable man. The look Mr. Cunningham gives him with his pale blue eye as he passes—that's surely not a kindly twinkle, is it? A coldly gauging eye, cold as the polar wastes.

Ram watches him as he totters down the stairs to the street, watches him somewhat tensely, because he's poised for something he's only half-consciously waiting for, something he's only half sure he's felt, on previous occasions like this. A kind of *wake* that follows the old man.

And there it is—isn't it? Following the old man a few slow heartbeats behind. A faint, airy commotion, an invisible hastening of multiple feather-light feet, hustling inaudibly down those same stairs, and out the door behind him, and into the street.

*   *   *

> *In Netherlands did old Van Haarme*
> *A vasty boneyard till and farm . . .*

On the keys, with what work just as well as fingers, he punches out truth now, not trash. There is only truth now, space without limit, time without end. This truth surrounds the poet, breathes in on him from all sides through the weathered, gappy planks of his walls. Black space un-bounded surrounds him, littered with the slow-turning wheels of stars, the scattered springs of eternity's clock.

> *did plough and plant a funeral field*
> *where gnarled lich was all his yield*

The poet, in his life before, loved rooms not wholly unlike this one, sheds and shacks, lofts, garages. Lovely, shabby, lonely places where the words can be forged, the images assembled, where patiently, privately, he can make his own piece of the world.

> *and parched cadaver all the crop*
> *that e'er the ghoul did sow or reap*

Does that off-rhyme work? He likes it. Its jangle drives home the spiteful deformity of the Master's enterprise. Or does it limp? He will come back to it. Time enough to polish, revise. Time and time and time enough.

> *But Carnival Town in latter years*
> *is where Van Haarme now scythes and shears*

He pauses. He has the rest already and sits weighing it, savoring it. He smiles, with what work just as well as lips. A nice little almost-sonnet. Bald and nasty. None of the trumpets of glory in it, the rousing call to the bold of heart that the Master likes in his copy. The Master will reject this poem in anger, will dash it down like a mirror that has failed to flatter his unspeakable visage.

But what can the Master do? Bar him the feast for an eon or so? Deny him the red riot, the stealthy rampage through the huddled cities, the glut of appetite amid the helpless struggles of the prey?

But what is an eon or so? At least the poet can run (unlike Bill), can see (unlike Cozzens) when he's let off the leash again. As for the hunger—what's a few eons of hunger?

It won't kill him.

> *The boggy graves of his natal fief*
> *he has quit for the Carnival's shadow-strife.*
> *It's Poortown's earth that he seeds now, and tills,*
> *where the shambling shadow-folk drift without wills.*

End

Printed in the USA
CPSIA information can be obtained
at www.ICGtesting.com
CBHW051312040924
14049CB00035B/385